MY ONLY SON

****

A NOVEL BY
CHRISTOPHER J. GAMBINO

To Frank, My Good Friend, Thank you for Everything and Becoming my Family! Regards, Warm Regards, CJ Gambino

This is a work of fiction. Names characters, places, and incidents are the product of the author's imagination. Any resemblance to real persons, living or dead, locales, or actual incidents, is entirely coincidental.

All rights reserved
Copyright 2004 by Christopher J. Gambino
No part of this book may be reproduced or transmitted in any form or by any means, electronic, or mechanical, including photocopying, recording, or by any information storage and retrieval system without permission in writing from the publisher.
ISBN 0-9759085-0-2

ACKNOWLEDGMENTS

* * * *

MY DEEPEST THANKS and unending gratitude for all who supported and helped me from the time I started my literary journey until the vision that was so clear in my mind matched that which I committed to paper. Everyone gave me the inspiration without which, I could not have completed this difficult but extraordinarily rewarding task.

Teri Perrone, Chelsea, Carol Demeo, Anna, Cathy and Cruz, Michael & Mary Barth, Ashyln, David, Opa & Omi Barth, In Loving memory of Steven Barth, Christina, David & Ann Darwin Michael, Ashley, Kayla, Anthony, Garry D'Amato, Joseph "Joey Pins" Haley, Joseph Dobbins, In Loving memory of Margie Dobbins, Jane, Billy and grandchildren, Frank Sinatra Jr, Heidi Fleiss, Eddie (The Mechanic) Cox, Armando "Tommy Pip" Pipolo, Antonio & Grace Ricatti, Pat (the water guy) Desimone, Father Francis, Mary Stone, Jonathan Pennell, Alda Witterberns, O. Carm., Rev. Richard Champigny, St. Jude Catholic Church, Don "Duckman" & Kelley Vitucci, Michael & Anne Franzese, Lewis & Lil Michael Franzese, Danny "Dapper" & Peggy Giurleo, Georgio "Hollywood" & Elizabeth Gambino Panagiotou, Maria Gambino Panagiotou, Michael Panagoitou, Jay & Mary Klein, Wally Vincenty, Micah & Simone McCarter, David Lee Roth of Pure & Pristine, Christopher Joseph Gambino III and Bella & Meke "My Malteses."

SPECIAL THANKS

* * * *

Steven and Lori Weiss

Jake and Katherine

Steve, my friend and personal attorney. Through the difficulties we went through together you stuck by my side and helped me follow through on this dream. I am grateful, and if I had to do it all over again, I would want you by my side.

Thank you sincerely with
all my heart.

DEDICATION
* * * *

This is dedicated to the memories of the past, however painful, for they served a purpose.

To my wife Evelina:
Tough guys have hearts, I love you!

To my son Christopher Joseph:
You are gifted and blessed. If you follow your dreams, believe in yourself and trust God within your heart, you can do anything you set your mind to. My favorite saying from you is, "it's all gravy Dad"!

To my son Anthony Christopher:
Though we have been a part for a long time, there is not a day that goes by that I do not think about you or wish that I could hold you in my arms. I miss you.

To the most precious thing in my life, my daughter Alexandra Nicole:
There is not a second that goes by that you do not enter my mind. You are the light that shines in my life. You are a daughter that everybody should have, kind, sweet, warm, understanding, loving and talented. You have helped your father become the person he is today. I am so proud of you.

To my son Nicholas Joseph:
Though your life just began Daddy loves you.

For my loving mother:
Trouble started the day I was born. Soon, I was on a path that was leading me to destruction. After many years of getting into "trouble" and wondering where my life was heading, one day, unexpectedly, something happened deep inside me, which changed my soul. I knew I would become somebody of influence and make a positive difference in the lives of those I loved and even those I did not yet know. This manifestation of "goodness", led me to create a book from my life experiences. My life "stories" turned into a book of deep feelings and passion, which I wanted to share with the rest of the world. It became a dream for me.

It started with you mom, and it ends with me telling you I am sorry for the pain and many sleepless nights I have caused you. I love you and thank you for loving me, no matter what. You can be proud of who I have become, a writer.

* * * *

FROM THE AUTHOR

* * * *

MY ONLY SON is a novel about organized crime. As you will quickly determine, I am including realistic information, which as far as I am aware, has not been published before. Rather than just describing "what" happens in the novel, I go further into details of "how" and "why" decisions are implemented by my crime characters.

In the first three chapters, you will meet Vinny Denucci, the son of the most powerful crime boss in New York City. Vinny had been isolated from his father's work while growing up because his uncle was to be the successor. On his twenty-first birthday, Vinny's father tells him that he must abandon his plans to become a lawyer and instead replace his uncle and become the new successor. "In the real world it is forbidden to have your son become a "made man." It is against the rules." Reluctantly, Vinny participates in his assigned birthday ritual, which requires him to kill a disloyal family member. As a "made man" and the family successor, Vinny must watch his father's organization while his father takes care of a "business" problem in Florida. When his father is gone, Vinny slowly transforms from a man who must morally justify his actions into a man who, because he cannot trust his acquaintances or even his father, becomes more callous, paranoid, and impulsive. He comes to learn the true nature and consequences of being part of the Mafia and understands why his mother warned him to be strong and resist the lure of "easy" money and power.

In the end, Vinny is set up by a friend and goes to prison. While serving time, he experiences the truth about prison and the legal system: crime life continues unabated and any privilege can be bought for a price. Despite this, he re-establishes his earlier values and sense of justice and begins to plot the downfall of his father's empire. He combines his mother's guidelines and his father's ruthlessness to become a man who is honest, honorable, and admired. Only in completing his plan to destroy his father and free himself from the Mafia can he regain his self-respect—even if the price is his life. In the novel, I delve into the media myths about the Mafia: for example, that the Italian Mafia does not sell drugs (they do), that Mafia bosses always wear suits (only on special occasions). Rituals are explained in detail as are the solutions to some of New York's unexplained crimes. The bosses, along with the loyalties, payoffs, and tradeoffs that Mafiosi commonly do to avoid punishment, discuss legal maneuvers. Most interestingly, I show how my characters live their lives, including the daily routine of pickup and delivery of money and services. I hope you will find my novel fascinating. I promise that it shows a side of the Mafia that, to my knowledge, has never been seen.

* * * *

TABLE OF CONTENTS

* * * *

Chapter 1: **The Beginning** 1
Chapter 2: **The Family Gathering** 21
Chapter 3: **Learning Street Smarts**...................................39
Chapter 4: **Felicia's Embarrassment** 81
Chapter 5: **My Father, Mafia Boss** 91
Chapter 6: **The Truth Unveils** 111
Chapter 7: **Mother's Death** 129
Chapter 8: **The Initiation** 135
Chapter 9: **Life On The Streets** 151
Chapter 10: **Making A Name** 169
Chapter 11: **A Lesson Learned** 183
Chapter 12: **The Drug Trade** 195
Chapter 13: **The Girls** 209
Chapter 14: **Scared To Death**..219
Chapter 15: **The Homecoming** 237
Chapter 16: **Debbie** 245
Chapter 17: **A War And A Bust** 255
Chapter 18: **Corruption In The Court** 273
Chapter 19: **Prison** 295
Chapter 20: **The Truth About Family** 325
Chapter 21: **No Turning Back** 347
Chapter 22: **The Setup**...353

CHAPTER 1
THE BEGINNING

* * * *

VINNY WOKE UP DAZED to hear loud banging coming from what sounded like the front door. Vinny, thirteen years old, had short black hair and a mole on his right cheek. He had big brown eyes that seem to have a mystery behind them. He was tall for his age. Vinny was skinny. He could eat all day long and not gain an ounce. Slightly annoyed, he threw his arm over his eyes and moved restlessly to grab a pillow. Attempting to hide from the noise as long as he could, he sat up and tried to get his thoughts together. Maybe it was just a dream. Yawning and stretching, Vinny pushed his fingers through his hair and rubbed his eyes to get a better look at the faint green florescent light illuminating the alarm clock. The hands pointed to 3:30 in the morning...and more banging. Who could be at the door at this time? Vinny sat there in silence for a few minutes and wondered if his father heard the noise. He knew he would not be happy if someone was at the door. Vinny's father did not like unexpected visitors. "I am coming!", his father yelled. Vinny heard his father mumble as he passed his bedroom, "this better be fuckin' important!" His father sounded pissed.

Vinny stumbled out of bed and crept over to his bedroom door to see if he could find out who was making the entire ruckus. He did not dare open it or make noise himself because he was afraid his father would hear him. Putting his ear against the door, he quietly listened for a moment but only heard silence. Kneeling down, Vinny put his head on the floor to see if he could see what was going on through the crack under the door. Luckily, there was enough space for him to get a clear view of the front door entryway. He watched his father pass as he stomped down the hall, tying his black silk robe around his waist and cursing the night's interruption.

Sonny Denucci was six-foot-two, and weighed around 210 pounds. He was a well built, striking man who looked liked he worked out, but had never had any use for a gym. His black hair was starting to turn gray at the temples, which somehow made him look even more powerful. Sonny's light brown skin was always clean-shaven and he had deep brown eyes that could turn almost black when he was angry, those eyes would sometimes look right through you. Vinny hated that look. However, there were other times when he reminded Vinny of a gentle cat, so loving and with a hug a kid could get lost in. For Vinny, Sonny Denucci was bigger than life.

Vinny fantasized about the day he would wear the heavy gold crucifix and Italian horn that always hung from Sonny's strong neck. Vinny loved his father despite the fact that he was moody and hard to figure out. He had a short temper, which he seemed to thrive on at times. One minute he could be playful and fill the kitchen with his deep, hearty laughter, then, for no apparent reason, he would start screaming at the top of his lungs. The roar of his voice made Vinny's mother Felicia cry. A fit of anger triggered by something as simple as him not liking the flavor of the meat Felicia put in the spaghetti sauce. To Vinny, it seemed like his father would make such a big deal over nothing and was usually sorry later. However, Sonny could always make his wife forgive him, no matter what he did. He would just look at her with what Felicia called "those bedroom eyes of his" and she would melt, crying into his arms. On the other hand, at least she used to.

Sonny had charm. Everybody said so. He always had the charm to make people feel good, especially women...even the women Felicia did not know about. It must have been one of those 'Italian' things. No matter who else was in his life, Sonny always came home. In Sonny's world, family was family.

Sonny walked down the hallway and flipped the light on, slamming open the front door locks and yanking the door wide open. "What is it? You had better have a damn good reason to wake my family and me up in the middle of the freakin' night! Get your ass in here!"

Sal Nicoletti, one of Sonny's friends, stood frozen in the doorway, staring at Sonny's outraged face. Rain gently fell around him, making soft patters against Sonny's anger. Sonny grabbed him by the coat and pulled him inside. He kicked the door shut behind him. Sonny shut the locks and turned to Sal. He was more composed and spoke calmly, "Okay, tell me, why I deserve this unforeseen freakin' pleasure in the middle of the night?"

Sal was out of breath. His face was ashen and the scar under his left eye looked swollen and almost purple. His stocky chest was heaving as he tried to catch his breath. His clothes were drenched from the rain and his blue shirt was hanging out one side of his pants as if he had been in a scuffle. Water dripped from the edges of his coat, piddling on the floor at his feet. His black shoes covered with globs of mud that dissolved as the water dripped on them. Sonny looked down at the mess Sal was making on his entry floor then back at Sal. Sal looked scared. Vinny thought his jet black eyes looked like shiny marbles and his hair, cut short above the ear, reminded him of the crew cuts people get when they join the Army. Sweat mixed with rainwater poured off the top of his head, running down the sides of his cheek as if somebody had poured a pitcher of water over him. Sonny grabbed him by the shoulders, smacked him across the face and yelled, "Hey, get a hold of your self. I have never seen you act like this."

Sal looked at Sonny like seeing him for the first time. "One minute... please," he said. Sal walked into the living room and fell into a chair. Vinny could still see them.

Sonny asked, "You need a drink?"

"No, thank you," Sal replied and kept staring at the floor for what seemed like days. A few seconds later he gasped out, "Sonny, they just killed Mac Valenti! It was a horrible scene. Four gun shots to the back of the head. The hole was the size of a tennis ball. Blood splatter all over the place, you could hardly tell it was Mac. I knew it was him. I recognized his uniform." Vinny's father looked puzzled.

"Calm down and keep quiet," Sonny said as he looked back toward the hallway where he assumed his family was sleeping. Sonny went to the hallway bathroom and grabbed a towel from the wall. Coming back, he tossed it to Sal.

"Who killed who?" he asked calmly as he seated himself in one of the room's easy chairs.

Sal took a deep breath and wiped his face, "You know Mac Valenti from Queens?" Sonny said nothing. "You know the tow truck company guy. Speedy Mac's Tow Trucks… The company we helped a few days ago. We loaned him thirty grand to get his business started."

Sonny scratched his eyebrows and rubbed his forehead, "Yeah, I remember. I did not remember his name. He was my brother Nunzi's guy. But, who killed him and what does that have to do with me?" Sonny was starting to get impatient. He liked to grasp the situation immediately, with as few words as possible, and Sal was not making a long story any shorter as far as Sonny was concerned.

Sal said, "All I know is some guy named Ricky Burke is a distant cousin of Vito Scarabelli and he's here to do vengeance on whoever killed him. He was asking all sorts of questions around town and in the local bars. The information I gathered so far from the regulars at Cubby's Bar said Burke double parked his black Corvette in front of Mac's tow truck. Mac got a call and the son-of-bitch would not move it. Mac screamed at the guy, if you do not move that fuckin' car then I am going to move it for you. Burke told him he did not like threats…one thing led to the next and Burke pulled out a gun. The rest is history. Bang-bang, Mac's dead."

Sonny sat down, "Do you think this is a problem?"

"I don't know, but this guy seems to be trigger happy. He popped Mac right there in the street. He could turn out to be a problem. He is also asking questions about Don Vito."

"Burke is? He must be an Irish prick with some bullshit pride. You are right this might be a problem. This piece of shit must be working to score some points with a crew. The only time a person whacks you and does not give a fuck is trying to make a reputation for the skippers. Does he have anybody else with him or what?"

"I don't know yet." Sal said.

Sonny was letting everything sink in, "So, do you think me and my family are in danger?"

"I don't know. But let's get prepared for this crazy lunatic anyway."

Sonny got up, "Call Charlie and a few other boys and have them cover the place to make sure everything is okay."

Sal was already on his feet, "You got it. I'll handle everything."

Walking Sal to the door, Sonny spoke almost to himself, "Why some dumb shit wants to prove something to the other families just so he could be known as a tough guy and earn his badge?" When you become a "made man", the Mafia uses a term "Badge." It lets other families know, if you are a "made man" or not. Some other signs are if you meet a guy who you think is made he will make a sign of the cross over his heart. A real made guy is not allowed to tell you he is made. The associates are supposed to tell you that or your skipper will if you are part of a crew.

As Sal walked outside, he looked back over his shoulder, "I'll call when I need to get back in."

Vinny's breath came in little puffs as he tried to keep quiet. He watched his father scratch his head as he paced back and forth. Vinny was trying to figure out why Sal was so upset and what did it have to do with his father? He had never heard of Mac Valenti and apparently, his father hardly knew him either.

Just then, Vinny's father yelled out to his mother, "Felicia!"

In a sleepy voice, she yelled back, "What's the matter?"

"Get up and take Vincenzo with you to my brother's house."

Vinny's mother came storming out of the bedroom, tying the sash to her old blue robe, yelling at Vinny's father. "Sonny, I can't take this anymore, it's the middle of the night. When are you going to stop this? You are playing games with these people and you are going to get us killed. What are you going to do about your son?"

Ignoring her, Sonny picked up the phone and dialed. He glared at Felicia with a look that said he wanted to kill someone and started screaming at her, "Felicia! Just do what I fucking tell you to do." Going back to his phone call, Sonny spoke to his brother, "Nunzi, we have a problem. The family is on the way over. I will explain what is happening when I see you. Just keep your boys on alert. I'll talk to you later." He hung up the phone.

Felicia stood in the hall glaring at him with her arms crossed. Sonny shouted, and started clenching his fists, "Felicia! I cannot deal with your fuckin' attitude right now. Move your goddamn ass and do what I say." Walking over to her, Sonny's voice sounded deadly, and he got right in her face, "If you ever raise your voice to me again, so help me God, I'll just get rid of you. You know I can. Get your stuff and my son and get the fuck out of here and over to Nunzi's."

"Wow", Vinny thought, "Things must be serious if we're going to Uncle Nunzi's house at this hour. He lives all the way out in Long Island." Vinny shuddered. He had a frightening thought that sent chills up his back. What if Sal plans to kill that Scarabelli person and he wants his father to help him? Why would his father hang around Sal if he were involved with those kinds of crazy people? Vinny could not wait to get out of there and away from Sal. That guy is probably looking for him too, he thought.

Hearing his mother's slippers rasping toward his door, Vinny leaped into bed. When she came in, he looked wide awake, but she did not seem to notice. Felicia Denucci was a petite five-foot-two, 135-pound woman. She had long black hair that rested on her shoulders with a slight curl at the bottom and her soft hazel brown eyes were always full of love for Vinny. When she spoke, her Italian accent made her voice melodic in Vinny's ears. At first meeting, people would think she just got off the boat from Italy. She seemed to be an innocent of the world she was in, kind and sweet. She was a church going woman who believed strongly in her Catholic faith. She had a heart that was warm and understanding. She would do anything for anybody. Neighbors were always in Felicia Denucci's warm and inviting kitchen, which was always filled with the aromas of her famous cooking; telling their tales of woe while Felicia patiently listened and offered an occasional warm and loving touch. She always dressed in her favorite color black, which she said made her look thin; she started pulling clothes together for Vinny.

"Vincenzo, get up! Get up, we have to go." She tossed the covers back and pulled him upright by the arm. Tossing him some things from the closet, she was upset and in a tremendous hurry. "Here, put these on," she said, handing him his shoes. "Where are all your books for school? We should take them just in case you need to be dropped off at school tomorrow morning and we can't get back by here."

Vinny stood in the middle of his room feeling overwhelmed, a pair of jeans dangling from his hand. "Mom, where are we going? What's wrong?"

"Don't ask questions," she said, "Just get dressed." Her fear and anger were rising. She found Vinny's books and stuffed them into his gym bag. "Vincenzo, one day you will understand all of this. Just keep quiet for now. Your father hangs out with a group of men and they do very stupid things to one another to prove who is more macho and has more control. Innocent people get hurt." Mumbling to herself, she continued, "One day you can turn around and find you have nothing anymore... no security, no love, no future...nothing."

Putting on his clothes and grabbing his gym bag, Vinny said, "Mom, I don't understand what's happening. What group of men does my father hang around with? Like the Knights of Columbus?"

Vinny's mother rubbed her forehead, a slight smile creeping across her face at his youthful innocence, "Vinny, my love, you're too young to be hearing this. Please, just tie your shoes before your father gets angry. Go and kiss him goodbye, then grab a snack to take with us. I have to finish getting ready."

When Vinny went out to the living room, Sal was back. He and Sonny were standing by the window, looking out and talking quietly. Vinny was not hungry so he just went and sat on the couch and waited for his mother. After a few moments his father came over, sat down next to him, and put his arm around his shoulders, "Vincenzo, I don't ever want anything to happen to you or for you to get hurt. I'm sending you and your mother to Uncle Nunzi's house."

"Why are we going there? Why can't we stay here, with you?"

"When you get a little older I will explain some things to you about this family. You're my only son." His father said.

Vinny looked at his father quizzically, "What do you mean about 'this family'?" Sonny avoided the fear in Vinny's eyes, "Vincenzo don't worry about it." Seeing his father upset, Vinny said, "Dad, don't you worry, I'll watch out for mom." Filled with love and concern for his son, Sonny pulled Vinny close and hugged him tight.

It was still dark outside when Felicia came out, dressed and ready to go. Sal took car keys from his pocket and Felicia's suitcase from her, "Sonny. We're ready to go whenever you're ready."

Sonny stood up and looked Sal straight in the face, "Sal, you'd better guard Vinny with your life. I know you understand how important he is to me."

"Mr. Denucci, you can count on me."

"Sal, I don't know what I would do without you. You have been loyal to me and I owe you. I won't forget that."

Sonny went to kiss Felicia good-bye, but she turned her head away and started toward the door. He looked angry, but this was not the time for family scenes. "Felicia," he said, "I'll call you when this is all over. Stay with Nunzi and Sal, okay?" Felicia looked back at him, her face red from crying. She wiped away her tears, her voice thick with emotion, "Sonny, you promised me. You promised that you would stop this and now you are endangering Vinny and me. When are you going to keep your word? You talk about keeping your word to your men. Your word to your family means nothing. You expect everybody to keep their word with you, but you don't keep yours with me."

Sonny exploded, "Felicia, Don't you fuck with me! I do not need this shit from you. Just get the fuck out of here before you piss me off even more." Sonny started clenching his fists and pacing like a caged animal. Fearing his father might hit her; Vinny got off the couch and quietly took his mother's hand while looking obediently at his father.

"Be good, Vincenzo, listen to your mother and Uncle Nunzi. We'll talk when you get back." This last bit said with sheer hatred toward Felicia, who turned pale, squeezed Vinny's hand to give her strength and rushed them outside.

On the way over to Uncle Nunzi's house, Vinny asked his mother when they would be able to go back home. He wondered if this was going to mess up the family's Sunday gatherings or if his parents would get divorced. However, Vinny knew, in his heart, that they would not. Divorce was out of the question in the Denucci household. Sonny may not act like a good Catholic, or honor his wife as the Bible directs, but to him, tradition was tradition and family was family. However, as much as Vinny loved his father, sometimes he wished they would divorce. His mother seemed so unhappy most of the time. Vinny looked up into the rainy sky and wondered if God would punish him for thinking that way.

Vinny tried to make conversation with his mother. He could see how upset she was but Vinny did not want her to know what he had overheard earlier. Sal drove frantically to Nunzi's house. Felicia sat there in silence with her head against the window, a handkerchief in her hand, dabbing at her eyes and nose, twisting it into a knot with hands that were shaking. Vinny felt saddened in his heart as he watched the tears rolling down his mother's face. He reached over, took her hand and held it tight. Felicia looked at her son with pride as she listened to his childlike voice say with protective authority, "I love you, Mom. Everything is going to be all right." She kissed his cheek and, with the saddest face, Vinny had ever seen, put her head back against the window, letting quiet tears spill into her lap.

It was daybreak when they finally arrived at Nunzi's house. Nunzi greeted them at the front door. Uncle Nunzi stood there, tall, handsome, in a black and red robe, and expensive black slippers. A cigar dangled from his mouth, a surprising contrast to the conscientious man who worked out at the gym every day. Already clean-shaven, a certain style to him spoke of authority and trust. Vinny loved hanging around his Uncle Nunzi. He never got angry and he never yelled. It was hard to believe Nunzi and his dad were brothers.

Felicia got out of the car, threw her arms around Nunzi and burst into tears. He held her close, comforting her until she slowly regained her composure and stopped crying. Aunt Catherine came out from the kitchen and took Felicia by the hand. "Everything is going to be okay," she said, leading them into the house. Aunt Catherine looked cheerful in her white terry cloth robe with a yellow daisy on the lapel. Vinny was happy to see her. A petite woman who was quiet and understanding, Catherine had shoulder length black hair and green eyes full of wisdom and peace. "Everybody should have had an aunt like her," Vinny thought as he fell in step behind the two women he loved most in the world. Reminiscing for a moment in the quiet of the morning, Vinny's thoughts turned to a Christmas holiday when his aunt Catherine cooked leg of lamb that he did not like. Sonny was forcing Vinny to eat it, but he did not like it. Every time Sonny turned to speak with another dinner companion, Aunt Catherine would take pieces of lamb off Vinny's plate and eat them herself. She would give Vinny that knowing wink of conspirators in crime. She always looked out for him.

Breaking away from his daydream, Vinny heard Aunt Catherine's voice reassuring his mother, "You'll be safe here and then it'll be over and you can go home."

Nunzi hugged Vinny and took hold of his gym bag. He greeted Sal and shook his hand warmly, "I'll get everyone settled and then we'll talk," he said.

"That's just fine, Nunzi. I think I will drive the car into the garage and have a smoke. Give me a few minutes to look around and to see that everything is okay."

Vinny looked from Nunzi to Sal thinking that was strange. Why would Sal be worried about making sure everything was okay? Vinny could not figure out why Sal was with them rather than being with his father. However, considering Sonny's anger this morning, maybe this was better. His father's anger would not color Vinny's time with his aunt and uncle.

It was still early and Vinny just wanted to get back to sleep. Uncle Nunzi took him up to his son Robert's room where Robert was sound asleep. He quietly helped Vinny climb onto the top bunk bed and kissed him good night. "Don't worry about anything, Vinny. Just go back to sleep and your father will be here to explain everything soon, okay?" Vinny nodded and settled down. The last thought Vinny had as he drifted off to sleep was that Robert was sure going to be mad when he realized he slept through all the excitement.

Vinny abruptly awoke to yelling coming from downstairs. He looked over and saw that his cousin Robert was still sleeping so he climbed out of bed carefully so he would not wake him. Opening the door quietly, Vinny walked over to the top of the stairs and sat down. His father had arrived and was yelling at his mother in the library downstairs.

"Felicia, why do you do this to me?" Vinny could hear his father ask. "Every time there's a problem you give me shit. Is it hard for you to keep your mouth shut for once? You keep threatening me and wanting to take Vinny. I have told you a thousand times. Do not ever threaten me! In addition, do not ever threaten to take my only son. You do not seem to get it. You don't have power to do anything! I own your fuckin' soul!"

He paused and for a minute, all Vinny could hear was his mother sniffling. "I'm sorry I hit you, but you know this is my life and I can't have you in my way."

Vinny thought for a second. At that moment Vinny's throat got dry, tears rolled down his face, his stomach ached with knots and a part of him felt emotionally hurt. He wanted to go downstairs and scream at his father, even hit him to see how he would have liked it. Vinny hated him when he hurt his mom. He crept slowly down the stairs so he could listen better and see if his mother was OK. Felicia was red in the face, still crying, sitting with her legs crossed, looking toward Sonny. From where Vinny hid, he could see her, but she could not see him. Sonny was sitting drinking orange juice making announcements: "I want what is best for him. I know what is best for him. You have no idea!. You know what I am all about and I am not going to change and not in this fuckin lifetime! I am not going to change for you. I like who I am and people depend on me to run this family. I am the fuckin' boss of the largest organization in the United States and I am not taking shit from you or anybody. You ought to respect the position and me. The way you act, you are embarrassing me. I have people with power respecting me but my own wife is constantly whining and crying. What am I going to do with you, Felicia?"

Vinny could hear him pacing and saying some more things that he could not understand. When Felicia spoke, Vinny could barely hear her, "Sonny, I'm your wife." Then her voice rose with a little more conviction, "You married me in church in front of God." Although her speech was strong, she was still shaking. "Vinny and I should be the most important thing in your life, more important than your work. You just want to be the king and you could not love us or you would give up your wicked, ugly, immoral life. You are going to go to hell and I will not let you take Vinny with you! Vinny is not going to be like you and your slimy friends. He is going to be a lawyer and you are not going to stop him. He is going to college and he is not going to be like you. You'll have to find someone else to train to take over."

Suddenly, Sonny slammed his fist down on the table, breaking the glass. Vinny was certain Sonny's voice could be heard by the neighbors all the way back home, he was yelling so loudly, "You'd better get your priorities straight woman or I'll stick you in the fuckin' ground! I mean it, Felicia. You stand in my way and I'll fuckin' take care of you. I am sick of your sass, your ingratitude and your threats. You listen to me bitch, I am not just threatening you, I am fuckin' promising you, and you got that? You had better change your attitude and you had better change it fast! I'm not going tell you again."

Felicia was crying so hard it broke Vinny's heart. He could not believe what he was hearing and started to cry. He wanted to go downstairs and tell them to stop fighting but Nunzi grabbed him from behind, put his hand over his mouth and led him into his bedroom and closed the door behind them. He sat Vinny down on his bed, and then he sat down next to him. Putting his arm around Vinny's shoulders, a million thoughts went through Nunzi's mind. How are kids supposed to deal with this shit?

"Vinny, I'm sorry you had to hear that. I know how you must feel inside."

"Uncle Nunzi, why would he hit her? Why would he want to hurt my mother? He said he would kill her...what organization are they talking about? What's happening?"

"I can't explain it to you right now, but, I promise you I won't let your father hurt your mother anymore. I just want you to forget what you just heard and do not think about it. Do not think of your father as a bad person, he is a good person. He is just mad and he is not thinking straight. Sometimes adults get angry at each other and they do not think about what they are saying. Think about how nice he is at Suffern."

For a moment Vinny lost focus of what was going on between his parents and thought about a special place they all went to sometimes. Suffern was a family retreat in upstate New York where they spent just about every weekend in the summer. Vinny's grandfather took his father and family there when they were young and gave the property to Sonny when he died. It was a family getaway in a secluded area covered with many trees and creeks. It had tennis courts, a pool and barbecue pits. It was nothing like home. Nobody seemed to fight there. It was just a fun place to visit.

Thinking about facing his mother and father, Vinny grabbed Uncle Nunzi's arm tight, "Will you go downstairs with me?"

"Sure." As they walked out of the room, Uncle Nunzi shouted, "Sonny, I'm bringing Vinny down." When he saw his mother, Vinny ran over to her. She was sitting at the kitchen table. She gave her son a big hug. He could see her eyes were red and swollen with a slight bruise developing under her left eye. She tried to smile at him and held him tight as she whispered in his ear, "I love you baby boy." Vinny's mother always called him 'baby boy'. "We're going to be okay," she whispered softly again. "Don't worry; we'll work it all out. Your father is a stubborn man, but I think he will do what is best for us. He just doesn't like to admit when he is wrong."

"I know. I love you, too, mom."

Sonny watched them with an expressionless face, "Hey, Vinny! What...your father doesn't get a hug and a kiss?" Vinny reluctantly went over to Sonny's outstretched arms, walking stiffly, hesitantly and scared. He hugged him and kissed his father's cheek dutifully, even though he did not want to. He was still upset over his father hitting his mother and wanted him to know that he knew what he had done to her.

"So, Vincenzo, what do you think about going home this morning or do you want to stay here through the weekend with Robert?"

"Is mom staying?" Vinny asked, looking at her with pleading eyes. He wanted to keep her close to him, protect her.

In the background, Vinny heard Nunzi clear his throat and he looked at his mother again, expectant. Gracefully, Nunzi tried to change the atmosphere in the room and asked Felicia, "Are we still on for Sunday at your house or would you guys like to come here?" Reluctant to make a decision, Felicia looked at Sonny, "Well, Sonny, what would you like to do?" she asked in a small voice.

Sonny smiled confidently. "Everybody over at our place, Felicia will cook a terrific meal. Right, Felicia?"

Felicia paused for a moment, lowering her head because she was unable to hide her growing distain for such an abusive man. Then choking on a smile she said, "Yes, Sonny, a terrific meal, as always."

Sunday was a day that the family always got together at one house or the other. Depending on the sports season, feasting and football went on all day. If it were the Denucci's turn, Felicia would get up early and make her delicious pasta sauce with veal meatballs and Italian sausage. Sonny would pace back and forth watching TV and waiting to see if his bets would come through. He even had conversations with the teams, screaming at the coaches and players on the little glowing screen in the living room. Things could get intense if Sonny's team was losing. Between yelling at the TV and yelling at his bookie over the phone, Vinny and

Felicia avoided the living room. Vinny never understood what was going on; he just assumed his dad was a sore loser.

"Felicia are you ready to go?" Sonny asked.

"Yes, Sonny," she said, as she picked up her purse and headed to the front door. Sonny grabbed Vinny by the hand and they went outside to the car. As they drove away, Vinny could see that Felicia was looking up at Aunt Catherine, standing at the living room window. Catherine's face was full of pity as she briefly raised her hand to wave, then turned and moved away.

On the way home, it was quiet in the car. Nobody was talking. Sonny and Vinny sat in the back seat while Sal was taking side streets and repeatedly looking in his rear view mirror. Felicia, in the front seat with Sal, kept glancing nervously between him and the mirror. Vinny could tell it made his mother nervous. She reached down and turned the radio on to soft jazz music, interrupting the strained silence in the car. Vinny was looking at comic books he had taken from Robert's room in anticipation of an uncomfortable ride home. He glanced over to see his father nodding off to sleep. Every once in awhile, Felicia would turn to look at her son and blow him a kiss. Whenever she did that, it always made Vinny smile. Traffic seemed unusually heavy. It seemed like they would never get home. The music lulled Vinny to sleep and he slumped against the door, the comic book slipping to the floor. He awoke as the car pulled up to their house. Sal opened the doors and stood nervously, his eyes darting as Sonny pulled a sleepy Vinny from the car and gave Felicia a small push toward the house. Once inside, Felicia hustled Vinny upstairs and into his bed, he barely felt her brush a kiss over his forehead before he drifted back into sleep.

Sunday dawned bright and sunny. It was pasta day at the Denucci house. Felicia had gotten up a little earlier this Sunday to start cooking so she would not miss church. Her mother, Gina, usually came over to help cook around eleven-thirty. Felicia enjoyed the company. Her mom was a sweet old woman who always dressed in black as though she was still in mourning for the husband she had lost many years before. She could not have weighed more than ninety pounds and had several little whiskers coming off her chin. Vinny was curious about the little flask grandma always carried. When he used to catch her taking a sip, she would always rush to hide it from him in the folds of her black dress. He asked her one day what was in the container and she replied, "Its Grandma's medicine, it keeps my heart ticking." Vinny just laughed knowing she was teasing him. Sometimes Grandma Gina would promise to give him a quarter if he did not tell anybody, and Vinny would smile and say, "Okay grandma," then give her a big hug and kiss. He would never tell nor did he care that she smelled like the whiskey bottles his father kept in a locked cabinet. Grandma Gina was something special.

Another regular Sunday dinner guest was Uncle Joe, Felicia's brother. As Sonny would say, "He was a real piece of work." He never worked and that used to drive Grandma Gina crazy. Part of her frustration was his laziness and the other was his appearance. How could he get a job when he was such a mess? He looked like a hippie from the sixties, wild curly long hair that rested on his shoulders. He had a big nose that leaned to the left and was always using some type of nose spray. To Vinny, Uncle Joe's nostrils were so big that he could envision fitting a marble up into each side. The thought always made Vinny laugh. Uncle Joe's eyes always seemed to be glassy and he had bad acne, as if he never washed his face. He would sit alone reading the newspaper for hours until Grandma Gina could not stand it anymore. She eventually made him, "join the family." Sonny avoided Joe whenever possible. He called him "the bum." He could not stand him.

Early that Sunday morning Sonny and Vinny got up around nine-thirty and Sonny drove everyone to Mass at St. Joan of Arc Catholic Church in Queens. Sonny did not like to miss church. He preached to his family the need for everyone to confess all sins and accept the body of

Christ or they would rot in hell. Vinny figured his dad had to confess a lot because he was swearing and yelling at Felicia all the time. Nevertheless, it was still nice to see the family all go to church together every week.

Vinny liked Father Michael, the priest. He was about five-foot six, balding and resembled Bozo the Clown without the big nose and make-up. He was not a fat man, but you could tell he liked to eat. Father Michael always made everyone feel good, as if each of us were special to him. He was soft-spoken, intelligent and at times funny when he told the jokes that he had heard while traveling as a missionary in other countries. Vinny could listen to him tell his stories for hours. He always made Vinny feel good about himself and seemed to have the right answers no matter what questions Vinny asked. Vinny would call him sometimes when Sonny seemed out of control, yelling or hitting Felicia and Father Michael would tell Vinny to calm down and assure him that everything would be all right. When things got bad, he would send a cab to pick Vinny up and take him to the church office where he put on some relaxing music and explain that sometimes people learn life lessons the hard way. Maybe Sonny had gotten off his path.

"Don't judge him, Vinny," Father Michael would say. "He's only hurting himself and wrestling the evil spirit that dwells in him. He is fighting his demons. Just forgive him and try to be good. Read your Bible, go to church, and obey the Commandments... I will pray for you and your father and mother, and I want you to pray everyday too. Never let God out of your heart. He will always be there for you. Life has many lessons and we do not always know what to do until we have confronted them. We have to accept that God often tests us to see if we can stand by his beliefs. Sometimes life has difficult moments and trouble arises, that makes life seem like hell. But, you must remember, God never lets us down and we must always have faith." Vinny thanked God for Father Michael every day.

Sunday was the best day of the week for Vinny. He always felt great after church. Felicia was a great cook and Vinny loved her kitchen. The two of them had memorable times together. Vinny acted as her soux-chef, preparing all the garlic, opening the cans of tomatoes for the sauce and getting the water ready for the pasta. Cooking became a favorite hobby of Vinny's and Felicia taught him every Italian dish she knew.

She told him, "Vinny, one day you will make some girl real happy. It's romantic for women to watch their man cook, especially if it means your future wife doesn't have to make dinner every night." Then she laughed and patted Vinny's face. Even though he did not understand what she meant about all the 'being romantic' stuff, it sounded good, so he just smiled and pretended he understood. Vinny did everything to spend time with her.

Vinny's favorite dish was shrimp scampi. It took some time to prepare, but it was well worth it. His job was to peel and de-vein the shrimp, which could take almost two hours when he was making enough for eight to ten people. Vinny sat at the kitchen table with a bowl of shrimp in his lap and sipped the iced tea Felicia had steeped with fresh oranges. The kitchen was steamy hot and the tea was fragrant, cool, and delicious. Felicia also showed him how to make delicious desserts like Tiramisu, which she said meant, "Lift me up." It was ladyfinger, espresso coffee, mars Capone cheese and a splash of rum. It was Sonny's favorite so tonight was the perfect night to serve it. Maybe it would improve his mood.

Felicia also made the best marinara sauce in the world. She would add just the right ingredients and remind Vinny, "Vinny, don't ever add too many spices or cook the sauce too long, it won't be good."

While they cooked together, they talked. Felicia told Vinny how much she loved him and how she knew that, he would be successful at any career he wanted as long as he believed in his own abilities, as she did. She assured him he was a special child and that God had wonderful plans for him. Felicia was a firm believer in God and was determined to instill this one area of stability in her son's life especially with things being so crazy in this world today. She told Vinny, repeatedly, that if he ever had any problems that he did not think he could handle, he just needed to ask God to guide him. "God will never let you down," she said. "He might not answer you right away but he will eventually."

When Felicia caught Vinny staring at her as he often did sometimes when they cooked together, she could always make him laugh, "What? Am I better looking than those shrimp?"

"You just look so beautiful with your hair coming loose in the heat, wiping your hands on your apron." With that, Felicia did a little sashay around the kitchen and gave Vinny a big hug until they were both full of laughter.

"I love you mom and I'm so proud you're my mother." Every kid should have had a mother like her, he thought. Then he got more serious for a moment, "I will always be around to take care of you and won't let anything happen to you mom...ever. I promise." Felicia had tears in her eyes as she hugged him even tighter. "I know you will, son. God be with us."

CHAPTER 2
THE FAMILY GATHERING
* * *

VINNY WAS ALREADY AWAKE WHEN HIS MOTHER came into his bedroom.

"Good morning Vincenzo."

"Good morning, Mother."

Felicia bent over to kiss him on the forehead. He closed his eyes and felt her warmth. He loved when she woke him in the morning. She walked over to open the window and let in some fresh air, "Breakfast will be ready in thirty minutes. Keep moving..."

After she walked out of the room, Vinny stayed in bed for a couple of minutes to breathe in the crispness of the day. He liked when it was cold. It made him feel totally refreshed and clear-headed.

When he remembered that they were going away today, Vinny jumped up and ran out onto the balcony in his pajamas. He stood outside as his feet stuck to the frosty landing and took in deep breaths of cool fresh air. He could see his breath form little white clouds as he enjoyed the nippy morning. He pulled his pajama shirt over his head and threw it on the lounge chair behind him. Looking down at himself, he was proud of the small patch of black fuzz developing on his chest. He was becoming a man. Sitting down in the chair he put out on the landing, he could feel the start of a cool winter. Goosebumps covered his body, making the black fuzz on his chest bristle out. October was such a gorgeous month. The leaves were already showing shades of bright orange clipped with gold and copper. He loved to look at the trees against the background of tall skyscrapers, a mixture of country and city. Some of the grass was still green, but fading fast. A squirrel has scrabbled around the bushes and scurried up and down the trees. The color in the sky started to change from the deep blue-black of early morning to light gray, with shades of white. The air was brisk and it felt like the world was fresh and clean. Sitting atop his balcony, Vinny felt like this place was a million miles away from the realities of his home.

Today was going to be a great day because the family would be together. Once a month Sonny would arrange for the family to go to Suffern and today was the day. Even the three hour ride did not bother him. It was worth it. Suffern was a town in upstate New York. Sonny told Vinny that he loved Suffern because it allowed him to be himself and not some 'everyday boss.' Vinny never entirely understood what he meant when he said that, because he never saw his dad working. He was reluctant to ask questions, so he just accepted whatever his father said and was happy to be with his family. Sonny never seemed to get mad when they were in the country.

That morning, everyone seemed to be in great spirits. Felicia was even singing. Vinny sat in the back seat and kept himself busy with his etch-a-sketch when Sonny decided to get very chatty. He had a lot to get off his mind after the rough week they all had. Maybe he felt bad for what he had done to his mother.

"Vincenzo", Sonny said, "Life holds many challenges and sometimes you get caught in shit you never expected, then you don't know where to turn. That's when you look for peace and quiet."

Vinny thought, That explains why we get away and here comes my fathers thoughts on life.

"You're my only son, and when I'm with you and your mother like this, I feel close as a family. I wish we could live in Suffern all the time because that is where I'd rather be, but I've got responsibilities."

Vinny could tell that there was more meaning behind what Sonny was trying to say than his words were conveying, but when Vinny asked him why they couldn't go to Suffern more often, Sonny simply said

Vinny was too young to understand. Even though he was fourteen, Vinny was already familiar enough with the phrase, 'too young to understand' to know that his father was probably right. Besides, he had a feeling he did not want to know.

There were so few times that they all got along and enjoyed themselves as a family. Vinny did not intend to make waves with questions that might anger his father. Suffern was the only place where they could get away from their regular lives and have fun together. Sonny seemed to open up more to Vinny there. He always shared his philosophies and theories of life during the car ride. He spoke of trust and loyalty. He would say, "Trust no one but the family because if you can't trust them, then whom do you trust?" Street survival was another lesson, not that Sonny thought Vinny would end up in the streets. However, he thought that street smarts were practical insurance for any kid.

"When you have street smarts," Sonny would say, "You can survive anywhere. Your decisions are smarter and you can handle situations better and faster than the next guy."

Everyone in the family met at exit seventeen off the freeway. They would all grab a bite to eat and follow each for the last hour of the trip together. Sonny always seemed to like it best when everyone arrived. Uncle Nunzi brought the steaks, hot-dogs and potato salad. Aunt Catherine baked apple pies that everyone agreed were 'out of this world'. Vinny thought it was nice how everyone seemed to contribute to the weekend except Uncle Joe. Then, nobody ever expected anything from Uncle Joe anyway.

Aunt Catherine seemed quiet today. Vinny was surprised she did not say much except "That's nice" to just about anything anybody would say to her. She was also reminding Vinny to pray to God every day. Although he knew Aunt Catherine was religious, he wasn't used to her being so preoccupied with it like she was today. She wore a strange smiling expression on her face like she was either afraid of something or something bad was going to happen that she was trying to be polite about. Vinny could not figure her out.

Grandma Gina rode with Nunzi's family since they went right by her house on the way. She brought a pasta and peas dish that was always so good that everybody in the car had already picked at it so much during the ride that by the time they sat down for dinner, it was almost gone. You could tell that Grandma Gina was right off the boat from Italy. She was always pinching Vinny's cheek saying, "That's my grandson." Moreover, he loved her broken English as it rolled off her tongue.

Feasting was part of the weekend. Felicia made great pasta dishes, too, because Sonny was spoiled. As long as Vinny could remember, he never saw his dad eat fast food or anything else for that matter. Only Italian food entered his body. Uncle Nunzi brought hot-dogs and hamburgers for the kids knowing Sonny would not touch them. Felicia would stay up all night preparing outlandish dishes like veal parmesan, hot sausage and peppers, with stuffed shells. Even though Catherine contributed, family meals were Felicia's responsibility and she took that responsibility seriously. She did everything to make Sonny happy and comfortable. It was easier that way. Vinny had no idea how much Felicia operated out of sheer fear of his father. He just thought his mom was great and he hoped that one day he would find a wife as caring, loving and supportive as she was.

Vinny and Robert decided to get out of the way while everyone was getting settled and preparing the food. Although Vinny liked Robert, he was a sarcastic kid, always wanting to start a fight for no reason. It was as if he had a big chip on his shoulder. He always thought he knew everything, "Fifteen-going-on-twenty-seven", Aunt Catherine would say. Did that mean a twenty-seven year old was a bigger jerk? Vinny hoped not.

Sometimes Vinny thought of him as a skinny little black haired twerp who always had to have the last word. Robert was about five-foot three and probably weighed about a hundred and thirty pounds. He had short black hair and unusually thick eyebrows. However, as frustrating as Robert could be, Vinny still thought of him as a brother. After all, they had practically grown up together.

Suffern allowed the boys to go on great expeditions. They would go hiking and pretend to get lost in the wilderness. It was fun unless Robert got pissed off at Vinny because he could not be 'the leader'. This would always perplex Vinny. After all, there were only two of them. How much 'leadership' did climbing rocks and hiding behind trees take? It also bugged Vinny when Robert would tell him that Vinny was not 'leader' material since he was too honest and acted like a momma's boy. How can you be too honest? Vinny would wonder.

Quiet times always made Vinny fantasize about what he was going to do when he got older. He knew he was going to buy a big house and have fancy exotic cars like Lamborghinis and Ferraris. He also thought he could make a difference in the world somehow. Not always save it, but do his little part to help. He wanted to be a good person that did well. He wanted to earn the respect of others. Vinny did not want people to fear him as they did his father.

This time, when Robert and Vinny went on their hike, Vinny told Robert that he had decided he was going to be become a lawyer.

"Lawyer!" Robert chuckled. "You're lucky if you become a garbage collector!" Robert barked at him.

"Why can't I be a lawyer?" Vinny asked. He stopped, his hands on his hips, staring Robert down.

"Because you don't have the smarts and you're not tough enough. The only people you would represent would be the ones your dad sent over and they would walk all over you. Why would you want that humiliation?" Robert sneered. His mouth had twitched to the side as if he was hiding a smile. He knew he had hurt Vinny.

Vinny stayed quiet for a while. Robert hurt his feelings again. He was always doing that. Somehow, Vinny knew Robert acted that way because he was jealous of him for some reason. Why did everything with Robert have to feel like a competition?

Robert turned his back on Vinny and strode away. Vinny followed, quietly. Later, they found a little outhouse behind a burned out cabin. Robert pulled out a pack of firecrackers and some matches. Grinning at Vinny, he jerked his head toward the outhouse; he wanted to set them off inside it.

"You better not" Vinny told him.

"Who is going to know? It will look like it burned down with the cabin."

"It's wrong and it could start a fire out here. Besides, I am not taking the blame for you. Your dad is going be mad if you destroy someone else's property and you know it. I don't know why you'd want to do it anyway; it's nothing but a fire."

"I just want to see how things blow up. Besides, if I get in trouble, you can defend me, "Mr. Lawyer"!" Robert was always looking to make problems for himself. To Vinny, it seemed that Robert wanted the attention or something. Vinny gave up, "Do what you want." He shrugged his shoulders and started walking back toward their house. He heard Robert make an angry snort behind him and he yelled something incoherent in Vinny's direction. Vinny could hear him getting more furious as he watched Vinny walk away.

What a goodie-two-shoes., Robert thought. He knew if he blew up the outhouse, his dad would give him a lecture about how childish he was and how grown up and responsible Vinny always appeared to be. Robert was so sick of the comparison. Who was Nunzi Denucci's son anyway? He was, not Vinny.

Robert found himself running after Vinny. When he caught up to him he grabbed the back of Vinny's shirt, pushing him to the ground. He reached in his pocket and pulled out the matches, and lighting the firecrackers he had in his hand he threw them at Vinny. Before Vinny could get up, several of the little explosives went off with a loud bang and burned a hole in his shirt and jeans leg. The edges of the burned holes caught fire and he started to scream and roll in the leaves. This made the leaves started to burn, but his rolling extinguished them. By this time, his screams had brought his mother and father running out of the house, shouting his name. When they found the boys, Vinny was sitting on the ground, still crying and a little in shock. All the little fires were out. Robert was alternating between smiling smugly and looking toward Sonny nervously.

"Are you okay? What happened? We thought we heard gun shots."

Tears rolled down Vinny's face, his heart was beating fast. His hands were shaking and he realized that he had peed in his pants. He was so embarrassed that he stuttered when he answered his father, "Rob-Robert threw firecrackers on me."

Sonny looked disgusted and asked, "That's all? Why didn't you get up and kick the little shit in his ass rather than crying like a baby?"

Vinny hung his head, feeling totally humiliated by his father's outburst. "I don't know," he said.

Sonny grabbed him by his shirt and jerked him to his feet. His fingers bit into Vinny's shoulders as he shook him. His eyes narrowed as he looked at Vinny with anger.

"Vincenzo, what are you?" he shouted, "A fuckin' sissy? Am I raising a little girl or what?"

Vinny just stood there surprised that his father was yelling at him and calling him names. Robert had realized that he was home free and was openly smiling at the result of his bully tactics. The look on his face was smug. Uncle Sonny appreciates me more than he appreciates my dad, Robert thought.

Felicia went to Vinny and hugged him whispering in his ear, "Don't listen to him, Vinny. Robert is acting like an idiot as usual. I love you; let's get you into the house." She took Vinny's arm as he limped from the burn on his leg, but Sonny pulled her away from him, yelling that she was the reason he was so weak.

"Quit babying that boy, Felicia. No wonder he's got no guts." Then, he turned to Vinny, "I ought to whip your ass for snitching on Robert. I do not like snitches. You have to learn to take what comes like a man, Vincenzo. Be like your father... tough! If you don't toughen up soon, I'll have to toughen you up myself." Then Sonny grabbed Felicia by the arm and jerked her toward the house, leaving the two boys alone.

"Yeah, I'd want you to be my lawyer." Robert said, pointing to Vinny, "He did it your honor!" Robert said, his voice high pitched and mocking. "What a wimp." Robert turned and walked back to the house alone strutting in his arrogance. Vinny stood alone in the clearing staring at Robert as he retreated, wondering how much longer they would be in Suffern this weekend. Jeeze, we just got here, he thought. To think I was looking forward to this.

When Vinny reached the barbecue area, everybody was sitting around talking. Uncle Nunzi motioned Vinny to come over and then asked what had happened.

"Nothing, Uncle Nunzi," Vinny said. His voice was low and he turned his eyes away from Nunzi's stare.

Uncle Nunzi wasn't buying it. "Are you sure of that, Vinny?"

"Yes, nothing happened—it was just a little accident. That's all." Vinny said. He saw his father out of the corner of his eye, closing in on him.

"Good, you're learning." Sonny muttered, walking past them to get a drink.

"Hey, don't be afraid of me" Uncle Nunzi said. "If Robert did something to you, I want to know."

"I'm not a snitch, Uncle Nunzi." Vinny said. He raised his head and stared at his uncle whose face was impassive, hard.

"It's not snitching, Vinny; when someone already knows something happened. I mean, look at your clothes. You didn't get messed up just walking down a path."

Vinny looked down at the burn holes in his shirt, "It's okay, we were playing, but nothing happened."

From the drink table Sonny shouted out, "Hey, Nunzi! Leave the kid alone! He said nothing happened right, Vinny?"

Nunzi looked over at his brother, "Sonny, mind your own business! We're talking about something important here!" Looking back at Vinny, he lowered his voice, "Sometimes your father gets a little hotheaded and he doesn't think clear. Therefore, when he is pissing and yelling, just forgive him and overlook it. "Tell me what happened?" Nunzi asked quietly.

Vinny looked from his uncle to his father. Sonny stared at him, no emotion showing on his face as he raised the glass to drink. He nodded at Vinny. "Nothing," Vinny replied, his eyes still on his father, "I just wanted to check out the firecrackers Robert had and dropped them on me. It my fault. That is all. Okay?"

Without waiting for Nunzi to answer, Vinny walked over and sat down by his Uncle Joe who was reading the newspaper. Uncle Joe always kept to himself. To Vinny, he acted as if he was on another planet all the time. Glancing up at Vinny as if he had not been listening to all the conversation around him, Joe said, "You all right, Vinny?"

"Yea." Vinny said, his eyes returning to his father who stood staring at him, sipping at his drink.

Still reading, his face hidden behind the newspaper, Uncle Joe said, "You know, you should put your foot up Robert's ass so he won't pick on you. He'll back off."

Vinny looked down at Uncle Joe, surprised that he had an opinion at all. "I'm okay. I just don't like to fight." Vinny said as he sunk down next to him on the grass.

"Well, I got some bad news for you, kid", Uncle Joe said, as he put down his paper. "Your father's a bastard and an asshole. He's going to teach you to do many things you won't like to do; one of them is going to be how to fight back and not take shit from anybody."

Vinny glanced quickly at his uncle Joe. He had never heard anyone call his father a bastard or an asshole. In addition, he never thought he would hear something like that from Uncle Joe.

"I'll worry about that when the time comes." Vinny said.

"Okay, we'll see," Uncle Joe, said calmly as he went back to his paper.

"So, what are you reading, Uncle Joe?"

"There's a story about some Mafia guys," he said as he looked over at Vinny's face for some reaction. He saw none.

"Mafia, I don't understand? I've heard about it, but that is all. "What is it?" Vinny asked him.

"Well, Vinny, it's something that started a long time ago in Italy. Some men got together from different towns in Italy and formed what they called 'La Familia'. Each family was made of Bosses, Captains, and Soldiers. The leader of the entire family was the 'Boss'" Uncle Joe explained. "Under him was the Captain, under him, the Soldiers. These men did many illegal things that got the attention of the cops and eventually the FBI. The Feds gave the collection of crews a name. They called them the 'MAFIA'. How they picked the word Mafia is a whole other story going back to a time when the French invaded Italy."

Vinny stared at Uncle Joe, fascinated. He could not believe Uncle Joe knew all this stuff. Uncle Joe never knew anything according to his father. He was just 'the bum'.

"So anyway, these crews would go out and terrorize small business owners then offer them 'protection' from the terrorism for a price. That meant that if the businesses paid up, the crews would leave them alone. The bosses wanted to be the most powerful and richest men in the world. They would have their crews steal from everybody, then go and sell whatever they stole, sometimes even back to the person whom they stole it from. They would threaten people, even have people killed if they did not get what they wanted or if the people did not do what they were told to do. If you were a soldier and you did not make money for your Boss, you could be killed. They intimidated everybody. If you were in business making money the Mafia wanted a piece of your business. Sometimes one crew would make more money than another would and that would set off a war between them. They would start killing each other because they were jealous of who made the most money. They would use tactics that were so devious and underhanded it would make you puke. Later, they found they could make money here, expand out, so they came over to the United States and started setting up their operations. The Mafia is the biggest and strongest criminal organization in the world and it's growing stronger every day."

"What's happening is that there are many jealous wiseguys, that's what they call the crew members, and they want what the other family's wiseguys are getting, so they're killing each other over it. To put it in perspective, they are fighting over sections in New York, which are broken up into five areas, the turf: The Bronx, Brooklyn, Queens, Long Island and Manhattan. Five families control the Mafia organization. They split up the turf and every business category is assigned to the families as to who controls what. One gets construction, one gets the garbage contracts, some take the sports action or prostitution and the massage parlors. They decide who should control the drugs; who should run the gambling casinos; and everything else. It's a complicated thing."

"How can they get away with that stuff?" Vinny asked. He was shocked, this was something that he had never known, and it surprised him that Uncle Joe seemed to be an expert in it.

"Well, here, read this." Uncle Joe handed Vinny the newspaper. The front-page headline said in big bold letters, MOB THREATENS NIGHTCLUB OWNER. Vinny read, "Vito Scarabelli, the new Mafia

Godfather, is showing signs of what this new Boss is all about. According to police sources, members of the Scarabelli family allegedly sent two unnamed representatives to the new jazz nightclub, The Blue Note, located in Queens at the west corner of 36th and Crescent Street. According to witnesses, the men assaulted the owner because he failed to let Vito Scarabelli know of his intention to open a nightclub in Scarabelli's neighborhood. Mr. Otis Jerkins, owner of The Blue Note quoted as saying that he was, 'Furious and not going to be bullied around by un-American gangsters who don't even pay taxes.' He further plans to take any needed legal action against the two men cited in the police report. Mr. Scarabelli denies these allegations and responded with a slander lawsuit against Mr. Jerkins for referring to him as 'un-American'."

"Wow, Uncle Joe," Vinny sat there in shock. He got goose bumps down his back when he remembered that 'Scarabelli' was the name of the person Sal was so upset about when he came to the door the other night. Vinny shook his head to himself, 'But, that couldn't be the same 'Scarabelli', he thought. 'How would Sal and especially his father, know someone like that?'

"What does this mean Uncle Joe? They going to court?" he asked.

"No, Vinny, I doubt that. I'll bet those guys will teach that club owner a painful lesson for that bit of public disrespect."

"What type of lesson?" Vinny was fascinated by the story. It was too much like the movies to be real. Like most kids, Vinny never read the paper and this was his first exposure to the way powerful men acted and how those same men could control the world around him.

"My guess is that they'll blow up his nightclub with him in it." Joe said matter-of-factly.

"Are you serious?" Vinny asked, stunned. "Why would they do something like that? You can't just kill somebody because he didn't ask permission to open a business."

"Vinny, you have to understand, to these guys it's their neighborhood and they don't want anybody moving in or opening businesses unless they go and talk to the Boss first. Get permission for their business to be there. The Bosses think they are protecting the neighborhood by only allowing businesses to operate that pay for the privilege. They are also prejudiced. They do not want blacks or foreigners in the neighborhood, running it down…just their own kind. The Mafia likes to protect its own. They only want to live around other Italians and sometimes Jews. The Jews seem to understand them and give them the respect they were looking for. These guys may be crooks and thieves, but at least they're only crooks and thieves in their own neighborhoods."

Vinny just listened, feeling a twinge of shame that he was Italian. Did average Americans think all Italians were like this? Vinny hoped not. He knew he did not want to live in any of the neighborhoods Uncle Joe described and he could not imagine why anyone in a regular neighborhood would want an Italian to move in. Vinny thought, "What if the neighbors in our building thought that his family was in the Mafia?" Where **could** he live when he grew up?

Uncle Joe could see Vinny was upset at what he had learned. Reaching out, he turned the paper quickly to another page and said, "Vinny, you just forget about this and don't let your father know I told you. He'd be mad that I showed you that story."

"Uncle Joe, do you know Mafia people?" Vinny asked.

"Yea, but I stay away from them. I'm not going to tell you who they are because you wouldn't know them anyway, so go away and be quiet." Uncle Joe waved Vinny off and went back to his paper seemingly forgetting Vinny existed.

"Okay." Uncle Joe was like that. He could be friendly and fun for a short while until he remembered whatever it was that made his life so sour, then he'd shut you out. Vinny felt that Uncle Joe cared for him, he just was not the type that could be nice to anyone for long.

Vinny got up and brushed the grass from his pants as he went over to his mother. She was sitting at the table stirring her coffee with Aunt Catherine and he leaned against her chair, "Mom, do you know Mafia?"

She gasped and quickly put her hand over Vinny's mouth, "Don't you ever let me here you say that again!" she hissed, her eyes darting to Catherine, fear on her face.

Vinny gave her a puzzled look, "Why not?" he asked. He looked over at Aunt Catherine who had her eyebrows raised in a questioning look, her face alert and observant.

"Well, Felicia?" Aunt Catherine finally said, waiting for her to respond to his question.

"Well, nothing!" said Felicia, angrily throwing down her spoon and glancing up, "Vinny, I don't want to discuss it and I don't want you to ask anyone about it. Is that clear?"

"Yeah, mom, okay, okay. I hear you." Vinny said. He backed away from them, shaking his head, wondering why it was such a big deal. His mother's reaction had made him curious though and he was now more determined than ever to find out what this was. He found his father at the barbeque grill and asked if he would cook a steak for him. Sonny always cooked steaks on request because he could not stand to see a good piece of meat drying out on the grill. Sonny has weird rules.

Vinny studied his dad's profile while he seasoned the meat and positioned it just right over the coals. He wondered again why Uncle Joe said not to ask his father about the Mafia. It seemed like Sonny was the logical person to ask, being a successful businessperson and all. Vinny looked over at his mother who was intently watching him as though she knew what he was thinking. When Vinny's steak was ready, he thanked his dad and went to sit under a tree alone. Maybe he would talk to his grandma about it. She would usually listen and tell him what he wanted to know. In any event, Vinny decided to keep his ears open for more information he could gather about the Mafia.

Finishing his steak, Vinny leaned back against the tree, wondering what to do. He did not want to search out Robert. In addition, there was not anything around he could do on his own, so he decided to follow up his questions and find his grandmother. Still avoiding his cousin, he took his plate into the kitchen where his grandma was washing dishes. Even though they had a dishwasher, Grandma Gina believed it never got the plates clean enough to eat off, so she would not use it. Since they were alone, Vinny thought this might be a good time to see what grandma knew.

"Do you know Mafia guys grandma?" he asked as he slipped his plate and utensils into the soapy water.

"What? Where did that question come from?" Grandma Gina picked up a dishtowel and began to dry the bowls.

"I don't know. I was just reading an article in the newspaper about it and wondered if you knew... that's all."

Grandma Gina just shook her head, "I don't know what to tell you, Vinny. Do not worry about those things. You just go to school and study hard."

Vinny saw she would not answer anything else on the subject so he just kissed her on the cheek and wandered back outside. Perching under the tree again, he pulled a piece of grass out and started to chew on it, thoughts wandering through his head as the warm air and the food worked together to slowly close his eyes. Shrugging mentally, his last thoughts before he drifted off were, 'Oh, well, it had nothing to do with my life anyway.'

The next day, Vinny was leaning against the window in his bedroom, watching the rain hit the windowsill. At least he had been able to hike a little this afternoon before it started to rain. Rain always depressed him. It was hard to feel positive and happy on a day when everything around him was gloomy and gray and not likely to change. He tended to stay in his room and think on days like this, but not anymore—thinking was becoming depressing too. Why were his mother and father not getting along anymore? They seemed to be fighting a lot lately. His father and uncle had not been getting along as well either. Sonny seemed to be so much on edge that he fought with everybody. Vinny had been glad everyone left Suffern a little early since he and his parents were going to stay at the cabin a few extra days. Now he was not so sure. It was raining and there was nothing to do.

After a couple of hours of feeling restless and bored, Vinny got up and went into the kitchen to find something to eat. Snapping on the light, he went to the refrigerator and pulled open the door, sticking his head inside to look around.

"Hey, Vincenzo!" Vinny turned around, startled. His father was lounging in the dark kitchen. Sonny was sitting on a chair, he was leaning back, had his feet propped up on the table, and he was drinking a glass red wine. Vinny thought the bottle on the table looked empty.

"Jeeze, you scared me, Dad!" Vinny said.

"Sorry son. What are you doing?"

"I'm looking for something to snack on."

"Okay," he said, rising. "Don't stay up too late, we're leaving in the morning and don't make a mess for your mother to clean up." Despite his father's short temper, sometimes he was a good father and husband. It was nice to hear Sonny speak in a manner that showed he cared about them for a change.

"See you tomorrow, Vinny. I have to go and make some phone calls."

"Goodnight dad." Vinny said as Sonny walked out of the room. Vinny smiled, he loved his father, especially at times like this, when he was calm and not yelling about everything.

Vinny rummaged through the refrigerator and decided to fix some left over baked ziti. He took the chair near the window where his father had been sitting and glanced at the newspaper lying on the table. The headline caught his attention and he slowly put down his plate to read further. The article read, Mob Boss Killed! The Mafia was still having a street war over who killed the Godfather, Vito Scarabelli. Jim MacKay of the Daily Tribune, who had been following up on the brutal murder of the Mob Boss, wrote that there were hit men coming in from all over the United States to find the person who pulled the trigger. Apparently, they were sure an ambitious local Boss did the killing.

MacKay continued by writing, "Whoever killed The Godfather is going to pay a pretty heavy price and I would guess his family may end up dead too. In an interview, one of the reputed Captains in the Scarabelli family, known as "The Duke", said, "The bastard who did this better kill himself or disappear from the face of this earth before we find him. He has to be a real low-life son-of-a-bitch to kill a good man like Vito Scarabelli."

There was a picture at the bottom of the article of two men laying face down in a pool of blood at a nightclub called Dreamland, found on 57th and West Broadway. The paper said the men were shot twice each in the back of the head.

Dear God, what sick people we have in this world. Vinny, thought as he put the paper down to finish eating his pasta. He gobbled his food quickly, got up and put his dish in the sink, then headed for his bedroom. He went into the bathroom first to wash his face and brush his teeth, and then got into bed. Saying his prayers, he tucked his arms behind his head and relaxed into the pillow. Vinny was still surprised that people could run around killing each other in public places and get away with it. Do the hit men think they will find the killer before the police do? And, how would a newspaper reporter even know that hit men were hired? All these questions went through Vinny's mind as he drifted off to sleep.

CHAPTER 3
LEARNING STREET SMARTS

* * *

VINNY HAD JUST TURNED 15 YEARS OLD when his father started taking him to the horse track. Every Wednesday, Sonny would gamble. Sal usually had some inside information on a few horses that were going to win, so Sonny would keep Vinny home from school and take him to the track with him. Felicia argued with Sonny constantly over his taking Vinny out of school but Sonny was thick headed and she had no choice but to let it slide. Vinny would complain that he needed a note for his teachers; otherwise, he would get into trouble, so Sal made a phone call to the school. Vinny never had to take a note again. Sonny influenced many people.

Vinny never knew why his father wanted to take him to go gamble. It was okay, but it could get a little boring for a kid. Vinny would try to stay home sometimes but Sonny would say, "My son, this is a learning experience and you are going." Vinny never understood what the learning experience was, but when his father said he had to go, he went. However, all he ever learned was that there was a room filled with smoke and men screaming at a television screen that showed horses running around a track. It did not seem like much of an education to him.

The Denucci's went to a place in Queens called an OTB, or off-track betting, parlor. OTB's were outlets set up all over the city so people could place bets on horses without going to the racetrack. To Vinny, the racetrack seemed like a cool place to be, better than the OTB's. 'Wouldn't it be more fun to be there in person than this smelly place,' he wondered.

Sonny told Vinny that these places were located all over New York City and they made it easy for degenerate people to lose their money.

If they were losing their money, why would they go there then? Vinny thought. In addition, why are we here? Some of this made no sense to Vinny.

Arriving at the O.T.B. around noontime, Vinny could watch the horses run around the track on big screen TVs set up everywhere. The room filled with people who looked like they lived there and that they never took a shower, and smelled like it too. Most of the people cursed every time they lost a race and then walked around telling everyone whose horse they were planning to bet on in the next event - as if anyone would take the advice of these people!

Some of the gamblers had such gross vocabularies; Vinny knew that if Grandma Gina were there, everybody would have to have his mouth washed out with soap. "Goddamn" seemed to be everybody's favorite word. The smoke from cigars and cigarettes was so thick you could not see the door from the other side of the room. Vinny wished they would go to a real horse race track where he could see the horses in the paddock and hear the crowd roar as the winning horse thundered past the post.

Sonny told Vinny to go and sit down in the corner with Sal. Sal did not talk much, he just looked around as if he were a seeing-eye dog, and making sure his master would not get into trouble or go off in the wrong direction. Sonny was talking to a person in a wheelchair named Smitty. Smitty placed bets for Sonny while he walked around and talked to other people. Smitty was an unhealthy and nasty-looking man with thin scraggly hair and a long gray-red beard that had grown way down his chest. Vinny guessed that he had to be about fifty-five years old and had no legs. He was wearing some old rags. When Sonny came around to where he and Sal were sitting, Vinny asked Sonny what had happened to Smitty's legs. During the Vietnam War, they were blown-off in an explosion. Vinny felt sorry for Smitty even though he looked right at home in this sleazy place. Maybe this was his way of dealing with his injury. Maybe it was some type of therapy.

After about two hours of betting, Sonny got hungry and Sal drove them to a local restaurant called Benito's. Benito's was a small Italian café located on Mulberry Street, in Little Italy. The atmosphere was nice. The smell of roasted garlic filled the room. Italian music played softly, a giant wine rack stretched from floor-to-ceiling, completely taking up the back wall. The hostess, a tall, thin, longhaired brown-haired woman, always greeted everyone at the door. "Buon giorno!" which Sonny told Vinny meant 'good day'.

Benito's was Sonny's favorite place and always the highlight of Vinny's 'afternoon with dad'. The chef never failed to come out of the kitchen and greet Sonny, respectfully asking, "How are you today, Mr. Denucci?" Chef Gino, a big three hundred pound man, was short with a full black and gray beard and heavy Italian accent.

"Fine, thank you, Gino, I'll have the usual." Vinny was always impressed that they never looked at a menu.

'The Usual' consisted of a little of everything from soup to pasta and dessert. Starting with a cup of minestrone, then some roasted peppers soaked in lots of garlic, Gino would serve sliced homemade mozzarella in olive oil and fresh basil that was delicious too. There was always bruschetta on the table, which were pieces of Italian bread topped with chopped tomatoes, onions, basil anda more garlic. Next came a Caesar salad and the main dish consisted of angel hair pasta with a light pink sauce along with whatever meat the chef thought was prepared special that evening. Sonny finally finished with a cup of decaf coffee, complete with a splash of sambuca liquor and a slice of homemade cheesecake.

Whatever Gino thought Sonny would like, he would bring out. Sonny had a healthy appetite so Gino would say, "Please try this, Mr. Denucci. I would much appreciate your opinion." Sonny would taste everything and the chef seemed to be sincerely interested in Sonny's evaluation. One night while dining at Benito's, Gino created a dish that was made with chicken, potatoes, and small pieces of ham with peas, onions and garlic. Vinny thought it was okay but Sonny raved so Gino thanked him repeatedly, then later put it as a regular item on the menu. Sonny was pleased about that. He would point that incident out to Vinny as a good example of the restaurant's respect for a successful and conscientious businessperson of good taste.

The next few hours, after a fabulous meal at Benito's, Sal drove Sonny and Vinny around to different businesses, 'visiting friends'. Vinny asked his father why he did not get out and say hello to everyone, Sonny replied, "Vinny, it's like this; we are all friends and we don't have to see each other just to say hello. It is like, they know I am out here in the car and they give me their regards through Sal. Just knowing I'm here is good enough for them."

Sal pulled up in front of a travel agency, turned to Sonny and asked, "How much do I give Lenny?"

Sonny replied, "Five thousand, and give him a five point vig."

Sonny and Vinny sat in the car waiting, "I need to explain some of the things I do so you start to understand a little about my business," Sonny said. "Sometimes people want to start a company or they get behind in debt or they go to a bank for a loan and get turned down, that's when I help them. I have the word put out on the street that if anyone needs money they should reach out for one of my people. I have my people then set up appointments with them and loan them money. I charge a little interest. I then give them a payment plan so they can pay back the loan. If they miss a payment, I add on some more interest. Sometimes I take collateral if I am not comfortable with the person. I am not friends with any of them, it's just business. But, I was there when they needed me and they remember that."

"Is this legal?" Vinny asked.

Sonny looked surprised at the question, "Why would you ask a question like that?"

"Well, it just seems odd that you would lend money to people you don't know." Vinny said, as he shrugged his shoulders.

Sonny laughed, "You think banks know everybody they lend money to? Vinny, you're still a little too young to understand what I'm going to tell you, but, I am a Boss of an organization who's name I'm not at liberty to say right now. We are an organization who helps people out. Everybody needs a little help now and then and when they do, I'm there to provide it."

"Why would banks turn people down?"

"Some of these people don't have enough of collateral or there credit history is not that good. If you have excellent credit or something like property to use as collateral to secure a loan, then you are a good risk and the bank will lend you money. If you do not have decent credit or collateral, then the bank will not. That is the way it is. Nevertheless, I trust people and see their mere existence in life as a valuable asset, so I give them what they need. It's good business."

"Yeah, I guess when I make money as a lawyer, I can do the same like you and lend out money to help people too." Vinny said, his face serious. Sonny began to laugh and Vinny could not figure out why his father thought that would be funny.

Sal got back in the car and Sonny told him to drive over to a bar on Staten Island called 'O'Toole's'. When they arrived, Sonny let Vinny come in with him and Sal. Vinny could tell this was an Irish joint because of the green clover they had painted on the window. When they walked inside, it was dark and smelled like beer, piss, and mildew. Vinny thought he might puke up his dinner, the smell was so bad. It looked like a basement that had not been cleaned out in years; cobwebs all over the place, dark, dingy and with a sticky floor. The bar had about eleven bar stools and several tables stood around that were all crooked and mismatched. Vinny did not know how his father could stand it in there and tried to be polite when Sonny introduced him to the bar's owner, Joe Francis.

Joe was about two hundred pounds of solid fat. He was missing a few front teeth, his gray hair covered his partly bald head, and he dressed as if he was living in the sixties, complete with bell-bottom pants and a colorful polyester shirt. Joe looked like he did not shave too often either and smelled like his bar: disgusting.

Joe shook Vinny's hand and said, "Glad to meet you," then, leading the way to the corner of the bar, Joe offered everyone a seat and a drink.

Everyone said, "No Thank you."

Sonny turned to his son. "Mr. Francis has our pinball and poker machines, Vinny. We rent them to him and whatever the machines earn; we split the money, 50/50. One day you'll own this route and it will all be yours." Vinny was shocked, "How much money does this route earn?"

"About five thousand dollars a week," Sonny replied.

"Wow, this is going to be mine?" Vinny had a smile on his face. Suddenly the place did not look so bad.

Sonny was pleased with his son's response, "Yes. Go with Sal and wait in the car while I talk to Mr. Francis. I won't be long." Sal and Vinny headed toward the front door. Vinny had excitement in his eyes as he pushed opened the door. Then he opened the back door and climbed in. Sal walked around the front of the car looking both ways as if to see whether there was anyone was watching them. Sal got into the car and rolled down the driver window. He positioned the rear view mirror so he could see if anyone was going to creep up on them.

While waiting, Vinny asked Sal about the bar, "Isn't that a lot of money?"

"Vinny, you're going to be lucky," Sal said. "You don't know half the stuff that goes on with your father."

"What do you mean? What stuff?"

"Your father has about three hundred machines located all over New York City, Queens, Brooklyn, and the Bronx."

"Sal, are you kidding?"

"No." Suddenly conscious that he was talking too much, Sal hastened to add, "But don't say that I told you about that."

Vinny sat in the back seat thinking about all the money the machines would make for him. Sal said he had 300 of them! 300! Vinny smiled with excitement. Settling back to contemplate his future wealth, he could not wait to join his father's organization. 'My father must make a lot of money,' he thought. He was aware that they lived well. Their condominium was big and spacious, high up on the twenty-first floor of a beautiful twenty five-story building, with a view everyone said was "to die for." They had expensive marble floors, imported leather furniture, a TV in every room and a Jacuzzi in two of the master suites, one of which Vinny occupied and one in his mother's that did not work.

It is true that Vinny never had to worry about money, but he knew other kids who seemed to have more spending cash than he ever got. Vinny decided that maybe his father thought he was mature enough to learn the financial success so he could be just like him.

Sonny came out, got in the car, and told Sal to drive them home. Sonny was tired and Vinny was excited to tell his mother the things he had learned today. Rush hour was over but traffic was still horrendous. There must have been an accident. It seemed to take forever to get home and Vinny was anxious. Sonny opened the glove box, pulled out a cassette and put it in to the player. Frank Sinatra was Sonny's idol. Then Sonny leaned back and nodded the entire trip home. Once there, Vinny dashed out of the car, hearing Sonny shout behind him, "Slow down boy!"

Running into the lobby and straight to the elevator, Vinny got to the twenty-first floor and ran all the way down the hall to their apartment. He unlocked the door and dropped his key on the foyer table, running through the house shouting, "Mother! Mother! Where are you?"

"Vinny, I'm here in your room putting away your clothes." Her voice came muffled from down the hall.

Vinny ran into his room, out of breath and hugged his mother. "Did you know that Dad has pinball and poker machines all over New York City and they make money? He told me that they are going to be mine! I will be rich! Isn't that great?" Felicia stared at Vinny, she did not look too happy.

"What's wrong, Mom?"

She shook her head, "Vinny, come here and just let me hug you tight. I am just sad because you are growing up fast. You won't be my little boy much longer."

"I love you, Mom. I will always be here to take care of you. When I am rich, we will go on trips and buy nice things. We'll have so much fun." Felicia smiled at that. She always wanted to travel but Sonny did not like to. He was always too busy.

"Felicia!" Sonny's voice boomed from the hall.

"I'm here, in Vinny's room! I'll be there in a minute," she said as she hugged Vinny once more.

Sonny came into Vinny's bedroom. "I'm hungry. I want something light tonight because we ate earlier. I'm going to take a quick shower first, and then I want to go to bed so hurry up and cook something."

"Okay," she said and quickly finished putting away Vinny's socks then kissed him on her way out.

Vinny watched his mother scurry to the kitchen and thought, sometimes his father was a real asshole. He had a habit of ordering Felicia around as if she was his servant. After all that they ate tonight, Vinny could not figure out how his father could still be hungry.

Vinny changed into shorts and a T-shirt and went into the kitchen to see what he could do.

"Do you need help?" he asked her.

"Sure! Open those cans of tomatoes and pour them into the pot." Felicia smiled at him, waving her hand vaguely in the direction of one of the cupboards.

When Sonny came into the kitchen, he was quiet. He went over to the cabinet where they kept the wine glasses, then poured him a glass from an open bottle of red wine. Vinny thought that he seemed to be drinking more than usual lately. Not saying a word, Sonny took his bottle and his glass with him to the dining room and seated himself at the head of the table, waiting like a king for his food.

The water started to boil and Vinny added the pasta. His mother got some lettuce and cucumber out of the refrigerator to make a salad. Vinny checked the pasta to see if it was cooked enough to his father's likes. It was still a little hard but the sauce was just about ready. It had started to boil. Vinny got his mother the big serving dish, cut up some bread and drained the pasta. He put it onto the platter so his mother could pour the sauce over it and took it into the dining room. His mother followed with the salad and bread. Felicia sat down slowly, and looked nervously at Sonny. Vinny sat down next to her, wondering what was wrong. Sonny bowed his head and began to pray.

"Thank you God for our food and my son. Amen," Sonny made the sign of the cross across his chest and then folded his hands. No matter how much of a jerk he could be, Sonny always said grace before a meal.

They all sat around quietly eating their dinner. Sonny ate fast. The sauce was all over his mouth. Sonny finished first then excused himself, kissing Felicia goodnight on the forehead. He then turned toward Vinny, sauce dripping off his chin.

"Vinny, I'll see you tomorrow. You did well today. Do not stay up too late watching TV. Okay?" he said. Vinny nodded to his father, but he had already left the room, not looking back to see if Vinny had even heard him.

Felicia got up too and told Vinny to go and study while she did the dishes. Vinny took one more bite, dropped his plate off in the kitchen, and then went out on the balcony off his bedroom to study. However, instead of studying, Vinny could not get his mind off the bar and all the things he intended to buy with the money that would someday be his. The first thing he was going to buy was a heart pendant for his mother that he would have inscribed with the words, "I love you, Mom." He thought about some fancy clothes for her too, and a bracelet for himself with his name spelled out in diamonds, or maybe, a fancy sports car. He would have a nice looking girl who would be proud to be with him and they would hit all the fancy nightclubs in town. Thoughts of this fantasy money were going to his head. Tomorrow he was still Vinny Denucci, student, so, tonight he had better read a little of his history book and get his head screwed back on straight.

His mother knocked gently on his door. She came into his room to tell him it was 9:30 p.m. and to warn him not to stay up too late.

"I only have ten more pages, mom, then I'll go to bed." Vinny had a quiz the next morning that he had not studied for but at least he read the chapter and he could get by. Felicia kissed his cheek. She was so proud of him.

Around 1:00 a.m., Vinny was stumbling into the bathroom when the doorbell started to ring and ring. He stayed in the bathroom, quietly, with the door opened just enough to hear what was going on. His father finally got up to answer it. Vinny figured his father must have been expecting someone because he did not cuss at all.

Standing at the door was Sonny's friend, Charlie. Charlie always wore black puma sweat suits and was like Sal, always hanging around with Sonny. He was six-foot and about two hundred pounds of solid muscle. Charlie liked to work out a lot. He wore his brown hair in a short crew cut and was intimidating. When Charlie was in the Navy, he had gotten a tattoo of a battleship inscribed on his right arm. Vinny put his ear to the door and heard Charlie tell his father that Joey Pineta from Chicago was coming to town to teach some guy named Winston Lamont a lesson for trying to rip off money from one of his friends.

Vinny thought that he was having deja-vu. Not again, Vinny thought. Vinny listened with his ear glued against the door. He listened to their plans for teaching somebody 'a lesson' and could not believe this was happening for a second time. What was his father really involved in? This did not sound like normal business procedures. It sounded like the stuff Vinny had been reading in the paper, the stuff about the Mafia. Things started to make a little sense. Vinny's mind began to put pieces together. No wonder nobody wanted to admit knowing Mafia people. It was probably because his dad was one! Everything he knew about them and their organization pointed to his dad's activities; lending money and painful lessons for past-due clients were Mafia characteristics. It seemed to be coincidental that Sonny would get visits, all hours of the night lately and always talked privately to his 'friends'.

Vinny knew his imagination was probably working overtime, that he was seeing things that were not there, but there was something going on and he was going to figure out what it was. After all, lawyers have to know all the facts to present their case.

Vinny heard his father's voice, "Why doesn't he just send somebody to do the job?"

"He's going to make a statement with this one so he doesn't get fucked anymore. He doesn't want anybody to try anymore bullshit." Charlie said.

"Where is he going to be at?" Vinny heard his father ask.

"He's coming here first to get your approval before he goes and wastes this guy."

"Here? Oh shit!" Sonny shouted. "Charlie, get Sal and the boys together. Let us be ready for anything. I know he is on our side, but I don't trust nobody anymore, especially some of these assholes who get their fuckin' rocks off killing people." Sonny said, "Why don't they make other arrangements"? I could give a fuck less what they do."

Vinny stood behind his door, shocked. He could not believe he had just heard his father say that someone was going to be murdered and Joey Pineta was coming here to get Sonny's permission! What was going on? Who was his father, anyways? Vinny was scared to death to have this psycho in his neighborhood, much less his house. He could not imagine why his father would hang around with these people. Vinny started to tremble, his mouth got dry and he felt like he had a lump the size of a grapefruit in his throat. He had even more questions, but did not know who to ask for answers.

Opening the bathroom door Vinny slowly tip-toed out and into his room. Jumping back into bed, he said The Lord's Prayer to himself three times before he could fall back asleep.

The next morning Vinny heard laughter coming from the living room and he wondered who it was. Hoping it was not the murderer he had heard about last night, he got out of bed, threw on some clothes, and walked into the living room. Sonny was talking to a police officer! Vinny's heart just about leaped out of his throat!

"Good morning," he said as casually as he could.

"Good morning, Vincenzo. Say hello to Detective Calloway."

The detective turned toward Vinny and, relieved, Vinny recognized him, although he was not used to seeing him in uniform. Jack Calloway was a detective from the 115th Precinct who came by frequently and talked to Sonny. Sometimes he even came to their parties and other family gatherings. Vinny could even remember him up at the Suffern house once. Jack was a part of the family and Sonny trusted him, thus he was welcome.

Detective Calloway was about six-foot four, middle-aged, with a potbelly like an overstuffed cowboy. Every time Vinny saw him, he was wearing cowboy boots, a big belt buckle and a plaid shirt. He chewed tobacco, which Vinny thought was disgusting. 'How could anybody chew anything that makes your teeth turn brown, and makes you look like there's a golf ball stuck inside the side of your mouth? And, as if that isn't bad enough, tobacco chewers were always spitting brown crap everywhere. Jack would wear what Vinny thought was a ridiculous straw cowboy hat which made him look like a hayseed farmer even though he was a nice friendly guy. The uniform he had on today was an improvement.

Jack and Sonny talked for a while longer and finished their business. Jack excused himself to go to the bathroom and Sonny turned to Vinny.

"Vincenzo, you remember that man, don't you? If you ever need help, you can rely on him, okay. Do not trust anybody except Detective Calloway. He shows up when I want him and when I need information on anybody, he gives it to me. He is always professional, and he is a good person to have around. That's why I keep him on the payroll."

"What do you mean, 'he's on your payroll'?"

At that moment, Detective Calloway walked back into the living room, "Sonny, do you think you should be telling your kid about me?" he said. His voice was low, and he stared at Vinny.

Ignoring him, Sonny said, "Time for you to leave Detective. If I need you, I'll call."

"Goodbye, Mr. Denucci." Detective Calloway nodded his head and walked to the front door.

"Vincenzo, listen up! Many cops like to gamble. It is against the law and their policy. If regular citizens can gamble, the people who protect us should be able too, right? Therefore, I arrange for the cops to bet horses and sports through Jack and we keep it among ourselves. That's what I mean when I say 'he's on our payroll'."

"Our payroll" Vinny said.

"No, I mean my payroll. I pay him for handling the odds and payoffs for me. However, as my only son, you share in my income so I can say 'Our Payroll."

Therefore, Jack was a dirty cop. Vinny knew enough to realize that a cop who took money to do something illegal and persuaded other cops to do it too was corrupt. Funny, you never believe that the stuff you see on TV happens in real life, but it does. Thank God for 'America's Most Wanted'!

Vinny lost all respect for Detective Calloway now. He wondered how many others were like him. What is their motto? 'To protect and serve'? On the other hand, is it to protect and serve them? Vinny was mad and thought it was a shame that his local law enforcement was going to hell, and that his father was leading the way!

Vinny went back into his bedroom to get ready for school, his mind whirling. He had to know more. When putting on his clothes, he thought he might do some research on the New York based Mafia. It was getting late. He rushed out the door and stood outside for a couple of minutes before he finally flagged down a cab. He told the driver, "Manhattan High School, and make it quick please."

"No problem," said the cabby and, twenty-four minutes later, Vinny made it to school just before the bell went off. He ran up the stairs and walked into his classroom. Sitting in math class, waiting for the teacher to start, a new student walked in. The teacher, Mr. Torrez shouted for everyone to settle down and welcome the new boy.

Mr. Torrez asked, "What might your name be young man? Do you have paper work for me?"

"My name's Al Brennen, sir." Al seemed to be shy and looked scared as he handed Mr. Torrez his transcripts. "Mr. Brennen, 4.0 average", Mr. Torrez said. "Make your way to the back of the class and find a seat.."

Vinny could see that by the way Al was dressed that he fit the profile of a 'goody-goody'. He could also tell Al was a real geek. However, he was a smart geek. He was dressed in a blue and yellow plaid shirt, dark green pants and skips, which meant his parents did not have much money. Skips were cheap sneakers that people bought at the five and dime store. He had blonde hair and a few freckles spattered across his nose and cheeks. He had blue eyes. As he walked down the aisle, he kept staring at the floor until he reached the back of the room. Coming to a new school must have given him butterflies in his stomach, because Al had all the signs. Somehow, Vinny felt sorry for him. As Al started to walk toward the back of the class to find a seat, Vinny stood up and motioned him over to his side of the room, "Al," he said. "Come over here and sit by me." Vinny had decided that, geek or not, Al could use some new friends so he might as well be the first one.

Henry leaned across the aisle whispering, "Hey, Vinny! Does that new person look like lawyer material or what? Maybe he'll be your roommate in law school!" Henry laughed uproariously. He seemed to think that he was hilarious.

"At least he's going to be something when he grows up, unlike some people I could name." Vinny retorted.

Henry was the first person Vinny met when he came to this school. Some person started to pick a fight with Vinny and Henry jumped in and saved his butt. Nevertheless, Henry could be a real jerk sometimes, too. He was five-foot ten and super skinny. He lived off junk food that contributed to a bad case of acne. He had black hair, something fuzzy that he called 'a mustache' above his lip and wore a hanging dead man for an earring. Henry was not the sharpest knife in the drawer, but Vinny liked him, obnoxious tendencies and all. Vinny even tutored Henry right before big tests and, in trade, Henry had taught Vinny how to fight.

After that first day of school, the two boys became good friends. Henry was not bright, but was funny as hell and always hustled to make a buck. Even though he was quick with a smart remark, Henry had friends and was the man to see if anybody needed anything.

Al walked over, grabbed the seat on Vinny's other side and said, "Thanks. What's your name?"

Henry butted in, deciding to answer for him, "You got the number one man in the school, my friend. Meet Vinny Denucci. I'm Henry, his partner-in-crime."

"You just move here?" Vinny asked Al.

"Yeah, I live over on 24th street and York Avenue."

"Hey! That's up the street from me," Vinny replied. "I'm on 21st and York. Well, we have to be friends," Vinny reached over to shake Al's hand. 'Shake a hand, make a friend', that was one of Grandma Gina's words of wisdom.

Al and Vinny hung out together for the rest of the day and when it was three o'clock, Vinny told him, "I got to go out the front. If you want a ride, my father sends one of his friends to pick me up. I could have him drop you off if you want."

"Great. Are you rich or something?"

"No," Vinny said, "My father is just protective."

When they walked outside, Sal was waiting. Vinny went over and tapped on the window, "Is it all right if we drop Al off around the corner from the house?"

Sal consulted his watch, "I don't think your father would like that."

"Come on, Sal. The guy is harmless. He just moved here and we go right by his place." Vinny said.

Sal got out of the car, walked over to Al, and frisked him. Al allowed it, but looked surprised and Vinny was mortified.

"Sal, is that really necessary?" Vinny croaked. His embarrassment showed in the red flush that was slowly creeping up his face.

"What do you think? Do you want me to give him a ride or not?" Sal asked.

"Yeah, okay. I got the idea."

"Then let me do my job. The kid is clean. Okay, get in." Sal opened the door and the two boys hopped in the back of the car.

Vinny decided the shakedown was too embarrassing so, tomorrow he and Al would take the train. Vinny sensed that Al was shy and made sure he had his number before he left the car.

"Call me later." Vinny yelled as Al got out of the car and began to walk away.

"Sure, see you tomorrow." Waving at Sal, Al said, "Thanks a lot for the ride."

When Vinny walked into his house, he went straight into his father's den. His father was bent over a desk and going through a pile of papers. He had a calculator in one hand and a pencil in the other. Without a greeting, Vinny shot out "Why does Sal have to pick me up from school? I want to take the train just like the other kids."

"I told you before, there are crazy people out there and I don't want you to get hurt," Sonny said, his head never rose to look at his son.

"Please. I would rather take the train. I met this kid named Al and he seems cool. He is smart and I am probably going to be studying with him a lot so, I will be safe. We would take the train together. Okay?"

Sonny looked up at Vinny for a moment, then returned to his paperwork, "Let me think about it," he said. Vinny knew he would not get an answer if he kept after him; all he would do was to make him mad and get him yelling again. He turned on his heel and went to his room, tossing his books on the bed. Walking over to the window, he stared out, thinking about what had happened. Normal people did not frisk a kid. That paranoid behavior pointed to even more evidence that something was wrong with his father's business.

Al called Vinny later that evening and they swapped stories, sharing their plans for the future. By the end of the conversation, the boys were fast friends. Vinny was excited when Al said he was going to become a lawyer. 'It must have been fate that we're friends,' Vinny thought. He told Al that he wanted to become a lawyer, too. They just laughed. Vinny said they should go to the same law school so they could study together and help each other out, be best friends. As best friends do, they made a pact, no matter who made it as a lawyer first; they would look out for each other —forever. They would apply to the same college and hoped to open up a law firm someday. 'Denucci and Brennen', the boys agreed, it had a nice professional ring to it.

As soon as Vinny hung up the phone, his father came into his room. "I've thought about it and I don't like it. No train and that is final. Al can ride with you and Sal as soon as I've had him checked out." Vinny knew protesting would do no good, so he nodded and went back to his books. At least he and Al would get to ride to school together, even if it was not on the train.

The next day, Al and Vinny studied together at school for the entire day. They joined the debate team so they could improve their 'lawyerly speaking skills'. For the next few months, they helped start a fund-raiser for deprived children and set up a private tutoring class during lunch period for students who needed extra help with math. Al was a wizard at math and shared the little money they charged with Vinny since he was the one who knew everybody and set up the schedules.

The boys were inseparable and Vinny thanked God every day for his friend. The two boys hung out after school with each other, went to the movies and to the gym together, and studied together almost every night. Although not athletic, Al was on the soccer team and needed help so Vinny would study books on soccer techniques, then coach him with whatever he had learned. Everything to them was fun, even the bets they made with each other over which one of them would grow hair on his face first. Vinny won.

For Vinny, friendship with Al was like having a brother. The boys talked about everything together. Vinny taught Al how to dress. Al taught Vinny how to tutor math and they took their first foray into dating together. The boys laughed about Al's first ride home the day they had met and Al started to tease Vinny about needing a chaperone to tag along every time he had a date. Sonny did not even trust the girls Vinny dated and, although he would laugh too, Vinny hated it. It made him feel like a kid. At least Sal did not frisk the girls.

Al even learned how to make himself useful in Felicia's kitchen. Felicia liked Al and thought the boys were good for each other. The first time Felicia made ziti with meatballs, Al was hooked from that moment, as he tasted the sauce to his lips. He was proud anytime she referred to him as her 'adopted son'. Nevertheless, Vinny's father did not like Al at all. Sonny did not like anybody who was not Italian, and he did not know anybody that knew Al's dad. That meant Sonny did not trust the boy or his family. Vinny did not care. Al was his friend anyway.

Through the next summer, Al spent a lot of time over at Vinny's house while his parents were out of town on business. Al's mother and father were involved with medical supplies and they were always traveling somewhere doing trade shows for the products they sold. One night, Al and Vinny decided to go to the movies to see Rocky III and to try to pick up some babes. When Vinny was waiting in line for popcorn, he started talking to the girl in front of him. She said her name was Marlene and she was a knockout!

Marlene was petite, had long gorgeous brown hair and a beautiful olive complexion. Vinny could not take his eyes off her. Her beautiful smile revealed her perfect white teeth and the cutest dimples he had ever seen. Built to perfection from top to bottom. Vinny could get lost in her big brown eyes. He asked what movie she was going to see and he was disappointed when she told him she was going to see, "Nightmare on Elm Street."

"Want to get together some time?" Vinny asked as she picked up her soda.

"I'd like that," she said, her voice soft and gentle. She stood at the counter writing her phone number on a napkin. Handing Vinny the paper, she said, "Why don't you call me when you get home tonight?"

Vinny smiled and forgot about his popcorn. "It's a date," he said.

Vinny ran back to tell Al and Al called Vinny 'one lucky guy'. When the movie was over, Vinny stood outside with Al for a few minutes, hoping Marlene was still there, but they did not see her. Vinny flagged down a cab and talked about the movie all the way home. Vinny wanted to be like Rocky. He felt Rocky was a super hero.

"It's only a movie, Vinny. Jeeze, snap out of it!"

The cab dropped Al off first. When Vinny got home, he did not even take time to say hello to his parents, he just walked into his room and picked up the phone to call Marlene.

Marlene's voice came on the other end of the phone, "Hello?"

"Hi. It's Vinny."

"Who is this?" she asked, a puzzled tone in her voice as she struggled to match the name with someone she knew.

"It's Vinny... the guy you met at the movie snack counter. Remember?"

"Oh, yeah... you didn't tell me your name." Marlene laughed, and Vinny felt like such a jerk.

"Oh, I'm sorry. Let me properly introduce myself. My name is Vinny Denucci. I was wearing a red and green polo shirt."

"Yes," Marlene said laughing, "I remember you. I am glad you called. I am on vacation from Italy with my family and I do not know anyone. Maybe you will show me the city while I'm here?"

Vinny's heart skipped, he thought it sounded like she had asked him out. "When are you going back?"

"In two weeks," she said.

'Oh, wow,' Vinny thought. His heart sunk. Two weeks! How was he going to get this girl to kiss him before she went back home in two weeks? She had such beautiful lips. Vinny began to pray.

"Vinny? Are you still there?" she asked.

"Uh, yes... I'm just wondering when we can see each other."

"What about tomorrow? Maybe I could meet you over at your place?" Marlene's voice sounded hopeful, and Vinny's heart rate shot back up.

"Sure...great." Vinny stammered, "I'll call you tomorrow and send a car for you. Okay, great, see you then."

Vinny wait, don't you want my address?" she said with a laugh, "It will help your driver find me."

Vinny's face began to burn. What a jerk I am, he thought.

"Yeah, I guess that would help wouldn't it?" Vinny laughed with her, his nervous heart tapping out a slower beat as he wrote down her address.

"We'll get something to eat or... something," he told her.

"Okay, I'm looking forward to it. See you tomorrow. Is around 5 okay?"

"It's great, Vinny." She said, "See you then. Bye."

Vinny laid the phone back in the cradle. It was late, but he was so excited that he could not sleep a wink all night. He kept thinking about Marlene. This was the first time that he had ever been attracted to someone and wondered if that was what love felt like. Eventually, sleep claimed him and his dreams were of an olive skinned girl with long dark hair.

The next morning, Vinny raced out of bed and headed for the bathroom. He took a quick shower, brushed his teeth not once but twice and flossed them so much that he could squirt water between them. He looked in the mirror, slapped on some Old English after-shave, slicked his hair back with some gel and blew a kiss at the mirror.

"You're looking fine, Denucci," he said to his reflection.

He tried on about six different outfits before he decided to wear a pair of blue jeans, with a cream-colored polo shirt. The girls at school seemed to think he looked hot in it. Vinny went into the living room and called Marlene. He told her to give the driver his address and he would meet her downstairs. He was so excited; he could not even eat all morning. He could not even sit still.

His mother sat at the kitchen table and watched her son as he paced between the refrigerator and the door, glancing up at the clock like he thought it would jump off the wall at him. Finally she could not stand it anymore, "Vinny, why are you pacing back and forth? You are making your mother dizzy. Are you okay?"

"Yes, Mom, I'm fine, great. It's just that I have this girl coming over."

Felicia's eyebrows rose, but her son did not see he was too busy staring down the clock. "Well, I have to go out with your father, so you two will be alone. You offer her something to drink and eat, okay. Don't forget your manners."

"Oh no, Mom! I forgot to tell him. He does not know she is coming here. Do you think Dad will be mad? I mean he does not know her. But she is Italian, she told me she is, and she's only visiting for two weeks." Vinny's eyebrows knitted close together, he had not thought about his father's reaction.

"Don't worry about it. You're a big boy." Felicia said. "It will be fine."

She gave him an encouraging smile and Vinny felt a lot better. He went back to his pacing and watching the clock. Felicia smiled at him, shook her head and left to get ready for Sonny. Her son was growing up.

When Sonny arrived, Felicia met him at the door. "Your only son has invited a girl here tonight. Please, Sonny, he is so nervous about this. Talk to him and let him know it is all right. He's worried about what you might say."

Sonny looked down at Felicia and started to say the normal rhetoric about not knowing strangers and he did not know this girl. However, Felicia looked at him, her eyes pleading and for once Sonny gave in. "Okay, Felicia, this one time. But if I don't like her, she doesn't come back. Understand?"

Felicia's face lit up and she stood on her tiptoes and kissed him on the cheek, the first time she had done that voluntarily in a long time. "Thank you, Sonny. It means the world to him. You should see him. He has almost worn a hole in the kitchen from pacing. Go talk with him."

Sonny turned away and walked into the kitchen. Vinny was standing there staring at the clock, bouncing up and down on the balls of his feet, his hands patting out a tune on his legs as he watched the second hand creep around the dial.

"Your mother says you got a girl coming here? Do I know this girl?" Sonny said.

Vinny jumped and turned from the clock, "Dad. No, you don't. Her name is Marlene and she is from Italy and I met her at the movies in line for the popcorn and she's beautiful and…" Vinny ran on, his eyes bright as he tried to fit everything in before his father yelled. However, Sonny just smiled, and a look of relief stopped Vinny's explanation.

"Italian! Well, that is good. This one is one of us. Well, have fun! Your mother and I are going out. Treat this girl with respect, do you understand, or else. Do not disgrace the Denucci name. Understand?"

Vinny shook his head, relief running through him, God was truly on his side tonight. Even his father approved.

Vinny took the elevator with his parents to the garage, then down to the lobby to wait for Marlene. He saw the car pull up and his heart started to pound. Looking in the lobby mirror, he saw his face and was appalled that it looked as red as a tomato. He started to blush even more. 'Get a grip, Denucci', he thought.

Walking to the door to greet her, Marlene was already out of the car and looked even more amazing than she had the night before. He thanked the driver and threw him a twenty-dollar bill. Never taking his eyes of her, 'she's breathtaking' was all his mind could say.

Marlene was about five-foot-two and the jeans she wore showed every curve. Her long, wavy brown hair went down to her butt and her lips were the color of red roses. Long thick eyelashes made her eyes stand out even more than Vinny remembered and her smile made him blush again. As they rode up in the elevator, they could not seem to take their eyes off each other. Vinny was amazed at their chemistry; it was almost like an electrical current running between them. When he looked at her she smiled, and he was sure Marlene was feeling the same intense feelings he felt.

The elevator door opened and he escorted her down the hall to his door. He opened it and allowed her to walk past him, he admired the way her hair swung over her hips and the way she moved, with a sway to her hips that made his heart stop beating for a moment.

"What a beautiful place you have." Her voice was like magic. "Is anybody home?"

"No, my parents went out," he replied. He could not take his eyes off her as she stood in front of him. The shape of her pricked at his desire and he felt himself grow warm inside.

"I'm glad." She said. She turned and reached out a hand to him, "Why don't you show me around?"

Vinny linked his fingers with hers and led her in. They took a quick tour. At the door to his room, Marlene looked in. "So, this is your room?"

She walked in and for the first time Vinny noticed all the kid stuff he still had lying around. He swore that the models and baseball pennants were going into the closet tomorrow! Marlene sat on the bed and crossed her legs. She smiled at him. Vinny stood in the doorway in shock. Was this girl in his bedroom?

"Vinny," she said, "I am attracted to you and it is making me want to kiss you. The only problem is I have never kissed anyone. I mean, I have never French-kissed anyone. Does that turn you off?"

"No of course not." Was he sounding cool?

"Well, once I let this boy back home stick his tongue in my mouth, but I pushed him away. The boy wasn't sexy like you."

Grinning, Vinny said, "I have some news for you, too. I have never kissed anybody like that either. To be totally honest, I don't date much."

Marlene just giggled, "Well, do you want to kiss me?" Vinny walked over to the bed and sat down next to her. "You can put your arms around me if you want to."

"Okay." He put his arm around her waist slowly, feeling the warmth of her skin through her blouse. Her hair brushed against his wrists and he suddenly found himself sliding his fingers through it. Her hair was slinky, cool and soft. He wound a curl around his hand, feeling the texture on his fingertips. He leaned forward to kiss her and saw those beautiful eyes flutter closed as she lifted her face to him. His breath caught in his throat as he lowered his head to her. She was gorgeous.

Vinny kissed her gently, his lips lightly brushing hers. She wound her arms around his neck pulling him closer. It made him crazy. He pulled her head back slowly, her hair still wrapped around his hands. Those eyes sent blood to his heart, which made him want her! She was staring. Kissing her lips softly with his tongue, Vinny was in a daze. He could not think. He just wanted to gather more of her against him. He could feel her breasts against his body and felt himself start to swell. This was the first time he had ever felt a girl's breasts. They felt wonderful even through the fabric of Marlene's blouse.

"Marlene," he whispered into her ear, "You feel wonderful next to me. Can we lie down on the bed? I want to feel your whole body next to me."

"Yes, Vinny," she breathed back.

Marlene lay back with a natural sexy awareness of her beautiful body. She kicked off her shoes and looked up into Vinny's eyes. "Go ahead, Vinny. Kiss me more."

He could not help himself. She was driving him crazy. Leaning on one arm, he ran his fingers down her cheek, tracing her lips. Looking down at her, he felt dizzy, like he was falling into her eyes. He bent over her, his lips and tongue following the path of his fingers until he pressed her lips with his, his tongue darting out to lick at her mouth.

"Oh, God, Vinny," she said between breaths. "The way you kiss me and lick me with your tongue... you sure you've never kissed like this before?

"Never, Marlene...it's because of you..." he whispered.

Vinny placed little kisses across her jaw line and down her neck. He began licking and nipping her ear lobes playfully. Marlene began to move slowly against him, back and forth. Vinny was tickling her and she could feel the effect he had on her clear through to her core. She reached up and ran her fingers through his hair until it gave him goose bumps. Their breath was coming in small gasps. The room felt too warm all of a sudden. Marlene sat up and moved around behind Vinny, reaching for his shirt. She tugged it over his head and tossed it to the floor. Gently, she ran her fingers down his back, scraping him. Her fingernails felt good across his back. Vinny turned to her and reached for her blouse, unbuttoning each button slowly, watching her smooth skin appear inch by inch. Vinny slowly pushed her top from her shoulders and it joined his on the floor. Marlene sat there on her knees in front of him in her bra. Vinny's eyes wandered over her, drinking in the sight of her. God, she was sexy.

He reached for her and pulled her to him, holding her tightly against his bare chest, feeling her nipples through the thin material of her bra. She wrapped her arms around him, dropping light kisses on his neck and shoulder. He ran his hands up her back, stroking her and she moaned. He heard himself moan in return. Vinny did not know how much longer he could control himself.

Marlene pulled away from him and stretched out on the bed. Her movements were sensuous. "Oh Vinny, I am glad we met."

Vinny stretched out, half on, half off her. She squirmed around, moving under him until he was laying on her. Her hands never stopped moving as she rubbed her body against his. Moving her hips under him instinctively, she could feel him swelling against her abdomen.

"Take off your pants, Vinny. I want to see you."

Vinny rolled to the side and tugged at his belt, undoing the button and zipper on his jeans with fingers that shook. Beside him, Marlene did the same, wiggling out of her pants and kicking them away. Vinny looked at her as she lay there in her bra and underwear. She was beautiful. He reached out and pulled the straps of her bra down, baring the top of each breast. She arched her back and reached behind her unhooking the clasp and pulling her bra off with slow movements. Her eyes never left his. Vinny thought he would die. Her breasts were perfect, not large, not small, and the nipples were erect, a dusky pink in color.

Vinny reached out and ran one finger lightly down her breast to the nipple. Marlene arched her back and gave a short gasp. Vinny quickly pulled his hand away, wondering if he had done something wrong.

"Oh god Vinny don't stop... keep moving... that feels good," Marlene whispered. She reached up for him, pulling him down to her. Her kiss was deep and borne of instinct.

He could not believe what was happening. He was lying on top of this amazing creature. Her breasts bare on his chest, her body wriggling under his. He moved with her as he felt her hips begin to press into his. Frantically, with desperation, he felt her hands move over him to his underwear. She pushed at it, trying to get the offending cloth off. Vinny quickly rolled off her and pushed down his underwear. Marlene began to do the same, but he stopped her, holding her hand.

"I want to do that." His voice was low, husky, and he was not sure it was his. Nevertheless, nothing mattered except Marlene. He pulled at each side of her panties, tugging them down her hips. He watched as a triangle of dark curls appeared. He could not believe he was doing something like this. Marlene raised her hips as he slid the panties lower, over and down her legs until they joined the ever-growing pile of clothes on the floor. He ran his hands back up her legs, feeling the silky skin. He was shaking. Wanting to do this right, but not knowing what right was.

Marlene solved his dilemma by reaching for him and pulling him on top of her again. Vinny placed little kisses over her neck and shoulders, slowly moving over her breast and catching a nipple in his mouth, swirling his tongue around it, savoring his first taste. Marlene moaned again and arched her back into him. He licked her breast and then kissed her deeply on the lips, his tongue darting in her mouth. He knew what he was doing so far was "right."

She pushed at him, rolling him off her and onto his back. Her eyes ran over him, stopping when she saw his erection. A smile broke out over her face and she glanced up at him through her eyelashes.

"I never saw one on a boy before, just my aunt's baby. It didn't look like much, but I like yours." She said.

Reaching out, she stroked her fingertips down the shaft making him jerk in response. She felt the silky texture, the ridge running down the outside. Her fingers circled it, holding and stroking. Vinny moaned and reached down, staying her hand.

"What's wrong?" she asked.

Vinny looked down at her, his mind a blur of sensations "Nothing. Nothing's wrong. Everything is right."

Marlene started to rub her hands up and down Vinny's enormous erection.

"It's beautiful," she said. "I never thought it would be beautiful. But it is."

"Not as beautiful as you..." Vinny said as his eyes devoured her. He reached down, pulling her on top of him, feeling her silky skin slide over him. All of a sudden, Marlene bit down on his shoulder and he pulled back slightly. The friction was grating and delicious. She stared down at him, licking her lips, smiling.

"I want to feel you inside me. I want to see what it feels like. I want you," she purred.

Vinny slowly ran his hands down her body to the top of that triangle of curly hair. He cupped her, rubbing his hand between her legs. Marlene's hands grasped his arms, her nails biting into the flesh and her eyes closed, a small sigh escaping her lips. Vinny felt damp hair, skin and withdrew his hand. He may not be experienced but he had heard things from other people, she was ready for him, she wanted him.

He circled her waist with his hands and lifted her from him and to the side to lie on the bed next to him. Moving over her, he felt her legs part and she reached for him. Her eyes opening, bright with an intensity he had never seen in anyone, she pulled him toward her. Vinny could feel the head of his penis touch those damp curls and finally the wet skin under them. Vinny gently pushed into her, feeling her open and stretch, feeling warmth surround him. He thought he would release right then, but gained control and pushed further. She was warm and welcoming. As he pushed he felt resistance, a barrier. He pushed harder and felt her gasp, her eyes flying open, her nails biting into his back. Vinny stopped moving and raised himself on his arms.

"Did I hurt you? Marlene are you alright?" he asked. Worry washed over him. He never wanted to hurt her. He only wanted to make love to her.

"A little," she said, "but I knew it might. My mother explained it to me. It can happen the first time. I'm okay, thank you for asking."

"The first time," Vinny asked. He was the first! She had been a virgin.

He felt her hips move under him, pushing him further inside her warmth. Vinny did not hesitate. He moved slowly, pushing in until he buried his penis inside her. Pulling back they found a rhythm; withdrawing until he could feel her clench and pull him back, then sliding back into her, feeling her rise to meet him. For what seemed an eternity, they moved with each other until he heard her moan loudly and clench on him, holding him. A huge wave of sensation overtook him and he could not hold on any longer. She knew and he knew. Together they set up a faster rhythm, stroking until the wave overtook them both.

Marlene said "Now!" and Vinny exploded letting out a loud cry that he was sure the neighbors could hear. His head was spinning, and his body was tense pushing into her as hard as he could. It felt so good that he did not want it to end. Marlene was bucking up against him, her legs wrapped around his waist holding him to her.

"Oh, my God...my God...Vinny, what are you doing to me? I...I...I'm coming and I can't stop!" He kept stroking inside her, still enlarged and hard, rubbing against her as she grasped him. Slowly, the waves subsided for both of them until they lay in each other's arms, spent and trembling.

Breathing heavily Vinny marveled at how good it felt to hold her. His heart was slowing; going back to normal as he held her tight to him, her breathing even and quiet. Her breasts rested against him, one leg thrown across his and moving up and down, teasing him. He leaned over and sucked her nipples tenderly until he felt them perk up. He was starting to get excited again. Marlene just smiled and held his head against her breast, guiding him from one nipple to the other. She kissed him, nibbling on his neck, sucking his nipples in return. They lay there teasing each other, exploring with hands and bodies and mouths. Vinny played with her breasts until she thought she would scream with delight. She stroked him with her soft hands until he thought he would explode. When he leaned over to put on some music, they smiled at the perfection of the song Frank Sinatra's "I Did It My Way." Within minutes, both were ready for each other and the passion overtook them again.

An hour of music and exploration flew by. Marlene had to go home. Reluctantly, they dressed, touching each other at every opportunity, reluctant to part. Later, Vinny called her a cab. He walked her downstairs, kissed her good-bye and told her that he would call her during the week. What a night. How was he going to tell Al about this?

Vinny sprinted upstairs, he had so much energy. He closed his bedroom door. He called Al giving him a full description of what just happened.

"Al, I think I'm in love. You remember that girl I met at the movies?" Vinny said. He was breathless, excited.

"Yeah... so keep going..." Al said.

"We just spent the last three hours rolling around on my bed, driving each other crazy. We kissed, I felt her breasts, next thing I know, she wants me inside her," Vinny said.

"No shit, Vinny! C'mon. You are just jerkin' me! No way would a girl like that do that." Al said. However, there was a hint of believability in his voice.

"I am not jerkin' you, Al. She was here. We did it. Would I lie to you about something like this? It is like a fantasy come true, man. I'm in love."

"So Vinny, I guess you're a stud muffin huh?" Al chided, "You going to talk to us mortals anymore?

Laughter escaped Vinny's lips.

"Yeah, well... I could not wait to tell you what happened. Next time, we will get two. Hey, by the way, how about going hunting with me and my dad this weekend?"

"I don't know. I will have to ask my parents. I think it would be great but, let me check," Al replied.

"Okay. I had better check with my dad too. I'll let you know if it's okay for you to come, but, I'm sure it will be."

"I'll call you at eight tomorrow and...Vinny way to go you sex machine," Al said.

Vinny laid back on his bed, arms under his head, a smile on his face, reliving his first sexual experience. He was still feeling the aftermath of love and great sex when his dad came home.

Vinny jumped up and went into the living room as his parents closed the door. "Can Al go hunting with us this weekend?" he asked.

"Sure, if he can take all the blood," his father said almost nonchalantly.

Vinny thought his father was kidding and laughed, "I am sure he can. Al's tougher than he looks." He waved thanks to his dad and went back to his room to call Al and tell him it was okay.

"Great, my dad said I could go too. I'll see you in the morning."

Vinny hung up the phone. He realized it was late and he was tired. Sleep would come quickly, and dreams would be of a dark-haired girl with a body to die for.

The following morning Sonny woke Vinny up very early. It was 5:00 am when Vinny glanced at the clock. He groaned. He had been having a nice dream, and reality sucked sometimes.

"Vinny, get up and call your friend. Tell him to be ready in thirty minutes." Sonny said. "And don't wake your mother. She's still sleeping."

"Okay." Vinny rolled over and grabbed the phone, dialing Al's house. While Vinny was calling Al, Nunzi arrived. Vinny heard Sonny say he was surprised that his son, Robert, was not with him.

"He didn't want to come," Nunzi said as Vinny came walking down the hall. "Morning Vinny."

"Good morning Uncle Nunzi," then, turning to his father, "Al's all set."

"Are you ready?" Sonny asked.

"Yes," he said.

"Okay, you two better be quiet. Don't wake your mother—we had a late night last night. Vinny, why don't you leave your mother a note and I'll call for the car." Vinny wrote a quick note to Felicia, telling her he loved her and he would miss her and left it on the kitchen table.

"Let's go," Sonny said as he ushered everyone down the hallway.

"Al will be waiting outside," Vinny told his dad as they got into the car. Nunzi was surprised someone else was coming.

"Who's Al?" he asked.

"He's a good friend from school." Vinny told him, "My best friend."

"Vinny, remember this," Sonny said as he turned to face him, "There are no such things as 'good friends' or 'best friends'."

Al was standing outside his house as they pulled up. "Morning everyone," he said as he got into the car. "Good morning Sir," he said to Sonny, shaking his hand. "Good morning. I'm Al, sir," he said to Nunzi.

"Nunzi Denucci, Vinny's uncle," Uncle Nunzi said shaking the boy's hand.

"I have heard a lot about you. It's a pleasure to finally meet you."

"Likewise. I am always glad to meet Vinny's friends."

Al sat in the back with Vinny while Nunzi and Sonny sat in front. Silence ensued for several minutes until Vinny asked "How long is the trip Uncle Nunzi?"

"About three hours," he said." "Why don't you boys catch up on a few z's'? It'll make the ride shorter." Both boys agreed, leaned back into their respective corners and fell asleep right away. Before they knew it, Sonny was shaking them. They had arrived at Bear Mountain Park.

It was a perfect day. All they could see for miles were mountains and trees. The air was cool and the woods filled with a fresh pine scent that made Vinny feel healthier every time he inhaled. It was quiet too. No honking horns, yelling people, or cars rushing past you on the street. All Vinny could hear were insects buzzing and birds singing. He wished he could live in the forest forever.

The hunter's station was a large log cabin situated among the trees in the middle of a clearing. They filed inside to register and be outfitted for the day. The proprietor behind the counter took everyone's sizes and left for a few minutes, leaving Sonny and Nunzi to look over the gun selection. He returned with bright orange jumpsuits and handed them out. Vinny and Al started to laugh as they held them up.

"We have to wear these?" they said. The boys looked at each other and burst out laughing.

"Yep," said the man behind the counter. "You do if you don't want to get shot. You think you are the only people out there hunting today. That orange jumpsuit is the only thing that separates you from the game. You gentlemen picked out your rifles yet?"

"Yeah, we'll take the Winchester 30/30's." Sonny said.

While the man removed the guns from the cabinet, they all slipped into the bright orange jumpsuits. "We look like a bunch of giant carrots," said Vinny, doing up his zipper. Al laughed and pulled the hood of the suit over his head making him look even more like a giant carrot.

Sonny and Nunzi were handed each a map. It showed the grounds of the park on one side and an explanation of the gaming rules on the other. The papers told them that the park closed at 8:00pm in the evening. Everyone grabbed their backpacks and went outside to head up the trail into the wooded mountains. Vinny was excited and almost ran up the trail with Al, his father and Uncle Nunzi behind him.

Sonny told the boys, "If you spot a deer, don't move. Just stand still until we can see if one of us can get a good shot at it." The boys agreed. "Hunting is more than a sport, boys. You can learn a valuable lesson about survival here."

Vinny wondered what his father meant. He figured Sonny must have meant the deer's survival. He knew how quick they were. Nobody in the group expected to kill one out here. Vinny was out to have a good time, and not learn lessons in survival. Besides, he did not want to kill an innocent deer. He just wanted to spend time with his father and play 'hunter.'

They had walked about six miles into the park when they decided to pair off and go in two directions, agreeing to stay within voice range since the boys had never hunted before. Everyone seemed to be simply enjoying the wonderful outdoors. Vinny was standing in a group of trees when a young buck walked out of the trees opposite him and into the clearing. It was grazing on a patch of wild flowers. Its dainty muzzle clipping off the heads of the flowers without pulling the stems from the ground.

Vinny raised his rifle and looked through the scope, targeting his prey. He wanted to kill the animal and make his father proud, but he hesitated before he pulled the trigger. He watched the gentle beast through the red targeted X of the eyepiece mesmerized at how beautiful it was. The deer and nature seemed to be one.

The buck must have sensed Vinny's presence because he stopped and looked directly into Vinny's gun site. Then, suddenly, it bolted. Its white tail held high over its back. Automatically, Vinny pulled the trigger and the gun went off. The loud shot scared the piss out of him, and he saw the buck drop. Oh, God, what had he done? He had just killed one of God's creatures and God saw him do it. This was the first time he had ever fired a rifle. Would God punish him? Vinny was nauseous and his head was spinning. It took everything he had for him not get sick on the spot. The gunshot was still ringing in his ears when he heard his father yelling.

"Vinny are you okay?" Then Sonny saw the animal stretched out on its side, "The first one is always the hardest, son."

Al was behind a tree, vomiting up his guts. He had no idea what he thought they would be doing today, but this was not it. Sonny and Nunzi went over to the deer and could see that it was still alive. Its sad eyes looked right into Vinny's, and he knew he had done something terrible. His mind kept repeating, 'God, I'm so sorry, I'm so sorry,' repeatedly. Sonny kept saying something to him but all he could do was stare at the poor animal.

"Vinny you have to finish him off. Go ahead and shoot it in the head."

"What?" Vinny squeaked. His mind not comprehending what his father had just said.

"Shoot it in the head," Sonny repeated

"No, Dad....I can't do it. I can't just kill it while it's looking at me."

"Yes, you can. You have to finish the job you started." Sonny's voice was stern, a hint of anger present.

Sonny wore a mixed expression on his face, one of anger and another that showed complete disregard for the animal in front of them on the ground. Every time Vinny looked at the deer, his heart pounded harder and his mouth went dry. Sonny was growing increasingly impatient.

"Vinny, shoot that fuckin' deer. Look, you want to be somebody in this life; you never show signs of weakness. You want to be a leader so people will respect you. Then, you do what you got to do….SHOOT IT!" This was an order from a man who never took no for an answer.

Vinny fired. His range was too close and the deer's brains splattered all over his boots and pants. He watched the deer's body began to jerk and twitch. It seemed like forever before it finally stopped. It was such a sad sight. Vinny turned away with such disgust for himself, his stomach roiling. Hunting was supposed to be a sport, not a life or death situation. There was nothing fun about this. Vinny wanted to lash out at his father too. Sonny knew why he took Vinny hunting. Why would a man bring his son here to do this? Was this the great 'lesson' Vinny was supposed to learn? What animal was his father, anyway? Sonny showed no emotion at all and that beautiful deer was lying there dead, its brains and blood splattered all over Vinny and the ground. Sonny walked over to the buck and looked down. He shook his head in affirmation.

"Nunzi, give me a hand here. We have to bring this down to the cutting house so they can skin it for us. Vinny, you too, let's move this thing." Sonny said.

The three, two men and a boy, lifted the buck. Its head dropped down, blood and brains dropping to the ground as they carried it. Vinny could hear Al in the background getting sick again.

They half carried, half dragged the deer to the cutting house. Vernon, the cut man, walked around the deer lying on the floor of the cutting house, sizing it up. "Nice kill...who's the shooter?" Vinny reluctantly acknowledged himself as the culprit.

"This your first kill?" Vernon asked. Although it was obvious from the pallor of Vinny's face that he had never harmed even a fly.

"Yeah." Vinny gulped, "My first."

Vernon stared at the boy, sizing him up, seeing the regret and disgust on his face. "We have a tradition around here which has been around for years," Vernon continued. "To be a real hunter, you must drink the blood of the first animal that you kill."

Vinny looked at Vernon in complete disbelief, "Are you nuts? What do you think I am, some kind of animal?"

Sonny gave Vinny a little shove, urging him on. "Its tradition son! We all did it once in our life, so you have to do it. You should be proud!"

Vinny looked at his Uncle Nunzi who just shrugged his shoulders like to say, Yeah, it is true. Nothing you can do about it. Vinny heard Al choking in the background. This gross conversation about drinking blood sent him running into the bathroom at the back of the store.

Seeing Vinny's reluctance, Sonny tried to be supportive, "Okay. If you drink the blood, so will I."

Vernon grabbed a cup and a thin curved knife. Quickly he slit the throat of the deer in just the right place. Blood dripped from the wound into the cup until it was half-full. Vernon handed the cup to Sonny. Sonny slowly put the cup to his mouth, drank a little, and passed the cup to Nunzi. Nunzi also slowly sipped the blood from the cup, his eyes looking over the rim at Vinny. Slowly he lowered the cup and handed it over to Vinny. Vinny looked down at the ugly reddish-brown liquid remaining in the cup. It smelled so bad he almost vomited on the spot.

"It's not so bad, kid. Go ahead," Vernon encouraged him.

Vinny took a deep breath, put the cup to his mouth, and took a sip. It was sour and salty and immediately turned his stomach. His father watched as Vinny drank, and then burst out laughing. "Vinny didn't I just tell you to be a leader? Why would you trust someone you don't even know and drink that shit?"

Vinny was flabbergasted, "YOU drank from this cup!"

"No, Vinny I did not! It may have LOOKED like I drank it, but I did not. Neither did Nunzi." Vinny was furious at his father.

"What are you saying? You tricked me?" Vinny said, his voice rising in anger and pain.

Vernon laughed, "Yes! Indeed we did," he said.

"Well," said Vinny with renewed bravado, "I should be laughing at you because you are not real hunters. You were chicken. I was a man."

Sonny humored him, "Vinny, one day you'll understand." Vinny just looked up at is father with disgust. How could a man trick his own son? Why do I always have to prove something to him? When Al came out of the bathroom, Vernon handed him the cup.

Al said, "No fuckin' way! I'm not drinking that."

Vinny took the cup from Vernon and put it on the counter, "Don't worry about it, Al. It was a joke." However, Al still looked a bit green as he noticed the blood on Vinny's lips.

Vernon bent down and manhandled the deer onto his back, disappearing into a curtained room off to the side of the shop. Hunting day was over and it was time to wash up. On the way to the cabin, Vinny was quiet. He felt betrayed. His father should have stuck up for him, not humiliate him like that.

The cabin was peaceful and Nunzi brought in wood for a fire. The room warmed quickly and the boys laid out their sleeping bags. Vinny collected his thoughts and decided he was not going to let this incident spoil his weekend. The cabin was cozy. A little out-dated, but it served the purpose. They were hunting and this is how you have to live if you live in the woods. Tomorrow had to be better than today.

Al sat down on his sleeping bag, as Vinny unzipped his and crawled inside, pulling the bag up to his chest. "Are you all right?" Al whispered, looking over his shoulder at a sleeping Sonny and Uncle Nunzi.

"Yeah, I'm just tired. See you in the morning..." Vinny muttered. His voice was short, low. He did not want to talk to anyone right now. He zipped his sleeping bag up over his head and rolled away from Al.

"Goodnight, Vinny." Al stared at his friend for a while then crawled into his sleeping bag and fell asleep, visions of blood and deer haunting his dreams.

The next morning, Vinny woke before the rest of the party. Slipping quietly from the cabin he stepped into the clear cool air, breathing deeply. Maybe a walk would chase the last vestiges of the nightmares he had had away from his roiling mind. He had not slept well and wanted some quiet time alone with God.

Bear Mountain Park felt like the heart of God's country and Vinny had some sins to recount. Sitting next to a bubbling creek, Vinny started to pray. He prayed for the deer that he had killed, for his family, for his mother and for his friends. He thanked God for everyone's good health and for giving him a wonderful life. He asked for guidance and help dealing with his father. He wanted desperately to live up to Sonny's expectations, "And help Dad too," he prayed, "Help him be a nicer man. Help him love my mother and not fight so much with her. Help him want to be proud of me for who I am, not because of the stuff I do that would make him mad."

Sonny called from outside the cabin door, which interrupted Vinny's praying. Vinny gave God a quick, "Amen." and answered his father, "Coming Dad."

Sonny was packing up the car, "Where were you?"

"I went for a walk." Vinny said, looking away from his father and out into the forest.

"Well, go and get packed. I want to get an early start back home."

"I thought we were staying all weekend." Vinny asked.

"Well, you thought wrong. Go get packed." Sonny said, not looking at Vinny.

Vinny went into the cabin and started gathering his stuff. Al already had most of his gear ready and started to help Vinny pack up.

"Where did you go?" Al asked.

"I went for a walk by the lake." Vinny said.

"We're leaving." Al said, "Do you think it is because of what happened yesterday with you and your Dad?"

"I guess. I do not know nor do I care. Here...help me tie up this bag."

The men stopped to check out at the hunter's station and return their gear. They went into the back of the station and picked up the deer that had been skinned and slaughtered. The meat was wrapped in heavy butcher paper. It was then placed in a Styrofoam cooler with dry ice for the ride home. Al looked at Vinny and jerked his head toward the car. The boys took off at the same time racing each other back to the car.

"Okay, last one in the car smells like shit." Al yelled as he ran into the car ahead of Vinny, using his hands to buffer his quick stop.

The two boys jumped into the back of the car. Sonny sat with Vinny for the first hour home. "Do you know why I took you hunting?" Sonny asked suddenly, not looking at Vinny.

"Yes, I do... to pretend to hunt and make a fool of your son in front of everyone." Vinny said sarcastically.

"Watch your mouth, boy. Don't disrespect your father." Sonny snapped. "No, Vinny that's not the reason. I wanted you to see how living things bleed to death. I wanted you to see how flesh splatters when it is shot. This is a lesson for you to remember and remember well. Human flesh does the same thing as that deer."

"Why are you telling me this? Is this another sick prank?" Vinny asked. His head hung, he had no idea why it mattered that he knew these gruesome facts.

Sonny's voice got deathly quiet and he became serious. "Yesterday was an important lesson for you, Vinny. You never know when you'll have to kill someone, and I want you to know what it is to watch something bleed."

Vinny's blood ran cold and all the color left his face. His father was serious. He did not know how to respond. "I get the message," was all he could say.

For the first time, Vinny thought his father might be crazy. Under what conditions could anyone find himself 'needing to kill someone'? The whole idea was too much for him to consider. He fell quiet and sat still beside his father. He was happy when they stopped to get lunch and he could ride the rest of the way home in the backseat with Al.

When they finally reached Al's house, Vinny helped him carry his stuff.

"Thanks, I'll see you at school next week." Al said. His voice strained and Vinny knew he had heard what Sonny had said.

"I'm sorry about this weekend, Al. I didn't think this trip would turn out this way." Vinny apologized.

"No problem. You had better get back to the car before your dad gets mad. Bye." Al walked into his house, waving over his shoulder, his eyes sad.

Home was a welcome end to a strange weekend. Vinny walked inside and found his mother. Hugging her tight, he recounted the events of the last two days and told her what his dad had said in the car on the way home, which made her cry. Vinny felt even worse. He did not want to upset his mom. He felt she had enough problems of her own being married to his father. He told her he was tired and had studying to do and did not want dinner. Hugging her again, he wished her goodnight.

"I'm just happy that you're okay," was all Felicia could manage to say.

Vinny walked into his bedroom and dropped his bags. Hanging his coat up in the closet, he opened up a drawer and pulled out his Bible.

Sitting on the edge of his bed, he started to read. It did not take long before tears rolled down his face. He put his head down, closed his eyes and sat that way for a long time.

"Please God; forgive me for what I have done."

After a few minutes, Vinny opened his eyes and got undressed. He pulled the covers back on his bed to lie down. Bed was a welcome relief. He gently closed his eyes and quickly fell into a deep sleep but woke up in a panic, drenched from sweat. The clock said 2:26 and his heart was pounding. His dream made him relive the hunting expedition all over again. Vinny immediately got out of his bed and dropped to his knees.

"Dear God, I promise on my own life, I will never hurt another living thing as long as I live," he prayed.

As he knelt there with his hands folded in front of him, he became aware of yelling coming from his parents' room. Not wanting to hear another one of his parents' arguments, he got up and opened the window to let in the fresh night air and the sounds of the street. Pulling over a chair, he sat down and let the cold breeze wash over him until he was almost frozen. The arguing was getting louder, drowning out the city noises. Grabbing the covers off his bed, he pulled them over his head to try to drown out the raised sound of his father's voice against his mother's growing defiance. Sitting like a cocoon in the corner of his room, knees drawn to his chest, Vinny rested his head on the windowsill and fell back asleep.

CHAPTER 4
FELICIA'S EMBARRASSMENT

* * * *

SONNY SURPRISED HIS FAMILY when he decided to take them to one of his favorite restaurants, Victor's Cafe. It was a regular hangout for many of his friends and a special treat for Felicia and Vinny. A five-star Italian restaurant specializing in seafood, Victor has created an elegant dining experience complete with marble floors and beautiful Italian murals hand-painted on the walls and ceiling. It was located on the upper West Side in Manhattan, on 82nd Street and Broadway. Felicia appreciated the crystal glasses, gold plates and fancy silverware. It made her feel special as if she were on vacation in a fancy hotel. She also thought it was a nice touch that there were different china patterns and nouveau place settings at each table. Sonny was not interested in the details, but liked the private booths where conversations remained private. The atmosphere was stylish and quiet and Sonny thought his family could use the treat.

Just as everywhere else Sonny went, he knew everybody. At Victor's, Sonny was treated like a king. The owner came to greet him, fussing over his family as if they were royalty. They were immediately ushered to Sonny's own private table in a back corner where he could keep an eye on the other patron's arrivals and departures. Like most of Sonny's regular restaurants, he never needed to see a menu. The chef always prepared his favorite foods and knew how to please him. Sonny loved all the attention but Felicia thought it was a little overwhelming and embarrassing at times. Vinny always enjoyed going to Victor's. He would want this classy upscale place if he owned a restaurant. A place with just the right touches of class and modernism, blended into an atmosphere that immediately put a person at ease.

Chef Gabriel came over to the table, bowing his head respectfully, "Good evening, Señor Denucci. It is always so nice to see you again. May I make a few suggestions for you this evening?" Vinny had a hard time understanding him; his Italian accent was so strong.

"Please, Gabriel." Sonny inclined his head in Chef Gabriel's direction, making the man beam with pleasure. A nod from Sonny Denucci carried high praise, most of the time.

"Tonight we have a nice veal shank served with a side of angel hair pasta topped with fresh tomatoes and basil. We also have our regular menu items if anyone would care to see a menu or I would be happy to make you whatever you're hungry for if there is something special you would like."

"Thank you, Gabriel. My wife and son will have lobster Fra-Diavolo. I'll try your special." Sonny said.

"Thank you kindly sir," Chef Gabriel said. "I'm going to send out some bread and olive oil, and for you, Señora Denucci, I'll be sure to send one of my flavored butters that you enjoy so much."

Chef Gabriel enjoyed pleasing his customers. He specially enjoyed pleasing the wife of Sonny Denucci! His culinary conversations with her pleased them and she was pleased that the Chef took her culinary likes so seriously.

"Thank you," she said, a smile lighting her face.

"Perhaps, Señora Denucci, you'll be able to guess which oil I added this time. Here is a hint; I have mixed it with a nice herbal blend. Let me know what you think and, Señora Denucci, I will have the waiter bring your usual wine. Enjoy your meal."

The waiter brought a bottle of red, 1954 Lambrusco from the owner's private reserve. Sonny loved good wine, especially red wine. The waiter opened the bottle and poured a little into Sonny's glass for tasting. Sonny smelled its fragrance, and then sipped slowly, swishing it around in his mouth a few times before spitting it out into another glass. He sat back for a second, making his evaluation. "Excellent!" he pronounced.

The waiter inclined his head and poured them each a glass. Vinny was always impressed with the traditional routine Sonny went though with the wines he drank. He would have to remember the technique. It would make an impression with the women.

After enjoying his wine for a few minutes, Sonny sat back, the stem of the delicate wine glass twirling between his thumb and fingers. He cleared his throat and looked at Vinny.

"Well, Vincenzo, what are your plans after school? Have you thought about it?"

"Yes, sir, I have… I want to become a lawyer." Vinny said quickly. He was proud of his choice—it was something he had dreamed of since he was a child. Felicia smiled at Vinny. She was proud of his choice. Sonny did not look as pleased.

"Why do you want to be a lawyer?" he questioned.

"For one thing, they make good money. And two, I want to help people get the best advice without somebody taking them for a ride." Vinny stated.

Sonny took a sip of wine, watching Vinny over the rim of the glass, "Are those the only reasons?"

"Yeah, I mean… I think I could help you dad, as Max Delaney does. Sometimes I hear you and Mr. Delaney talking and it seems like he helps you get out of trouble when you need it or he keeps people from taking advantage of you when it could hurt your business. Someday I want to do that." Vinny looked at his father, sincerity in every word. He DID want to help people and his father if he needed it.

Max Delaney was Sonny's private lawyer. Sometimes he came over to the house to talk out problems. "I don't know a lot about your business,

Dad but Mr. Delaney seems to have all the answers when you need his help. I want to be like him."

At that moment, Felicia started coughing and could not stop. Tears welled in her eyes and spilled out.

Sonny shot a look at her and pushed her glass of water toward her, "For God's sake, Felicia. Don't just keep coughing, drink something." She drank in big gulps, finishing the entire glass. She seemed to recover, but her makeup ran a little, so she excused herself and went to the ladies room to repair it. Sonny watched her walk away.

"We'll finish this conversation later," said Sonny, catching the eye of the waitress and motioning her to come over. She was a middle-aged woman with thick, black shoulder length hair, big brown eyes, a pointy nose and large breasts. Vinny was surprised that she seemed so happy to see his dad. He did not think she was attractive and he became aware she was flirting with Sonny. It was something Vinny did not like, and he frowned as he watched the two of them. Sonny put his arm around the woman's waist and squeezed her butt. He laughed at her false expression of surprise then seemed pleased when she leaned into him and gave him a seductive smile.

"Make some time for me next weekend, sweetheart. I have some clients coming in from out of town and I want to be sure they're shown a good time." Sonny told her.

He patted her on the butt again, "I'll call you, honey. Okay?"

"You know the number, Sonny," she laughed and shifted her butt against his hand. She did not seem like she was in a hurry to leave the table. Vinny was glad his mother was in the bathroom during this little display, but, as he looked down the hallway, he saw Felicia walking toward them. She was not smiling. Vinny wondered how much she must have seen and could not believe that his father was not asking the waitress to leave their table. His father had no respect for his mother. This was embarrassing...especially in front of everybody in the restaurant. Nobody was looking at their table but you could tell they were deliberately not looking. Vinny could sense people watching his mom out of the corner of their eyes then quickly turn away before she made eye contact. Vinny felt so bad for her.

Felicia marched over to the table with a look of complete disgust on her face. "So, Sonny is this one of your whores?" When Sonny responded by sipping his wine Felicia spoke to the invading women with contempt, "Don't you have respect for yourself or another man's wife?"

Eyes never leaving Felicia's face, the waitress removed Sonny's hand slowly off her butt, smirked at Felicia with a superior air, and walked away with complete indifference, her hips swinging. It was obvious that Sonny was not going to try to cover up the situation nor did he apparently care how Felicia felt about it.

Felicia turned on Sonny. "Well?" she said, her voice high pitched and strangled.

Sonny looked up at her. "Felicia!" he hissed. "Sit down and shut your fuckin' mouth. I was only teasing her."

"I don't care what you think you were doing, I can't stay here." Felicia said. Vinny could hear pain in her voice and he wanted to go to her and hug her, and make it all go away for her.

"You're embarrassing me. Sit the fuck down. We're not going anywhere." Sonny's voice had begun to rise, drawing surreptitious looks from the closer tables.

Felicia moved around the table and sat next to Vinny. Tears of anger and frustration streamed down her face and how could he publicly humiliate her like this was all Vinny could think about. The three Denuccis sat in silence, Sonny nonchalantly sipping his wine, Felicia's tears slowly drying on her cheeks, and Vinny looking from one to the other not knowing what to do or say.

Dinner mercifully arrived a few minutes later, much to the relief of Vinny. He was not sure how much more of this strained silence he could take. The waiter served Felicia first, as was fitting, then Sonny, with Vinny last. He discretely placed the plates without comment. It was apparent that even he was obviously uncomfortable. Sonny's behavior and Felicia's outrage had far-reaching consequences in an establishment such as this. Everyone ate his or her meal in silence. Although it was her favorite food, Felicia pushed most of it around her plate. All the beauty and class of the restaurant and the ease of the family's evening was destroyed and Vinny felt ill at ease. His mom's face was red and tears silently welled in her eyes and spilled out as she stared at her plate. Sonny ate with his usual relish, seemingly oblivious to any stress from the other two. He seemed to have no regrets about being disrespectful to his wife. He kept his head up and even smiled and nodded when someone he recognized bowed in his direction.

Vinny tried to change the mood at the table. He asked his father, "How is your veal shank?"

Sonny turned to him with such a hostile look on his face that Vinny withdrew the question and quietly ate his lobster. This was one of those times that Vinny could not figure his father out; he had just embarrassed the family yet he was the one with the attitude. Vinny couldn't figure out why Sonny had even brought them here knowing his lady friend would most likely be working?

When Sonny finished, he signaled the waiter to remove everyone's plates and ordered coffee and dessert. Vinny could not wait to get out of there, but it looked like Sonny wanted the meal to last as long as possible. Why? Was this a punishment for his mother over something?

On the way home, Vinny could feel the tension building between his parents. Felicia sat on her side of the car, legs crossed, shifting as far away from Sonny as possible. She seemed more angry than hurt. Vinny sat in the back seat, behind his father, and was glad that he could not see Sonny's face. Vinny wished he were not there at all.

Sonny was driving fast, cutting in and out of cars. His anger showing in the way he clenched his hands on the wheel of the car, his knuckles white from the effort. Finally, his bottled up emotion exploded. He turned on Felicia, "The next time you embarrass me in front of anybody, I'll kick your fuckin' ass, Felicia, and do you hear me? You seem to keep forgetting, I am the fuckin' boss and I will do what I want, when I want and with whoever I want and it is none of your fuckin' business. Do I have to give you another lesson for you to remember that? Do you forget who I am? Wives are to keep their mouths shut and look dumb like they don't know what's going on and do not make a fuckin' scene in public over nothing. You had better remember where the fuck you came from! I took you from the Goddamn projects and gave you a beautiful life with fancy cars and a nice place to live. I give you the best and you embarrass me in there with your big mouth. Who the fuck do you think you are?," Sonny shouted.

Felicia had heard enough, "Listen, you son-of-bitch, don't you ever talk to me that way in front of our son! Did your mother ever teach you how to respect a woman? I am not one of your goons that you can just order around. My parents were poor, but we got by and my dad never disrespected my mother the way you disrespect me. I was going to college on a scholarship when I met you! I did not need you! I married you because I loved you and thought that you loved me enough to make a normal, happy life as a family. All your money cannot buy you class, Sonny. I'm supposed to be your wife and I won't have your whores shoved in my face for the entire neighborhood to see."

Suddenly Sonny jammed his foot on the brakes and the car spun around in a complete circle. Vinny held on tight waiting to hear the inevitable sound of crunching metal. Surely, they would hit something. When the car finally came to a stop, Sonny raised his right hand to back slap Felicia across the face but, when he saw Vinny's terrified face through the rearview mirror, he stopped. He put his arm back down and took a deep breath, while he continued to look at Felicia with rage in his eyes. Putting the car back in drive, he stepped on the gas and no one spoke a word all the way home.

For the next several months, Sonny and Felicia fought at the top of their lungs whenever they were together. Sonny made threats about wanting her dead leaving Felicia and Vinny physically ill. The two were living in fear. Although Sonny spent most of his nights out of the house, Vinny and Felicia became reclusive, staying in their respective rooms most of the time. There had not been loving and happy times in the kitchen. No more family visits. Vinny's grades were falling badly in school and he simply could not concentrate enough to do anything about it. Al spent time over at the house, which took some of the pressure off Felicia. It was hard for her to see Vinny suffering as he was, even though she was living in her own tormented world. Spending time at church was helping, but Felicia was having a difficult time coping with the destruction of her marriage. Vinny tried to comfort her, but she would emotionally push him away saying, "Vinny, I need time alone. Please be patient with your mother. This is not about you...I will always love you. I just need to be by myself right now."

Vinny prayed every night that things would get better. He was beginning to feel that he lost his mother and his father since neither of them seemed to be available to him anymore. That changed a few weeks before Vinny's seventeenth birthday.

For no apparent reason, Sonny decided to work things out with Felicia. He came home one night with flowers and a beautiful diamond ring that he said was to signify a new beginning for them. He put out more effort than Vinny could imagine convincing Felicia that he was genuinely sorry for his behavior. He vowed repeatedly to her to do better. Everything seemed to be back to normal. The whole family came over the following Sunday and that afternoon felt like a celebration. Even though Felicia was glowing like a new bride over all the attention Sonny was bestowing on her, something was not sitting right with Vinny. He was thrilled that his parents were back together again. In fact, it was what he prayed for...wasn't it?

CHAPTER 5
MY FATHER, MAFIA BOSS

* * *

It was Vinny's seventeenth birthday. All the family came for a celebration dinner and Vinny was beaming. Sonny and Uncle Nunzi had a special surprise planned after all the guests went home. The birthday cake was served to the family and guests. The last guest left around ten o'clock. Sonny was anxious to get going.

"Vinny, go change your clothes, nice but casual. Sal, go get the car and we'll meet you out front."

When everyone got downstairs, there was a beautiful white stretch limo waiting. Sal was standing by the limo door, "Happy birthday, Vinny!"

Sonny hugged his son, "Happy birthday, Vincenzo! Have fun!" He hugged him again and kissed his cheeks, "You're my only son and I love you. Just remember, I only want the best for you." Vinny was a little confused. Everyone was acting as if he was going somewhere alone.

Uncle Nunzi hugged him, too, "Good luck, Vinny."

"Thanks, Uncle Nunzi." Vinny looked back at his father as Sal opened the door to the limo, "I love you too, Dad. Thanks for the great birthday."

With that, Sonny and Nunzi just smiled, "Son, you have no iidea."

Vinny bent down to get into the car. When he looked inside, a sexy and beautiful woman was waiting for him. He looked back up at his father with the biggest grin Sonny had ever seen. Vinny was going to heaven. Sonny and Nunzi were laughing as Sal closed the door. The boy was on his way.

The driver spoke through the intercom, leaving the privacy window up.

"Excuse me, Mr. Denucci?"

"Yeah?" Vinny replied, his eyes never leaving the woman who was sitting beside him, unbuttoning her blouse and exposing her beautiful breasts.

"My name is Sergio and I'm taking you to the Waldorf Astoria in Manhattan, so just sit back and enjoy the ride."

"Okay, thanks."

The beautiful blonde was sitting with her back to the corner of the limo; her legs crossed and stretched out toward Vinny. She wore a tiny pink lace bra that could not contain her perfect breasts as her nipples poked teasingly out the top. They mesmerized Vinny. He could feel himself getting aroused, which embarrassed him a little, but the women looked pleased. Noticing his discomfort, she slowly uncrossed her legs and pushed off her shoes. She reached over with her toes to poke playfully at Vinny's crotch. Since her smile was so inviting, Vinny relaxed and eased into the corner of the car opposite her to watch her performance. With one leg up on the seat still toying with Vinny's growing excitement, he could see her panties squeezed between the soft folds of her body.

"I have a message for you," she said, her eyes never leaving his. She lifted up her mini skirt further until Vinny could see the 'Happy Birthday' embroidered on the tiny triangle of the panties that barely covered her. Her skin was bronzed from the sun. She licked her lips slowly. Her blue eyes sparkled seductively and never left Vinny's face. She was hot and she knew it.

"What's your name?" Vinny asked.

"Dominique," she said, fingering her nipple until it formed a taut, hard peak. "I already know your name—Vinny, right?" Her hand trailed along her belly and over the edge of her hiked skirt until she slipped it under the edge of her panties. She began to move her fingers and hand, seeming to enjoy herself. Vinny watched her hand move as she pushed the panties to the side with her finger.

"These are in my way, Vinny," she said, pouting at the naughty panties. "Can you help me remove them?"

Vinny leaned forward to pull down her underwear and leaned even more into Dominique's toes. He was so hard he thought he would explode. Her scent was intoxicating as she opened her legs wide, her fingers continually moving between her legs.

She smiled up at him as he leaned back into his seat, the panties dangling from one hand as he watched her. "I think you'd be more comfortable if you took those off, don't you think?" she said. Her hand never stopped moving, her fingers tickling herself.

Vinny quickly unzipped his pants and began to remove them, a smile on his face. Dominique leaned forward and kissed him ever so softly. Her tongue moved, outlining his lips before she began to probe his mouth deeper. She leaned into him, pressing her breasts to his chest, her hands resting on his waist. Vinny stroked her breast as he kissed her with more urgency. He could feel her hands moving lower as she felt for him. He thought he would explode right there, but she pulled away.

Dominique eased him back to lounge comfortably on the seat and moved over him, one leg on each side of his body, straddling him. His lips moved to her breasts and as she leaned toward him, gently taking a nipple and sucking. He could get lost in the softness of her. Dominique reached down, grasped Vinny's penis gently, and played with the droplets of cum at the head. Vinny moaned and took a deep breath, holding on to his control, determined to make this moment last forever. Vinny was overwhelmed just looking at the beauty whose sole purpose was to please him.

She unbuttoned his shirt and leaned down, licking his nipples. Her breasts rubbed against his erection and Vinny slipped himself between them, rubbing up and down. Her tongue moved to his neck and ear, teasing him. She eased herself down Vinny's body, kissing as she moved. She reached his manhood and took it softly into her mouth, kissing the tip and licking the drops of cum from him. She moved up and down the shaft giving him little soft suckling kisses. Vinny put his hands on her head and stroked her hair, watching her make every inch of his body scream with awareness. It was bliss to lay there, eyes closed, being driven mad by a beautiful woman. He liked that she knew what he wanted.

Vinny felt powerful. For the first time he understood his father and why he protected his position. Power and control—this is life! Vinny could have that control. He had that control now!. He realized Dominique was there just for him alone and had to do anything he wanted. He felt almost high with the power he had over her.

He looked down at her as he felt her tongue lick his balls and her hand was slick from stroking him. Suddenly, it was all too much. Vinny grabbed her by her hair and pulled back up, pushing his penis into her mouth. He could feel her surprise and resistance. She was confused with the sudden change in command. Vinny pushed deeper into her mouth and held her by her hair. He would not let her up because it felt so good. The sensations her mouth created along with his new sense of power made Vinny push harder and harder into Dominique's mouth. She started to gag, then relaxed and took him inside with reluctance. He felt her teeth rubbing against his penis, but did not care. Even the biting and struggling felt good to him. He thought, 'She wanted to suck my cock, I'm going to give it to her all the way down her throat.'

He was almost ready to cum. Vinny bucked himself into Dominique's mouth until he could not hold back any longer. He could feel his cum shooting deep into her throat and the spasms seemed never-ending. He held his hand on the back of her head so she would not move and made her swallow every drop. This was what control felt like and Vinny could not get enough of it. Dominique knew who was boss now. He would let her go when he was ready, no matter how much she struggled. In fact, her struggle had a different appeal to Vinny all its own.

When Vinny finally laid back, Dominique spit him out and began coughing and choking. Cum was running down the side of her mouth as she looked at him with disgust. He did not care. It just made him get hard again. He looked down at his growing penis with pride. This was his show. Dominique was sitting on her knees, trying to compose herself. Vinny could see her nipples were still hard and her face flushed. She eyed him with a new respect as she turned her back and moved to sit toward the front of the limo. Vinny took one look at her gorgeous behind and quickly moved off the seat. Keeping her on her hands and knees, he moved behind her, kissing her back, feeling between her legs to see how wet she was. Cum was dripping down her leg. She was excited and Vinny went crazy.

He turned her over and spread her legs wide. Grabbing her wrists, he held them over her head and slammed his penis into her. She pushed up against him, wrapping her legs around him as he violently stroked her until she came, screaming in ecstasy. He released her arms and grabbed her legs, pulling her up until they were across his shoulders. He rammed her, bearing down as much as he could, until she started to scream. Vinny could not stop and he did not think Dominique wanted him to anyway. She was too wet to pretend that she did not like it.

Sweat and cum covered them as Vinny fucked her, holding her by the hips until he exploded into her once more. Dominique collapsed, her legs sliding from his shoulders to the floor of the car. Turning away, she hid her face against the back of the seat and would not look at him. They lay like that for a few minutes until Vinny pulled away and got dressed. Dominique did not move. Vinny tossed her panties at her and she looked at him to see if she should put them on. He nodded silently. She sat up, found the rest of her things and finished dressing. Neither of them said anything but Vinny could feel that she had a new respect for him and he liked it. On the other hand, did he? The emotions rushing through him were confusing. What did he just do? Where did that come from? He could have hurt her and did not care…that is not who he was. That is who his father was. Suddenly he felt sick inside as he did when he killed the deer. He looked over at Dominique but her eyes were avoiding him. He reached over to tell her he was sorry, but she just kept quiet and turned away.

"We're almost at the hotel, Mr. Denucci," the driver spoke through the intercom.

"Thank God," Vinny said, too quietly for the driver to hear.

The car came to a stop and the driver opened Vinny's door. He was surprised to see his father, Sal, Charlie and someone he did not recognize waiting for him.

"Was she good?" Sonny asked, eyeing Dominique as she stepped from the car.

"The best! Thank you," he said, projecting the bravado he thought his father expected.

"Good, Happy Birthday! I have to go and take care of some business. Sal will take you home."

Vinny glanced from the car. Looking back at his father he said, "Why can't I come with you?"

"Vinny, you're not ready for my personal business yet." Sonny said.

"I think I'm old enough. I've proven myself to you." Vinny jerked his head back at the limo door.

Sonny took a deep breath and hesitated a few minutes. He looked long and hard at his son, reluctantly he said, "Okay, but keep your mouth shut and don't ask me questions."

"No problem." Vinny said. Suddenly he felt a part of his father's life. Vinny thought, "a night out on the town with my father and his friends." This was the best birthday ever!

Sal went to go and park the car while Sonny made his introduction.

"Vinny, this is Salvatore "Hacksaw" Riccio, a good friend from Detroit. He helps with the construction company's hiring and firing of union men."

Vinny shook Mr. Riccio's hand then stepped over to speak to Charlie while his dad finished the conversation he had been having when Vinny arrived. Charlie could see Vinny's confusion.

"What's up?" Charlie said.

"Why do they call him 'Hacksaw'?" Vinny asked. He glanced at the two men talking, confusion in his eyes.

"A guy was working for Mr. Riccio on a building in Detroit and told him he would have it finished in two weeks. Well, a week went by and the guy did not show up. Then, three more weeks and he did not even bother to call. On the fourth week, Mr. Riccio was at the job site going over some plans in the construction trailer and in walks the guy. He tells Mr. Riccio that he had hurt his hand, which made him unable to work. Mr. Riccio went nuts. He grabbed a hacksaw out of one of the worker's toolboxes and grabbed the guy's hand. He started screaming at the guy, 'You're going to have a real injury now,' and proceeded to saw all five of the guy's fingers off.

"God," said Vinny. "That is a sick person."

"You never know who you're going to go up against in this world, Vinny." Charlie warned.

Vinny wondered to himself, 'Where does my father find these guys?' He looked at Mr. Riccio and went cold. 'That is what a killer looks like', he thought. 'And, he's my father's friend.'

Sal pulled up in the car and everyone got in. Sonny and Salvatore Riccio sat in the back to continue their business discussion. Sonny reminded Sal that the next stop was The Diamond Club on 54th and 10th Ave. Vinny strained to hear the conversation coming from the back seat. Mr. Riccio was quietly talking about a person named Tony Defranco that was messing up some construction job and thought Defranco would benefit from one of Sonny's visits. Sonny was happy to oblige and they agreed that Tony's lifespan was not going to be too long the way he was going. Vinny stopped listening, none of this made sense to him. He did not want any of it to make sense.

Two large door attendants greeted their arrival at the club. They pulled open the doors of the car and stood ramrod straight beside them as the passengers exited.

"Good evening, Mr. Denucci, it's nice to see you. I hope you win tonight," one of the men said.

"Thanks, Danny," Sonny said, shaking the door attendant's hand.

Vinny was confused. Were these men there on business? Vinny thought. This sounded more like a gambling trip than a business meeting.

The club was crowded and noisy. A gorgeous brown-haired woman wearing a black velvet leotard and spike heels came to welcome them holding a tray of champagne glasses.

"Good evening, Mr. Denucci," she said.

"Hello, honey. Tell the manager I am here. We'll be at my usual table," he said without stopping.

The group made their way to the back of the club where two black double doors marked the entrance to a private room. An intimidating, six-foot-five, three hundred pound Maitre D', dressed in a black suit stood guard. The person reminded Vinny of a wrestler he had seen on TV. The man inclined his head to Sonny, "Wait here please, Mr. Denucci," he said. "Let me see if your table is ready."

Vinny looked at his father, "How do you know these people? They treat you with such respect."

"I come here often and they appreciate a good patron. That's good business, Vinny," Sonny replied.

The Maitre D' had returned, "Mr. Denucci, if you'll please follow the waitress, your table is ready."

Sonny nodded and motioned his guests to follow. Stepping through the double doors was a transformation Vinny could not imagine. He was not certain they were still in New York! The men and women were dressed in gowns and tuxedos, both dripping in diamonds and other jewels. Women in skimpy, sexy, black and white outfits and net stockings were serving drinks. The room was enormous in size and had high ceilings with massive chandeliers, royal red plush carpet. Slot machines, craps tables, roulette wheels and black jack tables, all filled with hopeful gamblers, were wall-to-wall. The noise from the slot machines filled the air and everybody seemed to be having a good time.

Sonny's table was on an enclosed glass platform area at the back of the room overlooking the casino floor. They sat at a large round black marble table, already catered with gold plates of delicious appetizers complete with tall fluted crystal glasses filled with champagne. Vinny was impressed with the fact the bottle sitting in the ice bucket was Dom Perignon. That was the name of Champagne that even Vinny knew was expensive.

"Wow, this place is great," Vinny, said his excitement overflowing. "How did you find out about this place? Have you ever brought Mom here?"

Frowning at his inappropriate, child-like enthusiasm, Sonny was short with him, "Vinny, I told you... No questions."

"Okay," Vinny swallowed his other questions, realizing how he sounded. He sat back, feeling quietly dejected.

Mr. Riccio watched the exchange between father and son, he leaned toward Sonny, and "Does Vinny know anything?" he asked.

"No, and that's the way I want it until I'm ready." Sonny barked, his eyes never leaving the floor of the casino.

Reaching into his pocket and pulling out a large roll of bills, Sonny handed two to Vinny. "Here are a couple hundred bucks. Go and play. When I'm finished talking business with Mr. Riccio, I'll send for you."

Vinny was surprised that they would let him on the casino floor because of his age, but took the money from Sonny and went to the cashier's window. When he asked for two hundred dollars in chips, she never questioned his age, just handed him his chips and put his money in the drawer. He walked straight over to a roulette table and placed one ten dollar chip on his mother's birthday, number nine. He stood with his fingers crossed and watched the man spin the roulette wheel. The little ball went round and round until it landed on number twenty-seven. Damn.

At first Vinny was disappointed, but after a few tries he decided it was fun and exciting. He could see why his dad could get used to going to this place regularly. Glancing around the room, Vinny thought he would try his hand at blackjack. There was an older man sitting with a young woman who proudly displayed gigantic breasts. The man's stack of chips was large, so it appeared to Vinny that the man was lucky in many ways. Vinny sat next to him, hoping that some of his luck would rub off.

While glancing at his cards, the man leaned over to speak with his woman friend who was looking up at the private glass room, "That's the top boss up at that table," Vinny heard him whisper.

"Impressive," she said. Vinny glanced in the direction the women was looking and realized that they were referring to his father's table.

"The tall good looking one right, who is he?" she asked.

Her escort looked at her in disbelief, "Don't you read the papers?"

"No," she said, embarrassed.

"That's the most powerful man in the US," the man said, scooping up more chips from another win.

"What do you mean? Is he some rich politician?" Her eyes glued to Sonny.

"He's Mafia. That makes him rich AND political. He is what they call 'the Godfather', which means he controls all the money and the politics in the city.

"That guy in the spiral tie is the Godfather? He looks like just a regular guy," she observed.

"Well, looks can be deceiving. He's a powerful Mafia boss, trust me." The man nodded his head, punctuating his words.

The woman looked at him with wide eyes, "Wow, that's exciting."

The man noticed the dealer had moved closer, eavesdropping on his conversation with the woman. He became uncomfortable with the dealer's interest in their conversation and quickly changed the subject. "Yes...yes...winning is exciting," he said. The dealer simply smiled and shuffled the next hand.

Although Vinny won his first hand at blackjack, he was having trouble even seeing his cards. His head was spinning. The thought of Mafia kept running through his mind! His father is the Godfather written about in all those articles he read. Those heartless killers and thieves worked for his dad. Vinny could not understand how he and his father could both live in the same house and he was not aware of something like this. He wondered if his mom knew. Maybe the man was mistaken or trying to impress his girlfriend. However, now that Vinny thought about it, it did explain many crazy things that did not make sense before. The late night visitors, Sal's presence everywhere his dad went, strange business meetings...none of his friend's fathers did business as Sonny did.

Vinny lost interest in the cards and went to sit in a lounge area where he could watch his father's glass room. He could see many people come in and out of the dining suite, just to say 'hello'. They would shake Sonny's hand when they came in, and then kiss his cheek when they went out. From where Vinny sat, his father looked like he moved in a separate world and Vinny suddenly realized that in actuality, he did. He was saddened to think that, at seventeen, he did not know anything about his father at all. By 3:00 a.m., Vinny could not keep his eyes open any longer, propped his head on his hand, and closed his eyes. It seemed like mere minutes had gone by when he felt Sal waking him and leading him to their car.

When Vinny woke the next morning, his mind recounted the events of the following day and he was not sure if it was a dream. The dinner... the limo... the girl... the sex... the casino... his dad's private room... 'Could his dad be the Mafia boss?' he wondered. Where would that leave him? Did that mean that Vinny had no choice but to eventually be part of his dad's organization? Vinny's mind reeled. What about the plans he had for his own future. Vinny had too many questions and the likelihood of answers was not great. Vinny was willing say little, but would be more aware of what was going on around him after last night. After all, he did not have a choice.

Al and Vinny were halfway through their senior year of high school and were already making plans for college. Christmas had been extravagant in the Denucci house this year. It seemed like Sonny was trying to make up to Felicia for the tough year they had shared while showing Vinny how prosperous and successful he was as a provider for his family. Theirs was a lifestyle that anyone would envy and was not easy to duplicate with an ordinary, nine-to-five job. Sonny pointed that fact out to Vinny with great regularity.

New Year's Eve was one day away and Vinny wanted to go to a club in the city called Fantasy with his cousin, Robert. The greatest challenge he faced tonight, however, was to convince his father that he did not need a shadow like Sal or Charlie to tag along with them. It was not going to be easy to be free of "the goons" as Robert called them, but it was worth a try.

Sonny came home about eleven o'clock and Vinny wasted no time.

"Dad, when you get settled, can I talk to you for a minute?"

"Sure Vinny, give me ten."

Vinny sat on the balcony waiting. Part of him was ready for a confrontation, another part of him questioned if the argument that was inevitable was worth it. He was still wrestling with his thoughts when Sonny came out of the bedroom.

"What can I do for you, son?"

"Robert and I are going out for New Year's Eve and I don't want the guys to go along."

"No fuckin' way," Sonny said.

Exasperated, Vinny looked at his father, "Why, Dad? When are you going to trust me?"

"Sorry, Vinny I don't trust anyone."

Vinny waited for a minute, took a deep breath and stood up to his dad, "Well I 'm going and I don't care what you say. You're not going to stop me from having a good time."

Sonny's eyebrows rose a bit. He was surprised at the confrontation and felt a mixture of anger and pride. He stared at his son. Rather than blow up, he thought he would play this one out.

"Vinny, I'm sorry. I need you alive and I do not know who might be trailing you on a night like New Year's Eve. You wouldn't know how to handle things if something came up," he explained.

"Dad, I am a big boy. I can handle more than you give me credit for. I watch. I see. I'm not as naive or unaware as you might think."

Sonny smiled at that. 'The boy's coming around,' he thought.

"Okay son, I tell you what. Against my better judgment, I'm going to let you go, but under one condition." Sonny said, he raised his finger as a punctuation mark, and then pointed it at Vinny.

"What?" Vinny said.

"You can go to one club. I want to know where it is, what time you are going, and what time you plan to head home. That way, I know when you get home safe."

"No problem. Thanks dad. This means a lot to me." Vinny shook his father's hand and turned to leave the room.

"And, Vinny..."

"Yeah?"

"Watch out for Robert. He can be a little obnoxious and sometimes his attitude cause's trouble," Sonny warned.

Vinny grinned at his dad, "I know, Dad. I'm sure we'll be fine but, at the first sign of trouble, I'll call you."

Vinny could not wait to call Robert and tell him the news. The boys felt like that they were being set free. 'How ironic,' thought Vinny!

The next day filled with personal preparations for that night. Vinny got a haircut and bought a tuxedo. He went to three different stores until he found the right pair of shoes. For some reason something felt different about tonight and he wanted to look good.

Robert called from the lobby at nine. He was waiting with a taxi and told Vinny to hurry. When Vinny got in the cab, Robert handed him two condoms.

"I doubt that I'll need these. Thanks anyway," Vinny said, handing them back to Robert.

"You never know. You've been known to get lucky."

Vinny smiled. Robert knew about Vinny's birthday present.

The luck started when they arrived at the club. Vinny was so concerned about not having the 'goons' with them; he forgot that he was underage. There were butterflies in his stomach and his palms were getting damp as he stood in a line with Robert that went clear around the block.

"God, will you look at these girls?" Robert said as he was sizing up the crowd. As they slowly advanced toward the club entrace, Robert began talking to small groups of women along the way. Each time he flirted with a new group, he would motion Vinny to join them. Vinny was surprised that the rest of the people in line did not mind their rapid advance toward the front.

The next thing Vinny knew, Robert was talking to somebody at the door that was checking I.D's. Robert and his new friend were laughing while the guy stamped Robert's hand and motioned Vinny to come over and have his hand stamped too.

"Happy New Year, gentlemen," the door attendant said as he opened it for the boys.

Vinny turned to Robert and was impressed, "How did you do that?"

"Vinny, someday you'll do the same." Robert winked at him.

Vinny was confused. What was going on? Who the fuck was Robert to go waltzing into a club like that? Vinny was immediately drawn into the atmosphere and excitement of the nightclub. The place was overcrowded with people. Women were dancing on the tables and the music was very loud. Beautiful women appeared to be standing in clusters all over the room. The club was dark with light shows everywhere, illuminating the place enough to be able to appreciate the sexy and skimpy outfits adorning the women servers. Women were dancing in cages wearing bathing suits and transparent lingerie. The walls were covered in mirrors so Vinny could enjoy the views of the dancers from every angle. He felt like he was becoming an expert in the evaluation of the female anatomy.

Some people had even come in costume. Vinny especially liked the matching lionesses that sported big breasts and long tails. A huge disco ball hung in the center of the dance floor and sent prisms of light everywhere. They even had dry ice machines that blew out clouds of smoke that billowed around the stage floor and gave the appearance that everyone was floating. This was a dream world.

While Vinny was getting a drink, he watched his cousin roaming the floor like a bloodhound, in search of some poor, lonely girl that he could take home and fuck all night before putting her in a cab home. Robert treated everybody badly and thought he was God's gift to women. But he was the only one who thought so. He branded anyone who appeared not to like him, "a jerk or a bitch" and would proceed to belittle them in front of everyone.

Vinny lost sight of his cousin, but it was not long before Robert came back down to the bar to get him.

He reached out and tugged at Vinny's arm, "Vinny, I just met two beautiful Latino babes. We're getting laid tonight, man."

"You can have them; I think I'll stay here with that cute little barmaid. She seems pretty interested." Vinny grinned.

"Fuck the barmaid! She will have to work all night and besides, she is probably a whore working in this joint. I bet her pussy has more mileage on it than your father has on his car." Robert sneered at the barmaid, letting his eyes roam over her, liking what he saw, but just as quickly rejecting her as not good enough for him.

"Nice choice of words, Robert. Moreover, maybe she is a virgin putting herself through college by working nights so her days are free to go to school and study. You know, some people work for a living." Vinny retorted.

"Vinny, you're a moron. Watch this," Robert said as he waved toward the barmaid. "I'll prove she's a whore, and then we can go upstairs, get a little drunk and go fuck the two Spanish broads in a hotel room right down the street. I've got it all figured out."

Robert continued to flag down the barmaid. A little curious, Vinny asked him, "What are you going to do?"

"Just watch... Excuse me, honey," he said, directing his voice to the barmaid.

The barmaid walked over with a friendly smile. "What can I do for you?"

"See, Vinny? She already wants to do something for me." Vinny just grinned.

The barmaid was a cute strawberry blond with an average build and a great smile. She was thin, but not too tall and wore a delicious ruby red lipstick that Vinny was certain tasted as good as it looked.

"My friend and I have this bet going. I say you sucked cock before and he says you haven't." Robert said with a straight face.

Vinny put his forehead down on the bar with disgust and embarrassment. How could he have asked her that? Nevertheless, then again, Robert had no class.

She frowned for a moment then said, "How much is it worth for you to find out?"

Robert said, "$100.00 dollars and I'll let you suck my cock for free."

She looked directly at Vinny and said, "Sorry, you lose. I have sucked several cocks," then turning back to Robert "Where's my hundred?"

Robert paid her on the spot, "What about my free suck?"

"Got another hundred?" she asked.

"No."

"Well, come back when you do," she turned and walked away to wait on another customer.

Vinny sat shaking his head and finishing his drink. 'You've got to hand it to Robert', he thought. 'The guy's got balls."

Robert recovered quickly and looked at Vinny with a grin, "Vinny, they're all fuckin' pigs. Can we go upstairs and nail those two broads?"

Grinning, Vinny got up and followed Robert to the second floor. Two women were sitting at a table—they looked up and smiled when they saw them coming. Vinny could not understand Robert's excitement, neither of them were much to look at. The women were a little too heavy and had too much makeup and cheap jewelry. Vinny was glad that it was dark. He could see that Robert had no taste in women, whatsoever.

"This is Maria and Carmen. Ladies, this is my cousin, Vinny." Robert said to them.

The women looked grateful for male companionship and smiled at Vinny. Robert was subtly motioning toward Maria to let Vinny know that she was the one he wanted. Vinny reluctantly sat down next to

Carmen thinking that 'this scene is a waste of time' when a slow song began, luring Robert and Maria out onto the dance floor.

"Want to dance?" Carmen asked Vinny with a Spanish accent so strong he could hardly understand her.

"No, thank you. I am somewhat thirsty. Can I get you a drink?" he asked. He would do anything rather than dance with Carmen. This was not turning out to be a good night.

"Sure a gin and tonic please," she replied.

Vinny walked over to the bar, placed an order for two gin and tonics, and then carried them back over to the table. He raised his glass to toast the evening, "Cheers."

She tapped her glass against his and drank the iced liquid in one continuous gulp.

Vinny stared at her. "Do you always drink that fast?"

Carmen looked straight at Vinny, the smile she had disappearing from her face. "Vinny, let's cut the bullshit, It's about quarter to twelve and I want to be drunk enough so you can take me home, suck on my pussy, fuck me a little until I get tired of you, then get you out of my house before my boyfriend gets home from fucking some other whore tonight rather than me."

Offended, Vinny still felt sympathetic for this woman, "Sorry, but I'm not going to do that. What makes you think I would want to sleep with you anyway? I don't even know you."

Lighting a cigarette, Carmen was indignant, "When's the last time you saw a face on a pussy? Turn us upside down and we're all sisters, right?"

"Are you always this blunt? Where is your self-respect? You are a woman, for God's sake, be a little more mysterious. Guys don't like cynical, unhappy, dissatisfied women."

"What? Are you a priest? Men are pigs, so I treat them like pigs. My boyfriend could not take me out tonight 'cause he wanted to fuck someone different on New Year's Eve so I told him I'd go out and do the same. You don't have to worry, Vinny, I'm a clean girl."

Vinny drank the rest of his drink and got up, disgusted, "Well, good luck tonight in finding your prey. I am sure you will not have a problem, but it is not going to be me. You could ask my cousin though, he'd probably be happy to help out."

"You're serious? How could you turn down pussy? No man ever turns down pussy." Carmen's face dropped, her eyes wide.

"That's just it. I am a man, not a pig—you know the difference."

Carmen was quiet for a moment. Then she said, "Well, good-bye then. I'm kind of sorry it's not going to be you." Vinny leaned over, kissed Carmen's cheek and walked by the dance floor on his way back downstairs. 'It's depressing,' he thought. His thoughts ran to Marlene. He missed her. He was certain that they could have had a future if she did not have to leave. Oh, well.

Robert was leading Maria back to their table, his arm around her waist, "Where's Carmen?" he asked.

Vinny whispered quietly, "There's no chemistry so I told her to split and that's what I'm going to do, too. If you can find her, she has an interesting reason why she wants to have sex tonight. Maybe you can work them in together."

Robert asked with interest, his eyes sliding in the direction of the table. The men hugged, Vinny bid Maria 'Good-bye' and went outside to catch a cab. He was not enjoying the dating scene as much as he thought he would. Men and women had no idea what the other wanted. They just used each other and still were not satisfied. What a waste.

As Vinny stepped outside into the crisp night air, he could hear everyone inside shouting, "Happy New Year."

"Yeah, Happy New Year," he said as he got into the cab.

CHAPTER 6
THE TRUTH UNVEILS
* * * *

School was going good and Vinny was looking forward to summer. He got home around four in the afternoon and walked in on his father talking to a strange looking man. He was huge with a slicked back ponytail, sunglasses and sporting a scar on his right cheek that continued back along his face until it stopped just above the missing part of his left ear. 'That missing ear must make wearing those sunglasses even more challenging,' thought Vinny, wondering why the man would be wearing sunglasses in the house anyway.

"Hello… Excuse me for interrupting." Vinny said.

"Vincenzo, come over here. I want you to meet a good friend of mine."

A friend! Vinny thought. Why would anybody want this person for a friend?

"Vincenzo, this is Mr. Capers."

Vinny reached over to shake the man's hand. It was smooth and he was disgusted at how sweaty it was, "Nice to meet you, sir." Vinny replied.

"Thank you," Mr. Capers said, his voice polite but impersonal.

"Mr. Capers is in the disposal business." Sonny said.

"Like garbage?" Vinny asked.

Mr. Capers looked at Sonny and smiled, "Yeah I dispose of all trash."

"Oh." Vinny could not imagine how he was supposed to respond to that.

"Okay, Vincenzo, go to your room and study."

"Go study" was Vinny's cue that he was no longer welcome to stay in the room when Sonny had guests. Every time Sonny conducted business with someone in his home, Vinny immediately left the room. Vinny knew his father was hiding something but he was getting less and less interested in what that 'something' was. After the night in the Diamond Club when the old man said Sonny was Mafia, Vinny watched for signs. Knowing little about how the Mafia worked, he did not know what signs he should be looking for.

Vinny felt his relationship was different with his father. It was more distant, but with a subtle sense of expectation. There was no need for Vinny to try to figure it out. His dad would let him know whatever he wanted him to know, whenever he wanted him to know it. Besides, Vinny did have a lot of studying to do. Finals were coming up soon.

Reading volumes of notes from class made Vinny tired. He closed his eyes for a minute, just to rest them and ended up falling fast asleep at his desk. He felt he was asleep, yet he was aware of someone nudging him. He could also hear a voice that sounded far away but shook it off. The nudging and prodding became more persistent as Vinny became aware of someone's presence in his room.

"Wake up, Vinny"

Ignoring the voice, Vinny tried to go back to sleep.

"Vinny, wake up your dinner is going to get cold. Come on, dinner's on the table."

Nothing....he just laid there quietly!

"Vinny!" Felicia shouted.

He woke with a jolt, "Okay! Okay! What's the big deal?"

"I want us to eat before your father gets home," she said, satisfied that he was awake, as she walked out of the bedroom to go back to the kitchen and finish preparing dinner.

"I'll be right there," he called loudly behind her.

Stretching and yawning, Vinny walked into his bathroom and put his head under the cold faucet. The shock of the frosty water brought him back to life and he stood, bent over the sink, letting the cool stream hit the back of his neck. He could not understand why he felt so tired. He combed his hair back, dried his face and smiled into the mirror. For some reason, he felt good.

Vinny walked into the dining room where his mother was sitting, all alone.

"Where's Dad?"

"Out for the evening," she said. "Sit down and eat your pasta and peas." Felicia looked disgusted.

Vinny asked, "Are you okay?"

As a tear rolled down her left cheek, Felicia put her hand to her mouth, "No."

Vinny went to her and gave her a hug, "I love you, Mom. Don't be upset."

"I don't want to talk about it, Vinny. Eat your dinner," she said.

They were quiet for a while then Vinny tried to make small talk. "Did you see that 'Mr. Capers' guy? What's with the shades in the house?"

"Your father has animals for friends. Mr. Capers is just another of his menagerie. Do not get mixed up with them, Vincenzo. You're better than them put together and don't you ever forget it." Getting up from her seat, Felicia started to gather up the dishes.

"You want dessert?"

"No, thank you mother, Why don't you go relax for a while, I'll clean up," Vinny replied.

"No. I would rather stay busy. Finish your homework and go to bed." She took his plate and gave him a kiss, dismissing him for the night as she walked into the kitchen.

Vinny's alarm went off at seven the next morning. He dressed quickly and went into the kitchen, giving his mom a good-morning kiss.

Felicia seemed a little better today, but Vinny thought she was also a little jumpy.

"You get your homework done last night?"

"Yes I did mother." She put eggs and toast down in front of him.

"Eat your breakfast." Felicia sat down with Vinny, her voice was serious and to the point. "Vinny, I know you see a lot money and flash, but school is what's important. If you want to be somebody you need an education. There are no short cuts in life. Study hard and make your momma proud."

"I know Mom. I like school and I am looking forward to college. You sound funny. Is this about that Mr. Capers guy?"

"It's about you. All you've got to worry about is getting good grades and everything will be okay." Felicia got up, "Time for school."

Vinny put his plate in the sink and kissed Felicia goodbye. 'That was a strange conversation for breakfast,' he thought.

That night, Sonny and Felicia were back at it.

"Don't you even think about screwing up Vinny's mind? Those people you keep introducing him to are just making him curious. He is a good boy, Sonny. Let him finish school." She pleaded with Sonny.

"This isn't for you to decide, Felicia."

"He's my son too, and I want a better life for him than that."

"There's nothing wrong with your life." Sonny retorted, "Is there?"

"Vinny deserves a chance. What future is he going to have if you pull him out of school?"

"Okay. I will let it go for now. He might as well stay in school anyway because I am not ready for him yet. However, I am telling you right now, Felicia, when it is time, it is time. I will tell him what his choices are and that is it. He does not have all the facts to make a good decision, so he is safer where he is. But soon, he'll have to come around with me and I don't want to hear more of this shit from you when he does," Sonny warned.

Vinny hated these conversations. They created so many questions that he was unable to ask. He wondered what his father meant by 'safer'. He lay in bed, questions tumbling around in his head until he fell asleep.

The next morning he got ready for school and went into the kitchen for breakfast. Hugging his mother he asked, "Why were you fighting with Dad again?"

"Oh, Vinny your father is a royal pain in the ass. I guess that's just what parents do." She seemed resigned and tired. She did not want to talk about her concerns with Vinny this morning.

"Give me a kiss and get to school. It's getting late."

As Vinny stepped into the elevator, Larry Friedman, a sixty-two year old, hard-of-hearing busy-body neighbor was telling another tenant about the 'Big Mafia Boss' living in the building. Nobody took Mr. Friedman seriously. He dressed like a street vagrant with mismatched clothes and two-toned shoes, he was a retired airline captain who misunderstood most of what he heard and couldn't remember what he'd said much less to whom from one day to the next. People called him the Walter Winchel of the building because he was always providing 'news flashes' to anyone who would listen.

More than once, Mr. Friedman had stopped Vinny in the hall to tell him that neighbors were complaining about how loudly he was playing his music and that he should stop before they called the police. Another time he remarked how, if he were younger, he would kick all the little teen punks in the ass just to teach them a lesson. Vinny found Mr. Friedman's threats as entertaining as a comic routine. The old man took himself so seriously. Sometimes he would get so worked up, he would shake so hard he could barely stand and spit would come flying out of his mouth when he talked. Vinny assumed he liked having a few young people in the building because it gave him something to complain about. He used to complain that pets were not allowed—then he moved on to anyone under twenty-five who was not married. Mr. Friedman never knew who any of the kids were. So they all got together and decided to credit the acts Mr. Friedman complained about on a fictitious kid named Jimmy. Vinny used to feel sorry for the old man, but listening to him in the elevator, he thought he was just a nasty geriatric who liked to stir up trouble.

Vinny decided to confront Mr. Friedman this morning and he asked him, "So, who's the Mafia boss in the building?"

"Mind your own business, kid. No one's talking to you anyway," was his reply as he scurried out of the elevator to try to catch the door attendant away from his post at the lobby door. It was his second favorite thing to do, next to complaining.

Vinny was super-sensitive to the Mafia issue. Like someone who buys a new car because they like that it's unique, then they see them everywhere on the road after they take delivery, Vinny was seeing Mafia articles in the paper or hearing about them on TV constantly. It seemed to Vinny as if the organization was always accused of some heinous crime, but somehow they were never convicted. The news never told who they were, where they lived or what their family members did. Apparently, there were many bosses around, but no one seemed to know who they were, except maybe the FBI, and they didn't seem to be able to do anything about it.

Vinny once read a profile by the FBI about why tax evasion was the easiest way for the government to convict Mafia offenders. It talked about how greedy they were, getting unearned pieces of other people's businesses, and how they did not pay taxes. The profile showed the players spent too much on things that were traceable. Even though they had a small annually reported income, they lived well beyond their means. They said that when someone makes a lot of money illegally, it is difficult to spend it. The government wants to know where people's money comes from. Purchasing big-ticket items like houses or cars requires ownership registration. How can someone pay cash for a three hundred thousand dollar house when their income was only fifty thousand dollars a year?

It made sense to Vinny that high cash profit businesses were the ones the FBI watched for Mafia activity. Businesses like casinos or restaurants had many cash transactions. It was easy for them to say they had a 'better night' than they had and funnel illegal or 'dirty money' though legitimate channels, making it available to the owner for spending.

Vinny found the whole thing fascinating and could understand why there was so much interest. Politicians could base their entire platform on cleaning up the Mafia. They were easy to criticize. Nevertheless, what the people may not have known is that the Mafia financed most of their election campaigns and practically owned the politicians. Having politicians in their pocket gave the Mafia a greater stronghold into a city's activities.

As Vinny left the building, Sonny was talking to a group of nicely dressed men that looked out of place on the street. Sonny had many friends like that. When he was younger, Vinny never questioned that his dad did not seem to need an office. He went to work every day. Vinny never knew where his fathers work was. Vinny was older and these things disturbed him. How can his dad conduct business as a "financial consultant and investor" without a business address? Sonny looked up and waved at Vinny when he noticed him leaving the building, then went back to his 'meeting' on the street.

Vinny got home that night around five-thirty and found Felicia in the kitchen, crying. As soon as she saw her son, she rushed over and hugged him tightly. Her heart was pounding and she was clearly fearful and upset.

"Mom, what's the matter with you?"

"Vinny, I have to talk to you about something and you must promise me that you won't say anything to your father or he'll hurt me."

"Mom..." Vinny thought she was being a little dramatic.

"This is hard for me to explain to you, Vincenzo, and I wanted to wait until you were older but I have no choice." Felicia's voice was desperate.

"What is it?" Vinny asked.

"After the argument your father and I just had, I know I have to tell you."

"Tell me what?"

"Your father is involved with some nasty people. You've met a few of them - Mr. Capers, the one you were so fascinated with is one of them." Then speaking almost to herself, Felicia said under her breath, "God help me if Sonny finds out that I told you this..." she whispered.

"Mom, tell me. Dad won't find out, I promise." Vinny reach out for her, but she took a step back and looked at him.

"Vinny, your father has other plans for you than for you to finish college." Her eyes revealed that much more needed to be said.

"Why? What plans are you talking about?"

Felicia pulled out a newspaper clipping that dated three days earlier. She had cut it from the paper so Vinny would not see it, but thought it best that now he did. Handing it to Vinny, it read:

"As the Italian Mafia Grows, So Do the Bosses"

"Sonny Denucci, Godfather who took over the New York Mafia crime family five years ago, is becoming the most powerful boss ever. Insiders describe his unique way of force as 'incredible' explaining further that it has said to be 'the boss's way or death'. Sonny Denucci is the youngest New York Godfather in the history of the family; he is also the only boss who has never been to prison. Sonny Denucci's brother, Nunzi Denucci, is second-in-command as trustee and will replace his brother in the event of Sonny Denucci's untimely demise. However, reliable sources say that Sonny's son, Vincenzo Denucci, who is not yet involved with the family, will retain that position over his uncle. Our inside sources say that when young Vincenzo is ready, Sonny will retire from routine local dealings, passing the torch to his son, and handle only major family business."

"Does this mean what I think, Mom?"

She started to cry.

"Is this true, Mom? Do I have to do this? What about my plans to become a lawyer? Just because everyone else thinks I'll just go along with this, that doesn't mean I will." Vinny was getting upset. He was also furious at his dad.

"I don't want his life. He knows that." Vinny's voice rose. He was frightened of the implications of this.

"Vinny! Please calm down." She was crying hard. The reality and enormity of what they were going to have to face was crashing down on them. They sat in silence for a long time.

"You must never tell your father I showed you this article. You have to pretend you don't know," she begged.

"Why?"

"Your father is a dangerous man and I cannot begin to tell you how angry he would be. He would hurt me! Vinny promise me you won't say anything."

"Oh, God, Mom, what are we going to do?"

"I don't know. I have been worrying about this for years and now that it is in my face, I don't know what to do. Before, you were too young to help him, but you're old enough to start learning his business and he wants you to quit school at the end of the quarter."

"Before I graduate?"

"Yes. However, he might let you finish high school. I'm not sure."

The enormity of all that Vinny was hearing was overwhelming.

"Is there anything else you need to tell me while we are alone?" he asked. He felt dead inside, numb.

"Yes." Felicia was hesitant, but continued, "I'm worried about your Uncle Joe. He got involved with your father somehow, he will not tell me how, but something happened and now your father is upset. He said he's going to teach Joe a lesson."

"What lesson?"

"I don't know, but he's angry, and I don't like what that means." Her fingers were clasped together tightly.

"Is there anything I can do?"

"No, But I want you to tell me if you overhear anything so I can warn Uncle Joe that you know who your father is, you keep your eyes open and your mouth closed do you hear me? The men that work for him, like Sal or Charlie, report everything back to him. Never discuss your father or me in front of them. They're loyal to Sonny."

"That I do know." Vinny agreed.

"Did you know that your father has you followed everywhere you go to see you don't get into trouble with any of the other members in his organization?"

Vinny's head was spinning, "It's hard to believe that he didn't find out any of this until now. How did dad manage to keep all this quiet for so long?" Leaning back in the chair, Vinny let the enormity of all he had learned wash over him. He clinched his fist and felt the anger rush over him. Suddenly he slammed his fist on the table and began pacing like a caged animal around the kitchen. Felicia did not know how to comfort him. For the first time, she could see a little of Sonny's temperament in her son.

"People believe what they want to believe, Vinny. Sonny makes it clear that he does not like questions so nobody asks them. After a while, people just assume he's just another guy who provides well for his family." She clutched Vinny's hand tight, "You be careful, the worst is yet to come."

"What?" he asked with curious dread.

"Your father plans for you to take over as boss someday. That means no law school. Being a boss is about threatening and killing people. It is a lifetime of ducking the FBI, lying, cheating, even potential jail time. I do not want that life for you Vinny. I don't know what I can do about it...but, I don't want that life for you." Felicia grabbed her apron from around her waist to wipe the tears that rolled off her face.

"He can't make me."

"Yes, he can, Vinny. Believe me. I wish it wasn't true but he can." Felicia sighed.

"No fuckin' way, Mom! This is America, we'll go away somewhere." Vinny said.

"He'll find us. He has millions of dollars and people at his disposal. If we move every week, he will find us. If we change our names, he will find us. You will never rest. Your life would be miserable. You couldn't have a family without worrying about them," she warned.

"Then I'll stay and find a way to avoid it. Maybe Uncle Nunzi can take over."

"No, Vinny, you're his only son. He wants you." She paused, and then said slowly, every word weighed and spoken with a flat finality, "Vinny, we fight all of the time about you. I do not want him to ruin your life, but this is your father's way and I cannot stop him. I can only hope you can be strong enough to handle it. When you were younger, I thought about running away to protect you. I always hoped some other boss would come along and kill him. I love your father, but I love you more."

Vinny picked up her hand and kissed it gently. "Mom, I love you, too. I will find a way. Everything will turn out all right, I promise you."

Vinny went to his room and sat in the chair by the window to think. Everyone was right...the man at the club, even crazy old Mr. Fridley. At least the puzzle was starting to fit together.

The next morning, Vinny walked into the kitchen to find his father reading the newspaper.

"Good morning, Dad."

Sonny looked up, "Good morning, Son."

"Can we talk, please?"

"Sure," he said. "What's the matter?"

Vinny drummed up his courage and blurted out his question, "Are you involved with organized crime? Are you a Mafia boss?"

Sonny put his newspaper down abruptly, "Did your mother tell you that?"

"No, I overheard a conversation in the elevator yesterday morning. One of the tenants mentioned your name. And before, when we were at that casino, one of the people playing blackjack was pointing up at your glass room, telling his girlfriend that a Mafia boss was there that night. I did not know then he was pointing at you. Was he?" Vinny waited for his father to speak. When Sonny did not, Vinny continued, "I would like to know who you are because I don't have any idea. Up until now, I thought you were a financial consultant or something."

"Well, Vinny, I don't think you're old enough to understand. But, as you get older you will." Sonny said.

"Dad, remember when you told me about trust? If you cannot trust your family, whom can you trust? Was that a lie?" Vinny was getting frustrated. Sonny was not taking him seriously and Vinny was almost yelling "So who the fuck are you?"

Sonny was on his feet, knocking the kitchen chair over in the process, "Don't you ever talk to me in that tone of voice again or I'll kick the shit out of you. You want to know who I am. I will tell you. I am the boss of a secret society, which we call the Mafia. So there you have it. Do not ever fuck with me. I'll give you answers when I'm ready, not before, so go to your room and don't ask me questions."

Vinny looked at his father and saw an anger and disgust that he had not seen before. He saw him as a king who needed an heir but was afraid to say too much in case the heir wanted to be king too soon. Vinny marveled at how his father could shut him out of his life when he chose, and then expect him to be eager to give up the life he always wanted for himself just to get involved with his father's business. Vinny knew little about the Mafia and even less about his father. However, he would find out. He excused himself and left for class.

After school, Vinny decided to go to the library and do research. He wanted to get a better understanding of the life that may be ahead of him and, more important who his father is. It occurred to Vinny that strangers knew more about his dad than he did.

Walking into the library, Vinny started to sweat. He stood waiting for the clerk to help him and became embarrassed, wondering how he was going to ask about crime bosses and organized crime without her connecting him with his request. After what his mother had said, Vinny thought maybe everyone knew he had a crime boss for a dad.

Vinny scanned the library for signs of his dad's goons. What if they followed him there and reported Vinny's research topic back to his father? Vinny was getting paranoid and he did not like the feeling. He was in the school library, for God's sake. There were more than a few dozen kids doing projects in the place, why should he assume someone would think his motives were anything except homework? He started to settle down.

Mrs. Clark, the librarian, came out from the back room carrying an armload of books and smiled when she saw Vinny.

"Hi, Vinny... what can I help you find today?"

Vinny did not know what to do. He knew Mrs. Clark and assumed she would make the connection. He was hoping to keep his request anonymous, but he liked the librarian and felt like he could ask her almost anything. She did not seem like the judgmental type...did she.

"Vinny, are you all right?" she asked.

"Yes, ah, fine. Um...Ms. Clark, I need information on the Mafia...for my social studies class." He stammered. He hated to lie to her, but it just seemed to come out by itself.

Ms. Clark hesitated a minute, looking at Vinny, "Row five, Section G, in the cabinet marked 'Mafia'."

"Thanks," Vinny turned quickly and walked to the direction she had pointed him too. He thought he could feel Mrs. Clark watching him, which made him uncomfortable. Section G had a number of books covering Mafia history and there was an additional filing cabinet filled with newspaper clippings. Vinny thought he would start with the clippings first. That was the most likely place to find things on his dad.

He found the section and the right filing cabinet. Vinny took some deep breaths one —two—three. He wanted to get the queasiness out of his stomach. He wanted to prepare for the worst. He reached up and slipped a hand through the handle. Vinny pulled out the cabinet drawer. All the files were in alphabetical order. He fanned through until he reached S. Scarabelli. Pulling out several newspaper clippings Vinny looked around for a seat where he could read in private. Spying a private booth near the window, he walked over slowly. His heart was pounding. He sat down and unfolded the paper. He started to read some old articles from the local newspapers saying who was dead and who was moving up in the Mafia world. From what he read there was a lot of violence.

He read some more articles until he came to a headline that read, "Mafia Boss Beats another Indictment, Will They Ever Convict the Godfather?" There was a picture of Sonny leaving the Federal courthouse with his lawyer, Max Delaney. Vinny read the following editorial column written by Jim McKay and it said, "Sonny (The Penman) Denucci, the most powerful of the Mafia bosses, escapes yet another murder conviction because of lack of evidence and witnesses. Does he have the public scared? Reliable sources say he has threatened the victim's family so no one would testify against him. Sonny's lawyer Max Delaney denies these allegations against his client. Delaney contends that his client was out of town when the murder took place. According to Delaney, Mr. Denucci has no idea why someone would kill Mr. Otis Jenkins, owner of The Blue Note, a jazz club. Mr. Jenkins was found outside his bar at 3:45 a.m. last night, slumped over in his car with three bullets to the back of the head.

Sources say that Sonny Denucci loaned Mr. Jenkins money to get his club started and when Mr. Jenkins could not pay it back, Denucci taught him a brutal lesson so other borrowers would know if you could not pay it back, do not borrow.

However, also related to this same club, was an altercation between Mr. Jenkins and the previous boss, Vito Scarabelli, who allegedly sent the boys over to let Mr. Jenkins know that his club was not welcome in the neighborhood. However, Mr. Scarabelli was later murdered by an inside rival thought to be Denucci, who quickly assumed control. Current FBI reports suggest that Denucci helped Mr. Jenkins set up an order to test Scarabelli's control. When Jenkins refused to pay his loan back because he thought he had strong information against Denucci regarding Scarabelli's murder, Denucci killed Jenkins. I suppose the amazing thing is that Denucci did not try to pin the murder on Jenkins before he got rid of him, but even Sonny Denucci makes mistakes. He'll soon make a mistake that sends him to jail where he belongs."

Vinny thought he might throw up. This was much, much worse than he had thought. He put the newspaper down. Vinny could not believe what he had been reading for the past couple of hours. His father is just like them, only worse because he leads them and wants to drag me into his game. A sign of relief came over Vinny for some reason. He felt like the cat was out of the bag. He did not have to pretend to be this well liked person. People are scared shit of his family. He walked back over to the cabinet and put his head down on top of it with disgust. Vinny opened the drawer and shoved the newspapers back in, not caring if they were in the right place or not. Closing the drawer slowly, he turned and walked toward the front door with a tear rolling down his face. He was hoping that no one noticed him as he walked out the door. Looking up at the sky, Vinny asked God, "Why me! Why me! My poor mother!

Vinny ran to the bus station. He sat down on the bench to wait for the bus, his head in his hands. When the bus arrived, he got on, deposited his seventy-five cents, walked to the back of the bus and sat down. He thought about his mother, what to do to help her. Slowly his eyes closed and he slept until he got home.

For the next couple of days Vinny watched his father closely. He realized that sometime in the last couple of years he had become an arrogant, ruthless person. He seemed to be always yelling at or threatening somebody. The house seemed like it had a revolving door; people would come over all hours of the night. He felt sorry for his mom. She cooked twenty-four hours a day for him and his men. Ever since he learned that his father was involved with the Mafia, he spoke a little more freely around the house. Vinny felt that he could be himself now that he knew.

Every once in awhile Sonny would sit down with Vinny and tell him to pay attention. "There is only one way to control people: Make them fear you. It's always better to have people fear you," he told Vinny. "You gain more respect that way and it keeps people from getting greedy." Vinny nodded as if he was eating it up but in his head, he was still trying to work out a way to get his mother and himself away from Sonny.

A few weeks later, Vinny read an article about how his father became boss, written by a guy who had turned witness for the Feds. "Sonny was into construction and remodeling, and would get a percentage of the jobs through the union. At a meeting one day with the families that controlled the organization, Sonny told the Godfather he thought he deserved a bigger cut than he already had. Vito Scarabelli, who at that time, was the big boss said, 'No, you get enough.' (Sonny collected forty-five thousand dollars a month from contractors and all he had to do was just make sure all Union people were working rather than non-union members.) Sonny wanted more, so he decided to put together his own little crew and plan the disposal of Vito Scarabelli. On Friday, August 10, 1977 at Dreamland, a club in New York City, Sonny paid a door attendant $25,000 to open a back door to Vito's private room. Allegedly, Sonny Denucci snuck up behind Vito and shot him three times in the back of the head, killing him. He also shot and killed Mario Nanzetti, Vito's right hand man and under boss. Sonny Denucci was brought in for questioning about the murders, but the D.A. could not find anyone to testify against him or place him at the scene of the murder. Two weeks later the D.A. dropped the case. The D.A. knew Sonny knew something about the murders. Word got around that whoever did not walk behind Sonny would find death around them soon, too. So the families joined in and made him the new Boss of all Bosses and he's been untouchable ever since."

Vinny remembered that article he had read when he was younger about Vito Scarabelli and being awakened in the middle of the night by Sal, one of his father's friends, who he knew was his bodyguard. Sal was worried about some hit man named Ricky Burke. Therefore, it all added up.

As Vinny analyzed his father's kingdom, he realized that it was strong because of the terrible things his father had done back then. Knowing that one day he might have to run this organization frightened him, but he did not know if he would have a choice. Vinny was afraid of what his father would do to him if he knew that Vinny knew how ruthless he was. He was frightened, but he would never let Sonny know that.

Time was passing and Vinny's 18th birthday was coming up. He did not know how he was going to handle the situation. "Could the organization be salvaged if a different, more honorable man led it?" Vinny thought. Was Vinny going to be the boss or his father's puppet?

CHAPTER 7
MOTHER'S DEATH

* * * *

THE HOARSE SOUND OF HIS FATHER'S VOICE echoed in the apartment. What could it be this time? Vinny wondered. He lay sleepily on the bed, vaguely trying to figure out the words that were penetrating his sleep-fogged mind. Suddenly he jerked awake. He thought of his mother. Why does he do this? He could here her voice mutter softly. He heard their bedroom door open and quick footsteps down the hall. His bedroom door swung open and his father rushed in, eyes wide with panic.

"Vincenzo! Vincenzo!" Sonny shouted.

Vinny feigned sleep until his father shouted in this ear, and he jerked upright at the words. "Get up, Vinny. I am taking your mother to the emergency room. Did you hear me? Your mother needs a doctor. Get up, we have to go."

Vinny glared at his father, his eyes cold and hard. "Why does she need to go to a hospital? Did you hit her again?"

Sonny pulled back and looked at his son. His face-hardened like a rock. "I will call you from the hospital. Just stay here by the phone."

Vinny stared at his father's retreating form as Sonny rushed from the room. He got a cold feeling that he was never going to see his mother again. Goose bumps covered his body and his heart began to race. Vinny felt the beat pound harder and harder against his chest until he thought it would explode. Grabbing pajama bottoms from the edge of the bed, he struggled to pull them on. Hopping on one foot while tugging at his clothes he started out after his father. Vinny had almost reached his door when he tripped over his own feet and hit the floor heavily on his right cheek. The front door slammed shut. Vinny lay there and burst into tears, screaming out his frustration and anger.

"Mother! Mother!"

He lay with his fists clenched, banging on the floor like a spoiled kid. Spit drizzled out the side of his mouth. He kept thinking that his father must have hurt his mother, and he had not been able to stop it.

He got up slowly and went into the bathroom. Flicking on the light switch, he looked at his face in the mirror. He could see a small bruise high on his cheekbone where he had hit the floor when he fell. He turned the cold water on and splashed it on his face with his cupped hands. The water felt soothing on his hot angry face. Grabbing a towel, he dried off and headed for the living room. In his mind, Vinny kept hearing the crying voice of his mother from the last fight she had with his father. Why had he not heard her this time? Something was wrong.

Vinny slid into his mother's favorite chair, a rocker his grandmother had given her when she had first married and was pregnant with Vinny. Picking up the phone, he dialed the hospital. A recorder came on saying please call back in five minutes. He called Uncle Nunzi's house, no answer. Finally, out of desperation to hear another voice, he dialed Al's house - another answering machine. Where the fuck is everybody, he thought to himself. He wanted to call his grandmother, but was afraid the news might give her a heart attack. Vinny called the hospital again. Again, he got the same recording. He called the hospital every five minutes until he finally got through. He needed to check on his mother, to see if she was okay, but nobody would give him information. He was in tears when a nurse said, "We are doing the best we can."

Vinny said, "What do you mean?" His blood turned to ice water in his veins.

"Sir, call back later please. I am sorry. I'm not at liberty to say anything right now." She hung up the phone.

Vinny slammed the phone down with disgust. The chill in his blood overcame his body. Sitting in silence, Vinny picked up his mother's rosary beads from the basket of knitting she kept by her chair and started to pray. He prayed that she was okay. He prayed it had been him rather than her. He prayed for her life. Glancing into the kitchen, he gazed up at the clock. Two am in the morning. It had been a long night so far and he watched the second hand move slower and slower.

Vinny waited patiently until early in the morning. Suddenly he heard the front door open and his father come in. Vinny hesitated then dashed to him. He could sense that something was wrong. He stared down at the floor. Vinny looked at his father and asked him how his mother was? Vinny started to cry.

His father put his head down and said, "Vincenzo, I have bad news."

"What, Dad?"

"Vinny," his father said, "let's go out on the balcony." They went out and looked at the few lights still on. "I don't know how to tell you, so I'll just give it to you straight. The tears rolled down his face. Vinny had never seen him like this. Sonny sat down on his chair, his movements slow and pained. He leaned over and rested his elbows on his knees. His hands held up his teary face. He took a deep breath. "A few years ago your mother was diagnosed with cancer and the doctors told us she only had a few years to live. For the past couple of months she has been in a lot of pain and her medication was not helping much. She died from the cancer at 4:30 this morning."

Vinny sat there stunned, and then started to cry. Sonny grabbed him and hugged him to his chest. He whispered in his son's ear, "Its okay, I understand. You can cry. I know how much your mother meant to you. You and she were close."

"Why didn't you call me? I would have come to see her before she died." Vinny sobbed. He felt so terrible that he had not gone down to the car when she left or tried to find out how she was doing. "I should have taken a cab to the hospital rather than waiting for you to call me. This is my entire fault."

"No Vinny!" Sonny said.

"Yes! Yes! God, why my mother?" he shouted. "Please bring her back! God please!"

"Vinny! Get hold of yourself." Sonny pushed him away, shaking him by the shoulders. But all Vinny could do was cry.

His father walked him to his bedroom and helped him into the bed. He lay there shaking and trembling, not wanting his life to go on.

Sonny gazed down at his son and said, "Vinny, I'm here for you and we'll get through this together. Your mother said to tell you that she loved you. You know that she just wanted you to be happy. You have to remember all the good times and close feelings you shared."

He paused and added softly, "I have to remember that, too. Your mother and I did not always get along, but I loved her. I will always regret that on her last night we argued. I guess that's God's punishment for me not making her happier." He put his arms around his son and hugged him hard one last time. Straightening he ran a hand through his hair and turned away, leaving Vinny with his grief.

Vinny cried the entire night. His father went into the bedroom he and Felicia had shared and closed the door behind him. Vinny could hear the creak of the bed as he lay down on it, then for about an hour that night he cried. Then silence. No sounds from behind the closed door. Vinny felt resentful that his father had been so vicious with his mother. Who knows, maybe all that abuse wore her down and the cancer grew.

The next day Sonny arranged for a private service at Jacobson Funeral Home, in Queens. Jacobson's was just like other funeral homes: quiet, with flowers around and candles burning in the corner. Family members came to the funeral. Only family members went up to the casket. Sonny had arranged a closed casket so no one could view the body, not even Vinny, whose grief overcame the strangeness of not being allowed to see his mother. When he finally confronted Sonny and asked to view his mother's body one last time, Sonny shook his head no and told him this is your mother's wishes. Vinny accepted his words with a grain of salt, kneeled by his mother's coffin, and cried. He prayed that she had a peaceful death and thanked God for such a wonderful mother. He prayed that God would help him keep the promise he had made to her to live a good, honest life.

Vinny kissed his mother's coffin, got up, and went to stand next to his Grandma and Uncle Joe. Uncle Joe was pissed off more than sad. Every time Sonny glanced over where they were standing, Uncle Joe looked at him with loathing. Vinny guessed Joe was angry that his father had not made his mother happy and now she was dead and it was too late. Uncle Nunzi came over and hugged Vinny and they cried together. He said, "Vinny if there is anything I can do, just name it. Robert was teary eyed too, and came to say he was sorry. Vinny guessed that maybe somewhere deep down inside Robert had a heart.

The funeral was even more heartrending because the family had just attended his Aunt Catherine's, who had died three months earlier. Superstitiously, Vinny wondered who was next. They say death always came in threes. Vinny shook himself out of his stupor. He knew his mother would never have approved of his thoughts. Rather than getting morbid, he wanted to remember her sweet, thoughtful ways. A sad smile crossed his face.

CHAPTER 8
THE INITIATION

* * *

VINNY COULD HEAR A FAINT SOUND coming from his father's room as he walked toward the kitchen. Today was the big day; it was Vinny's 21st birthday. He began to feel an excited nervousness. He had cottonmouth and even his eyes felt dry and scratchy. Vinny stared out the window and wiped away a solitary tear. He had no idea where it came from but in his heart, he felt a loss and it was his mother he cried for. At that moment, his father walked in to the kitchen.

"Vinny, my boy, today is the special day when you and I will become more than father and son. We will become one and someday you will inherit the largest, most successful business in the U.S. So, get dressed. We have to go to Long Island. I have a special gift for you." Sonny clapped Vinny on the back and left the kitchen. Vinny had not seen his father this happy in a long time.

Vinny's mind reeled. "What does he mean, inherit the largest successful business in the U.S? He could not be referring to his organization. Who the hell would want to inherit that bullshit?" he thought, "What a fuckin' nightmare."

"Okay," he replied. "I need about twenty minutes to get ready." Vinny's heart beat hard, once, twice. Was this the way he was supposed to feel on his 21st birthday? He did not think so. He thought he was going to be sick.

Vinny moved quickly into the bathroom and turned on the water in the sink. Leaning over the sink and letting the water run through his fingers, he raised his head and looked up at the mirror. Funny, he did not look different. He thought something special was supposed to happen when you turned twenty-one. Cupping his hands, he filled them with water and splashed it gently on his face. Slowly drawing his hands over his face, he began to tremble. A lump rose in his throat. He stared at his reflection, water dripped from his cheeks and nose, falling back into the sink. He reached for the towel and dried his face with jerky movements. He knew he needed to be strong. What happened to his dreams? To the dreams his mother had had for him? Was he going to give up on them, on her memory?

Vinny flung the towel into the hamper and turned away from his reflection, hating what he saw. At that moment, he realized the dream he had of becoming a lawyer was gone. He realized it had never existed, not in his father's world, and now, not in his. His mother had been right. His father has taken over his life. There would never be a chance to follow his dreams. He no longer had dreams; they had become his father's dreams—and Vinny's worst nightmare!

Soon his life might be over, too. Vinny was scared and wished his mother were there to guide him and give him strength. He started to pray to the Virgin Mary under his breath. Vinny closed his eyes and leaned against a wall in his room. He kept muttering the first two lines repeatedly. Suddenly he realized he could not remember the rest even though he had probably said a million Hail Mary's in his life.

Vinny heard his father shout out for him, "Vincenzo! Let's go!" Whenever Sonny had that deep tone in his voice Vinny knew he was serious.

As Vinny and his father exited the building lobby through the front door Sal Nicoletti and Charlie Manzo greeted them.

Walking toward the garage, Sal looked Vinny up and down, like measuring him and said, "Congratulations."

Vinny looked at him in surprise, "For what?"

Sal gave a little grin and shook his head. "Vinny," he said, "Someday I'll be working for you. Or didn't you realize that?" Vinny stopped and looked Sal in the face, trying to see if he was joking. He was not. Vinny gave a weak smile and turned away. The walk to his father's Lincoln Continental seemed longer for some reason. Vinny had learned that all wiseguys drove Lincolns; it was like some trademark for them. Sal climbed in behind the steering wheel with Charlie in the passenger seat. Vinny and Sonny took the back seat and settled in. Pulling the Lincoln out onto the main street, they headed toward the Queensboro Bridge. Vinny stared out the window until Sonny started to explain why today was so important to him. Listening to his father, the thought crossed Vinny's mind that Sonny was only thinking of himself.

Vinny stared at his father and thought "What about me? His whole life I'm only his reflection, never myself." However, he could not say that to his father, he just sat there dumbly and listened.

"Vincenzo, for the past ten years I have been the boss of a powerful organization. The reason I have been here so long is that I have been loyal and I get the job done. You will read many articles about me in the paper, but it's just hearsay and bullshit. The news media just likes to give the people something exciting to read. I have never hurt anyone who did not have it coming to them, who had not hurt me in one way or the other. The life we live is a dangerous one, but if you have men with you who are loyal and honest, it can be peaceful and rewarding. Can you understand that, Vincenzo?" Sonny turned to look at Vinny, his brows knit together, his eyes questioning. Vinny nodded his head and his father looked satisfied for the moment.

Sonny continued with his explanation, "Sometimes you have to make a point to gain respect and make people fear you so they know you mean business. What I am telling you might upset you or you might hate me, but it is time you know the truth about me. I have killed people, Vinny. I have had to kill many times in my life, not because I wanted to but because I had to. Someday you'll have to do the same."

Vinny sat there and stared at Sonny. He was sick with shock. His father had calmly admitted that he was a ruthless killer with no mercy. For what! Respect! Then he had the nerve to say that Vinny would have to kill. He must be out of his fuckin' mind! Vinny knew he could never kill anyone even if his life depended on it. He knew everyone has the capability to kill, but he also knew he did not have the heart for it. He could not believe what his father was suggesting.

He went on, "I'm 50 years old and when I go, I want you to take over as the head of all the families from New York to California. I know my brother Nunzi is next in line, but I have made the decision that I want you. I have to look out for what is best for the Family and what is best for you, son. He's my brother, but he's soft."

"Vinny, you listen to me. You are going to have to learn street smarts quick. Rule #1: whatever I tell you remains between you and me. You never discuss our Family business with anybody. If you ever need advice, you come to me. Rule #2: is never talk over the phone about anything to anyone. There are many rats out there and the FBI is always trying to put together a case against my organization and me."

Vinny looked at him and said, "Who would rat on you?"

"Some of our guys can't handle prison so they become informants for the Feds and they go around snitching on everyone. This organization does not tolerate rats. You know your friend Al?"

Vinny's head snapped around and he glared at his father. "Yeah! What about Al?"

"He's a fuckin' rat!" Sonny spit out.

"There's no way!" Vinny yelled. "First off, how could you come to that conclusion, when for one you don't even know Al and second, he is one of the most innocent guys I know. Al would never be involved with illegal shit. Or with the people who do it."

Sonny turned toward him and raised his hand, pointing his finger at Vinny's face. His voice was a little hoarse when he finally spoke, "Vinny, trust your father's instinct. Why don't you ask him this the next time you are together, if both of you rob a bank and he is caught, would he give you up to the cops. If he hesitates more than a second he's a fuckin' rat."

Sonny settled back into the seat of the car and turned his head away. "If we find out you ratted you automatically get a death sentence. But some people you don't have to worry about, like I'm not worried about you because you're my blood and my only son and I know you would never rat on me or the Family. I know it's going to take you some time to adjust, but it will all work out."

He kept quiet; he did not know what to say. He stared out the window, his mind reeling and his heart racing.

"Okay," his father said. "Rule #3: If the Feds ever pick you up for anything, you keep your mouth shut and don't answer questions until your lawyer is present. Last, but not least, Rule #4: If you ever have to do anything, you do it by yourself. Don't ever leave witnesses behind that can testify against you and don't ever trust anybody, especially a woman."

His father continued, "Your Uncle Nunzi is loyal, but he doesn't have it in him. He does not believe in violence or making a point. He gives too many breaks to people who fuck up, and Robert has too many problems. His fuckin' attitude is going get him killed someday." Sonny explained in detail what part wiseguys played. Here is what makes up our family.

Listen carefully,

The Commission:

The Commission handles inter-family disputes and sets general policy for La Cosa Nostra. It acts as more of a forum of Family Bosses than a board of directors. And, there are two Commissions: the Eastern Commission is based in New York and addresses concerns of the eastern Families, and the Western Commission is based in Chicago and handles concerns of the western Families, such as Kansas City, Denver, Detroit,

Los Angeles, San Diego (San Jose), St. Louis, Milwaukee, and San Francisco. Not every Family has a seat on the Commission. For instance, the Genovese Family on the Eastern Commission represents all the Cleveland, Buffalo, and Pittsburgh Families. Vinny, just sat there with a scared look on his face. Sonny continued explaining who is in rank.

THE FAMILIES:

Boss
Also called Don, he is the man with the power in the Family. He gives the orders and the rest of the Family is expected to follow them without question.

Underboss (Sotto Capo)
He is the second-in-command. He is usually the word on the street, so to speak. He controls the day-to-day operations of the Family.

Consigliere
The consigliere acts as a "counselor" or "advisor" to the boss. He is directly under the boss in terms of the hierarchy, but he does not normally give orders.

Capo
Short for capodecina or capo régime, he is a leader of a "crew" or decina (literally, "group of ten") of ten to fifteen soldiers.

Soldier
These are the guys that do the dirty work. They are still "made" guys. In addition, each soldier may have a few associates hanging out with him.

Associates
These guys do the real dirty work. Associates are not "made" guys; they just hang around with the crew. They often are willing to do anything to be "made", and therefore handle many hits.

As Vinny sat there and listened, his heart started to pound. He knew he was in a situation where he had no idea how to get out. What was he going to do? Was this what he wanted to happen? How could he stop this?

At that moment, he realized what his mother had meant. He had no choice. His fate had been determined with his birth.

He was the next Mafia Boss.

For the next half hour on the expressway, it was quiet in the car. He kept thinking, "Doesn't my father care about me? Dose he love me enough not to jeopardize my life? He does not think my Uncle Nunzi can run the organization. What makes him think I can do it?"

He looked over at his father and asked, "What about my plans? I have put four years into college and enrolled in law school. Would I have to give that up?"

Sonny did not look at Vinny; his eyes stared straight out the window. He replied without hesitation, "Yes! You will make more money with me than a lawyer and I want you to be street smart. Lawyers are no fucking good anyway. They can't be trusted. End of discussion."

Vinny kept silent. He wanted to speak his mind, but how could he reason with his father. The last thing he wanted was to get Sonny pissed.

The ride seemed to go on forever, but they finally arrived at Uncle Nunzi's house in Selden, Long Island. You could tell people in Selden had money. The houses were beautiful, the lawns were lush and well groomed and the cars sitting in the driveways spoke opulence and money. Uncle Nunzi's home was always getting bigger, better, and more beautiful by the year. He was always sinking money into it to make it the best. This was a large two-story brick house set on a nicely manicured two and a half acres of land that included a lake. Vinny had never realized how good his uncle lived. He walked in, took a good look around, and realized it was funny how you never notice something until it concerns you personally. His uncle's house was furnished with the best money could buy.

He had beige Italian marble floors throughout the house, plush Berber carpet, a Picasso over the fireplace, and even an enclosed, heated swimming pool and Jacuzzi out back. Nunzi's new silver Lincoln Town car sat parked out front of the massive four-car garage. Vinny suddenly realized that Nunzi bought a new one just about every year. The estate had security cameras everywhere; a wrought iron fence with a massive gate encircled the entire grounds. Bodyguards appeared out of nowhere and stood next to the gates when they admitted anyone. As they drove up the long, paved driveway, Vinny spied men standing to the side in the shade of the trees. Bodyguards were here, too. As they pulled up to the house, more guards appeared at the foot of the steps leading into the house.

Uncle Nunzi's drive and house were mobbed with limos disgorging men onto the portico. Vinny noticed there were no women present anywhere. This was something for the men, not the women.

Nunzi and Robert greeted them at the door. Men were dressed in black, single-breasted suits, dark ties and shoes so black and shiny you could see your reflection. The four embraced and made their way around the room. They always kissed on the cheek as a sign of respect. Vinny never realized there were so many wise guys, and they all turned to look at him when he walked in the room. Everyone looked dead serious in their dark pinstripe suits and shiny shoes. "This is going to be a fun party." He thought sarcastically. He had been to funerals where the crowd was livelier than this.

While he was looking around at the men gathered in the room, Robert slid up next to him and said, "So you're finally going to be one of us."

Vinny looked back at him, his brows together as he tried to hide his anxiety, "I guess," he said. Vinny could hear his own voice, it was dead, as dead as the dreams he had held onto for so long.

Vinny could feel his cousin was upset with him. He knew he wanted his father to take over so he could move up. Robert always had a nasty attitude with him. He was 24 years old, sharply dressed and he thought he knew everything. Robert always liked to throw his father's name around. He thought he should get more respect and he had to have the last word. Vinny had heard people call him "Mr. Fucking'-Know-It-All" but Robert was his cousin and blood. He accepted the way he was even if he was a jerk. Little did Robert know that if he had the position he craved so much, he would find it was not what he thought it was or what he wanted.

Suddenly the room became deathly quiet. His father stood up at the long table that had been placed in the middle of the room. "It is time that my only son sets the record straight. Come over here."

As Vinny walked slowly through the crowd of men, his entire body was shaking. He started to get a sick feeling inside and his head began to buzz. He walked to the table where his father was seated. Four other members of his organization were also present and Vinny bent over to pay his respects one at a time. No one smiled. No one acknowledged his tribute. It was a privilege for someone to approach them. Sonny introduced them one at a time, in a solemn voice that showed the mood of the room around them.

First, to his father's right, was Joey (The Snake) Pineta from Chicago. Vinny had read an article about how he had gotten his nickname. Joey Pineta is the enforcer of the five families and when somebody needs to be whacked, we call Joey. He would wait like a snake, quiet and still, and then attack his prey when they were the most vulnerable. Most of his victims never knew what hit them. Joey prided himself on being well groomed, his hair and clothing were always immaculate and in the current style. He appeared to everyone to be a well-to-do businessman. Then you looked in his eyes—they were dark, cold, emotionless, like a snake. Those eyes gave the impression that he was waiting for somebody to screw up so he could rub them out or torture them. Vinny remembered a time when he was younger and Joey had come over to get permission to kill some person for stealing money from him. Vinny had not understood what was going on then, but he did now. Joey's position was part security, part enforcer. He provided all the security and bodyguards for the five Families. Vinny knew that if the Family wanted someone to cease to exist, it would be Joey's pleasure to accommodate them.

Next to Joey was Salvatore (Pasta King) Riccio from Detroit. He got his name from the pound of pasta in front of him at every meal. He was short and fat, with no neck, more round than he was tall. Salvatore had been with Vinny and his father when they had gone to the Diamond Club on Vinny's seventeenth birthday. Salvatore been obsessed by food, no matter where he went he always had something to eat. Salvatore spared a glance at Vinny and nodded, his fork never missing the mark as he kept stuffing his face. Vinny could not imagine Salvatore as a top Boss, but he was head of the Family unions and controlled all the construction that went on around the U.S. with the help of some politicians in his pocket.

Next was Anthony (Ringman) Perconti from California. Anthony got his name from always flashing his rings around. He would always bullshit about how much he spent on his rings and how many he had in his collection. Vinny had never seen him wear the same ring twice with a few exceptions. He was a $2,000 dollar suit man, with a smooth, polished appearance that complemented his good looks. He wore a pinkie ring with a five-karat diamond that flashed when he moved his hand in acknowledgement to Vinny. Even his bodyguards were fashionable and dressed almost as well as the man they guarded. He smiled at Vinny; and for some reason Vinny felt as if there was something about him that he liked. He was a bookmaker and ran the casinos, took sport bets and loaned out money. The loans came with a high price, interest was always exorbitant: for every $500 dollars borrowed you paid back $150 interest. Vinny wondered who would borrow money from these people. However, he knew it was a lucrative business and a business that occasionally made use of Joey's services.

Next Vinny was introduced to the Family's drug connection: George (Candyman) Terranova. George had earned his name from his dealings with the cocaine and drug trade. On the street cocaine was known as nose candy and George was the Candyman that supplied it. He was a mean-looking man with dark circles under his eyes and a hollow look when he stared at you. He looked as if he had been up for days. He was slender and average in height, a non-descript man. You could tell George was from Florida by the way he dressed. He wore a bright lime green double-breasted jacket, with a black T-shirt underneath it, black jeans, no socks and loafers with a fringe. His fashion statement said it all, "I'm a drug dealer from Florida." Nevertheless, the bottom line was that he led most of the powerful men that surrounded his father. He would arrange drug distribution all over the U.S. In addition, it was a lucrative business; drugs made over half the money that supported the organization.

Vinny's father held the best position in the organization's hierarchy. Sonny was the BIG BOSS, (Capo De Capo) and he sat at the head of the organization to make sure these guys did the right thing. Sonny (Pinman) Denucci. He nickname was the Pinman because he controlled the pinball machines, video games, candy machines, and cigarette machines in the United States.

Vinny stood in front of the most powerful crime Family bosses in the U.S. These men controlled the Mafia world. As he looked at them he thought, "They are all ruthless killers and I don't want any part of it." Nevertheless, in his heart he knew could not stop what was going to happen. He stood quietly as his father embraced him and started to speak.

"Today my son, Vincenzo, becomes the number two man in the Family. You all know my brother Nunzi was supposed to take this position, but because of reasons, which I do not care to discuss, I have other arrangements. Treat Vinny as you would me; with loyalty and respect, and trust his judgment. He will be a great asset to us all. I know in this room we have a few disbelievers about Vinny when it comes to having heart and courage. So today I will satisfy all your minds."

Vinny sat there, listened to his father's speech, and wondered, "What in God's name am I going to have to do?"

His father looked at him and told him to put his hands together. He then placed a piece of paper in his hands. He lit the paper and said, "Vinny, repeat after me:

I, Vincenzo Denucci, do swear to abide by laws that protect my brothers and guide them into harmony. If for any reason, I need to use force I will take whatever action is needed, including the death of another human being. I will do what I have to do to maintain and nurture the respect this Family has earned. In addition, I will do what is needed for the protection and loyalty of the Family. I will go to the grave with my word." The paper burned slowly as Vinny juggled his hands back and forth.

Reluctantly, Vinny repeated the words. Sonny told him to give him his right hand, palm up. He took a knife and pierced his index finger, then passed the knife to the other Bosses who each pierced their finger. Vinny went to each one and touched his wound to theirs.

The last one he touched was his father.

They embraced and Sonny said, "It is done." In silence, everyone in the room raised a glass of champagne in salute. Vinny was relieved that it had not been as bad as he feared. Someone handed him a napkin to clean the blood that was still on his hand. He was so relieved that he almost missed his father's next words.

"And for the second part of the ceremony, Vinny will prove that he has the guts to be an enforcer." Sonny said. He turned to Vinny and motioned for him to follow.

Vinny was in shock. He had thought it was all over. He could feel the terror building in him and sensed everyone knew he was scared. He followed his father into the garage and the rest of the Bosses followed him. He saw a man sitting in a chair facing the wall. His hands bound so tightly that they were turning blue from lack of blood and his mouth taped with duct tape. The garage had no windows and it was dim. Vinny could not see the man's face. Vinny got a sick feeling that started in the bottom of his stomach. Realization set in. He thought "Please, God. Don't let this happen."

Then his father spoke, "Vincenzo, we all do things for a reason. We found out that one of our men was not so loyal. He's a fuckin' RAT!"

"You know what we do to rats, Vinny. Listen and learn. His life is forfeit according to our law."

Sonny looked Vinny in the eye, "We don't like it when you steal from us, and especially we don't like rats. If you play, you must be willing to pay. There's no second chance in our world."

Sonny reached inside his coat and pulled out a .38 Special revolver.

"It's up to you to prove to me and the other Family members that you have what it takes to one day become a boss and stand up person."

Vinny hesitated, unable to raise his hand to take the gun. His father could see it and said, "This is an honor and a privilege, Vinny. You cannot refuse. We can't just let you walk away at this point."

Vinny looked at his father with surprise, "Let me walk away? Dad, I do not want this. I do not want to kill anyone. You must be fuckin" crazy!
"

Sonny moved fast and slapped him across the mouth. "Vincenzo, I'm warning you. This is a fuckin' order not a request. Do it. Kill him."

Vinny looked into his father's eyes and he could see that he was not going to back down.

In the background, Vinny heard George Terranova yell at Sonny, "Hey, Sonny, he isn't going to do it. You have a fairy for a son. Maybe you should let Nunzi's son, Robert, be second in line."

Sonny turned to the men behind him, "Shut the fuck up or you'll be in that chair next!" his father shouted back.

Sonny turned back to Vinny. Slowly, quietly, and with the intensity of a snake, he hissed, "Vincenzo, you're embarrassing me. Get your fuckin' ass over there and do what I ordered."

Vinny raised a shaking hand and took the gun, his mouth was dry and for a moment, he remembered that prostitute that he fucked until she broke down. She had hated him the same way Vinny hated his father right now. He hated him for making him take someone else's life. In a part of his brain he could not believe what he had to do, He was scared, but knew that if he didn't do it he would end up in that chair. This was the next victim in his father's unrighteous world!

He walked slowly over to the man. He could hear him crying and choking on his gag. Pointing the gun at the back of his head, he looked at his father with tears in his eyes.

"Do it!" Sonny ordered. Vinny had the same look on his face as he had when his father forced him to shoot that deer. Sonny wanted this person dead. Moreover, he wanted Vinny to do it. Vinny remembered a promise that he had made to God never to hurt a living thing as long as he lived, and now he was breaking his promise. He asked God to forgive him. Vinny tightened his finger on the trigger, once, twice, three times. The shots ran through his mind like a death knell and echoed through the garage.

He started to shake, tears rolled down his face. His hand had gone numb from the tight grip he had on the gun. He had this loud ringing in his ears and a buzzing in his head. He felt like he was in a daze, or some weird dream. He turned slowly to look at everybody and everything seemed to be in slow motion. The Bosses were smiling and laughing like this was funny. Vinny snapped out of the daze and realized what had just happened.

He looked over at the body... blood was everywhere! The man's head bent forward and sideways. Blood ran from his head and Vinny saw the man's face for the first time. It was unrecognizable, most of it blown away by the shots. He thought he was going to get sick.

He looked at the Bosses. They were all smiling. Vinny had done their dirty work and now was a member of what they called a Family. He dropped the gun and heard it hit the cement floor. His right hand came up to cover his mouth, but it was too late. Vinny bent over and started heaving.

His father came over and said, "Vinny, it's going to be okay. It is always like this the first time. Trust me, it will get easier."

Sonny embraced him and said, "You are one of us. La Familia."

Vinny looked at him in shock and pulled free, running from the garage and into the kitchen, then into the bathroom. He was scared. He was sick. He wanted to die.

He sat on the floor in the bathroom, his head resting on the coolness of the porcelain toilet. A knock at the door startled him. He opened it to find his Uncle Nunzi there. Nunzi hugged him and said, "Vinny, it's all over. I hope you understand why your father and I do not get along. I fought with him for months over this. I told him never to involve you and to let you finish school, but he would not listen. He told me to mind my own business. Wipe your tears away and forget about this. It is in the past. You cannot change anything. Just don't ever put yourself in that position again." He faced him in the mirror and said, "You know, Vinny, I always thought it would have a lot more sense if you had been my son, and Robert, Sonny's." He smiled sadly and patted Vinny on the back as he left.

Vinny rinsed his face and went back to his father. Sonny looked at him with pride and said, "Son, I knew you had it in you." Vinny gave a feeble smile and looked away, praying to God to forgive him, but he did not think there was much hope for that. Slowly the Bosses filtered away. Cars pulled up in front of the house and each man left in a spurt of gravel. With Sonny's arm around him, Vinny walked toward the front of the house. Uncle Nunzi grabbed Vinny and pulled him away from his father who was busy talking with a departing Boss.

"If you need me, I'm here for you," he said. Vinny thanked him and almost ran from the house. He did not know if he could ever come back to this place without remembering the horror of this day.

On the way home all Vinny could think about was that man in the chair. He hoped that the person in the chair did not have a family. Vinny was confused and worried. "How will I be able to sleep tonight?" he asked aloud.

His father reached over, patted him on the shoulder, and said, "Son, I know the first one is the hardest, but they'll get easier—not that you have to kill again, unless it is necessary. Put your head down and rest until we get home." For a moment, Vinny got the feeling that his father was trying to show some sympathy.

He was still awake in his bed staring at the ceiling at three in the morning when there was a knock at his door. It was his father.

"Vincenzo, are you awake?"

Vinny mumbled yes and Sonny came and sat down on the edge of the bed. Sonny looked into his eyes and said, "You're my only son, and I'm real proud of you."

He bent over and kissed his forehead.

"I love you no matter what life brings us," he said as he removed his crucifix and horn necklace and put it around Vinny's neck.

"This was my father's and I'm giving it to you. Whenever you're in disbelief, remember me, no matter what you think of me, I'm still your father and I'm all you have."

Vinny wanted to cry! He wanted this nightmare over! He wanted his mother to appear! He wanted to crawl under a rock and never come out!

"Go to sleep." Sonny said. "We have a new beginning to start tomorrow and your new future."

CHAPTER 9
LIFE ON THE STREETS

* * * *

THE NEXT MORNING his father came into his room and said, "Get dressed. Today you are going to spend the day with me. I'm going to show you what the Family's all about."

Vinny was still wrung out over the killing the day before and this wake up call just showed what sort of day it would probably be. He had a burning sensation in his gut and he knew that twenty-four hours of rest was not going to cure it that fast. He knew he was going to feel like this for a long time. Naively, he thought things could not get worse. He dressed and headed for the kitchen for coffee. He heard his father whistling in the kitchen and he felt like he wanted to just fall back on his pillow and sleep forever. Vinny was depressed and amazed that Sonny was acting as if this was the most glorious morning in time. Killing someone was a good thing to Sonny, because it could only strengthen his empire. To him, this was just another day, only better.

As he walked toward the kitchen, tucking in his shirt, the doorbell rang.

"Vinny! Answer the goddamn door!" his father shouted.

Looking through the peephole, he saw that it was Sal. He unlocked the door and walked away before Sal even came in.

"Hey, Vinny," he said, shutting and locking the door himself. "How are you?"

What a stupid question. "I'll survive," Vinny said bitterly. It was a sarcastic tone, which Sal ignored.

"Is your father ready to go?" Sal asked.

"Ask him." Vinny turned on his heel and walked away. He had suddenly realized that even though Sal had been around since he was a kid and he should have felt affection for him, like an uncle, he did not. Maybe it was that he had such a boring personality, a dull reflection of his father. Sal had met Sonny when he was a teenager and with no other strong figure in his life, he had imprinted on Sonny and would follow him to the ends of the earth.

His father strolled out and they embraced. They were both dressed in white and black sweat suits with a gray stripe going up the sides. Vinny thought they must all shop at the same store.

"Today, Sal, we are going to take Vinny around and show him some of the operations. He needs to see how we conduct business and earn our money." Sonny announced. He was about to turn back to the kitchen when the phone rang.

His father answered, "Hello. Who is this?"

Sonny turned and looked Vinny in the eyes. It was a cold, hard stare.

"Hey, Al, you know what? Vinny is going to be busy! Lose his fucking number, you hear me? Good." He hung up.

Vinny just stared at him, "Why did you do that? Al is my friend. Why can't I have any friends?"

His father said, "Why? No friends, because I said so! I am still the fuckin' Boss of this Family." Sonny stared at Vinny, a challenge in his eyes.

"You got a problem with that?" Sonny asked him.

"No." Vinny let his eyes drop to the floor. There was not anything else to say. He needed to figure out what he would have to tell his best friend. They were supposed to go to college soon. He would have to tell him that he had a family crisis and would have to put school on the back burner for now. Later, Vinny would find time to call him and explain. Nevertheless, essentially, Vinny knew the friendship was going to be over.

Sal looked sorry for him. "I'll, uh, go get the car."

"Vinny," his father said, "I don't want you thinking about yesterday. The past is the past. Just pay close attention to what I am going to teach you and show you. I am going to teach you something more useful than anything you could learn from a book. I'm going to teach you to survive in this world, the real fuckin' world, not some TV land."

It was funny how normal suburban, working class lives only existed in TV shows and the violent life of crime was reality. Totally opposite from the view most of the country had. Vinny was descending into hell.

They got in the car and Sal drove out to Staten Island. Vinny sat up front with Sal and stared out the window. His father sat in the back seat, chauffeured around like Napoleon. He could hear him on the phone bullshitting with some goon.

They pulled up in front of O'Toole's Irish pub.

"Vinny, I want to introduce you to Joe Francis," his father said to him, putting down the phone at last.

He said, "Dad don't you remember I met Joe a couple of years ago? We came by to check on the poker machines."

"Yeah your right, however, this is different. You are number two."

Joe was the owner of an Irish Pub in Staten Island. O'Toole's was in an old neighborhood, run down and dirty. You could tell mostly poor whites lived there. Vinny did not think there was a new car within fifteen miles of that bar.

His father, Sal and he walked into a greasy smelling, dark bar that reeked of cigarettes and booze. An old person behind the bar greeted them. He looked groggy as hell, as if he had a nasty hangover from the night before and was drinking the cure.

"Where's Joe?" Sonny asked him.

"In the back room," he said, directing us behind him with his thumb.

O'Toole's was a small dark pub with a few scratched up pool tables and a cheap bar that seated about thirty people. The place was never full except for sport night. It was the neighborhood bar where the locals with their small paychecks and no ambition exchanged sob stories on Friday night. The lightning was dim and an odor of unwashed drunks, puke and piss almost gagged you. Exterminating was hopeless so no one bothered, and there were roach and mice droppings in the back hall.

His father walked through quickly, unconcerned about the smell. Not bothering to knock, he pushed open the "Employees Only" door that led to the office. Some guy was sitting back in a reclining chair with his eyes closed while a pale, skinny woman, naked but for a dingy bra, was sucking his cock.

"Hey, Joe," his father said. "What are you doing?" Sal snickered.

The girl jerked her mouth off him and his eyes snapped open.

He panicked and pushed her away, stumbling as he started pulling his jeans up. She just kept saying, "Oh my God, oh my God," while unsuccessfully trying to find her clothes.

"I'm sorry about this, Sonny," Joe said. "I didn't hear you come in."

"Don't worry about it, Joe. We all need a little action now and then." He looked the woman over. "By the way, is she good?"

"Uh, yeah. Do you want a blowjob? Susie will be happy to help out, right, Susie?"

Susie was scared, but she nodded.

"No," his father said, "But what about you, Vinny? You want a blowjob for breakfast?"

"Um, no. Thanks." He was embarrassed about the whole situation but his father and Sal seemed to think it was funny.

"Joe, do you remember my son, Vinny. He'll be coming around to take care of things." Sonny said

Joe shook his hand and said, nice and polite, like it was business as usual, "Pleased to meet you." Vinny noticed that Joe had aged a lot since he last saw him. His two front teeth were missing and he was skinny as hell. He was quickly losing what little gray hair he still possessed on his head.

Joe stood there and nodded inanely. He was more concerned about the broad standing by the chair with no panties on, just waiting for conversation to end so she could get back to what she was doing. Vinny looked at the two of them and thought, "What a life. Are these the kind of people I have to deal with everyday?"

Joe kept talking to his father. He smelled like week-old booze and could have used a case of mouthwash.

O'Toole's was going to be the first stop every day of the week. Joe had six poker machines in the back room, four pinball machines, and one cigarette machine, which belonged to his father. They collected about five thousand a week. Gambling isn't legal in New York, so his father had the machines rigged so that they only took special tokens that had the same shape and size as a quarter. The only machine that took quarters was the cigarette machine. They looked like the ones in Atlantic City and Vegas. If you wanted to play, you had to buy a roll of tokens. It was a nice way to make cash that Sonny did not have to claim. Every Thursday was payday for the winners. The machines were all fixed to pay off a certain percentage to the customers. They only gave back $350 dollars for payoffs and $150 of that went to Joe for his cut. Sonny told him they had over three hundred poker machines in Queens, Brooklyn, the Bronx, and Staten Island.

He could see that Joe was scared of Sonny. As they walked back to the car, Sal told him that Joe would tremble when Sonny walked in. Sonny told him that if the money were not accounted for that he would cut off his fingers. Fortunately, the money was always there. He felt bad for Joe; he seemed like a nice guy under all that dirt and grime.

After an hour of driving around with Sonny showing him all the stops he had to make, he finally showed him the apartment casinos. They were private apartments all over New York and set up with blackjack tables, slot machines, roulette wheels, and craps tables. All the apartments had plush carpet, bars, food, liquor and even sexy women in short skimpy halter outfits. Sonny spared no expense. The part Vinny did not like was that you could not see in or out because the windows were covered with black tint. Sonny knew what he was doing when he blacked out the windows. People would stay a whole day and not realize how long they had been there or how much they had spent until they were bankrupt.

He had to admit, Sonny was a smart businessman. He had built a multi-million dollar empire with his casinos. He even went so far as to make people buy membership cards for the privilege of playing. He made people fill out applications and then would send them downtown to his friends at the 109th Precinct. Sonny had police officers on his payroll, and some of them were the biggest gamblers. He would have potential casino members checked out. Once approved, one of the boys would notify you to come and pay your membership fee: $500 dollars for the year. All members were assigned certain casinos. You were not allowed to go to the other casinos even if you knew where they were. This kept the casino patronage exclusive enough to tempt people. The casinos were almost like a social club for the rich and famous, or infamous. All membership cards held up to a $50,000 credit limit. At the end of the night, you would have to pay the cashier if you lost or the casino would pay you if you won. There were few winners.

As they started to make their way to the next stop, the car phone rang. Sonny answered it and told whoever was on the line not to worry, that he would be there soon. He hung up the phone and told Sal to drive over to Brooklyn to Tony DeFranco's house. Vinny just closed his eye and thought to himself, "Oh shit, there must be trouble."

Sonny kept quiet the whole way over there. Tony (The Hustler) DeFranco was a weasel and a little troublemaker. He earned his name because he was always trying to hustle or swindle somebody out of something. He was in charge of the Family construction business, under Salvatore Riccio, the Pasta King. Tony was always trying to swindle the contractors to get them to bid the jobs cheaper. Then he would call Sonny and tell him he made money for him. He was always trying to get on Sonny's good side so that Sonny would think he was doing a great job. Tony was a want-to-be wise guy. He hoped to join the organization and to do that you have to work and hustle to make money for your boss. The more money you make for your boss, the closer he becomes to you and the more often he would consider sponsoring you as a member.

Vinny sat in the car and thought about the Family. The Mafia works on a simple basis: If they think you can make them money, they will wine and dine you and supply you with a car. They will be your best friend and as soon as you stop making money, they drop you like a bad habit and become your enemy. When it comes right down to it, the Mafia strives on money and power, nothing else matters. The Family, the oath they take to look out for one another was all bullshit. He realized they would gun you down in a heartbeat if you crossed them or were no longer an asset to the organization. If the Family blacklists you, you are down, and you stay down. You cannot ask for favors. Nothing, you are a piece of garbage to them. If an associate showed signs of weakness, they would take advantage of it and tear him apart. Setting someone up to take a pinch was a common way to get a liability out of the way. Vinny had always thought the Italians stuck together, but he knew that was bullshit too, they only look out for themselves. Everyone is expendable... even me.

Vinny kept asking himself, "Why did they have an organization? It was based on who had the most money and who had the biggest balls to take the other person out. The Family killed their own just to see who the toughest guy on the block was."

He thought Tony DeFranco, the Hustler, fit the description perfectly of an expendable associate. Vinny realized that when they were finished with him they would eliminate him. It made him sick to think of it.

When they arrived at Tony's house, it was obvious he was a small-time hustler because of the neighborhood and size of his house. Tony had a two-story row house in a middle class neighborhood where people parked on the street. In the Family, the bigger the house and the nicer the neighborhood designated your rank in the hierarchy of the Family. Tony was not high up. At barely 5'7", he was a small-framed guy who dressed in disco-fever fashion. His slicked back hair and his clothes looked like they came from an antique shop. He refused to dress with the times and preferred to look like he just stepped out of a 70's disco. When they pulled up Tony was sitting outside on his front steps. He looked nervous and you could see that he could feel somebody was going to get hurt.

Sonny rolled down the window and told Tony to get in the car. As he climbed in, he embraced Vinny and wished him luck in his new position with the Family. Tony had not been at the initiation, he was not high enough in the Family of Bosses, but he had heard the news.

Tony turned to Sonny and said, "I hired this cement company, Plako's, from Queens, you know the one."

"Nick Bilous, the Greek guy. Yeah," Sonny said, "And?"

"Nick came to deliver forty yards of cement for the building down on Fourth Avenue and Twenty Eighth streets, the roller rink job." Tony said. "I told him we pay $100 dollars per 20 yards. Nick turned around and said, 'You don't tell me what you want to pay, and I'll tell you what I want you to pay. In addition, I did not drive out here to get beat. You're going to pay $250 per 10 yards or I'm leaving.' I told him to pour the cement because he is holding up the fuckin' job. Therefore, he said 'pay me now.' I said no, pour the fuckin' cement or I will. Then I pulled him out of his truck, poured the cement, and did not pay him a fuckin' dime. Then he proceeded to tell me that I was dead and that we grease ball motherfuckers could go to hell. He pulled out a gun and said, 'I'll kill every one of you guinea bastards. Go call your fuckin' boss, because if I do not get my money I am going to kill you. I know Sonny—he is a greedy son of a bitch. He only lets the Italians make money, nothing for the Greeks. Tell him to fuck himself. Give him that message from me.'"

Sonny eyes were black with rage. He was furious. "Tony, how many times have I told you to use our own people! These other pieces of shit only make trouble and they embarrass me. I have to go and take care of this." Sonny was almost shaking with anger. "Sal, let's go to Queens."

Sonny reached in his brief case, handed Vinny a Colt .45, and told him to put it in his back waistband. Vinny started to get nervous. He had a feeling that another man was going to die. Vinny wondered why he did not hand the gun to Tony and he started to pray that his father would pick someone else to do his dirty work. His father picked up the phone and made two calls, telling the people to meet at the Red Wagon Diner. The rest of the ride was in silence, Nick too afraid to talk and Vinny sick with dread.

The Red Wagon Diner was a little hash house on a back street in Queens. Nothing set it apart from several of the other buildings on the crowded, dirty block except for a sign shaped like a covered red wagon that was painted. They met up with Angelo and Nino, two of the alleged "soldiers" in his father's army. Greetings kept to a head nod and grim looks. The two men followed them to Plako's construction yard, around the side where he kept his cement trucks. As they pulled in, Nick pulled in right behind them, blocking them in. Everyone jumped out of the car and formed a half circle around Sonny. These men were there to protect as well as enforce.

Nick was a tall, skinny greasy looking Greek. He looked as if he had not combed his hair in days. He had on dirty jeans that were falling off his waist, and a T-shirt with holes in it. He was the opposite of the men he faced with their suits and ties and gold chains.

Sonny said, "Nick! Why do we have to meet on these terms?"

"Why don't you get guys that are honest?" Nick asked.

"Why can't you compromise a little bit and work with Tony so we don't have any problems?" Sonny replied.

"Hey Sonny," he said, pointing to Tony, "this little shit is always trying to beat me out of what is rightfully mine. When do I ever get to have a say?"

Tony took a step toward Nick, his face red with anger, "Fuck you, you Greek bastard; we run the fuckin' show, not you!"

"Calm down Tony!" Sonny said as he pulled Tony back in line beside him.

"Hey Sonny, let me teach this piece of shit a lesson!" Tony yelled, "You see what I have to go through?"

"Shut the fuck up!" Sonny yelled at Tony. Turning to Nick he asked, "What do I have to do to make it easier for you and Tony to get along?"

"Sonny, I like you and respect you, but that little shit jerks me around, and tosses your name around like you work for him." Nick told them.

Tony made a sound somewhere between a choke and a yell and pulled out his gun. He aimed it at Nick's head and said, "Sonny, give me the order and I'll kill this fuckin' Greek right now."

Sonny looked at Nick and said, "Well, who should I believe, you or Tony?"

Sonny turned to him and said, "Vinny, here's your first lesson on the street. How would you handle this problem?"

For a moment, Vinny hesitated. If he knew anything about his father, he knew he would kill Nick. He just was not sure if that was the right answer and did not know how he could kill in a split second. While these thoughts rushed through his head, Sonny motioned to Sal by sliding one finger across his neck, and calmly said to Nick, "You fuckin' Greek. Goodbye!" Three shots hit Nick in the head. Nick's body fell backward from the impact, landing in a puddle of water and sludge. Vinny closed his eyes slowly and looked the other way.

Tony turned to Sonny and said, "You should have let me kill him."

Sonny replied, "This is the second time we have had a problem with you because you cannot handle business for me in a constructive manner. What will I do with you?"

"Sonny, please, I'll do the right thing." Tony begged.

"Tony when is the right thing going to happen?"

"Hey Sonny, come on, I'll make it up to you."

"Vinny!" Sonny barked.

"Yes! What's up?" Vinny said. He turned frantically in the direction of his father. He knew what was coming.

"What do you think we should do with Tony?" Sonny asked him.

He looked at his father with the same look he had the night he was initiated into the Family. Fear and disgust entered his body.

"Vinny, do what you have to do." Sonny said.

He knew it was unavoidable. Vinny reached behind him and pulled out his gun, pointing it at Tony. Tony dropped to his knees, tears running down his face, begging for mercy. Vinny felt sick inside.

Sonny yelled, "Vinny squeeze the trigger." The shot sounded like a cannon going off. The next thing Vinny knew, Tony was lying face down in a pool of blood. He would put all six bullets into Tony's head within a matter of seconds. He did not remember pulling the trigger that much, but he had and Tony was dead. Blood splattered all over the place and pieces of flesh were strewn across the ground and on the cars. The noise of the gun left ringing in his ears and his hand had a vibration, which left him shaking. He was a fuckin' mess.

He stood and stared in shock; Sal was shouting and tugging at his arm, "Vincenzo! Get into the car! We have to leave."

Vinny ran to the car and jumped in, sliding over to make room for his father. He was crying hysterically and could not stop. His father grabbed him and slapped him across the face, shaking him and shoving him into the corner of the car seat.

"Knock that shit off, Vinny. This is your new life and you are going to have to face that. Stop trying to fight what is in your blood. Your hands are dirty like the rest of us. You're a Denucci, act like one."

Vinny sat there shaking with fear. He felt as if he wanted to put the gun to his head right there and pull the trigger.

He heard someone moving Nick's car and felt Sal slam the car into gear and back out of the lot. Gravel and dust flew up from the tires obscuring the bloody scene from Vinny as they sped away. He dropped his head back and closed his eyes, not caring where they went.

They ended up going downtown to his father's favorite place, Bienito's Italian Restaurant. He stared numbly at the sign, not believing that Sonny had an appetite to eat. He was ashamed and sick to his stomach.

Nina, the host, met them at the door as usual. "Good afternoon Mr. Denucci, do you want your usual table?"

Sonny nodded his head as he moved past her. They sat in silence until the waiter came to take their order. Vinny stared into oblivion, not hearing when the waiter asked him twice what he wanted. When he looked up blankly, Sonny waved the waiter away. "What's wrong?" he asked his son.

Vinny's temper flared, his hand squeezed his glass of water until he thought it would break, "What's wrong? I just killed a man and for what? You don't have a decent ounce of sympathy in you," he lashed out.

"Keep your fuckin" voice down or I will kick the living shit out of you right here," Sonny threatened.

"Go ahead," Vinny, taunted, "Will you feel like a man?"

"Son, this is the last time I'm going to tell you this." Sonny bent over to whisper in his ear. "This is the life we chose and you do whatever it takes to build it right."

"No," Vinny interrupted. "This is the life you chose, not me."

"Shut up, Vincenzo, and let me finish. You never let them embarrass you. You take them out of the game right away or they will take you out. You had better stop feeling sorry for yourself and stand up for who you are. You must defend the Family name. No more discussion Go in the back with Sal, fix yourself up. Wash your face and come back, sit down and eat. What's more, Vinny, yes, you had better get used to this. I expect you to handle situations like this every day, because for you there is no choice."

Vinny escaped to the bathroom and stood in complete misery. What was he going to do? He thought about putting the gun again to his head right there and ending his life. He looked into the mirror and thought of his mother. "Vinny, be strong," she would say. "Sometimes we are put to the test and we have no control or understand why things happen. Remember, I love you and God will forgive you because your destiny has been chosen."

He pulled himself together and returned to join his father and the others at his table. He could not eat anything. He watched his father devour his shrimp scampi and wondered how he could eat?

Sal spoke softly, "Are we going to take Vinny to Delancy Street and show him the numbers spots?" Sonny nodded his head. Vinny thought to him self, "Just great, I need this like I need a hole in my head."

Delancy was the second worst part of New York City. Most of the buildings were condemned by the Health Department. Bums slept in the doorways and prostitutes walked the streets all hours of the day and night. It was filthy and overcrowded, which was a shame because the buildings were solid red brick with big windows. They were quality built, but somewhere along the line, the trash moved in and destroyed the neighborhood. As far as he was concerned, it was a slum area where drugs and gambling went on right on the streets. Even the police were frightened to drive down that way. Everyday the newspaper reported that someone had died there. He could not understand why his father and his crew would set up business in slum areas. Then he realized that the neighborhoods were so dangerous and full of desperate characters that it was the right place to be if you are selling cocaine and heroin.

Drugs were a part of the Mafia way of life. The Mafia controlled the drug market in New York City and it did not make a difference who they sold to as long as they were making money.

Sonny finally finished eating and motioned to the owner, Danny, to come over. He gave his thanks and sent his compliments to the chef, Gino, and left a nice healthy tip. Sonny never paid for anything, he just tipped everybody well. Sal pulled the car out front and they climbed in. They drove over to Avenue A, and Sonny got out of the car. He looked out of place in this slum area, but several men hanging out in front of a Latin grocery store greeted him. Miguel, the owner, an illegal Cuban from Havana, spoke broken English. He was a short, dark Cuban, with black nappy hair and a beer belly. Miguel took bets for Sonny. He was Sonny's Latin connection. Miguel liked Sonny because Sonny gave him respect and they made money together. Miguel was highly respected in his community and Sonny trusted him, so it worked out.

Sports and numbers were big business. Every day Vinny knew he would have to go there to pick up money. The odds there were the same as everywhere else, but the payoff was better, because the Spanish loved to bet on numbers, no matter how poor they were. They knew that if you bet on 215 straight, with the state lottery, you would get back $499 and you would have to report it. If you bet with the Family, your one-dollar would get you $600 and Uncle Sam never knew.

Sonny had over forty locations from Queens to Brooklyn to the Bronx. With each location earning $3500 or more each day, Sonny was making up to $140,000 a day. Even though he had payoffs to make, it was not a bad payday. He guessed his father was right when he said he could earn more with him than as a lawyer. Only lawyers slept comfortable at night and they did not go around killing anyone.

Making visits like this was what he had to look forward to as a Boss. Most Bosses did not go around to their sites unless there was trouble—they always sent somebody else to do it for them. But Sonny liked to make an appearance just to let people know he was a tough person and no pushover. Sonny thrived on perfection when it came to the laws in the family. He was leaving no stone unturned when it came to teaching Vinny the right way. He knew that there was no better teacher than the Big Boss. Vinny thought that this is how Sonny must have been taught.

They left Miguel with a smile and a pat on the back and drove over to Avenue C where condemned buildings were set up as drug houses. The myth that the Italian Mafia and drugs did not mix was bullshit. They kept it quiet because it was a lucrative business, but a dirty one, and even the Mafia had to play the game that drugs were off limits. They did not want the public to find out.

Vinny remembered when he was a teenager, Sonny staying up all night waiting for people to come over. He would look through the crack under his bedroom door and see them handling sacks of flour, which he found out later, were heroin and cocaine. Every time they went to the garment center, his father would stop the trucks at the intersection, pull off all those clothes and have his people take it to the flea market and sell the merchandise. He was building this empire. His father had just about everything sewed up, from construction to garbage to bookmaking. He was powerful and getting bigger by the minute. Vinny remembered him fighting with a rival boss because his father was taking to much money from the unions. He began to wonder how much money his father had. Some of the articles he had read stated that the Mafia thrives on the drug trade, which make them rich. With the heroin trade, they would pay $200,000 for a kilo. They would mix it up with other stuff and resell it for $5 a bag. One $200,000 kilo turned out to be worth over one million dollars a day.

In front of one of these places, his father looked at him and said, "Vinny, don't ever sell drugs yourself. Give it to someone else. If people find out you're selling dope, it'd be a disgrace."

Vinny listened as Sonny explained to him that a runner would work the street and pass the word that "copper" was coming. Copper was a code name for dope and the runners would say, something like "10:00 Am., outside, 375 on Avenue C." Then, at 375 Avenue C, another condemned building, there would be another runner inside and he would collect the money through a hole in the outside wall of the building. You could never get inside the building and they had guards on every corner and on the roof with machine guns. Once you dropped the money, you would walk around the outside of the building to another hole to pick up your dope. It was unbelievable because people would line up as if they were at the bank. Many of the customers were doctors and lawyers, prostitutes and people from all over, who you would never suspect did drugs. Sonny told Vinny that they had never been caught doing it this way, which surprised him.

Vinny sat in the car very astonished and could not believe that his father was not only a killer and a gambler, but a drug dealer as well. His father had chosen this life for himself. To him it was like playing Russian roulette every day. Vinny prayed to God for strength and for forgiveness for his father's pride in the evil he had created.

Sonny looked at Vinny and proudly asked him what he thought so far. He told Sonny that it had been an interesting day. Vinny sat quietly and thought for a moment what he wanted to say to his father. He wanted to tell him what a disgrace and immoral thing he was doing to the world and that he wanted no part of it. This is why he wanted to become a lawyer so he could put scum like this behind bars. However, he knew that if his father knew what he was thinking, he would probably kick the shit out of him. He actually did not know the answer that he was looking for, and his mind was anything but calm when the phone rang and

Sonny answered. It was quiet in the car for a moment; he wondered what the call was about and he hoped it was not bad news. Sonny hung up the phone and told Sal to drive home.

Sonny turned to him and said, "Vinny, I have to go to Florida on some business tonight which I can't explain. Sal knows the routine so you do your best and I'll call you later when I arrive."

"But, Dad," he protested, "I can't do this so soon."

"In this business, you have to adapt. I have trust in you," he said. "Everything will be all right. And Sal will help to guide you."

Vinny did not know what to think, so he just sat there and felt his stomach begin to curl into a knot. Sonny saw his expression and said, "Vincenzo, stop worrying!"

When they got home, his father called Florida again to confirm his trip and he went straight to his room. Vinny lay on his bed and stared at the ceiling not knowing what to do.

"Vincenzo! Come here!" his father yelled.

His father's voice echoing in the apartment startled him out of his reverie.

"What is it?" he asked as he walked over to him.

Sonny looked at his son and with a grim voice told him that his trip might last him a couple of months. Vinny was angry and upset. He got an awful feeling within him. He had hoped that this was not another test. He remembers the hunting trip, he had made him look like a fool and drink that deer blood. He remembered him telling him never trust anyone. Should he even trust his father? It seems he had no choice.

CHAPTER 10
MAKING A NAME

* * * *

THREE MONTHS HAD GONE BY and Sonny had still not come home from Florida. Vinny was alone and he did not feel good about it. He had lost his mother and now, even though his father was alive, he felt like he had lost him too. Uncle Nunzi and he were close, but he did not want to turn to him because he did not want to have a confrontation with his cousin Robert. Sonny called him from time to time to make sure he was okay. He was getting by, but he was depressed.

One day, when Sal buzzed up, Vinny told him to make the rounds alone.

Sal looked concerned. Vinny had not been looking well. "Are you okay? You want to see a doctor?" he asked.

"No, I just want to rest. I feel tired, that's all." Vinny said.

After Sal left, Vinny fell back into bed, full of self-pity. Vinny had fallen asleep when the phone rang—the sound jolted him upright and confused him. It took him a minute to realize where he was and to answer the phone.

"Hello?" he said

"Ah, Vincenzo, it's your grandma. How's my favorite grandson?" she asked.

He struggled to sit up. "Good, Grandma. How are you?"

"I'm fine… why don't you come to visit me anymore? I will make you your favorite pasta dish."

"That sounds nice, Grandma. How about I come by in a couple of days?" he asked.

"Why not today?" she said. Her voice reminded him of his mother's, and that hurt.

"Grandma, I'm just so tired. A lot has been happening."

"Okay, Vinny. We will talk soon. You won't forget?" she asked.

"No, Grandma. I'll see you soon, okay?"

He hung up and lay there, too depressed to get up. He suddenly wanted to talk to Al and see what he was doing. He dialed Al's number, but it just rang and rang. He realized that he was probably at class, but for some reason he felt upset and disappointed. He could feel the tears come and he started crying. It was too fuckin' much to take. His life was going to hell. He stayed in bed all day, alternating between sleep and crying, but it did not help much because the next day when he woke up, everything was the same and he still felt doomed.

It was late in the evening when an old friend named Henry called. Vinny was surprised, he had not heard from Henry in over three years.

Henry said he would stop by early that evening and said he was looking forward to seeing him. They had a lot to catch up on. Vinny wondered if Henry knew who his father was. As he started to get out of bed, the phone rang again.

"Hello!"

"Hey Vinny, it's me, your cousin Robert. I wanted to know if I could come over and to talk to you. Will you be at home?"

"Yes!" he answered, "I have an old friend coming over. Is that a problem? Did you want to be alone?"

"No. I will be there about 7:30am. See you then." Robert hung up.

This is strange he thought. Robert never visited unless it was on family business or Uncle Nunzi had sent him.

Vinny looked at the clock. It was 6:35am. Heaving a sigh, he thought he had better get up and get a shower. He rushed his bath and blow-dried his hair. He felt like he was getting ready for a date.

He was in the kitchen when the doorbell rang. Looking through the peephole, he saw it was Henry. He unlocked the door and smiled for the first time in weeks.

"How the hell have you been?" he asked as he hugged Henry.

"I am still hanging in there," Henry answered joyfully.

Vinny ushered Henry into the living room. A slow whistle escaped Henry's lips.

"Nice pad man," Henry said as he looked around.

Vinny laughed and slapped Henry on the shoulder, "So, how did you get my number?"

"I called Al, he gave it to me." Henry replied.

Vinny was shocked. He took two steps back and said, "Henry, you and Al never became close like we did. What made you decide to call him?"

Henry said, "I was looking for you."

"So how is Al? I tried to call him but never got through." Vinny said.

The two men sat down on the damask covered sofas while Henry replied, "He's doing just fine. He is still studying to become a lawyer. Said he misses you and he would like to get together with you someday."

Vinny thought to himself what it would have been like to finish school with his friends, then go off to college and become a lawyer. He felt hurt and betrayed by his father. He turned his head away from Henry as he wiped a tear away from the corner of his eye. Just then, the doorbell rang again. As he walked back to the front door he thought about how different Henry looked and acted different from the people that Vinny was used to dealing with on an everyday basis.

He looked through the peephole and saw Robert. He opened the door slowly.

"Hey, Vinny, let me just say this to you before I change my mind," Robert said as he marched through the door. "I want peace between me and you. No more fights." Robert's mouth was set in a grim line and

Vinny realized how much this had cost his cousin. The thought of Robert coming over to make amends after all these years of abuse was touching to Vinny in his state of mind. He forgave him and the two men hugged and kissed on the cheek as a sign of respect before walking into the living room.

Vinny did not know what had motivated Robert to call him, but the training his father had drilled into him made him aware that no matter what he felt toward Robert at this moment, he should remain on his toes. They walked into the living room and Robert introduced himself to Henry. Robert shook Henry's hand and they all sat down on the couch to talk.

"Vinny… when was the last time you were out? Robert asked.

The question startled Vinny. When he thought about it, he realized he had not been out of the house except on business since before his father had left for Florida. "I don't remember!" he said.

"Well, that settles it. We are going whoring tonight. Robert announced.

Vinny looked skeptical, "I don't know about this." he said. Henry and Robert cut him off. It seemed he was out-numbered. He gave in, agreed, and went to his room to change.

"Maybe I could use a night out on the town," he thought as he stood in front of his closet. It had been a long time since he had enjoyed the company of the people he was with.

He put on his white jeans and a black silk shirt and looked in the mirror. Going into the bathroom he put some gel in his hands and ran it through his hair, combing it back. Even he thought he was looking good! He came back out into the living room to find Robert and Henry smoking a joint.

"Do you want my father to kill me?" he croaked out. "Go and smoke that shit on the balcony."

Robert stubbed out the roach in an ashtray and dropped it in his shirt pocket. He flashed Vinny a grin and patted his pocket. "No problem, cousin, I'll just save this for later."

"Where are we going?" Henry asked. "Let's just go and look up some hookers."

"Good idea!" Robert agreed.

The vote was unanimous and the three decided to cruise 24th and Park Avenue to look at hookers. Just before leaving, Vinny called Sal to tell him he was going out for a little while. Vinny assured him he would call when he returned.

"Vinny, be careful and observe everything." Sal warned. Vinny shook his head as he hung up the phone. Sometimes Sal was like a mother hen, slightly protective.

Vinny phoned a limo service and they headed downstairs. Outside Henry spied a friend from his neighborhood, Ralph Ortiz.

Henry shouted out to him, "Hey, Ralph, where are you going?"

"Hey, Henry, just hanging out—not much else to do around her," Ralph yelled. He loped across the street toward the trio, dodging cars and flipping off those drivers that beeped at him.

Ralph was an unusual fellow who dressed liked he was from the fifties and acted as if he was Elvis Presley. He would walk that Elvis walk and talk with this deep voice the way Elvis did. He would wave to everybody as he walked down the street just as if he were the King himself. Even though he was a little weird, Henry liked him. He remembered all the kids picking on Ralph at school. Henry had stuck up for Ralph all the time in school as far back as he could remember. Henry liked Elvis and anybody who liked Elvis was okay in Henry's book.

Henry told Ralph that we were going uptown to check out the hookers and invited him along.

Ralph grinned, "Sounds like a better night than hanging around down at the bar."

Robert's face turned a little red as he glared at Ralph. He thought Ralph had the IQ of an ant and was pissed that Henry invited him, but Henry just grinned and threw his arm around Ralph's shoulder, not caring what Robert thought. Ralph was his friend.

The limo pulled up silently and the four men climbed in. Robert told the driver to go to 24th and Park Avenue. The driver just looked at the young men and shook his head. Vinny wondered what that was all about but dismissed it. On the ride, the four joked and told each other what they would do when they found one of the hookers that appealed to them. They turned onto 24th Street and stared. Up and down the street on both sides they saw some of the most beautiful women they had ever seen. They looked like they had just stepped out of the pages of Playboy Magazine. They were hot, even though they were hookers. Ralph was fascinated and could not keep his tongue in his mouth. He kept turning his head to stare at this one or that one and his eyes never kept still as he looked each whore up and down. He was like a dog in heat. Vinny laughed at Ralph and asked, "Haven't you ever fucked a hooker, Ralph?"

Ralph stared out the window, with sparks in his eyes, "No!" he breathed.

"Well, tonight is going to be your lucky night." Vinny turned to Ralph with a big smile. "Tell you what I'm going to do. Ralph, you pick the one you want and I'll pay for everything and take care of the hotel."

"Are you kidding me?" Ralph asked.

"No joke. Hurry up and pick one of those ladies before I change my mind."

Ralph looked out the window and saw a tall blonde-haired woman with a sexy look. The look that said she could give you the fuck of the century.

Vinny grinned when Ralph pointed to her. He leaned out the limo window, shouted out to her, and asked if she would like a good time.

The hooker looked the limo up and down, and then peeked in the window. "Do I have to do all of you? It's going to cost $1000.00 "

"No babe, just one of us. Get in! My friend is truly horny!" Vinny told her.

The hooker grinned and reached for the door as Vinny pushed it open. She slid in next to Vinny and he told the driver to find them a hotel. The hooker introduced herself as Sunshine. Vinny pointed to Ralph, and said, "For now, baby you are his."

Ralph just stared at her. He was not sure what to do. Sunshine slid away from Vinny and moved next to Ralph, pressing into his arm as she leaned over to whisper something in his ear. Ralph was so excited you could see it in his eyes. He told her to pull up her top, and when she obliged she showed a large, firm pair of breasts tipped by dark nipples. Ralph buried his face between her breasts, his hands kneading them as he moved from one to the other, sucking the nipples. He heard Sunshine give a little giggle, then sigh as she held them up for him to lick. The others just watched, but envy was evident as they saw Ralph take a nipple in his mouth and suck vigorously. Sunshine could see them watching and she lazily placed two fingers in her mouth to wet them, and then ran the tips over the unoccupied nipple, pinching and smiling at them. She knew how to play a man.

"They must be at least a size forty-D," Robert blurted out. Vinny and Henry burst out laughing. Robert turned beet red and grinned. Vinny pointed to Ralph and said, "Sunshine, it's his birthday, and you're his present." Sunshine smiled and tweaked a nipple, "Two-hundred and fifty and I'll suck every drop of cum out of him," she said. From between Sunshine's breast, Ralph moaned with excitement.

"Six blocks up on the left is a hotel, "Sunshine said." "I love getting fucked there." She put her hand on Ralph's hand and guided it across her tits in a circular motion. Ralph almost went insane. He grabbed Sunshine's hand and shoved it down the front of his pants. Vinny thought for sure he was going to cum now. The driver found the hotel and Vinny got out of the car to check them in. He put Ralph on the third floor and the rest of them stayed on the second floor right under his room so they could listen to the yelling and moaning going on. This sounded perverted, but after all Vinny and the boys needed some fun too, even if it was second hand. Ralph and Sunshine took off upstairs and the rest went to get a couple of beers from the lounge to take to the room.

Once inside, they crashed on the bed and cracked open the beers, flipped on some porno flicks on the TV and waited for the fun to begin upstairs. Vinny lay there with the cold beer resting on his stomach and stared at the TV with little interest. He thought for a moment this is the way life should be. He wanted to be hanging out with friends and having a good time. It felt good, but he knew it was not going to last long. Reality always came crashing back. He was taking another pull from the beer bottle when they heard Ralph scream out through the ceiling.

"Vinny! Vinny!" Ralph's muffled yell came through.

At first the guys just laughed, thinking he was being a jerk and just fucking around, so they blew him off and went back to the porno movies. Then Ralph screamed louder, "Henry, help. Please, someone help!"

The three men froze and looked at each other. As one, beer bottles went flying and they tore out the door and ran upstairs. Robert got there first and with the full weight of his body, he slammed into the door and sent it flying.

Ralph was up on the bed with a sheet draped across his body. He was crying softly and muttering under his breath, they could barely understand what he was saying.

"Ralph, what's the matter?" Vinny asked. He looked at the hooker across the room. She was completely nude with only a towel around her waist.

Ralph's eyes flew open and he gave them a wild look. "It's got a dick bigger than mine!" he yelled out.

"Huh? What was she going to do, shove a dildo up your ass or what?" Vinny said. He looked at Sunshine, she just shrugged, her breasts bobbing up and down with the motion. The men started to laugh until Ralph jumped off the bed. His face twisted in anger.

"She's a fuckin' man, you assholes! Look at it" he screamed. He pointed at Sunshine who stood there with no expression on her face. Vinny motioned to Robert and he jerked the towel from her waist and just stood there staring at her. They never would have believed it if they had not seen it with their own eyes. Miss Sunshine was Mr. Sunshine from the waist down.

The three men stood there and gaped at her/him. Disgust clouded their faces and Vinny thought he would get sick. Robert was the first one to move. He looked at Sunshine with hatred and said, "You're fuckin' dead, you worthless piece of shit." His arm came up and he backhanded Sunshine across the face. Sunshine's head snapped to the side and the back. Blood trickled from the corner of her mouth.

Sunshine raised a hand to the bruised cheek and wiped away the blood. She looked up with dead eyes at Robert and the others. "Didn't you boys know you were picking up a transvestite?" he/she asked. "24th Street is known for transvestites. I thought you knew that. I'm sorry, but a hole is a hole in the dark."

Vinny's face twisted with anger as he shouted, "Fuck you, faggot! Robert, take him down."

Robert grabbed Sunshine and wrestled him to the ground. It became a chaotic situation. The three men beat and kicked Sunshine into unconsciousness. Robert was delivering one last blow to Sunshine's groin with his foot when they heard someone shout that the cops were on the way. Grabbing Ralph and shoving his clothes in his arms, they ran out of the hotel. Vinny flagged down the limo and shoved Ralph's naked butt inside. The rest dove for the seats and Vinny yelled at the driver to take them home. They all sat quietly, avoiding each other's eyes. Ralph quietly dressed; his hands were shaking so hard he could barely button his shirt. When the limo pulled in front of Vinny's place, they said somber good-byes and each went their own way. Embarrassment hung over them like a cloud. Vinny turned at the top of the steps and watched his friends walk away. That was the last time he saw Henry or Ralph for three months.

One day, after things had returned to normal, and Vinny was back on the job, but none the happier, he stopped in to grab a cup of coffee at a downtown shop on his rounds. As he turned to leave with the hot coffee, he saw Ralph walk through the door with a newspaper under his arm. Surprise and delight lit his face and the two men greeted each other as if nothing had happened. Vinny was glad Ralph did not mention anything about the last time they were all together; he did not want to discuss it. The talked a bit and Ralph told him he was going to throw a party, "just for the hell of it." He invited Vinny and asked him to contact Henry and Robert and see if they wanted to come.

"I haven't seen them in awhile, but you got it. I'll give them a call tonight." Vinny promised as he waved to Ralph and exited the shop. Climbing in the car beside Sal, Vinny said a silent prayer that this party would be better than the last.

That night after the rounds, when Vinny arrived home he called Robert and Henry. He told them Ralph invited them to a party over at his house. Robert, in his usual surly manner, complained that he 'wasn't going to no fag's house.' Vinny bitched him out and told him Ralph was no fag and to shut up and do it for him. Reluctantly, Robert agreed.

They arrived at Ralph's about 9:45. Ralph greeted them at the door and thanked them for coming, "I have a treat for you guys later, when everyone else leaves," he said. "Until then enjoy yourselves." There were a few guests hanging out and some sexy-looking women. Vinny had not thought Ralph had this many friends, but maybe he had been wrong. Vinny, Robert, and Henry grabbed some drinks and hung around the edges of the party. They did not know any of the other guests so mingling was a little awkward. About an hour later most of the guests left except for three women who had spent most of the time sitting on the couch and sipping on wine. They seemed to be bored. Vinny was about to tell Ralph they were leaving too, when Ralph came over and said, "I want you all to meet the grand finale of the party."

Ralph introduced them as Veronica, Betsy and Margaret. "They are here to help you relax. Escorts for your pleasure."

Vinny looked at Robert and grinned, whispering under his breath, "I hoped he checked them out." Robert stifled a laugh and returned Vinny's grin.

Ralph walked over to a closet and pulled out a waist-high piece of plywood covered with a sheet. There were three holes through the sheet and the plywood. He stood it in front of them and explained the rules. Each of you has to stick your penises in the holes. He then motioned to the girls to get on the other side, placing the plywood between us.

Ralph looked at us and gestured to the three women sitting on the couch, "These girls give the best blowjobs. I want to make up for what took place in the hotel a couple of months ago."

Vinny looked at Ralph, "Ralph, you don't have to do this," he said. "It's probably going to cost a fortune."

Robert looked over at the women and blurted out, "I am not letting a chick suck my dick until I see if she has a pussy!"

"Hey, guys, don't you trust me?" Ralph asked. He put on his best innocent look.

The three friends looked at each other and then at Ralph. Their looks said it all, "You have to be kidding. No way you fucking idiot."

Vinny told him, "It's not that we don't trust you, Ralph, it's them." Ralph motioned to Veronica and the other girls. The girls stepped back from the board and pulled up the hems of their skirts. Not a penis in sight—just plenty of trimmed pussy. They were real women.

Ralph grinned and reached for some material that was lying on the table next to him. "Here, put these on." He said as he handed them each a blindfold. "Unzip and stick your penises through the holes in the wood."

Robert ripped his blindfold off and glared at Ralph, "No fucking way, asshole. I'm not putting' my dick in hole that don't have hair around it!"

Vinny started to laugh, "Just do it Robert, and shut the fuck up." Robert glared and jerked the blindfold back on, unzipped his pants and shoved his dick through the hole. "If he does anything to my manhood, Vinny, you're going be the one to die first," he threatened.

A rustling sound was heard and then each man felt a warm mouth surround his cock. The women began to suck and lick, quickly causing each of them to become hard. Vinny could feel the board rocking as one of the others moved back and forth in the whore's mouth.

After a few minutes, Ralph cleared his throat and interrupted the suck-fest. "You're going to switch. To see which of these ladies is best." The women rotated, each taking a turn on the men.

"Now, something different and no peeking or you're out of here and the rest of us get to enjoy this," Ralph said. They heard some more rustling and a muffled giggle. Vinny was seriously beginning to wonder what Ralph was up to when he felt an ice-cold mouth surround his cock. He heard Henry give a short yip of surprise and say "Hey you got to wait a minute it's too fuckin' cold!" then he began to moan. Vinny was shocked too, but the ice soon melted and warmth surrounded him again. Robert let out a loud moan and Vinny felt the board begin to rock harder. Vinny was getting into the different sensations, the alternate hot and cold, and felt like he could explode at any time.

Ralph said, "Hey, I want you to stick your hand in the hole, reach in to touch the girl and feel for something so you can remember something about her!" Vinny reached in and felt long hair, then made his way around to her face, when suddenly he felt a mustache above her lip. He paused for a moment to see if Robert or Henry made a move. He was in shock. He wondered how Ralph could fuck them like this. Then Robert shouted, "Vinny, there is a man sucking my cock!" He pulled off his blindfold just as everybody else did to find Ralph sitting on the couch ready to burst into laughter. Just as Robert went to grab him, all the girls stood up to show them they were wearing fake mustaches. They were also laughing. Robert made a charge at Ralph but Vinny grabbed his arm.

"Ralph, that sucks. This is not funny. We are out of here. Robert, Henry, let's go." Vinny said. As they got into the car, they were furious. Robert told the guys, "We will get even." Vinny and Henry agreed.

"One of these days I am going kick that fucker's ass," Robert said. Vinny agreed and the three thought of the best ways to get back at Ralph for what he had done. By the time they reached Vinny's they had decided that Ralph was not worth their time. The worst thing they could do to him was to keep him wondering what they were going to do to get back at him. He would be looking over his shoulder all the time and that was enough to drive anyone crazy.

About three weeks later Henry and Vinny ran into a friend of Ralph's. They asked how Ralph was doing. He shocked them both. He told them Ralph became gay and was living downtown with some person. They just laughed and thought life is a bitch and paybacks are a motherfucker.

CHAPTER 11
A LESSON LEARNED

* * * *

VINNY WAS STANDING IN THE KITCHEN the next morning when the doorbell rang. He walked to the door, sipping his coffee and peered through the peephole. It was Sal and Charlie. He opened the door and let them in. Sal walked into the kitchen and grabbed an apple off the table.

"We got a slight problem, Vinny," he said as he crunched another piece of apple. "I'm going to get the car and meet you out front. Charlie will wait here with you and explain what's going on."

Vinny got his things together as Charlie started to explain to him that one of their drug connections, Carlos, had not returned calls for the last couple of weeks. It was normal for Carlos to check in whenever a shipment arrived, so it was strange that he had not called. Vinny knew the cocaine shipments were regular and there had not been big drug busts lately, so Carlos should be getting stuff in.

The first stop was at a bar in Corona aptly named the Bucket of Blood. Corona was a suburb in Queens. Mainly Latinos from Colombia populated it. They controlled the cocaine industry, so Corona had come to be the Cocaine Capital. It was the drug dealer's neighborhood. If you wanted to get involved with drugs or the drug trade this was the place to go for your education.

Before reaching Corona, Charlie leaned toward Vinny and said, "Here, you need this," and handed him a gun.

"Charlie, you hold it. I'm not going to use that type of force." Vinny said, "I'm not my father."

"Take it, Vinny. You might need it in case there's trouble." Charlie insisted, "Just for protection."

Vinny took the gun and tucked it in his waistband. He could feel the cold steel of the barrel through his shirt as it pressed against him. He felt lightheaded and nauseated and wondered if he would be in a position to kill again. He recited the Lord's Prayer in his mind and hoped that God would understand and help him.

Vinny stared out the window as they approached the bar. People were sitting on doorsteps and leaning against the building walls watching them pass. When the bar was in sight Vinny could see a small group of men clustered around outside, most were drinking from bottles hid in paper bags and carrying on animate conversations that included arm waving and laughter. Sal pulled in front of the bar and stopped. He did a quick look around and then nodded to Charlie.

Charlie opened the window and shouted to one of the guys closest to them, "Is Carlos in there?"

The guy answered yes and Charlie rolled the window back up and turned to Vinny. "Sal will go in first, then you, then me. I don't expect trouble but we got to be safe," he said. Vinny nodded and the three climbed out of the car and headed for the bar. A loser couple named Heidi and Herman Lopez owned the Bucket of Blood. The bar was dingy and smelled like onions. It was the neighborhood bar where all the local scum hung out. There were seven or eight people hanging around playing pool and drinking. The only barmaid was laying out a lemon and a knife on the sideboard. Sal pointed to the end of the bar, where a person was sitting drinking a beer. Carlos. They walked slowly over to him. Charlie and Sal were cautious and checked out each person they passed. Vinny felt nervous, his palms were sweating and he rubbed them dry on his pants legs. Carlos looked pale and anxious. As they walked, Vinny turned to Sal and asked, "Let me talk to him. Ok? Let me do this or I'll never get to learn what my father wants me to."

Charlie looked at him and said, "Vinny, we can handle this. We have dealt with this kind of thing before"

Sal said, "Yeah Vinny, let me handle this!"

"No. I need to do this to make my name and for my father."

"Okay," Sal said, "but you don't have to prove nothin' to us."

"I know that. But I have to prove something to myself, and my father." Vinny felt good for a moment that they had some sympathy for him.

Sal and Charlie looked at one another and shrugged their shoulders in resignation. Vinny took a couple of deep breaths and covered the last few feet to the bar stool where Carlos sat.

Trying to be confident and firm like his father, he asked, "Carlos, what's up? Why haven't you returned our calls?"

Carlos looked at him and said, "I got big problems with some local guys. I do not know what to say, I guess it is somewhat personal. I don't think you'll want to get involved." Carlos looked like he had been up for days. His eyes were bloodshot. Several days' growth of beard shadowed his face, his breath smelled as if he had been drinking for days, and his clothes looked like they needed a good washing.

Vinny looked Carlos up and down, not bothering to hide his opinion of the way Carlos looked. "Well, I don't have all day to hear your problems. You know, I am sure my father would back you on anything you do, but you have to let us know what is going on. I am no mind reader. If there's trouble I need to know." Vinny said. "Take a couple of minutes to rethink what you want to tell me. I'm going to wash my hands, and when I return you'd better have some answers."

Vinny turned on his heel and walked with Sal down a dingy corridor to the bathroom. Vinny turned on the water in the sink and started to wash his hands. Sal leaned against the door watching him. He looked up at Sal's reflection in the mirror, "What do you think. Is he on the level?

You think he has problems with another drug lord or something?" he asked Sal.

Sal shook his head and replied, "I don't know, Vinny. Carlos is a good person. He always makes the pick-ups and deliveries on time. We never had problems with him before."

Vinny said, "Maybe he's using drugs and he doesn't know how to come clean with us."

"Maybe," Sal agreed. "But he doesn't look strung out, just tired, like he's been on the run for a few days."

Vinny was about to speak when they heard screams and the sound of glass breaking and what sounded like chairs being thrown. Scuffles and pleading voices. Someone's tortured scream through the door quickly cut off and then silence. At the first sound of trouble, Sal had immediately blocked the door and turned the light off. The two men crouched in the darkness, waiting. A minute passed then two, then an eternity. All the sounds they heard a moment ago turned to a dead silence.

Sal whispered into the dark, "Get ready, pull your gun and stay behind me."

Vinny's heart started to pound and he thought it was going to come through his chest. His palms got sweaty again. The fingers he wrapped around the butt of the gun felt cold and numb. It was hard to swallow past the lump stuck in his throat and he thought he was ready to piss his pants. The two men waited and listened for a few seconds more. An emptiness filled Vinny and Sal. Sal put his ear to the door and still no sounds on the other side. Slowly, Sal opened the door and leaned his head out to peek into the corridor. He could see nothing. He took a chance and yelled out to Charlie. Charlie did not answer.

"It's too quiet." Vinny said to Sal.

"Yeah, I know. But we got to get out of here and find Charlie." Sal said.

Slowly he inched the door open and they slid into the hallway. Sal took one side of the hallway and Vinny took the other as they slowly walked back toward the bar. In the room where the pool table sat nothing seemed wrong. A cigarette burned in the ashtray, a beer sat on the sideboard. Then Sal noticed that the person playing pool was slumped over the table. A pool of blood surrounded his head where it lay near the cue ball. The pool stick still clutched in his hand. Sal shouted one more time for Charlie. Charlie still did not answer. Sal waved Vinny over behind him and they slowly walked out into the main part of the bar. They stopped and stood in shock. There was not a living being in the bar. Everybody was dead. Bodies were scattered like broken dolls. Blood dripped from everywhere. It looked like a mad painter had taken buckets of red paint and thrown them on the walls, floor, and furniture.

Vinny grabbed some napkins off the bar and covered his mouth. He thought he was going to vomit. Everywhere you looked people's throats slashed. It was a fucking massacre. He spied Carlos' body. He was lying stretched out on the bar, his arms above his head and his legs straight as if someone had been holding him down. Carlos's throat was sliced wide open from one ear to the other. He had a deep slash from one side of his waist to the other and another cut right up the center of his chest all the way up. His guts had protruded through the deepest cut in his stomach and were spilling over his body like a grotesque animal emerging from its den. Someone had sliced off his genitals and stuffed them in his mouth. Blood dripped from the bar and landed with a soft plunk on the floor. Vinny closed his eyes and fought for control of his stomach. He looked away only to find Charlie slumped over the bar at Carlos' feet. His throat had a deep cut all the way across his neck. His head almost severed from his body. The head of Charlie tilted forward at an angle and was only held in place by muscle tissues and some bone. His eyes were open and staring at Vinny. Vinny thought there was a surprised look on his face. He turned to find the body of a woman who looked to be a few months pregnant. She was slumped across a table. Vinny could see that the women's stomach had been stabbed and slashed. Some of the cuts exposed her bones under the flesh. Her ring finger had been severed and had fallen to the floor beside her; a cheap gold band lay in a pool of blood at her feet. Her back was a mass of repeated stab wounds until her back was almost a mush of skin and blood and bone. He looked over the bar and saw the barmaid face down on the floor. It looked like the knife she had been using to cut up lemons was stuck in her back. A broken bottle protruded from her neck. There were others just as bad, and some worse and the only sound you heard were the drops of blood hitting the floor. The entire bar was dead.

Vinny felt Sal grab his arm. "Vinny, we got to go." Vinny and Sal heard the sounds of sirens faintly coming through the closed door of the bar. They sprinted for the front door. As they went through the door no one was on the street, but Vinny could feel people watching them. They rushed to the car. Sal slid across from the passenger side to the driver's side quickly. He shuffled to get the keys in the ignition. Vinny sat there looking at the door to the bar. Sal drove as fast as he could without drawing attention and they headed downtown to Manhattan. They passed several police cars but kept going, hell bent on getting away from the scene.

Once they were out of sight of the bar and well on their way, Vinny looked over at Sal and noticed tears running down the right side of his face. It hit him that Sal and Charlie had to have been close. They had worked for his father for as long as he could remember. Sal had lost a friend today. Vinny did not know what to say, he had never dealt with a death that affected someone else he knew. His mother had been personal and the stranger in the chair had been business, but this hit home in a way he had not expected. Someone he knew and trusted had died and he was not sure what to do about it. He cleared his throat and looked away from Sal. He knew he had to say something but he was not sure what.

Finally, he chose a safe, impersonal path and told Sal that Carlos must have had problems with his Colombian contacts because only Latinos used knives like that. Italians usually shot people. This had been a quick, organized kill. The people who did this had to be professionals, no witnesses and not even the unborn!

Sal glanced at Vinny. "What about Charlie? What are we going do about Charlie?" There were tears in his eyes again.

Vinny said, "I'm sorry, but I don't know what to do. I suppose the cops will notify his next of kin. We cannot have the Family involved in this. You know that. No one will testify we were even there. They do not want to get involved. In addition, you have to remember it could have been us instead of him. We got lucky this time." Sal just stared straight ahead with sadness in his eyes. He thought that for a Mafia boss' son, Vinny was still an innocent. Well, he had gotten an education today.

Vinny sat there in the strained silence as they drove toward downtown. His mind was reeling. He kept seeing images of Charlie and the surprised look he had on his face. He realized he had to make a choice: Either he got with the program or he would end up like Charlie. He knew he had to become a person like his father.

He knew he did not want the life of a wiseguy, but he also knew he had no choice. He was in too deep. After seeing that bar killing, he realized that he did not want to end up with his throat slit or a knife in his back, or strapped in a chair facing the wall. He realized that he had to have the respect and fear his father commanded and never let his guard down. He was angry at his life, but he knew he could use that anger to keep himself alive.

He asked Sal if he knew anybody that he trusted to replace Charlie. Sal just sat there and drove in silence. Vinny knew then that he needed to get his own people. Sal was his father's man. He did not know if he was doing the right thing, but he needed people he could trust around him. After today and the way Sal was acting, he was not sure he could handle it anymore. He had to decide right or wrong.

They arrived in Manhattan at a place called Café Milano, an authentic Italian restaurant. Mamma Theresa owned the café, and she reminded him of his mother. She was friendly and loved to cook and always had a smile on her face when he saw her. She was a short woman built like his grandmother. She was kind and sweet, and had a soft Italian accent. She always dressed in black and never failed to give him a kiss hello. He sometimes thought he used to go there just for that kiss. Milano's was a quiet place where he could think, and most important, a place where no wiseguys went. He knew there would never be trouble there. It was his favorite restaurant

Mamma Theresa greeted him as usual and escorted them to his favorite table.

"What do you like today, Vincenzo?" she asked. Her eyes took him in and her brow knitted. She could see he was a troubled man.

"My favorite, pasta and peas, with a glass of red house wine." He smiled up at her.

"And for you big guy what would you like?" she asked Sal.

Sal looked at her with a smile but Vinny could see her smile back was as phony as a two-dollar bill, "I'll have anti-pasta with a side of angle hair pasta and a Budweiser! And some of your wonderful garlic rolls."

Vinny sat in silence until Mamma Theresa left to place the order, then turned to Sal and told him of his plans to get his own people and make the changes he wanted in the way he liked to see things run.

"Why the sudden change?" Sal asked.

"I just don't want to end up dead," Vinny explained. "If I die, I want it to be because of old age not because someone chose death for me. I do not want to die because of somebody else's mistake. I am going to set up my own crew to move the drugs and write our numbers and collect our money. It will solidify my position in the city." Vinny knew his father's bosses had the rest under control and he knew he was not strong enough to tangle with them.

Sal disapproved the changes, but Vinny cut him short and said, "I'm in charge and you'll do what I tell you!" He did not know if he was making the right decision, but he felt like he had to take control of his life again. Vinny felt boxed in and the only way to get out was to be someone he was not. He buried his true feelings in the same way they would bury poor Charlie, deep underground, away from the light of day. He was learning to play a part. Someday he hoped to put this behind him and ask God for forgiveness, but this was where he was at the time and he had to make decisions.

That night Vinny called Henry. He explained the situation and Henry said he had just the right people. When he graduated high school, Henry chose to earn money the easy way, on the streets hustling. Vinny knew he was connected and he could count on him to join his organization if he needed him. He told him they needed some men to transport our drugs around town, and some to work the sports betting rooms and handle the illegal poker machines they had around the city. Henry said he would check a few things and would meet him the next day at a private club called Backstreets in Astoria. Vinny was familiar with the place and knew it was one of his father's many hangouts.

Vinny arrived early and chose a table with a clear view of all the doors. He sat with his back against the wall and waited, sipping a glass of wine. Henry arrived with an entourage in tow. Vinny knew everyone Henry had with him.

There was Lori, Henry's girl, she was a real tough bitch and she did not take shit from anybody. She was not pretty, but Henry liked her. Tommy and Louie came next. They were two guys he knew from high school. These guys always had the answers to the homework problems simply because they would threaten all the smart kids to hand over a duplicate of their homework, then one of them would go Xerox it and sell it. He thought they had good business potential. Frankie was a friend, too. In high school, he was on the wrestling team and was huge. Everyone thought he was big because he worked out so much, but the truth was Henry supplied him with steroids. When he won a city championship, his friends did not tell on him. The favor would be owed. Vinny was not close to any of them except Henry, but he knew them in high school and from them being involved with different deals over the last couple years, so he took a chance. Sal came in behind them. He did not look too happy, but Vinny did not care. This was his show.

 He greeted each person and after everyone grabbed a cold drink, Vinny began to lay out some of the plans he had. He told them he had a place for each of them, but it demanded their loyalty to him. He needed to know he could trust them to back him up. If they did, it would profit them. They all agreed, each one knew Vinny, and they knew his father, and knew that to cross the Family was to cause you grief. They also knew they could make money, and that more than anything agreed with them.

 He put Lori in charge of all the massage parlors they owned and let her take care of the call girls they had working for them. It was an easy decision to let Tommy and Louie handle all the loan sharking and casinos. They could handle a deal better than anyone Vinny knew. Frankie repaid him by being his bodyguard. He was a solid 220 pounds and wore his hair short, like the marines. He was good at intimidating people.

 When Vinny was talking to Henry about the organization, he noticed that he did not look too good. He had lost weight and his face looked haggard and old. His acne was bad from eating trash like hotdogs and French-fries all the time. Vinny had doubts about letting Henry handle the drug part of the business, he showed signs of being a junkie, but he knew he had done drugs deals before so he thought he would be okay to be in charge of all the drug transactions. Vinny just had to keep a close eye on Henry. He told Henry to recruit his own men and that he did not want to meet dealers or buyers, just him. Vinny's father stressed to him to stay out of the drug business and to keep his hands clean.

Vinny sat back and looked around at his crew. "One more thing," he said, "If I ever get the idea that one of you plans to set me up or if someone decides to rat me, I will stick you and your family in the fuckin' ground. Do you understand me?" The crew looked at each and nodded. Each one of them knew the penalty for betrayal and none wanted to face it. "But," Vinny added, "but, if I see you doing the right thing, then I will do the right thing and you will profit more. You play me fair, I will play you fair and we all make money." Everybody agreed heartily to that one. Money, after all, was the reason they were here.

That evening after he had returned home, showered and was relaxing, he got a phone call from his father. He told Vinny he thought he would be home in three weeks and asked if everything was fine. Vinny lied and told him that it was. He did not think it was the right time to tell him what had happened inside the bar or that Charlie his long time friend died. He and Sonny talked for a bit about everything and nothing and finally said good-bye.

"Be safe and I'll see you soon." Sonny said.

"You too Dad, Take care of yourself," Vinny replied.

He hung up the phone and leaned back in his chair. He was not sure how his father was going to react when he found out about the day's events. It seemed so far away. Almost as if it had never happened. Vinny wondered if that was how it was to see death and walk away from it. He ran a hand through his hair and pushed thoughts of the day into the recesses of his mind. Some part of him screamed out that he should be grieving, but the new Vinny had taken over, and the old Vinny had the door slammed firmly in his face.

CHAPTER 12
THE DRUG TRADE

* * * *

A WEEK HAD GONE BY and things were running as planned. Even Sal was impressed. He had not thought Vinny had it in him to run things the way his father did. Sal even told Vinny he was impressed with the smooth way things were going, and it helped Vinny to know that Sal approved, it boosted his confidence.

Sal and Vinny were eating dinner at Dino's Pizzeria in Queens when Frankie came in. Vinny waved him over and asked what was up.

"Henry needs to speak to you right away." Frankie said.

"Why? Is there a problem?" Sal asked. Frankie just shrugged

"Have him meet me at the bar over on 36th Ave and 39th Street in Astoria in an hour." Vinny said. Frankie nodded and hurried out of the restaurant.

Vinny looked at Sal, "What do you think? We got a problem."

Sal shrugged, "I don't know, Vinny. Maybe it doesn't sound good."

"Yeah, I know. Finish up and let's get out of here." Vinny tossed his napkin down hard.

Henry was there when they arrived. He looked worse than the last time Vinny had seen him. There were dark circles under his eyes and he looked like he could use about 12 hours sleep. Vinny and Sal sat down and ordered a glass of wine and a beer. "So what's up Henry?" Vinny asked.

"Our connection in Florida got busted bringing in 100 kilos of cocaine from Columbia. His brother-in-law, Diego Ramos, is taking over for now." Henry said.

"Do you know this guy? Is he capable? Will he deliver?" Vinny asked.

Henry shook his head, "Yeah, met him a couple of times. He seems straightforward and can do the job. But I don't trust him more than I trust any other supplier."

"We need to make sure this guy is on the level. We can't have fuck-ups." Vinny said.

Vinny did not know anything about Florida or the drug industry. That was why he had hired Henry. He had stayed out of the drug trade and stayed clean.

He thought awhile then said, "Sal, make arrangements for the three of us to fly to Florida. I want the first flight out tonight. Henry, set up a meeting with this guy Diego."

"Vinny, you're not fuckin' serious are you?" Sal asked surprised.

"Hey Sal, it will be all right," he assured him.

"You sure you want to do this, Vinny? It's not good to get involved with these guys," Henry told him.

"Yeah, I'm sure. Sal, book the flight. Henry, call me at home when you get everything set up with this person. I need to take care of some business, and then I'll head home to pack," Vinny said. Henry nodded and the three of them got up and left.

Vinny was still throwing things in a duffle bag when Henry buzzed up and said, "Let's go, we have a meeting! In addition, Vinny, bring a duffel bag with some old clothes you do not mind losing; we need this to look like a legitimate trip. Oh, and bring some cash. We may need a good faith offering," he said.

"How much will I need?" Vinny asked.

"Fifty thousand should do it. I don't think he will ask for more." Henry replied.

Vinny gave Henry the time and flight information and agreed to meet him at the airport. He shoved the last of his stuff in the bag, yelled for Sal. Vinny went to the safe his father kept hidden in his room and opened it. He counted out $50,000 in large bills and shoved them in the pocket of his coat. Grabbing his duffle, he looked around the house to make sure everything was okay and followed Sal out the door. Downstairs they climbed in the car and headed for the airport. Vinny and Sal did not say a word to each other during the ride. The airport was a forty-five minute ride. Vinny just stared out the window. He kept looking into the sky. He kept going over in his head what was about to take place. They had to meet Henry at the main kiosk, and then go get their tickets.

At the airport, Sal turned to Vinny and said, "I don't think this is a good idea, Vinny. You know the rules, no first-hand involvement in anything to do with drugs."

"Mind your own fuckin' business, Sal. I'm the boss, remember that." Vinny snapped. Sal just looked away, his face a closed mask. Vinny knew he did not like what was going down, but that was too bad.

They found Henry at the kiosk and the three went to pick up their tickets. Going through airport security, Vinny prayed that Sal had remembered to leave his gun. They all passed through without a problem and just made it to the boarding gate as they announced last call.

They had first class seats and settled in for the flight with a drink they ordered from the flight attendant. Henry leaned back in his seat and closed his eyes, a few seconds later Vinny heard a snore coming from him. Vinny smiled. Henry had always had the capacity to fall asleep anywhere, at any time. Vinny envied him. After a few moments dozed off. Vinny's sleep was interrupted with images of death and blood. It was something he could not get out of his mind. Vinny noticed Sal was also asleep, so he pulled a magazine from the pocket on the seat in front of him and put the headphones on, tuning into a gentle, classical station. He slowly went into a deep sleep. They arrived at Miami International Airport around eight pm.

The next thing he knew Sal was nudging him to wake up. Vinny unbuckled his seat belt and retrieved his duffle from the storage compartment. They were one of the first ones to disembark and the trio headed down the corridor of the airport for the exit. The airport was busy.

There were people everywhere. As they continued walking, there were police officers everywhere. Vinny started to get nervous. For some reason it seemed as if everyone was staring at them as they walked through the airport. He thought to himself that they knew he and Sal were there to meet a drug connection.

Turning to Henry, Vinny asked, "Okay, we're here. Where are we supposed to meet Diego?"

"In the second floor coffee shop, a place named Lil' Espresso." Henry said.

Vinny laughed. "What stupid name is that?"

"Probably some brain dead airport employee thought it was cute," Sal put in.

Henry just shrugged. "This is Miami. What can I say?"

They reached the café and Henry spotted Diego sitting in a corner. He was wearing an orange and white tropical shirt and a green and white baseball cap. He was facing the entrance but sitting near a rear exit door, which impressed Vinny as suitably cautious. As they walked up to his table, Vinny saw his eyes dart toward the concourse and he made a small motion to someone. A signal to let the person know we were here. Vinny did not want to turn to see if he was bluffing. It did not matter anyway, if anything went wrong Sal or Henry would have taken out whoever they needed.

"Gentlemen," Diego said in greeting. "Sit down; please have a cup of coffee. The espresso is excellent in this place." For a person who looked like a migrant worker, he spoke surprisingly cultured English.

Vinny reached out to shake Diego's hand, but was waved away. Diego said, "I know who you are or you wouldn't be sitting here, so let's get down to business. I do not deal in bullshit gentlemen, just cold, hard cash."

Vinny's face clouded with anger. With more control than he thought he could muster, he said, "I like to know who I'm doing business with and if you have a problem with that, we can walk away and consider our business over."

Henry jumped in and said, "Hey, Diego, you came highly recommended. We didn't come all this way for nothing."

Diego sat there, running his eyes over Vinny and deciding what type of man he was. Finally, Diego said, "Okay, Mr. Denucci. I have to protect myself, you know. You can't trust anybody in this business." He stretched out his hand and Vinny took it.

The three men sat down as the server came over and asked if they wanted coffee.

"My friend here has suggested the espresso," Vinny told her. He saw Diego nod, and knew that he had carved a path with him. She wrote down the order and left the men alone.

"Diego, we have problem since your brother-in-law got busted. We need some merchandise right now. We have obligations to keep. I am sure you understand."

"I understand perfectly, Mr. Denucci. After all, we are both businessmen. And business must go on." Diego smiled, "I have six kilos available immediately. I can arrange to get as much as you need, but you have to make your own transportation arrangements."

"Sounds good, but how do you suggest we transport the stuff?" Vinny asked.

Diego said, "The only way if you want this stuff now, is to strap it to your body, and walk on the plane."

The two men stared at one another for a few moments.

"I have a problem with that." Vinny replied, breaking the silence.

"That is the only way right now, otherwise rent a car and drive it up." Diego spoke in measured tones.

Vinny said, "We will figure it out."

"There is another problem," Diego said.

Here it comes, Vinny thought, the pitch for the up front money.

"I have never dealt with you before. Granted, I know of Henry from my brother-in-law and the few times I have seen him, but you are another matter entirely. I know of you, but I do not know you. I want to start off our business right." Diego said. He smiled at Vinny and sipped from the cup of coffee in front of him.

"I see," said Vinny. "Would twenty thousand dollars be enough to show my good intentions?"

"Forty thousand dollars," Diego looked at Vinny over the top of his coffee cup. His eyes grew cold. Vinny knew he was testing him.

"Thirty thousand dollars, But first I need to sample the merchandise. I am sure you understand." Vinny put on his most innocent look.

Diego gave a small laugh. "You are a hard man, but you have a deal, Mr. Denucci. Give me a moment and my associate will deliver what you need and collect payment if you are happy." He motioned again to the person on the other side of the concourse and gave a small nod. Vinny looked over his shoulder, saw a tall, husky man dressed in a shirt as ugly and loud as Diego's nod, and walk away. Diego just smiled.

"We all have our protection, Mr. Denucci," he said. His eyes flitted to Sal.

Vinny gave a short bark of laughter. "Yes... protection of all kinds Mr. Ramos."

The four sat and sipped coffee, Diego said he was going to the newsstand next door to get the local racing sheets. He left Vinny, Sal, and Henry and disappeared around the corner.

They sat there in silence. Something nagged at the back of his mind, but he could not figure out what it was. Vinny thought this was too easy, too clean. Diego seemed too anxious to do business. Maybe this guy is trying to set him up.

Vinny turned to Henry, "Are sure about this guy? I just have a bad feeling about him."

"Vinny, trust me. I had this man checked out and he is okay. He is taking over for his brother-in-law is all. I met him once, when I had a pick-up down in the Keys. It was a year or so ago and he was working with someone else at the time, but he seemed okay then. Trust me." Henry reassured him. "The real issue is how are we going to get this stuff back to the city? With delivery this fast I can't set up transport."

Vinny shrugged his shoulders; he had no idea how this was going to work out. It just happened so fast. "How had it been done in the past?"

"Well," Henry said, "Normally, I have a runner bring it up. However, that needs to be set up beforehand. I do have an idea though how most of my runners do it. We tape the kilos to our inner thighs where it does not show, get on the plane and fly home." Vinny and Sal did not look too sure about the idea, but they agreed. About ten minutes later, Diego still had not returned. Vinny was starting to sweat. How long did it take to get a paper? Just as he was ready to send Henry after him, Diego returned with a black duffel bag over his shoulder.

"Gentleman..with your purchase my friend has kindly included a jack knife inside. Sample the packages if you wish." Diego smiled as he set the bag next to Henry. He seemed to know that Vinny did not want to handle it.

Vinny motioned to Henry who picked up the bag and walked across the concourse into the restroom. A short time later, Vinny and Sal followed with Diego trailing. Sal entered first to check the stalls and motioned Vinny inside. Henry was waiting at the end of the room by the handicapped stall. Diego and Vinny went in together; Sal went back outside to watch for trouble and to keep an eye out for Diego's partner, to make sure he was not going to be a problem.

They went into the stall and locked the door behind them. Diego placed the black bag across the back of the toilet and unzipped it. Diego pulled out a brick of cocaine that was a two-inch thick by ten-inch square. The cocaine was in a plastic bag. The brick wrapped up in tape multiple times to keep it solid. Diego pulled the jack knife out of the duffle bag and cut a small hole in a tightly taped corner. He peeled back the plastic and cut off a chunk of pure white cocaine. He smiled as he handed it to Henry.

Henry smeared some between his thumb and his first finger grinding it into a powder and dropping it into his other hand. He put his hand to his nose and snorted some of the powder to check the quality. Immediately, his nose started to bleed. He quickly pinched it shut with his fingers as his head jerked back from the jolt the coke sent through him.

"Good, wow," he said, wiping his nose with a piece of toilet paper Vinny handed him. "It's good, Vinny," Henry smiled.

Diego nodded and pulled out the rest of the kilos and a roll of tape. "I do not deal in substandard merchandise. I take it we have a bargain?" He looked at Vinny, raised his eyebrows, and smiled.

"Yes we do." Vinny said to him. "And if the quality is like this on all your merchandise, we will deal again."

Diego smiled and handed the cocaine and the tape to Vinny. "Have your friend outside deliver your good faith offering to my friend. He will also give you the full price of the merchandise. I will expect payment in full tomorrow. Henry knows how to transfer the funds."

"No problem," he said to Diego. "Henry, go get Sal for me. And Diego, you'll have your money tomorrow through the regular channels."

"It is good doing business with you, Mr. Denucci," he said. He picked up the empty bag and walked out.

Vinny studied Henry for a minute. He was sniffing and bouncing on his toes a little. Vinny noticed the rest of the cocaine was gone from his hand. "Henry?"

"Yeah, What?"

"Are you okay? Will you be okay on the plane?" Vinny asked.

"Yeah, Yeah, no problem." Henry said.

"Ok, go get Sal like I told you," Vinny said.

Henry bolted out of the stall like a deer. Within seconds, he heard Sal enter.

Vinny pulled out the money he owed Diego and handed it to him. "Give this to Diego's partner. Make sure they leave. Then get your ass back in here, we have to catch a plane home in less than an hour."

Sal palmed the wad of cash and left, Vinny pulled a jumpy Henry back into the stall with him. "Henry! Get your shit together or you'll blow this!" he hissed.

"I'm fine, Vinny. Honest. It is just the rush. That is some good shit." Henry replied, blinking rapidly. "Don't worry. Have I ever fucked up before?"

Vinny just shook his head, gave Henry the tape, and told him to find the end. Vinny dropped his pants and placed one brick on the inner part of his thigh. He took the tape from Henry and wrapped it around his leg and the bag a couple times.

"Not too tight, Vinny, or your legs will be asleep before we get to New York," Henry instructed.

Vinny cut the tape with the jack knife Diego had left and then did the other leg. He pulled up his pants and asked Henry how it looked.

"Fine," Henry said. He was fumbling with one brick and the tape, his hands shaking as he tried to run the tape around his leg. Vinny grabbed the tape and quickly secured the brick to his leg.

"Quit fuckin' around, Henry. I'm going to get Sal."

He left the rest room and found Sal standing at the restroom entrance. He noticed the "Restroom Closed" sign had been set up at the door. Sal was not taking chances. He told Sal to get in the restroom and make sure he hurried. They were running out of time.

Sal and Henry came out a few minutes later and they headed back for the security checkpoint and the flight to New York. Vinny could feel his armpits sweating. His heart raced with anxiety and fear the closer they got to the security gates. No one said anything to each other as they walked, but Sal kept wiping the sweat off his forehead. Henry had the least fear. He acted as if this was nothing. Vinny figured the cocaine was still working or that Henry was so used to doing this that it did not bother him. He looked at the others as they stood in line at the checkpoint, only then did he see the fear that he felt being showed in their faces. They were scared; they just would not admit it.

Vinny took a deep breath as he walked through the metal detector. His heart raced, his throat was dry, and he could feel himself shaking.

Like in a daze, he walked through and did not realize he was clear until he heard the security screener say, "have a safe flight." She startled him for a second and he gave a little jump. Coming out of his daze, he realized he should probably say something to her, so he turned, smiled, and thanked her. He kept walking, and looked toward the windows lining the concourse to see Sal and Henry's reflection, to see if they were going to make it. They passed through without a problem and caught up to him. Henry flashed him a grin and bounced a little on toes. Vinny just shook his head and steered them to the gate. None of them spoke as they boarded and it was not until Vinny went to take his seat that he realized that he had been so uptight about this that he had never once put down the little black duffle he had carried.

They took their seats and Vinny looked at Sal and gave him a grin. They had made it. However, Sal did not smile back. Vinny could see his face clouded with anger and he gave Vinny a look that was part disappointment and part venom. At the time he had started this, Vinny had not thought about the risks, he did what he had to do. Sal, on the other hand, had made it clear from the start what he felt. Vinny had the strangest feeling he was going to have problems with Sal, but because of Sal's loyalty to the Family, Vinny was willing to play it cool until they got home.

When the plane landed in New York, they found the nearest restroom and removed the coke from their legs. Shoving it in the duffel bag Vinny had been carrying; Henry slung it over his shoulder and prepared to leave. "I'll take care of this and get back with you by the end of the day. I need to arrange the rest of the payment for Diego first." He paused to take in his associates. "Don't sweat it, Vinny. We did well. Diego was pleased or we never would have gotten this shit. "This cocaine is pure is and hard to come by." Henry said.

"Okay, Henry, Listen give me a call as soon as you take care of your connections. I just want to make sure the deal is done. I don't want Diego pissed because you fuck up and don't get him his payment on time."

Henry just grinned and waved as he took off down the concourse for the taxi stand to grab a ride to where he needed to go. Vinny and Sal recovered the car from the garage and headed back home. On the way home Sal was quiet as he drove, staring at the road like nothing else existed. Vinny knew he had to find out what was wrong, he thought he already knew, but he needed to see if Sal was going to be a problem for him.

"Okay, Sal, let's hear it. What's eating' your ass? You been looking like you're ready to bust for the last 3 hours."

"You're out of line, Vinny," he told him. "You got involved in that shit. You have disgraced the Family name. Did your father not teach you anything? He said to never personally touch drugs. He is going to kick your ass. And you know what? I don't blame him. You broke every rule he taught you about dealing with that shit. What in the hell do you think you were doing? Are you trying to prove something? You fucked up, Vinny; Sonny is going to be pissed when he finds out."

Vinny turned on Sal, "I'm the fucking boss here, Sal. I do what I want. You hear me. If my father does not like it, fuck him. He gave me this show, it is mine to run as I see fit. Do you understand?"

"Yeah, Vinny you're the boss," Sal said, shaking his head.

Vinny knew then that he had to put Sal in his place. When they got back to the house, he told Sal to spend the night because he had some business to take care of later and he would need him. Sal agreed and went to settle into a spare bedroom.

Vinny waited a few minutes, and then called Frankie. He told him to meet him at the Backstreets nightclub about 3:00 a.m.—there was something important he needed him to handle. Frankie said, "No problem, boss, I'll be there." Vinny went to his room and settled down for a short nap. It was almost midnight, so he had time.

Around 2:30 a.m., he woke Sal and told him to get the car and he would meet him downstairs. Vinny waited until he heard the door click shut and then called Frankie again. He told Frankie that there had been a change of plans and to meet him down by the cemetery under the Brooklyn-Queens Expressway at 44th Drive.

"You know the place," I said.

"Yeah," answered Frankie. "Same time?"

"Yes," Vinny said. "And don't be late, this is important."

Vinny hung up the phone and went into his bedroom. He opened up the top drawer of his nightstand and pulled out the .45 he kept there. He clicked off the safety and chambered a round, then slid it in his inside coat pocket. He walked out of the bedroom and headed for the front door. The phone rang, but he did not answer—he had more important things to do.

He walked out the front door just as Sal pulled the car up front.

Sal said, "Where are we going?"

"Drive over to 44th Drive," Vinny said. "Frankie is stuck with his car."

"What, he doesn't know how to call a tow truck?" Sal laughed. Vinny did not answer. He sat there in the back seat wondering if what he was doing was right. Nevertheless, he knew he could not trust Sal not to tell his father what was going on. This was Vinny's show and he had to prove he had control. If he let Sal tell his father that he disobeyed the rules, then he would lose credibility in the eyes of his people and the other bosses. Weakness was an automatic death sentence in the Mafia world. When we arrived, it was quiet. Sal pulled up under the bridge and killed the lights. Sal looked around and said, "Well, where the fuck is he?"

Vinny reached in his pocket and pulled the gun. Sal had started to turn around to say something and before he knew what happened, Vinny shoved the muzzle of the .45 against the back of Sal's head and pulled the trigger twice. The shots sounded incredibly loud in the closed car. Blood and brains spattered the front window as Sal's body slumped to the side, part of his face missing. Vinny started to open the back door just as headlights panned over him. Frankie pulled up beside Vinny's car and jumped out. He came running over and jerked the back door of the car open.

"What the fuck happened, Vinny? I heard shots. Are you okay?" he asked.

"I'm fine… just a slight problem to take care of. I thought Sal would give me trouble, so I did what I had to do," Vinny told him.

Frankie pulled open the driver's side door and looked in at Sal's body. "Shit, Vinny. He's making' a mess in there. We have to get him out and then get out of here."

Frankie grabbed hold of Sal's coat and pulled him upright, dragging him across the seat and out the door. Vinny grabbed Sal under one arm and Frankie took the other. They dragged him from the car and placed his body behind the bridge wall. His body made a dark lump in the night.

Vinny rubbed his hands down his pants leg as if trying to wipe away what he had done. "You're my new bodyguard, Frankie. If you ever fuck up, you are going to end up like Sal. Do we understand each other?"

"Sure Vinny. You know me. I won't fuck up," Frankie said. Vinny nodded and turned away from the sight of Sal's body.

"Vinny, we got to get out of here, though." Frankie said. "Take my car and go. I will clean up yours enough to see out the front window and get out of here. I know someone that will take care of fixing it up real good. Don't worry. I'll have it back to you by tomorrow night."

Frankie tossed Vinny his keys as Vinny retrieved his pistol from the back seat of his car. He shoved it back in his pocket, climbed in Frankie's Volvo, and drove away. He was feeling mixed emotions and was not sure if he had done the right thing. He knew that he could not have taken chances with Sal. He did not need Sal telling him that he was wrong or how he should run his business.

When he got home, Frankie called and asked him if he needed him to do anything else.

"Yes," Vinny said. "We're going to Miami tomorrow. So be here early with the tickets. One for me, Henry and you."

"You got it boss. Anything else?" Frankie asked.

"No. Just get some sleep, I need you on your toes and awake tomorrow." He hung up the phone and went to his room. He was more tired than he had ever been in his life. This week was going to be busy.

They took several trips that week to Florida to pick up cocaine and bring it back. Every time he got off the plane in LaGuardia Airport, he got a rush of excitement. He felt like he was one bad motherfucker beating the law. His confidence ran high and he felt like a real boss, getting the job done. He felt like his father, he was a killer, a drug dealer, the boss of his own gang, and nothing would stop him.

CHAPTER 13
THE GIRLS

* * * *

Several weeks after their first run to Florida, Henry called Vinny and said he needed to talk to him. "There's a problem, Vinny. I will explain when I see you. Can you meet me out front of Rose's?"

"Sure. Let me call Frankie and we'll be there in an hour."

Vinny called Frankie and told him to meet him downstairs. They drove over to Rosa's in Long Island City. Rosa's was a hangout for wiseguys that wanted a quiet place to meet and enjoy a good meal. Frankie pulled up and parked the car out front. They got out and looked up and down the sidewalk for Henry. Vinny was getting ready to go check in the bar when he heard Henry hail him from across the street. Dodging a taxi, they jogged across the road. Lori, Henry's girlfriend, was standing next to him, almost hidden in the shadows.

"Vinny, we got a problem." Henry said. He looked over at Lori and nodded his head. She moved into the light of the street lamp and Vinny and he could see she was angry.

"One of the girls called. Carol. Said some guy beat her up pretty good and refused to pay her. I put her up at the Midway Motel at Astoria and 25th Street. She is a mess, Vinny; he did her in pretty good. She's out of commission for a long while." Lori said.

"Fuck! Does she need to go the hospital? How bad is she?" Vinny was pissed.

"No, no hospital. One of the other girls is with her taking care of her. Nevertheless, her face is pretty messed up. It's going take awhile to heal."

Lori told him. "The fuckin' asshole told her she was lucky she got to fuck him and she should be paying him." Lori spit out.

"Okay, let's get over there. Does she know the guy?" Vinny asked.

"No, but he told her he was going to the Diamond Club and it was too bad she was so messed up or he would take her with him." Lori explained.

"I am going to need her to point him out. Let's go get her."

The four of them walked back across the street and got in the car. Frankie took off for the Midway while Vinny, Henry and Lori sat in the back and talked about Carol. Carol was one of their highest priced girls at $250 per hour. She was not just a hooker, she was an escort, and one of the few Lori had chosen that had the intelligence, poise, and looks to be seen with any of the businessmen and wiseguys that came from all over to do business in the city. She would go with them to parties and dinners and be able to talk and act like a woman, then back to their hotel for the night. She had bruises on her body and she would not be able to work.

They pulled into the Midway Hotel's parking lot and Lori directed them around the back to the last room. They got out of the car and she knocked on the door. A few seconds passed and a voice asked who it was.

"Pam, its Lori. Open up."

They heard the locks being drawn and a petite blonde-haired woman opened the door to them. Lori walked past her and the rest followed. Pam shut the door and locked it again. Vinny saw Carol lying on the bed. She was holding a towel to her face, obscuring most of her features. He could see bloody spots at the edges of the white material.

Lori sat down on the edge of the bed and gently pulled the towel away. What Vinny saw made him angrier than before. One of Carol's eyes was swollen shut, the other eye was discolored and puffy, and her cheek bore an angry-looking purple bruise that ran into her temple. Her bottom lip split open and swollen; blood was still oozing from the corner.

Bruises marked her neck where the man who beat her had held her down. Scratches showed here and there. Vinny figured they came from a ring the person wore when he hit her. One of her ears had the earring torn out and had been bleeding into her hair and the pillow beneath her head. He could see bruises on her wrists and arms; finger marks were clearly visible where she was grabbed. Her nose had been bleeding and swollen, probably not broken but close. He reached and pulled up her shirt—large, dark bruises covered her ribs and one breast covered in fingerprints where it had been squeezed.

"The fucker's dead. You hear me Carol. He's a dead man." Vinny hissed. Carol could barely nod...her swollen eyes barely registering that she understood. She was in too much pain to care. "I need you to point him out to me. Can you make it to the Diamond Club with us?"

"Yes." She murmured through split lips. Vinny figured she also had a few teeth loose from the way she talked. "You are going to get my money? He owes me."

"Fuck the money. He will pay, but it will not be in cash. Nobody beats up a woman like this, not even a whore." Vinny said. His mind reeled, images of his mother with a black eye or a swollen cheek from when his father had hit her came back to haunt him. Somewhere in the back of his mind, the old Vinny was sickened. How could a man do this to a woman?

"Vinny, let me get her cleaned up some more and into some clean clothes. She can't go out with blood all over her." Lori said. For the normal hard ass attitude that Lori portrayed, she had a soft spot in her. Vinny could see she felt bad for Carol and it hurt her to see this.

"Yeah, get her ready. We need to move fast though; he might not stay at the Diamond all night," Vinny said.

Lori and Pam helped Carol to her feet and supported her into the bathroom. Vinny heard the shower start and bloody clothes flew out the door to land in a heap. A few minutes later Pam came out and dug through a small duffle bag that was sitting on the floor. She grabbed a few things and went back in the bathroom. Vinny heard crying coming from Carol in the bathroom and the sounds of the other girls voices. The girls came out of the bathroom with an improved Carol, but not by much. Her face still looked like she had been through a meat grinder and she held a hand to her ribs, but she was walking on her own.

"Let's go. Pam, you stay here. We will bring her back when we are done. Then you take her home and watch her to make sure she's going to be okay," Vinny told her. Pam nodded and unlocked the door for them, bolting it soundly when they exited.

They helped Carol into the car and Frankie took off for the Diamond Club. Vinny could see his reflection in the rear-view mirror. His face was a mask of anger. It had never dawned on Vinny that Frankie would care, but he supposed the damage Carol had sustained would affect anyone with even a little bit of conscience.

They rode in silence. Carol would wince every now and then and place a hand on her ribcage. Vinny knew she had to have a couple of cracked ribs besides what you could see on the outside. They were lucky and Frankie was able to park almost in front of the Diamond Club. Vinny got out with him and the two of them helped Carol out of the backseat. A little gasp of pain escaped her lips as she stood and she made a grab at her ribs. Vinny led as they walked into the club. The place was busy, but the Maitre D' knew Vinny and immediately asked if they wanted a table. Vinny told him no, they were just looking for a friend. He turned to Carol and asked if she saw the guy that beat her up. She looked around and finally pointed to a guy sitting in the corner of the restaurant with two other men. Vinny and Frankie headed for the table with the two women following. Lori and Carol held back as Vinny got closer to the table. In the dim light of the restaurant, he was finally able to tell who it was that Carol had pointed out. It was a wiseguy named Tony (Big Mouth) Pinto from Brooklyn. He was a short fat guy who was known to throw his weight around and act like a big shot. He thought he was better than anyone else and if you were in his presence, you should consider yourself lucky. He never spoke to anyone in a normal tone of voice; he always yelled what he had to say, as if he wanted the entire world to know he was talking. Vinny guessed that is why they called him big mouth. He was a poor excuse for a wiseguy, throwing money around, fucking whores and then bragging about it, and impressing local bums with his big mouth and his superior attitude.

Vinny calmly walked up to him, "Hi, Tony."

He stood up, embraced Vinny, and smiled. "Vinny! How is your father? What can I do for you that would bring you out here tonight?"

"We got a problem, Tony. One of my girls got beat up real bad tonight. She is going be out of commission for a long while. She said it was you that beat her up. Is this true, Tony?" Vinny asked as Tony sat back down.

"Hey, Vinny, you come all the fuckin' way down here to ask me about some whore? She is a fucking whore! Who the hell cares what happens to them?" Tony yelled out, "She deserved it. Besides, who the fuck do you think you are?"

"She says you stiffed her." Vinny said quietly.

Tony started to laugh, and made a rude gesture toward the two women standing across the room, "Yeah, I sure did stiff her." He laughed again and looked across the room, "Didn't I stiff you a good one, bitch?" he yelled at Carol.

Vinny saw Lori make a move toward them, her eyes shot fire at Tony. He made a chopping motion with one hand and halted her. He reached down and grabbed Tony by the throat. "You didn't pay her, Tony and you beat the hell out of her so that she can't work." Vinny hissed. "That is costing me a lot of money. Why would you go and do that, Tony? Why would you beat up one of my girls, and then cheat me out of my money?"

Tony could not answer. Vinny's grip on his throat was too tight. He could barely breathe. Tony fumbled in his pocket and pulled out a roll of cash. Vinny knocked it out of his hand. Hundred dollar bills fluttered to the floor and table. Vinny reached behind his back and pulled out his gun, slowly bringing it up to Tony's temple.

"You think that's going to make it right? You cannot afford her, Tony. Her price just went through the roof." Vinny said. He shifted his grip to the collar of Tony's coat and with the gun to his head, escorted him through the restaurant and outside. All hell broke loose as they walked through. People were jumping up from tables and taking cover. Others were just sitting there in stunned silence. Two waiters dropped the food they carried and made a beeline for the kitchen and the Maitre D' fumbled with the door as Vinny pushed Tony through it.

Tony stumbled as he came out the door. Vinny held him up and yelled for Frankie. "Open the trunk. There is a chain and handcuffs in there. Get them out," he ordered. As his father said, shooting someone is too easy. Physical abuse is the only thing that deters people. Frankie popped the trunk and pulled out a six-foot length of chain with handcuffs on one end and a bolt on the other. "Hook it on the bumper and put the cuffs on his ankle," Vinny told him. He looked at Tony and smiled. "We're going for a ride, Tony."

As Frankie attached the cuffs to Tony's ankle, Tony sneered at Vinny. "Vinny, when this is all over, I'm going to get permission from your father to bury you, you no-good fuck. If he were here, you would not be pulling this shit. You're fuckin' dead, Vinny!" he yelled.

"Shut the fuck up, you slime." Vinny said, "'Cause I'm going to make sure you don't tell anybody anything."

Tony started cussing at him until Vinny punched him in the mouth with the butt of the gun. Tony stumbled away and glared at him. His eyes flitted past Vinny and widened before returning to stare at Vinny. Vinny turned and looked behind him. Everyone in the restaurant had filled the sidewalk and had been watching.

"This is what happens when you fuck with what is mine," he told them. "If anyone fucks with my girls again or takes it for granted that I'll cut you slack, this is what's going to happen to you."

He walked over and jerked the door of the car open. Frankie tossed him the keys as he got in. He started the car and slammed it into gear. It jumped ahead and he heard the chain tighten with a metallic snap. He looked in his rearview mirror in time to see Tony disappear from sight as his body quickly pulled down under the car. Vinny roared down the street to the next intersection, did a u-turn and came back to the club. He hit the breaks and squealed to a stop in front of the club. Several men and women turned their heads away as Tony's body came to rest between them and the car. Frankie ran over as Vinny flung open the car door and got out. Frankie was busy unhitching the chain from the bumper when Vinny reached Tony. He was laying face down in a heap of tattered cloth and blood. Vinny used one foot to turn him over so everyone could see the damage.

Tony's face was black from the street. Part of one cheek was scraped away almost to the bone and blood trickled out the side of his mouth. His chin was gone, only the blood added color to the exposed jawbone. His nose was crushed so badly it was unrecognizable and blood was pouring down his face from cuts and rips. His hands were black and blue, the fingers and palms stripped of flesh. Tony's coat and shirt had been shredded to expose his chest and stomach. It looked like someone had taken a razor blade to him, cuts covered most of his skin and blood flowed from everywhere. One elbow was protruding from the sleeve of his jacket, the skin ripped away to expose the bone.

Vinny grabbed him by the hair and held up his face to the crowd gathered outside the Diamond Club. A small moan escaped Tony's lips and his eyes fluttered open. Vinny dropped Tony's head back to the pavement. He reached in the car and grabbed his gun.

"This is what will happen to anyone that fucks with me." Vinny told them.

He pointed the gun at Tony's head and pulled the trigger twice. The impact bounced Tony's head on the pavement. The left side of his face exploded from the shells. Vinny looked down at him and then hocked up some spit from his throat and spit down on his face before he turned away and left him to die in the street. To whack a wiseguy in the street was the ultimate insult. It showed that the dead man was no better than the trash on the street. Consider a wiseguy lucky if he got to enjoy his last meal before being whacked. The person doing the hit wanted to make sure you ate a good meal before you passed through to the other side his father once told him. Vinny had no respect for someone like Tony.

According to Family law, unless you got approval from the council you cannot whack a made guy. If you did whack a made guy, you just handed yourself a death sentence. Vinny had broken that law. However, he figured that since Tony was a dirt bag that had cheated him, he did not need approval. He also figured since his father was the big boss, nobody would mind.

As he walked back toward the car, some person in the crowd shouted out "You're a dead man, Vinny!" He looked through the crowd, but did not see who said it and no one came forward. Henry came walking out of the restaurant with Carol and Lori and took them over to the car. Vinny sat in back with Carol. He put her head on his shoulder and told her to rest until they could get her home. Frankie slowly drove off, leaving Tony's dead body in the street.

They arrived back at the motel and dropped off Carol with Lori and Vinny told them not to worry, and if there was a problem to call him. They watched until Pam opened the door to let them in, then backed out and headed for home. On the ride home, Vinny kept thinking about the life he had. What a life he thought, beating people up, threatening, killing, walking around like some god, and for what, a position in the crime family! He sometimes wondered what he was doing, and why.

Frankie dropped him off at home then left to take Henry home. Vinny dragged himself into his room. He was undressing and decided he better check the answering machine for calls. There was one message on the machine. His father had called to tell him he would be home tomorrow on the 10:00 a.m. flight from Miami. He wanted Vinny to pick him up at LaGuardia Airport. Vinny sat there with his head in his hands. This was not what he needed after a night like tonight. He knew the shit was going to hit the fan.

CHAPTER 14
SCARED TO DEATH

* * * *

SOMEWHERE IN THE BACK OF A DREAM, Vinny heard a phone ringing. He tried to ignore it, to make it go away, but it persisted. Finally, his dream began to fade, but the irritating ring of the phone kept on. Startled from sleep, he realized the phone on his bedside table was ringing. He rolled over in bed and picked it up.

Still half asleep, he asked, "Yeah. Hello. Who is it?" His voice sounded rough and harsh even to his ears.

"Vinny? Is that you?" a voice said.

"Yeah! Who? Who the fuck is this? Vinny growled.

"It's me. Henry."

"Henry? What time is it?" Vinny asked confused. He glanced out his bedroom window. It was still dark, only the streetlights illuminated the night. What was Henry calling him about in the middle of the night?

"It's about 2:00am." Henry said.

"What are you calling me for at this time of the night? What do you want? And it better be good."

"I got a problem and I need your help!" Henry said.

"Again?" Are you okay? Did something happen with the girls?" Vinny sat up in bed and glanced at his clock. It was 2:08 in the morning.

"No, the girls are fine. I'm the one in trouble."

"Henry... spit it out. I do not have all fuckin' night. My father is coming home and I need to get some rest."

"I'm sorry, Vinny, but I have a guy over in Long Island City who needs some stuff and I'm tied up watching the house and can't get away."

"Can the guy wait until later today?"

"No! He needs it right now!" Henry sounded on the verge of panic.

"What would you like me to do? You know I don't make deliveries." Vinny put the phone to his other ear.

"Can you make an exception this once?"

"Henry, call Tommy!" Vinny sighed. How stupid could Henry be? He knew Vinny did not do deliveries.

"Vinny, Tommy don't listen to me, he only takes orders from you."

"Then I'll call him," Vinny told him.

"Vinny, I don't want to put Tommy down, but he's not too bright upstairs and I don't want him fuckin' up my deals. I got a reputation out here." There was a begging tone in his voice, and Vinny just sighed. He knew he was beat.

"Okay, Henry just this once I will take care of it. Do you have all the information ready?" Vinny asked him.

"Jeeze, Vinny, thank you so much, you just saved me. Yes, I got all the directions and stuff. Thanks boss!"

"Yeah! Yeah!" Vinny said, "So where the fuck do I have to go? And who do I see?"

"Okay, the guy's name is José. His address is 2906 Hoyt Ave South, Long Island City, Apt 3—phone number 392-3110 and ask for José. Have Tommy take you, he knows where it is. Tell José you're a friend of Smiley's."

"Smiley, who the fuck is that?" Vinny asked him.

"Vinny, that's my nickname on the streets."

"Smiley... it figures," Vinny laughed. "Okay, Smiley you owe me one!"

"Yeah, I do. I will call him and tell him to expect you to pick up a package. I have to go... business is picking up. I'll call you later." Henry said.

"Bye, Henry."

Vinny hung up the phone and called Tommy. Henry was right about Tommy, he was not very bright, but he was big, and he was loyal to Vinny. He might need some back up and Tommy was one of his guys that did not take shit from anyone. Vinny knew he could count on him to watch his back.

As he dialed Tommy's number, he thought it was a little odd that the guy José needed this stuff right now and could not wait an hour or two for Henry to be free, but he shrugged it off. They were drug dealers, and you never knew what was up with them. The phone rang about five times before Tommy picked up.

"Hello, who is it?" Tommy answered. His voice was deep and thick with sleep.

"Tommy, it's me... Vinny D."

"Hey Vinny, What's up?" Tommy yawned.

"I need to take care of some business for Henry and I need you to come along to make sure everything goes okay. Can you come on over?" Vinny asked.

"Yeah, sure let me get dressed and I'll pick you up in about thirty minutes," Tommy replied.

Vinny hung up, then called the number Henry had given him for José. The phone barely rang once when José answered.

"Yes, 'Hola! Como?" José's accented English made it hard to understand him, but Vinny got the idea.

"José, it's a friend of Smiley's. He said you needed some advice on some property and I am going to stop by in about forty-five minutes. Are you going to be there?"

José said, "Si, I'll wait for you. Henry called and said you could help me out."

"Do you have the papers I need to pick up?" Vinny asked.

"All the contracts are here, ready for you to look at," José answered.

"You're at 2906 Hoyt Ave South, right?"

"Si," he answered, "Apartment 3, on the second floor."

"See you shortly." Vinny hung up the phone and got out of bed. He groaned a little at the exertion, he was dead tired. He grabbed a pair of shorts off a chair and slid them on, then added a black t-shirt. He went into the bathroom and splashed water over his face and hair in an attempt to wake himself up. Running a comb through his hair to slick it back he stared at his reflection in the mirror. He noticed dark circles under his eyes and he looked like he had not slept in weeks. His face was thin, and had angles that made him appear older than he was. It made him very depressed. He had been on a roller coaster since his father had left town, and he realized that he could not remember the last good meal he had eaten. He turned away from the mirror and the face he did not want to see and went back into his bedroom. He grabbed his black duffel bag out of the closet and headed for the door. Half way there, he turned around and went to the bedside table. Opening the drawer, he pulled out his 9mm handgun and shoved it in his waistband, pulling the shirt over it to hide it. Better to be safe than sorry he thought to himself.

Vinny headed for the door when he heard the intercom buzz. It was just after 2:45. He slapped the button and said, "Yeah?"

"It's me, Vinny." Tommy said.

"I'll be right down," he said and pressed the button off. He locked the front door and walked over to the elevator. He waved at the security guard as he passed by and left the building. Tommy was parked out front, leaning against his car.

"Hey! What's up Tommy?" Vinny hailed.

"Not a thing!" Tommy shook his head and pulled away from the car, heading around to the driver's side. "Is Henry fucking up again?"

"No, he's watching the dope houses and can't get away, so he asked if I would make a delivery," Vinny explained.

"Doesn't he know you don't do this shit?" Tommy asked.

"Yeah, well. You know Henry, besides he owes me one. Just drive, I don't need the third fuckin' degree. You sound like my mother or something." Vinny laughed.

They went to the warehouse in Sunnyside Queens where he kept his drugs. He picked out two kilo's of coke and put them in the duffel bag. They headed for Long Island City and José's apartment. It took about thirty minutes to get there but Vinny kept getting a tight feeling in the pit of his stomach. Vinny did not get the normal rush; he had more of a sick feeling. He told Tommy to drive around the block a couple times to scope the neighborhood. Vinny never dealt directly with José and wanted to make sure they were not being set up. He knew the cops could pull off a decent bust if they had a dealer in their pocket. They were looking for vans with tinted windows, unmarked police cars, or people hanging out and watching José's house. If anything looked suspicious, the deal was off and they drove away. The neighborhood seemed quiet and no cars passed. One or two people wandered in and out of houses, but nothing that seemed out of the ordinary. However, it was quiet, Vinny thought, almost too quiet. Vinny adjusted his shirt and left it hanging so it would cover his gun. Tommy pulled up in front of José's and Vinny opened his door.

"Keep an eye out, Tommy. If you see anything you don't like, come get me." Vinny said. That tight feeling in his stomach got worse. "If I'm not back in twenty minutes, come and get me, something's wrong... go park around the corner so you can see the house."

"Vinny, you want me to go and make the exchange?" Tommy asked.

"No. I'll handle it, you just watch my back," Vinny told him.

Tommy just nodded his head, "You're the boss. I'll see you back in twenty."

"Yeah, I'm the boss, big fuckin' deal." Vinny's voice dripped sarcasm. "Go park it some place."

Vinny slammed the car door, took a deep breath, and headed for the stairs to the front door. In the background, he heard Tommy pull away and drive up the street. He hoped he stayed alert. In this business, you never trust anyone. He had heard many stories about guys getting sloppy and getting caught or dead because they made a mistake and did not pay attention to what was around them.

Vinny looked around every few seconds to see if he was being followed. The knot in his stomach was worse and he was feeling definitely sick. Sweat was forming in his armpits causing his shirt to stick to him and his palms were clammy. He looked at the front door and thought, "What the fuck am I doing?"

He climbed the steps and stood at the door for a few seconds. His heart was beating hard and fast and it felt as if it was going to burst. He took a couple deep breaths and tried to calm himself but it did not work. He realized what he felt was fear.

He reached up and pushed the button for José's apartment number. It was quiet as he stood there. He could hear his heart beating and feel the blood rushing through his veins. He was developing a hell of a headache.

With relief, he heard the buzzer ring and the lock click open on the door. He walked into a badly lit narrow hallway and looked around. The place was in need of a coat of paint to cover the ugly stains and dirt that had turned the color to a dark rusty orange shade. The floors looked like they had not seen a mop in a decade and were sticky. Every step he took made a crackling noise as it released the soles of his shoes. The floor creaked and groaned as he walked. The building smelled of age mixed with cigarette smoke, mold, and stale cooking odors.

He looked up the staircase and saw apartment number three at the top. Slowly he climbed the stairs, taking each step as if it were his last. He felt strange bringing in drugs, but business is business, and he needed to make money.

He reached the apartment door and listened for a second before he knocked. He heard a TV playing and voices speaking in Spanish. He knocked softly. Every sound in the apartment stopped.

He heard footsteps and saw the cover over the peephole open up. A man's voice behind the door asked, "Who is it?"

"I'm a friend of Smiley's. We spoke over the phone about your property," Vinny replied, trying to remain calm. He heard someone else in the background, a muffled voice in Spanish. The sounds of several door locks being undone before the door creaked open. Vinny thought how it sounded like the creaks and groans of the floor as he had walked across or the sound of an old coffin lid being lowered.

A voice from inside the darkened apartment said, "Come in. I'm José."

Vinny's eyes adjusted to the lack of light and he saw a dark-skinned man with greasy hair touched with grey at the temples. He wore a Yankee's t-shirt and a pair of jeans and tennis shoes. He motioned to Vinny and led him through a short hallway to a dimly lit living room where two other men sat on a sofa that was in desperate need of a good cleaning.

"This is Santos and Benny." José said. Vinny went over to the two and shook hands. He noticed they were well dressed compared to José. They were Latino's and Vinny could tell they were absolutely drug boys. Each of the men had a gold chain around their neck. The man named Santos had a heavy gold and diamond cross hanging from his. They each sported gold Rolex watches and Santos had a gold and diamond pinky ring. He noticed they wore expensive Armani suits. They looked out of place in this apartment and doing business with someone like José. Vinny's stomach started to knot again. If these people were major movers and were heavy into the business, why were they buying from him? They were more likely to be high rolling sellers than buyers.

José cleared his throat and looked at the three men. "Let's get this over with before my wife gets up."

Vinny looked over at Santos and said. "Do you have the money?"

Santos leaned forward and stared at Vinny. "Yes, in the other room." His eyes flicked over to José and then back to Vinny. "My partner will get it."

Benny stood and walked out of the living room into the hallway. José abruptly sat down and was acting nervous. His eyes darted from one man to the other and Vinny could see sweat forming on his upper lip. Something was not right. The knot in his stomach became painful.

"How long have you guys known each other?" he asked. Dread was creeping into his mind. He needed to know more about what was going on. Why would José keep these people's money in the other room where his wife is sleeping? Vinny's headache started to get worse.

Santos glanced at José and said, "A couple of years."

Vinny noticed José's hands were nervously rubbing together. They shook a little.

"José, do you have a knife?" Vinny asked.

José nodded and quickly left the room. He moved too fast and Vinny thought he looked like a man trying to escape an unpleasant situation. He did a mental shrug and decided that maybe José was just the nervous type or that he had been sampling the product he sold. Vinny unzipped the duffel bag and pulled out a kilo of coke. He set it on the coffee table between him and Santos.

José returned and handed the knife handle first to Santos. As Santos pulled the knife from his hand, he cut a deep slice in José's right index finger. Blood dropped to the table.

"José, I am so sorry. It was an accident." Santos said. He reached inside his suit coat and handed José a white silk handkerchief. "Please, wrap this around your finger to stop the bleeding. We would not want you to contaminate the merchandise or have you bleed to death." Santo's smiled at José who took the white silk and clumsily wrapped it around his finger. Vinny could see blood slowly soaking through the thin silk. José returned to his seat and said nothing, but his eyes never left Santos' face.

Santos started to cut into the kilo of cocaine. He neatly cut a small corner open and, with the tip of the knife, sliced off a small piece of cocaine. He pulled a small, capped vial from his pocket. It contained a clear liquid. He popped the cap and dropped the coke into the vial, recapped it and shook it. The clear solution turned blue. Santos smiled and pocketed the vial.

"It is good merchandise. We have a deal," Santos said. He closed up the cut in the kilo by folding the area over and pressing the excess tape together, then slid it to the side of the table.

Vinny watched closely, but was beginning to wonder why it was taking Benny so long. He glanced at his watch and was ready to say something to Santos when Benny walked back into the room. He tossed a thick, rubber-banded stack of hundred dollar bills at Vinny and said, "This is half."

"Half?" Vinny blurted out. "What the fuck do you mean?"

We have all the money back there." Benny said.

Santos waved a hand at Benny and pulled the vial from his pocket. Holding it up so Benny could see the blue liquid, he said, "It is good. Get him the rest of his cash." Benny nodded and left the room again.

Vinny pulled the rubber bands from the stack of money and started to count. He glanced at José and saw sweat dripping down the side of his face. He realized José had not moved since he had sat down, nor had he said anything. He was a statue, staring at Santos and clasping a blood stained silk handkerchief around his finger.

Santos smiled at Vinny and said, "It's good we can do business."

"Yes," Vinny said. He finished counting the first half of the money and shoved it into the pocket of his shorts. He sat back in the couch and looked around the room, feigning interest in the furnishings. In actuality, he was observing José. He noticed the sweat had begun to drip from his brow and his hands were visibly shaking. Something was certainly wrong here. Vinny glanced at his watch; ten minutes to go before Tommy came looking for him. He hoped Benny would hurry with the cash.

Vinny reached in his duffel bag and handed the other kilo of cocaine to Santos. Santos placed it neatly on top of the first then leaned back into the couch again, looking as if he owned the place. He just smiled at Vinny.

Vinny looked at his watch. Five minutes and all hell will break loose. Just as Vinny was ready to prod Santos along, Benny reentered the room with a silver metal briefcase. He sat down next to Santos, opened it slowly and said, "I owe you another eighteen thousand, correct?"

"Right... thirty-six-thousand dollars. That is the price my friend agreed to with José," he replied.

Benny nodded and reached into the briefcase. He pulled out another stack of hundreds with his left hand and in his right he held a .45 that he pointed at Vinny's head.

"Do not move or I blow your fucking head off!" Benny hissed. Santos pulled a gun from behind him, held it to José's head, and told him to stay quiet or die.

Vinny froze. His heart started to race and pound and the blood rushed to his head. His eyes clouded over and he thought he was going to pass out. He was scared to death. He had fucked up this time.

Santos grabbed José by the arm and threw him on the floor. José whimpered as he tried to stand. Santos pushed back down into a kneeling position and put the gun to his temple.

"Get the fucking money and coke and let's get out of here," he told Benny. Benny stuffed the kilos back in the duffel bag Vinny still had beside him. He never moved the gun from Vinny's head and kept his eyes locked on him. Vinny could just see the headlines that would greet his father when he stepped off the plane, 'Vinny Denucci found shot to death over a drug deal gone bad!' After all the times his father told him to never touch drugs. He should have listened.

Benny flipped the money into the briefcase and snapped it shut. With one hand, he scooped up the handles to the duffel and the briefcase and set them on the couch. His gun never moved more than an inch or two away from Vinny's head. Vinny's mouth was dry and he realized he had not taken a breath in more than a minute. Here it comes, he thought.

"Stand up and put your hands behind your back." Benny ordered. Vinny stood. His mind reeled and he thought about trying to jump Benny, but then he realized he would not have a chance, the gun pressed to his head underneath his left ear. If he made a wrong move, he knew Benny would not hesitate to pull the trigger.

Instead, he put his hands behind his back. He felt Benny grab one and the cold steel of a handcuff encircled his wrist. Benny clamped it down until it cut into his wrist and he instinctively pulled away. Benny jerked him back and shoved the gun into the back of his head.

"Don't move fuck-head, or I'll blow you away where you stand." Benny said. Vinny froze. Benny put the other cuff on him and moved around in front of him. He pulled out a handkerchief and shoved it in his mouth, then reached down and grabbed the one José had wrapped around his finger and tied it around Vinny's head and mouth. José kneeled on the floor and did not move. He just stared at the gun Santos had pointed at his head. Vinny could taste the blood on the handkerchief. He thought he was going to throw up.

Benny looked at Santos, "You going to do it or should I?" he asked. Santos smiled. From out of the blue, Vinny thought that he smiled too much. The thought came that he had never liked people that smiled all the time, you could never figure them out.

Santos looked at José and smiled again. José started to shake his head. Vinny saw tears well up in his eyes. Santos shrugged and pulled José to his feet. He put the gun in José's mouth. "No hard feelings, José, but business is business. You can join that pretty wife of yours that I enjoyed so much. She wasn't half bad for a fuck before I slit her throat." He pulled the trigger.

Vinny tried to look away, but he was not fast enough. He watched the entire scene as if it were in slow motion. José was still shaking his head; he could see tears rolling down his cheeks as Santos pulled the trigger. The back of José's head exploded. Vinny saw his eyes widen in surprise as it happened. The last thing José saw was Santos smiling at him. José's brains blew out the back of his head and spattered on the chair he had been sitting in just minutes before. Blood, bone, and brains hit the wall behind him. The force threw him back into the chair. His head rolled to the side, eyes open, as his body crumpled.

Santos walked over to Vinny and smiled at him. "What's wrong, Mr. Denucci? You look a little sick to your stomach." Vinny's eyes widened, these guys knew who we was. He had never identified himself when he came in.

Santos smiled again. "Yes, we know who you are. We didn't expect you, but a delivery boy of pedigree still serves the purpose, you stupid fuckin' guinea." Santos put the gun between Vinny's eyes, "It's your turn. How do you want it? I blow a big hole in your head. Maybe I shoot you in the heart to keep that pretty face of yours nice for the funeral."

Vinny's stomach and head began to hurt unbearably. He just stared into Santos' eyes with hate and thought, "fuck you!" Benny reached up and pulled Santos' arm down, "Santos, we can't. You know who this is?"

Santos glared at Benny, and then shook his head. "You're right Benny. Besides, he is not worth the bullet. Put him in the closet where the cops can find him. That will be worse than anything I could do to him."

Benny shoved Vinny toward the closet in the hallway and pushed him inside so hard he bounced off the back wall. Trying to regain his footing, he tripped over some boxes on the floor and fell. He heard Benny laugh as he shut the door, "You're lucky Mr. Denucci that you are who you are. I would like nothing better than to kill you."

Vinny lay there in darkness with a box corner sticking him in the kidney and the smell of dirty shoes and moldy clothing permeating his senses. He heard Benny and Santos walk past the closet to the front door. He heard the door bolts drawn and the door open and close. The sounds of people heard through the paper-thin wall, they were screaming in Spanish and he knew someone had probably called the cops. He could not believe this was a setup.

His thoughts went to Henry, "I am going to kill that fucker! If I get out of this, he's going to pay." He laid there in the dark for what seemed like an eternity, waiting for the cops to show up. He knew Tommy would come looking for him. He just hoped it was soon enough. All of a sudden, he heard gunshots. Maybe the cops were fighting it out with Benny and Santos. He tried to get the closet door open by kicking it with his feet, but he was lying at an angle that prevented him from doing more than he could without making noise.

He heard the door to the apartment crash open and he froze. Maybe he would get lucky and the cops would not look in here right away. All of a sudden, a familiar voice shouted, "Vinny! Vinny!" It was Tommy.

He struggled to force the closet door to open with his feet and then kicked it very hard. The sound was deafening inside the enclosed space.

Tommy jerked the door open and grabbed Vinny by the scruff of his neck, jerking him to his feet. "What the fuck happened?" he asked as he untied the bloody handkerchief and Vinny spit out the wad of material.

Vinny spit the taste of blood out of his mouth. He jerked away from Tommy when he began to try to get the cuffs off. "We can do these later. I heard gunshots. What happened?"

Tommy grinned, "I met your two friends running down the stairs. We 'talked' about the little problem they had with you. It was a quick conversation, painless."

Vinny returned the grin as he led Tommy toward the door, "Let's get out of here, before the cops show up."

As they passed the living room, they looked in at José slumped in the chair.

Tommy raised an eyebrow and looked at Vinny, "Boy, did he fuck up." Vinny just nodded and headed for the open door.

They sprinted down the stairs two at a time. He saw Santos and Benny lying face down in a pool of blood at the bottom.

Tommy said, "I wasn't taking chances. They looked too suspicious."

"You did well, Tommy. They were scum. "As he walked past the bodies he spit on Santos. "Hey Santos, at least he did not mess up that pretty face of yours. No hard feelings Spic, but business is business."

Tommy grabbed the duffel bag and suitcase and they ran out into the car. Running across the street, he looked back and noticed lights were on all over the building. It would not be long before the cops showed.

Tommy jerked open the car door and threw the two bags in the back seat. Vinny turned his back to him, "Shoot these cuffs off. Then let's get the fuck out of here." He pushed his hands and arms as far away from his body as he could, Tommy shot once and they split in two. The two jumped in the car, Vinny slid across to the passenger side and Tommy folded his bulk behind the steering wheel.

"Where to, Boss?" he asked as he started the car and hit the gas.

"Let's go find Henry." Vinny said.

The car jumped forward just as they saw the cop's lights bouncing off the houses down the street. Tommy gunned it down the first street they came to and they disappeared from sight.

"Pull over at a phone, I need to call Henry." Vinny said.

Tommy reached in his inside pocket of his coat and pulled out a cell phone. "Use this. I don't want to stop right now, we're still too close." Tommy said. He pushed the on button and handed it to Vinny. "You need to get one of these, Boss. They come in handy." He grinned.

Vinny punched in Henry's number and waited. After five rings, he heard Henry pick up.

"Hello."

"Henry, you fucked up and I'm on my way over to see you!" Vinny growled into the phone.

"What the fuck. Vinny is that you?" Henry asked.

"Yeah, and you better be there when I get there. You fucked up, Henry."

"Vinny, I don't understand? What is going on? Is it the deal? What happened?" Henry sounded desperate. His voice was high-pitched and he sounded frightened.

"Henry, you better be waiting for us. We'll be there in about forty-five minutes." Vinny pushed the off button and handed the phone back to Tommy. "I'm going to kick his fuckin' ass when I see him," he muttered.

Tommy quietly took the phone and put it back in his pocket. He knew it was not a good time to say anything. When Vinny was pissed, you did not mess with him.

They got to Henry's dope house in less than the forty-five minutes. Henry was waiting outside pacing up and down the sidewalk and smoking a cigarette. He stopped when he saw the car pull up and started toward them.

Vinny threw the door open and ran over to him. Before Henry could react, he grabbed him by the shirt and punched him in the face. Henry threw his hands up to protect himself, but Vinny kept punching him, pushing him to the ground and straddling him as he rained blows at his head and ribs. The chains from the cuffs swung and sliced at Henry's face. Blood flowed. Tommy ran over and grabbed Vinny by the arms, pulling him off Henry. Vinny struggled to pull away, "Let me go, Tommy!" he yelled. "I'm going to kill him!"

Tommy's grip tightened, "Vinny, killing him won't do you any good. Just cool off and let's talk about this."

Vinny's breath came in gasps as he stood there. Anger still clouded his brain, but somewhere in the back of his mind, reason was emerging. Slowly, his body relaxed in Tommy's grip. He shrugged off the iron hold he had on him and said, "I'm fine. You are right. Killing him won't do me any good."

Henry rolled to his side on the ground. His arms encircled his ribcage as he started to choke and cough up blood. Blood flowed from his nose and stained the sidewalk. They could see his eyes were starting to swell and his face cut in several places. He started to choke and coughed up more blood.

"Vinny, what did I do?" His voice was harsh. As he spoke, blood spattered all over him. He coughed again, and then spit out more blood. He tried to rise but only managed to lean on one arm. He raised his head and wiped blood from his eyes, clearing his vision.

"You almost got me killed you dumb fuck! Those spics tried to rip us off. José has a hole in his head the size of a baseball."

"Vinny, I sold to José many times and I never had problems before," Henry rasped.

"Well this time José fucked up! It got him killed. It almost got me killed!" Vinny shouted. "Why didn't you fuckin' tell me there were other dealers there? These guys were high rollers. I thought you knew these guys."

"I'm sorry Vinny; I would never do anything to hurt you. You know that," Henry pleaded. "You're like my brother; I never knew José was into dealing with guys like that." Henry pushed himself up and stood there. Tears ran down his battered face. "You're my friend Vinny." He reached out a hand, but Vinny took a step back. Henry's face fell. He used the hand to wipe blood out of one eye. "Vinny, please I would never hurt you. You have to know that." He was practically whimpering.

Vinny looked at Henry and flashes of memories ran through his head. Henry had an expression on his face of disgust, as if he just lost his best friend.

"Shit!" he said. "I should kill you, Henry. You know that?"

Henry nodded, "I know, Vinny. I would if I were in your place."

"You better be sure you know who you're dealing with next time," Vinny warned.

Vinny ran a hand through his hair. His knuckles hurt and the chain on the cuff smacked him in the side of the head. He started to laugh.

"Okay! Okay! I give." He reached out and pulled Henry to him. "Just don't fuck up again." He hugged Henry to him, and then stepped back. "I got to go home and get cleaned up. My father's on his way home." He turned and headed back to the car.

Henry hailed him as he walked away. "Hey Vinny, you better get rid of the cuffs, I don't think your father will buy that they are a new fashion statement."

Vinny looked down at his wrists. "Fuck you, Henry!" he laughed. "Go get cleaned up and I'll see you later." He turned to open the door to the car, "Tommy, take me home. And figure out a way to get my new jewelry off."

He sat quiet all the way home. He knew he should have killed Henry for what happened, but for some reason, deep inside, he could not bring himself to do it right then. They drove in silence. When they pulled up in front of Vinny's place Tommy asked if he was all right.

"Yes. It has just been a long night. Go home and get some sleep, Tommy. I'll see you later," he answered. As he climbed out of the car, he felt like he was an old man. He hurt everywhere.

He took the elevator up to his place and slowly walked in. He looked at the time. It was 5:45am. If he was lucky, he could get a couple hours sleep. He figured he better call Frankie and give him the heads up. Then sleep. He dialed the number and a sleepy voice answered.

"Hello!"

"Frankie, is that you?" he asked.

"Yes! Vinny?"

"Yeah, I need you at my place at 9:00 this morning. My father's coming home."

"Sure, okay. I'll be there," Frankie said.

Vinny hung up and headed for the shower. He stood there and let the hot water wash the aches away. He eventually got out, set his alarm and climbed into bed. He was asleep before his head hit the pillow.

CHAPTER 15
THE HOMECOMING

* * * *

Somewhere in the back of a dream, he kept hearing bells and someone knocking. He tried to ignore it, but it was persistent. Slowly, he began to realize it was the alarm clock and that someone was banging on the door. He rolled over and slapped off the alarm. He was still foggy from sleep but somewhere in the back of his mind, he registered that it was 8:30. He woke with a start and rolled out of bed.

"Shit!" He had set the alarm for 8:00. He had slept through half an hour of it buzzing. He grabbed his robe and headed to answer the door.

He yelled out, "Who is it?"

"Vinny, it's me Frankie!"

Vinny opened up the door and said, "Good morning! I need ten minutes. Go and make some tea for me."

"I'll have it ready in a flash, Boss." Frankie said. "You know you look like hell don't you?" He yelled at Vinny who was walking away.

A muffled "Fuck you, Frankie," heard from the hallway into the bathroom. Frankie just laughed and went into the kitchen to get the tea. Vinny rushed through a shower and got dressed in record time. He came out and grabbed his tea off the kitchen table.

"Let's go. I don't want to be late and I don't know how bad traffic is this time of the morning," Vinny said as they headed for the elevator.

They rode down in silence and exited to the car Frankie had left parked out front. Vinny waved a hand at the security guard as they passed.

Frankie glanced over at him as they drove and remarked, "You're awful quiet today. Is everything all right?"

"Yeah, Frankie, everything is just fine. I just need some peace and quiet. Okay?"

"Sure Vinny, not a problem." Frankie shrugged, but he gave Vinny a sideways glance and frowned. He had a bad feeling deep in his gut that something had happened; he just did not know what.

They arrived at LaGuardia Airport in plenty of time, Vinny told Frankie to go and park and he would call him when his father arrived. He walked through the terminal and looked for the monitor to see if the flight was on time and the arrival gate. The flight from Miami was delayed by ten minutes, so he had time for a cup of tea and to figure out what he was going to say to his father. He found a coffee shop near the gate, ordered, and sat down.

As he sat there and waited, he thought of what he had been doing since his father had left. Sometimes he wondered if he was still sane. The old Vinny, the one who wanted to be a lawyer and save the world gnawed at the back of his mind. He stared down into the bottom of the teacup and wondered what he was doing to his life and where all his dreams had gone. Not so long ago he had been full of the aspiration to go to college and fulfill his and his mother's dreams. He just wanted to survive one more day without being killed.

He started to order another cup of tea when he heard the announcement that his father's flight had arrived. He got up, walked over to the gate, and stared at the doorway that would soon disgorge the jet's passengers. He realized he was nervous and shaking. So much had happened since his father had left and he knew there would be questions he would need to answer. He also knew his father would not like the answers he gave him. He saw him walk through the gate with his usual swagger. Sonny had a tan and it appeared that he had lost some weight, but his brow knitted and he seemed troubled about something. He looked up and saw Vinny standing there and he waved. Vinny stepped forward as his father reached him and gave him a hug and kissed his cheek.

"You look good, Dad. It's good to have you home." Vinny said. "Let's go get your luggage and get out of here."

Sonny hesitated for a moment and looked like he wanted to say something, then changed his mind, "Yeah, it's good to be back home. Have you taken care of everything while I was gone?" he asked.

Vinny turned with him and they walked down the concourse and headed for the baggage claim area. "Everything is fine," he told him. "I had some small problems but nothing I couldn't handle."

"So I heard," Sonny said. Vinny just looked sideways at him. He wondered how much his father knew about what had happened while he was gone. He should have figured someone would report in to Sonny and keep him updated—after all he was the Boss.

They grabbed his bags as they came down the chute and had a porter wheel them out to the curb. Frankie had parked in the loading area and pulled the car up when he saw them emerge from the terminal. He jumped out of the car, opened the trunk, and started helping the porter load up the luggage. Sonny glanced in the car and then at Vinny.

"Where's Sal and Charlie?" he asked.

"That's the problem I had." Vinny said. "Let's get in the car first and I'll explain."

Vinny reached for the car door and opened it as Frankie slammed the trunk closed and tipped the porter. His father slid in, across the seat to make room for Vinny and Frankie got in behind the wheel, and slowly started to drive away.

"So? Where are Sal and Charlie, Vinny?" Sonny asked again. This time his tone was stern. He wanted an answer.

Vinny stared his father in the eye, "Charlie got killed in a bar scuffle and Sal got out of line so I killed him." Vinny kept his voice even and steady, he thought he sounded like he was talking about the weather and not someone he had blown away.

Sonny's face turned red and Vinny knew he was in for it. His father shouted, "You killed Sal, what the fuck did you do that for?" Who gave you the order to do such a thing?"

"You're the one that left me in charge, Dad. I did what I had to do." Vinny told him. "Sal took liberties he should not have and I couldn't trust him. I recruited Frankie and he's doing a better job than Sal ever did." Frankie glanced in the rear view mirror at them. He stopped at a red light and turned to offer his hand to Sonny. Sonny just gave him a dirty look. Vinny looked at Frankie and shook his head. This was not a good time. Frankie nodded, but said "Good to meet you, Mr. Denucci. Welcome home." He turned back to the front of the car as if nothing had happened, but Vinny could see him looking at them in the mirror again, a questioning look in his eyes.

Sonny was quiet for a while and Vinny figured it was that he was trying to get his anger under control. Finally, he turned to Vinny and asked, "I heard you blew Tony Pinto away and in fucking public. Can you explain this to me?"

Vinny wondered how he knew about that. Then he knew with Tony being a boss it would get back to Sonny. You do not waste a boss, even an asshole one, without permission.

Vinny turned toward him "Tony beat up one of our high-priced ladies to the point where she could not work and then he did not want to pay her. He was disrespectful to me in front of my crew and some of his own crew. So I taught him a lesson."

"Do you know the fucking problems you caused me?" Sonny yelled.

Vinny just sat back and stared at him. He knew there would be trouble, but the decision had been his and he had done what he needed to. Sonny just shook his head and sighed.

"We'll have to have a sit down later with Tony's boss. You do not go around doing shit like that unless it is for a good reason. You have to keep the balance between bosses." he explained to Vinny.

Vinny just shrugged and stared out the front window. It was starting to rain. "Well, he beat me for $250 dollars and he beat my girl so she couldn't work. That cost me a lot of money. Fuck him and that whole crew. I'll whack them all." His finger pointed in the air like a pistol.

Sonny stared at him with a look of amazement, "Vinny, what the fuck is happening to you?"

"Hey, you wanted me to be like you, a boss, a killer that does what he has to do, so I am," Vinny replied.

His father just looked at him with disgust and ran a hand through his hair. They had arrived home and Vinny said he had business to take care of and would be home later for dinner. Frankie got out of the car and unloaded the bags. The door attendant came out with a dolly and they loaded them on and stood there waiting for Sonny to get out of the car.

Sonny sat there for a while then finally said, "Ok, you go take care of business. Stay out of trouble. We are going to talk later when you get home." He opened the door and got out. Sonny slammed the door without waiting for answers and walked into the building, yelling at the door attendant to hurry up. Vinny just shook his head. Nothing had changed with his father—he was still the Boss. Frankie got back in the car and they pulled away. Vinny thought to himself how ironic this whole thing was, he had turned into what his father had wanted, and now he wanted him to change back. Vinny also did not understand his father's reaction to Sal's death. It seemed that after years of loyal service from Sal his father did not care that he was dead or that it was Vinny that had killed him, he only cared about the peace with his men over the killing of Tony. It finally became clear to him that his father's talk about loyalty in the Family was a lie. Maybe his whole life had been a lie.

He shook off thoughts of his father. It was something that he did not need to think about right now. He had business to take care of. He knew his father was angry and he did not feel like confronting him so he decided to spend the night at a hotel. He figured that would give his father some time to cool down. He asked Frankie for his cell phone. Frankie smiled and reached over and opened the glove compartment.

"Here. I got this one for you. I figured you would need it one of these days." He passed the phone back to Vinny. "You'll get the bill at the end of the month," he grinned.

Vinny grinned back, "Cheapskate But thanks, Frankie! I haven't had time to get one and I can use it."

He dialed his home number and waited for Sonny to pick up. After three or four rings, a breathless Sonny was heard on the other end.

"Hello!" Sonny said.

"Hey Dad, is everything okay? You sound out of breath."

"Yeah, I'm fine, just in the shower and had to make a run for the phone is all. What do you need, Vinny?"

"I just called to let you know I'm going to spend the night out so don't wait up."

"Oh no you're not," Sonny shouted. "I just got home and we have things to talk about. You get your fucking ass home tonight."

Vinny felt the anger rise, "I'm staying out. I have things to do."

"Bullshit, Vinny. You obey me. Get your ass here after you finish your run!" Sonny yelled.

Vinny had had enough, "Fuck you!" he yelled in the phone. "You made me the boss and I'm doing what I need to do. I'll be home in the morning." He punched the off button on the phone and cut Sonny's reply before he could hear it. He shoved the phone in his jacket pocket and punched the seat in anger. Sonny was always trying to control him. Fuck him!

"Frankie, let's get this run over with. Then take me to the Midway Hotel on Astoria Blvd.," he said. Vinny knew a place where his father would never consider looking for him.

"Sure Boss. Problem?" Frankie asked.

"No. I just don't feel like dealing with my father. He's in a pissy mood."

Frankie nodded his head in agreement. "I understand. I got an old man, too. He's a pain in the ass sometimes."

"Yeah, well, let's get the run over with. Get a move on." Vinny told him, "I don't feel like fucking around all day with this."

Frankie nodded and sped up a little. They managed to hit all Vinny's places in record time by four o'clock in the morning; then they headed for the hotel.

"Stay near by," he told Frankie. "Get a room. I'll call if I need you." They checked in and went to their rooms. Vinny locked the door and pulled his gun out. He laid it on the nightstand and then stripped his clothes off and lay down on the bed. He was dead tired, but he could not sleep. His mind was in turmoil. He turned on the TV to see if the drug deal murder had been reported. He surfed a few channels but did not see anything. It would probably be on the late news if considered newsworthy. In this town a drug murder was not big news, it was normal. He found HBO and started to watch Smokey and the Bandit, about twenty minutes into it he felt himself drifting off, he let it happen and fell into a deep, dreamless sleep.

CHAPTER 16
DEBBIE

* * * *

VINNY WAS JOLTED AWAKE BY A SCREAM that cut through the early morning darkness. He jumped out of bed and looked out the window. By the lights in the parking lot, he could see some man beating a woman that he held by the hair. He raised his fist again and struck her in the stomach, doubling her over. Half-awake and dazed, Vinny threw on his pants and grabbed his gun off the nightstand. He ran across the parking lot in his bare feet and yelled out to the man just as he was jerking the girl to her feet to hit her again.

"Let her go!"

The man turned to him and jerked the woman around by the hair. He spat on the ground and yelled back at Vinny, "Mind your own fuckin' business!"

As he got closer, he could see the woman was beautiful. Long blonde hair tangled in the man's hand and her face stained with tears, but she was still one of the most gorgeous women he had ever seen.

"I said, let her go", Vinny repeated. He stood about six feet from the two. The parking lot lights illuminated the three of them and Vinny could see the woman's beautiful blue eyes tear up again as the man jerked her head toward him.

"Fuck you, who the fuck do you think you are?" The man spat at him.

Vinny's temper flared and he pulled out his gun. "Let her go or I'll kill you right now." He raised the gun and pointed it at the man's head. The man's eyes widened and he began to make sputtering sounds. He pushed the woman to the ground and fled down the street, glancing back at Vinny and expecting a bullet in the back.

Vinny stood there with the gun pointed until the retreating figure turned the corner at the end of the block. He tucked the pistol into the back of his pants and walked over to the girl. She tried to rise but stumbled and he grabbed her by the arm to steady her.

"You okay?" he asked. "What's your name?"

"Debbie Karls. Thanks, I'm okay. He didn't hurt me that much," she said. Her voice was soft and Vinny could feel it pull at him.

"C'mon, you can get cleaned up at my room," he told her. He reached to put his arm around her but she pulled back a step. "It's okay. I am not going to hurt you. I just want to get you cleaned up a little. You can't go anywhere looking like that."

Debbie nodded and moved into the circle of his arm. He gently led her back to his hotel room. He locked the door behind them after they entered then went over and placed his gun back on the nightstand and sat down on the bed. He was still tired and all he wanted to do was sleep, but here he was playing Good Samaritan.

"Go ahead and get a shower. There are plenty of towels and stuff. Just toss your clothes out here and I'll try to clean them up a little."

"Thank you," she said, and that voice pulled at him again. He looked at her as she walked toward the bathroom. Even after being beat up, Vinny noticed how beautiful she was. She shut the bathroom door behind her and he heard rustling. Suddenly the door flew open and her clothes came out flying to land in a heap on the floor. As Vinny picked them up, he could hear the shower start. He had this urge to open the door, and even went so far as to lay his hand on the doorknob. However, he pulled back. She had had enough tonight, the last thing she needed was him leering at her. He checked her clothing and found that they only needed a little brushing out to make them presentable. The labels were from a high fashion shop in Manhattan and he knew this was not an ordinary hooker type. They could not afford the price of the shoes she wore let alone the outfit. She did not seem the escort type either, but you never knew. She was absolutely in the wrong neighborhood. She was probably a rich bitch out slumming who got caught up in a bad situation.

He hung up her clothes and went back to lie on the bed. He was thinking of her voice. Her voice was soft like a rose petal. He began to wonder what it would be like to hear that voice say his name. He was just floating back into sleep when he heard the bathroom door open. He pulled himself up and leaned back on his elbows as she came into the room.

She was wrapped in towel that barely covered her, and another was turban style around her wet hair. She stood in the doorway and looked over at him. She had the bluest eyes he had ever seen.

"I want to thank you for helping me."

Vinny just shrugged, "I couldn't let that bum beat you up. No man should do that to a woman." He asked, "What were you doing out there with him to begin with?"

She crossed the room and sat at the end of the bed, one leg curled under her. "He was my boyfriend awhile back. He called and said he wanted to talk, so I met him. Everything was fine until I told him I did not want to get back with him. He got mad," she explained.

Vinny shook his head, "I can't figure out guys like that. Never could. You're better off without him around."

"I know that. Nevertheless, I didn't feel like I should not talk to him. After all, we were together for a couple years. I left because he started hitting on me a few months back."

"Well, I don't think he'll be bothering you again." Vinny laughed, "I think I scared the shit out of him."

Debbie laughed and smiled at him, he felt his pulse speed up and a stirring below the beltline. She was even more beautiful when she smiled.

He could not take his eyes off her and he had the urge to reach for her and hold her to him, to feel her skin against his own.

"You know it would be nice to know the name of the man that rescued me."

"My name's Vinny Denucci."

She said, "I know the name well. Your father is the Mafia Boss, right?"

"My father is a businessman, nothing else," he replied.

She smiled at him and said, "Yes, I can understand that, in the end isn't everything just business?" She slid a little closer to him and put her hand on his leg, "I do want to thank you, Vinny. You may have saved my life." She looked at him and smiled. He thought he had died and gone to heaven. She had a great body, blue eyes and such a sexy voice.

Slowly she stood up. She bent over at the waist and began to towel dry her hair. When she finished she dropped the towel and flung her hair over her shoulder, running her fingers through it to comb it out. She stood before him clad in the ill-fitting bath towel and stared at him. With movements that seemed to take an eternity, she reached up and loosened the towel, letting it drop to puddle at her feet. She stood before him, naked, her arms hanging down and her head cocked to one side.

"Do you want to make love to me, Vinny?" she asked.

He ran his eyes over her as she stood there. Her skin was smooth and creamy. She had breasts that were peaked with dusky rose nipples. He followed her stomach down and his gaze lingered on the light brown and blonde curls that resided between her legs.

"You don't have to do this," Vinny said. He sat up, swung his legs over the side of the bed, and stood. He wanted her to know he was sincere.

"I know that. I would not do this unless I wanted to. I want to feel you inside me." Her voice was barely a whisper, but to Vinny, it sounded like music. "I want to thank you. You saved my life."

She walked over to him and touched his face, running her fingers over his lips. He reached up and clasped her hand, holding it to his lips. She pulled it away and let it float down his chin and neck. Using one finger, she traced a path to his chest and made little swirls around his nipples. He had not realized it before but the top of her head barely reached his chin. He could smell the clean scent of her hair and body. She leaned into him and kissed his neck and chest, her tongue darting out to flick a nipple. He could feel her breasts touching him, soft and warm. Her hands were roaming over his chest and back until she finally reached up and pulled his head down to her. Her kiss was soft as she touched his lips for the first time. She almost seemed to hesitate, but a sigh escaped her and she opened her mouth, licking at his bottom lip. Vinny could not take it any longer—his arms crept around her and pressed her into him. Their kiss deepened and their tongues met willingly. He felt himself surge with desire and lust and he wanted to take her right there, standing up, but he pulled away knowing he did not want to hurt her.

She smiled at him as he pulled away. Her hands floated to his pants and she gently tugged open the button and pulled down the zipper. She pushed them over his hips and let them fall. Vinny stepped out of them and kicked them to the side, his hands continued to roam over her, and he felt the silk of her drying hair as it brushed against the back of his hands. Debbie let her body lean into him again, he was erect and his body was heating at an incredible rate. He could feel the silk of her skin as she rubbed against him, almost like a cat.

"I want you, Vinny. I need you inside me," she whispered.

They looked at each other with lust in their eyes. She slid from his arms, warm from the shower, and put her hand inside his shorts. She massaged him, and then gently pulled out his penis, pushing his underwear to the floor. She moved around him, guiding him to lay on the bed, her hand moving up to tug at his arm and pull him to her. Vinny lowered himself beside her on the bed, his hands gliding over her breasts and belly. She arched her back into him and her eyes fluttered closed. Instinctively her hips arched up and he let his hand caress between her legs, playing with the short curls and then going deeper. She moaned and opened her eyes. It was all there, no words needed. She reached for him, pulling him down on her, guiding him into her. She was warm and tight and Vinny thought he had gone to heaven. Their rhythm was slow and steady as he held himself over her. He looked down at her and saw the passion on her face, the excitement in her eyes. Gently, he rolled to the side and brought her with him until she sat upright. Her body was slick with sweat. He held her hips, guiding her on him, increasing the rhythm as she grasped his arms and panted with excitement. He knew he would explode, but he wanted this to last for hours.

She looked down at him and smiled, "Come with me, Vinny. I need to feel you."

Vinny moaned and bucked under her, she gasped and he could feel her spasm around him, feel her juices as they ran from her. It was enough for him. He rolled her onto to her back and thrust into her until they exploded together.

He slowly lowered himself to the bed beside her, taking her in his arms and holding their bodies tightly together. They rested until their breathing returned to normal and the sweat was gone from their bodies.

Slowly, Debbie ran her hand over his back, barely touching him. He could feel the desire begin again and he looked down at her. She was smiling. She began slowly leading him through different sensations, touching him with mouth and hands. She whispered to him, telling him how wonderful and heroic he had been. For a little while, Vinny almost believed her. Content to explore, she was creative and sensitive, moving here and there in answer to his responses.

They coupled then pulled apart, changed rhythms effortlessly, sliding deeper and slower with each meeting, until they were barely moving. It felt complete, harmonious. They fit together and knew it. She kept whispering how good he felt inside her and how great they were together. They did not scream, they sighed. There skin, so sensitive to each other's touch, was explored and tantalized. They rolled around together just to feel cheeks, arms, and thighs rub together like silk, like warm water. When the time finally came, they fell easily over the edge together, floating and drifting in that space between one heartbeat and the next. It took only a breath and they fell asleep entwined.

A knock at the door startled Vinny awake. He looked down at the sleeping woman in his arms. Her long hair spread on the pillow in a cloud. He pushed an errant piece from her face as he pulled away from her, gently laying her head on the pillow. He grabbed his shorts and pulled them on, tossing the sheet over her sleeping form. He opened the door as the knocking became more insistent. It was Frankie and he looked irritated.

"Your father has been calling you all night. I just got the messages." Frankie was scowling. "We got to get out of here. He wants to see you at the Palace!" Frankie peered around him and saw Debbie sitting up, rubbing the sleep from her eyes. He looked at Vinny and just raised his eyebrows.

"Never mind," Vinny grinned back at him. "Give me five minutes and I'll be ready. Go get the car. And call him and tell him I'm on my way."

He shut the door and turned to see Debbie sitting there with a quizzical expression on her face. "I have to leave. You can stay here and rest. Here's some cash if you need it." Vinny pulled his wallet out of his pants and took out five one hundred dollar bills, laying them on top of the TV. He hurriedly scribbled his home andcell numbers on a notepad from the bedside table, and handed it to her. "Call me if you need anything. I do not think your ex will bother you again. However, just in case, let me know. I'll handle it."

He finished dressing and kissed her good-bye. When he opened the door, Frankie was sitting in the car out front. He hopped in and they headed over to see his father. Frankie dropped him off outside and went to park the car. Vinny walked inside and saw his father sitting with some men over in the corner at the back of the restaurant. Vinny had been taught in life to sit in the back of the restaurants near the exits where he could feel secure. In reality, it did not make a difference where you sat if you were going to get whacked. The back door beside you and the front door in plain view was not going to save you if someone truly wanted you dead.

As he got closer to his father, Sonny motioned to the other men to get up and leave.

Sonny looked him up and down, "Good morning. You look like a slob."

"Thanks, Dad." Vinny laughed, "I have been up all night."

"You should come home like I tell you to," Sonny growled.

Vinny slid into a seat and looked at his father, "Dad, I just wanted to be alone."

"Well, Vincenzo, next time you want to be alone, take a vacation." Sonny placed his hands on the table. "I'm back and we're going to make some changes." Sonny stopped talking and stared over Vinny's shoulder.

A waiter appeared and asked if Vinny would like a drink. He ordered and Sonny waved the man away, scowling at him. The poor waiter scurried away, realizing he had interrupted the wrong person.

"Vinny, you tell all your people to get lost and stay out of my way or I'll bury every one of them. Do you understand? I want my own people in place, not some scum you picked up off the street," Sonny told him. "I also don't appreciate you transporting drugs like some fuckin' mule. You are too good for that and that is not the way I raised you. You broke the rules, Vinny. Don't do it again."

Vinny sat there and listened. He was pissed off at his father. Vinny knew he could not do anything against his father. His father was the law in the Family. He just nodded his head. The waiter appeared with his drink and vanished when he saw the scowls on the faces of the two men.

Sonny leaned forward and pointed his finger at his son, "If I find out you disobeyed my orders again, I'll kill you myself!"

Vinny could not believe what he was hearing. His father had just threatened to kill him. Vinny took a deep swallow of his drink and looked down at the table. When he raised his head, he nodded in agreement.

"Can I keep Frankie for my bodyguard? I trust him to watch my back," he asked.

Sonny nodded, "Sure, but not until I have him checked out."

"No problem," Vinny said.

Sonny pulled out his cell phone and dialed the police chief downtown. He was one of Sonny's old neighborhood friends. Sonny always said the man owed him, but would never say why. He muttered a few obligatory words and then asked him to check on Frankie.

"We'll know something in a few hours, until then; tell him to take a hike. We'll use my car and men."

Vinny nodded, he knew he had better not push it. His father would not stand for it and would not hesitate to berate him in front of the entire restaurant.

The two men finished their drinks and Sonny motioned the frightened waiter over. He shoved a hundred dollar bill in his vest pocket and told him he had done a good job today and that he would not forget him. The waiter went away smiling. Vinny thought it was ironic how Sonny treated some people one way and others he controlled with a steel fist.

CHAPTER 17
A WAR AND A BUST

* * * *

SONNY AND VINNY WENT TO MANHATTAN to check on the clothes they had for sale at one of the flea markets down around Aqueduct. These were top designer clothes, and Sonny's men would load extra merchandise on their trucks when the freight came in. When they left the dock, they would go to a pre-planned destination to meet a couple of sellers. The sellers would unload the merchandise and take it to the flea markets that populated the area. This went on every day with around twenty-five top design merchants and shippers. If the merchants did not agree to the terms offered to them, Sonny's men would hijack the trucks and shipments and the merchandiser would get nothing. If they agreed to this arrangement, they would receive some of the sales and it was tax-free. Sonny could arrange it so that designers and merchandisers could not operate their business in the city. A few had ever tried to defy him, and of those that did, he had made them offers, their life or their merchandise. In a way, it was cheaper for them to let Sonny take some of their stuff, they could write it off and make money, and Sonny could make money. Overall, it worked for everyone involved and no one was killed.

Everything was going smooth at the docks and at the market so Sonny had his driver take them downtown to meet Miguel, the bookmaker. Miguel had worked for Sonny for over 25 years and these visits were mostly one friend visiting another rather than checking up on him. Miguel was in Sonny's crew. Sonny never worried about him. Business was good and Sonny was happy.

As they left Miguel's, Vinny looked at his father and said, "I told you, everything's fine."

Sonny just shook his head, "So far. But we'll see."

The cell phone rang and it was Detective Calloway, one of the police chief's main men and another friend of Sonny's. Sonny listened for a few seconds then pushed the off button. "You can keep your bodyguard, Vincenzo. He checked out."

Vinny breathed a sigh of relief, he was glad, because he had other plans for Frankie. Vinny wanted Frankie to run his business for him without his father's knowledge. He had started an empire of his own and he was not going to let his father destroy that. He had worked too hard over the past months putting it together.

They made their way home in silence. Finally, Sonny turned to him and said, "We have to talk about this Tony Pinto hit. The Family is not happy about the way it was done." Apparently, no one cared about Tony because everybody knew he was an asshole anyway, but the Family did not like the public scene with all those witnesses.

Sonny said, "I took care of it this time. Just do not let it happen again. They will demand you come in front of them to explain your actions. That could be a bad thing. Come and talk to me if you ever get into a situation like that. And learn to hold your temper or it will get you killed one day."

Vinny said, "Sure, no problem. Thanks for looking out for me, Dad. It will not happen again."

Sonny shrugged, "You're my son. What else could I do? See that it doesn't happen again."

Vinny looked out the window. What else could he do? Hours before Sonny had threatened to kill him if he messed up again. He was acting like the protective parent. Vinny would never figure him out.

Once they were home, Vinny went to his room and called a meeting of all his people over at the Backstreets Bar and Grille for that evening.

He arrived early and ordered a drink. At the set time, they all walked through the door and headed for his table in the corner of the bar. He waited for them to settle in and get drinks before he started talking.

"Henry and Lori, you two need to keep it cool. Sonny is giving me shit about starting my own business. I want you to conduct business as usual, just keep it low key. For the high price girls, make sure you know the client. I do not want new ones they might be working for my father. If one of the girls wants to do it then let her make sure she collects and there is no contact between you and the john. You report to Frankie until I tell you to do differently. He will handle everything."

He turned to Tommy and Louie, "When you're taking bets, be careful. My father has many friends and he can easily find out if you are working for me. If you are not sure about the person, do not take his bet. " They both nodded. Everyone at the table looked grim. They knew their livelihoods and maybe their lives were on the line.

They sat and talked for a bit and in time, everybody left except Henry. "Vinny, I met a guy in Jersey who has one million dollars worth of phony travelers' checks, hundreds and fifties. It is a good deal and the phonies are as good as he had seen. It's quality merchandise," Henry told him.

"Okay, buy twenty thousand dollars worth. If they work out, we will buy the rest. I'll have Frankie get you the twenty grand to start with."

"Great, I will have them tomorrow. I'll call Frankie when the deal is done." Henry stood and waved a hand at Vinny as he left the restaurant.

Later that evening when he arrived home, his father was waiting up for him. He motioned him over as he came through the door, "We need to have a talk, Vinny. There's been trouble."

"What's going on, Dad? Are you okay?" Vinny asked him. His father looked bad, his eyes had dark circles under them and his brows knitted over his eyes in worry.

"Yeah, I'm fine. There is going to be bloodshed soon. Things are going to get rough. There's going to be a war with another boss." Sonny was sitting on the couch with his elbows propped on his knees, Vinny sat beside him and leaned back on a cushion.

"Why?" he asked.

"Because of greed and jealousy, nothing else," Sonny said. He ran a hand over his face and stood. He began to pace around the room, occasionally straightening an already straight picture or flicking an invisible piece of dust from a lampshade.

"My people in Florida informed me that the Ringman, Anthony Perconti, out in California is upset because I control everything. He thinks I should step down. Let someone else take over." He turned to Vinny. There was fire in his eyes and Vinny had never before seen his father this angry.

"What are you going to do?" Vinny asked.

"Nothing! I'll wait to see if he makes a move." Sonny spit out. "If the bastard thinks he can take me, let him try. I'll wipe him off the fucking map."

Sonny's anger was at a peak. Vinny realized then that if someone makes a move against his father they would be signing their own death warrant. It also made him realize that he should be extra cautious about what he was doing on the side. If he fucked up, he had no doubt that his father would bury him just as he had promised.

"What can I do?" Vinny asked him.

"You can be my son and not give me grief until this is over. If he decides to come after me, I will need all the help and men I can get to stop this before it gets started. I will need you beside me to help with this. And when it's over, your place in the Family will be assured," Sonny said. "Do you understand, Vinny? No fuck ups right now. Just keep your head down and duck when I tell you to."

"Sure Dad, you know I'll be with you. And I won't do anything without your approval," Vinny promised. He felt like a liar and a cheat, but right now he realized he had to hold on to what he had and keep his mouth shut.

"Go to bed, Vincenzo. It is late. If that fool decides to start a war, you won't have many more quiet nights to sleep." Sonny waved him away and Vinny got up and left. In his room, he undressed and thought of what his father had said. He figured he would lie there all night and worry but exhaustion took over and he was asleep before his head hit the pillow.

The alarm went off the next morning at six. Vinny rolled over and slapped it off, then lay on his back with an arm thrown over his eyes to block the sunlight peeking through the drawn curtains. He could hear his father moving about and the smell of fresh coffee permeated his fogged mind. He rolled out of bed and grabbed a pair of jeans and a polo shirt, and slipped them on. He padded barefoot into the bathroom and readied himself for the day. Grabbing his socks and shoes, he headed for the kitchen. His father was sitting at the table reading the Times with a cup of coffee and a plate of fruit on the table in front of him. He looked up as Vinny entered and gestured to the coffee pot, "Have something to wake you up, Vinny. What is on your agenda for today?"

Vinny poured a cup of coffee and went to sit opposite his father. He grabbed an apple from the basket on the table and bit into it before answering. "I need to check on a few things with one of the bookmakers, he had some problems a couple weeks ago and I need to make sure he got it straightened out. Then I am not sure. Maybe go downtown. Hang out for a while at one of the clubs. Why?"

"No reason. I just wanted to know what you were up to. I have been out of touch with you for a while. When was the last time you took a day off from this?" Sonny asked.

Vinny shrugged. He could not remember when he had a day just to himself. "I don't know, but I'll take a day off soon. I could use one."

The two men sat and talked about the weather, sports and everything but business. For a while at least, Vinny felt at ease with his father. They were just two men bullshitting about the world and complaining about the politics in Washington. He finally left the apartment when his father announced he had some calls to make. He left him finishing his breakfast and told him he would see him later in the day. When he left the building, he found Frankie out front, leaning against the door of a sleek, black stretch limo.

Vinny raised his eyebrows and looked at Frankie. "What's this? My birthday is not for a few months. Or am I paying you so much that you can afford a new car?" He laughed.

Frankie grinned at him and said, "Just get in, Vinny, and shut the fuck up. Can't I do something nice once in awhile."

He opened the door for Vinny and stood there smiling. Vinny raised his hands in surrender and laughed at him, "Well, if you are looking for a raise forget it. You take enough of my money as it is."

Frankie put on a hurt expression, "Would I do that to you? Just get in the car Vinny, please."

Vinny bent down and stuck his head in the car to find Debbie inside with Henry and Lori. He quickly slid into the seat beside Debbie and wrapped his arms around her, hugging her to him. Frankie looked in the car and grinned.

"How did you find Debbie?" Vinny asked him as he pulled away and looked at Frankie.

Frankie said, "I went back to check on her after I dropped you home. She was just leaving for home so I gave her a lift. She told me how much she liked you and what she thought of you. Therefore, I kept in touch with her to make sure she was okay and just in case you might want to know how she was."

"I was going to ask you to find her," he told Frankie, "But, I never expected this." He turned and greeted the others, then slipped an arm around Debbie and snuggled her close.

"We wanted to take you out because you've been good to us. You treated us fair. And in this business that's not what we expected," Henry said.

"Thank you," Vinny said. "You guys are my friends. How else should I treat you? So, where are we going?"

"We're heading for Atlantic City to gamble away our ill-gotten gains," said Frankie.

Vinny laughed and said, "Well, I guess that's what you can call them. And we may as well enjoy them!"

Henry reached under the seat he was on and handed him $50,000 worth of travelers' checks.

"What's this, spending money?" Vinny asked.

"It's part of those ill-gotten gains of yours." Henry laughed.

"Well, then, we might as well enjoy them. Let's go to Atlantic City!"

It was fun. They gambled in just about every casino and the phony traveler's checks never raised an eyebrow from one of the cashiers. They watched shows, ate lobster, and drank champagne. Vinny had the time of his life. As Vinny looked around at his friends, he thought that the life he had was not so bad.

On the way home Vinny thanked everybody and said that he would always be there. "As long as we stay loyal and honest there is nothing we can't do." He did not know if Debbie understood because she was not part of the crew he had built, but the others knew what he meant.

Debbie leaned over to tell him she wanted him to make love to her. He looked at her and kissed her on the cheek, "I'd like nothing better. However, I am having dinner with my father as soon as we get back. I somewhat owe him this—he has been away for awhile. I'll call you tomorrow."

Disappointed, she laid one hand on his cheek and said, "I understand. I'll wait for you to call."

Vinny turned his head, kissed the palm of her hand, and snuggled her close to him. He felt glad that she was not pouting and demanding like some of the women he had known. Her warmth next to him made him feel comfortable and he wished he could stay with her, but he knew he had other obligations that night and he did not want to disappoint his father.

After they dropped him at home, his father announced he was too tired to have dinner, and told Vinny to call his grandmother, Gina. She was expecting him to come over to see her. Disappointed, Vinny arranged dinner with Gina and spent a pleasant evening with her. They talked of the old times, when Vinny was young and none of the troubles had existed. He left her late in the evening with a promise to return soon and took himself home to bed.

When he lay down for the night, his mind was calm for the first time in a long while. He had a wonderful day with his friends and a great night with his grandmother. For the first night in a long time, he slept without the dreams of chaos that had been his life lately. All too soon, morning came and the chaos returned, only this time it was no longer just in his dreams. The war his father had predicted with Anthony Perconti had begun.

Vinny awoke to his father's raised voice and the shouting of strangers. He threw on some clothes and went into the living room to find his father and three other men arguing. It did not take long to figure out that they were some of Sonny's under bosses, the men he trusted to run his businesses. Vinny stood in the hallway, unseen by them, and listened as they described the deaths of five of their men to Sonny. This was not something fairy tales came from, it was the horror of every nightmare Vinny had ever had. During the last twenty-four hours, five of Sonny's soldiers were executed and there bodies were left in plain view. Anthony

Perconti was leaving a warning that the war had begun. Sonny's men wanted to know what he was going to do about it.

Sonny was red in the face and breathing heavily. Vinny thought that he was ready to have a fit of some sort until he realized that Sonny was suffering from nothing more than intense anger and frustration.

"He started this war, and I'll finish it." Sonny shouted. "I'll be damned if some two-bit son-of-a-bitch is going to go around killing my people and get away with it." The three men nodded in agreement. "Go home. I will call a meeting for later for everyone. I need to figure this out. And figure out how to bury Perconti," Sonny told them. The three filed out the door and Sonny turned to find Vinny standing in the hallway staring after them.

"Vincenzo, we need to talk." Sonny motioned him over to the couch opposite him and then started to pace up and down the room. "The Ringman has started a war. I warned you this could happen. It's going to get worse and I want you to watch what you do." He pointed a finger. "I want you to stay home as much as possible. Do not trust anyone and keep your guard up. This is no game, Vincenzo, no game. Ringman is out to destroy my family and I will not let that happen. Do you understand?"

Vinny nodded his head. He knew that shit was going to hit the fan. His father was out for blood and nothing was going to get in his way. He wanted Anthony Perconti dead.

"What can I do, Dad?" he asked.

"Nothing! Do you understand? You do nothing. Keep your head down and stay away from this, stay home and listen to me or you'll end up dead." Sonny's face was a mask of anger as he faced Vinny. However, there was also a veil of worry there. Vinny knew his father loved him in his own way and did not want anything to happen to him.

"What are you going to do?" Vinny asked.

His father looked down at him and just stared for a few seconds. "I'm going to bury him, Vinny. Bury him so deep no one will ever find his body."

Sonny came over and stood in front of Vinny, looking down at him. His face was a mask of anger and hatred, something Vinny had never seen before. "I'm warning you, Vinny, this is going to get dirty and rough. It's no game. No fuck ups from you, do you understand me?"

Vinny looked up at his father and nodded. He knew this was a warning, one he had better heed or he would end up dead by either Ringman's killers or by his own father. Sonny would not tolerate screw-ups from him or anyone else as long as there was war in the Family. This was going to be a rough time for everyone and the less noise he made about it the better off he would be. Nevertheless, he had a business, and knew he would have to be alert from now on, if he wanted to continue making money.

Afterward, when Sonny had gone out for the day, Vinny called a meeting and explained to his gang what was going on. He was still going to stay active and try to control everything, but he told them they might have to be ready to take over if it got too hot on the streets for him. Everyone agreed that they could handle it, and Vinny went home satisfied that his business would not suffer as long as he kept cool and kept his head on straight. War or no war, he had a business to run.

Several months passed, and things got worse. There were dead bodies turning up everywhere. Ringman was trying to get rid of his father's Family. He would execute one of Sonny's men, and Sonny would have some of his killed. It was not pretty to see two bosses fighting over money and power, but they did. In time, the murders escalated to the point where Vinny had to stop going out to communicate with his crew. He used his cell phone to keep track of everyone, but knew there were things he should be doing himself. Vinny told his father that staying home was like being in a prison.

His father just shook his head and said, "You'd better pray you never have to go to prison. I know guys who spent years of their life there, and it's a hellhole."

Vinny just blew it off. After all, how bad could it really be? He was tough enough to handle anything and figured he would never go to jail because he was the son of Sonny Denucci. That name made Vinny feel powerful. He did continue to heed his father's advice about going out. The killings were still going on and Vinny had no wish to wind up dead because of his father's war.

The next few days he spent at home so he could be with his father, but Sonny did not pay much attention to him. Men that Vinny had never met came and went at all hours of the day and night. Sonny spent most of the time talking with them in the den behind a closed door. A week passed and over breakfast one morning, a haggard-looking Sonny announced that the war was over.

"When? How?" Vinny asked him.

"Let's just say Ringman is buried deeper than the Devil himself. No one will challenge me again." Sonny looked tired and beat down. Vinny knew he had not slept a lot the last few weeks, and Sonny's years were beginning to show. Vinny breathed a sigh of relief. He was chafing at his confinement and needed to get out and see what was going on with his gang.

"I still need you to lay low for a couple days though," Sonny told him. "There is still a little clean up work to do. It should be fine to go out again by the day after tomorrow. Just keep one eye on your back. Ringman's crew had a long arm and many loyal soldiers. Revenge runs deep."

"Not a problem, Dad. It'll just feel good to get out of the house and back to normal again." Vinny bided his time and waited another two days until Sonny came and told him it was safe. He called Frankie and asked how things were and to let him know he was back on the job.

He said, "Okay, but I haven't been able to find Henry."

Vinny began to have a bad feeling, "Maybe he's in Florida."

Frankie said, "You're probably right. I'll try again."

"Yeah, do that. Give me a call when you find something out."

Vinny went out to make the rounds and check on a few things then back home at the end of the day to have dinner with his father. He was just settling into bed around 1:00 a.m. when the phone rang.

"Vinny, is that you?" he heard a shaky voice on the other end of the line. It did not sound like anyone he knew.

"Yes, who is this?"

"Me, Henry."

"Henry, do you know what time it is? Where the fuck have you been?" Vinny yelled.

"Busy, I'm sorry, but I need four pounds of cheese right now and Tommy won't go get it for me." Cheese was another code name for cocaine. Henry needed four kilos of coke.

"Henry, can't it wait until tomorrow? I have had a hell of a day and I wanted to get some sleep."

"No, the guy said if you get it for him, he'll pay an extra $10,000." Henry was insistent.

Vinny sighed, "Henry, remember what happened last time you called me?"

"I know, but this time is different."

"Are you 100% sure?"

"I swear, Vinny. It's cool."

"Why do these people like to do business at crazy fuckin' hours?" Vinny moaned.

"They're drug dealers. They have no brains to think, only to make money."

Therefore, he thought, an extra $10,000. "Okay, I'll call Tommy."

"Why don't you come out and meet this guy?" Henry asked. "He is going to be a good customer."

"Henry, you know I don't meet anybody, especially after last time," Vinny reminded him.

"Just one more time Vinny," Henry begged. "I know the guy real well. He's not all fucked up as some of them are. I'm going to be there with you this time," he added.

"No fuckin' way." he said. "I'll send Tommy with you.

"Okay" Henry said, "But I think you're making a mistake this time. This guy is a big player and he might be our ticket to the big league."

"Henry tell me the truth. Are you scared?"

"Shit! Yes, I am! Vinny, that's why I want you to come," Henry confessed.

"Then why are you giving me some bullshit?" Vinny said

"Because I didn't know if you would come."

"Well, next time just spit out what you want me to hear."

"Does this mean you'll come?" Henry's voice brightened. He knew he had talked Vinny into it.

"Yeah, I'll come. I'll be there in about 30 minutes. And Henry, if this is bullshit you get to go to heaven, you hear me."

"Loud and clear," Henry said.

He rang Frankie to get the car and then called Tommy. He told him to bring four pounds of cheese to the drugstore on 33rd Street and Astoria Boulevard and he explained that Henry was there waiting.

Frankie dropped him off to meet Henry and pulled up a little to wait around the corner, but in sight of Vinny. Tommy arrived shortly after. Vinny started laughing when he saw him. He was wearing shorts and the brightest Hawaiian print shirt Vinny had ever seen.

"Nice duds, Tommy. So who's your tailor?" Vinny asked.

Tommy just grinned and held up his middle finger to Vinny. It could be as low as twenty degrees and Tommy always dressed as if it was summer. The weather could never be as bad as his lousy taste in clothes! Henry just stood there as Tommy walked up. Vinny kept thinking he looked nervous, but he put it down to just jitters at doing a deal. The four men walked into the mouth of the alleyway and Henry finally introduced them to a person named Bob. He was a tall person with long hair and a thin face. He was acting nervous like this was his first deal, but Vinny figured he had been sampling too much of what he sold.

"Let's get this over with," he said, handing Henry a briefcase and an envelope. "Here are the hundred grand we agreed on and the extra $10,000 for early delivery."

Henry opened the briefcase and checked the stacks of cash. "I hope you enjoy it. I am looking forward to doing business. Tommy, give him his stuff."

Tommy handed him a duffel bag containing four kilos of cocaine. Bob took the bag and dropped it on the ground. He jerked out a pocketknife and poked a small hole in one of the kilos. Pulling out a small amount on the end of the knife, he dropped the powder in a vial of liquid he pulled out of a pocket. The clear liquid quickly turned blue. He nodded up at Henry and said thanks. He stood up and shook hands with each of them and said good-bye. He made a beeline around the corner of the building and walked quickly up the street, running a hand over the top of his head and pushing his hair back.

Henry still looked a little nervous as he watched Bob walk away, but Vinny knew he used to snort. Vinny turned and started to walk out of the alley when a bright beam of light hit him in the eyes. The whole street lit up and men with blue jackets were shouting, "FBI, FBI, don't move!"

Vinny froze and felt Tommy and Henry bump into him from behind. Six federal agents rushed them and threw them on the ground. They stuck a shotgun to the back of his neck and two agents held guns pointed at his head. Vinny lay there in shock, his face pressed into the dirt of the alleyway. He could smell gas, oil, and the filth of garbage. His senses went numb and he could not believe what was happening.

A voice above him said, "We've got you, Denucci! You're going to jail for a long time." He felt a punch to the back of his head that bounced his cheek and nose painfully on the pavement. He turned his head in time to see a booted foot aim for his ribs. They kicked him as he lay there on the ground. One of the agents put a booted foot between his shoulder blades to keep him down when he tried to roll away from the pain.

He started shouting, "Stop! I am not resisting you! What about my rights?"

Someone said, "You have no fuckin' rights, Denucci! So shut up. You're a murderer and a drug dealer." However, the kicks stopped.

Vinny froze when he heard that. Jesus, he thought, Where in the hell did they find out? How?

He tried to move his head around to see where Henry and Frankie were, but the boot pressed harder on his back and he knew if he tried to move the kicking would start again. He could see Tommy lying on the street in front of him; a shotgun pressed into his back as an agent pulled his hands around behind him and cuffed him. Tommy was bleeding from his nose and mouth where one of the agents had kicked him. Vinny felt his arms jerked behind him and fire shot down from his shoulders as they twisted his arms and hands. He felt the cold steel clamp around each wrist and they roughly pulled him to his feet by his arm, making him wince in pain. They put him in a patrol car and he could see the others being shoved into other cars that were blocking the street. He sat in the back seat with his shoulders and arms aching. His ribs felt broken in at least two places and it hurt every time he breathed.

A federal agent slid into the front passenger seat and turned to him, "Where do you get your drugs from?"

"I'm not answering anything until I speak to my lawyer," Vinny retorted.

The agent turned quickly and backhanded Vinny in the mouth, snapping his head to the right. He could taste blood and when he turned back to the agent, he spat at his face. The agent backhanded him again, harder, knocking him into the squad car door. Vinny jerked himself upright and started to lunge forward over the seat. He met the end of a gun barrel pointed at his head.

"Try it, Denucci. I would love to have a reason to blow your fucking head off," the agent hissed.

Vinny leaned back and glared at the agent. He knew he was not lying—they would blow him away for kicks if they thought they could get away with it. A uniformed officer got into the driver's seat and looked from the agent to the gun with questioning eyes. The agent gave him a dirty look and said, "Just get us the fuck out of here and back to the station." The officer grinned slyly and started the car, pulling in behind several plain black sedans that had already taken the lead. Vinny turned and looked behind him. Three more squad cars were following his with their lights flashing and sirens blaring. In the background, he could hear the F.B.I agent reading him his rights. He answered automatically that he understood, but the flashing lights and the unaccustomed incident of the moment mesmerized his mind... he wanted to say that he truly did not believe this was happening. However, the taste of blood in his mouth, the pain in his arms and ribs was all too real.

The news media was swarming the police station when the cars pulled out up front. The camera flashes were going off as quickly as fireworks on the 4th of July. The F.B.I. agents pulled him out of the car and led him up the steps and into the precinct. They put him in a cell alone where he waited to see what would happen. He half expected his father to come walking around the corner any moment and tell him he was going home. After all, he was Sonny Denucci's son and no one messed with him. But Sonny never appeared—only two uniformed officers came to his cell. They took off Vinny's handcuffs, and escorted him into a room. An officer walked over to Vinny and brought him to a table where they started fingerprints. Vinny then had a photo taken with a number on it. They led him into a room where they told him to strip. They took away his clothes, watch, necklace and all other belongings and made him sign a piece of paper saying they were his. Another officer came in and made him bend over and spread his ass checks for a body cavity search. They even checked in his mouth and under his testicles to see if he had drugs or weapons hidden anywhere. A guard tossed him a pair of dungarees, a blue work shirt, and a pair of deck shoes with no laces. They told him to get dressed and to wait until someone came to get him. No one smiled; no one spoke. Vinny tried to ask to use the bathroom but one look from a guard when he tried to speak and he decided it was not worth it.

A few minutes after he finished dressing, two federal agents came in and escorted him into a twelve by twelve room with a table and four chairs inside. A tape recorder sat on the table, there was a manila folder lying next to it with a bunch of numbers stenciled on the tab. They motioned him toward a chair. One of the agents pushed a button on the recorder and sat down opposite Vinny. The other agent paced the room behind him.

"State your name, please," the agent said.

Vinny looked at the recorder and back to the agent, "Vincenzo Denucci."

"Have you been informed of your rights, Mr. Denucci?" the agent asked.

"Yes."

"Do you understand those rights, Mr. Denucci?"

"Yes." Vinny stated.

"Good. This is FBI Agent Mark Harris, interview with Vincenzo Denucci. Witness, Agent James Ransom."

Harris folded his hands on the table in front of him and hesitated for a moment. He looked up at Vinny —there was anger and hate in his eyes.

"Vinny, we know you are dealing cocaine. We proved that tonight. What we want to know is about the murder you committed."

Vinny looked him in the eye—he could tell Harris was holding his anger in check.

"What murder? I never murdered anyone in my life." Vinny told him.

Harris' eyes flared with anger, "Two years ago, Denucci. A man was executed, murdered in cold blood by you."

"I never killed anyone. It wasn't me." Vinny said. He knew he had to remain cool. How had they found out? he thought to himself.

"We found this man tied to a chair in the East River. I think you know him." Harris said. He pulled a photograph of a man from the folder and slid it across the table to Vinny. What was left of the man's face was slightly bloated, a pasty-white color. He was still recognizable, but most of the top of his head had disappeared. His eyes were open and staring, bulging from his time spent in the water. Vinny stared at the picture and thought he was going to throw up.

"The coroner said this man had been dead for two days when he was found, which would put his execution, by coincidence, on the day of your 21st birthday." Harris said, slapping down a paper that looked like a coroner's report.

Vinny pulled his eyes away from the picture "I was with my father at my uncle's house in Long Island celebrating my birthday. I have never seen this man before. I don't know what you're talking about."

The detective said, "I think you do."

"I don't know him," he said.

"Well," the agent said, "His name was Joseph Loizzi. This is your mother's brother."

CHAPTER 18
CORRUPTION IN THE COURT

* * * *

HE SAT UP ALL NIGHT thinking how he put himself in this fuckin' eight-foot-by-eight-foot cell. It stunk of urine. There was a gray stainless steal bench attached to the wall and names burnt on the ceiling with a lighter. It was cold and damp and he felt like a caged animal. His freedom was gone and he felt like he didn't exist. He heard a guard call out his name and looked up. The uniformed officer tossed shackles through the bars and said, "Put these around your ankles and step back from the door." Vinny pulled himself off the bunk and shuffled over to where the shackles had landed. Every muscle in his body hurt and he moved like a man four times his age. He held a hand to his ribs where he had been kicked the night before. He knew they were not broken, but they hurt like hell. He bent down and fumbled with the unfamiliar shackles until he secured them on each ankle, then stepped back from the cell door. He stumbled from the restrictions of the chain that held his ankles together but managed to maintain his footing.

The officer waited until he was several feet away then opened the door and said, "Turn around, place your hands on top of your head and interlock your fingers." Vinny did what he was told. The officer pulled each arm down one at a time and handcuffed his wrists. Taking him by the arm, he escorted him down a short hallway and into the courtroom.

Vinny turned to ask the officer a question, but the officer told Vinny not to talk. He sat in a chair at the front of the courtroom at a table. He turned to look around the room—seated in the last row was the F.B.I. that had backhanded him in the squad car. Beside him sat a man Vinny didn't recognize, the two seemed deep in conversation. They must have felt Vinny's eyes on them because both looked up at him. The F.B.I. agent grinned slyly and said something to his companion. The other man was a young, nervous-looking type with dirty-blonde hair and pale skin. He nodded and rose, shaking Agent Harris' hand and grabbed a briefcase before he turned and exited the courtroom, throwing Vinny a glance as the door shut.

Across the aisle from Vinny sat a fat, balding man in his early sixties. Vinny recognized him from the times he had seen his picture in the newspaper as District Attorney Jack Calvin. Calvin smiled slickly at Vinny then stood and strutted around the table to talk to someone sitting behind him. He was arrogant and cocky, and looked ridiculous in an outdated gray suit that stretched across his paunchy stomach. He wore a loud red, blue, and green tie that almost made you dizzy when you looked at it. He knew enough about law to know that his attitude could be injurious to the case with the jurors, and he knew when to look and act the hotshot lawyer and when not to. Vinny knew he was a sly, smart prosecutor that could play a jury over to his side. He had a cut-throat attitude once he got you on the witness stand and was pulling himself up the political ladder one case at a time. He was clearly letting everyone know from the beginning that he was certain of his ability to handle this case, which would be a big political feather in his hat if he pulled it off right.

Vinny watched him talk to several other people and waited for about ten minutes until the door behind the bench opened. Jack Calvin quickly returned to his place behind the table and stood there solemnly with his hands folded over his stomach. A uniformed bailiff entered and said, "All rise. Honorable Judge Marsha Revitz presiding. Case Number 201-65-85. Government vs. Vincenzo Denucci."

The judge seemed preoccupied, shuffling papers around on her desk as she sat down, as if she was looking for something. Judge Revitz was a middle-aged woman who spoke with a slightly sarcastic snarl. She was dull as dishwater except for her fingernails, which were long and painted a loud red-orange. She had a strong sense of her power in the courtroom and used those fingernails as a pointer when she talked to people.

Vinny rose and stood there in his shackles and jail garb, listening to the opening ritual of his case in shock. He never expected to be on this side of the courtroom. He numbly listened to each question the judge asked.

"Mr. Denucci, this is an arraignment court. We are not here to pass sentence or judgment. Do you understand that?"

"Yes, Your Honor, I know."

"You are being charged with the following: possession of cocaine, which is a first degree felony and conspiracy to distribute cocaine, which is also a first degree felony. Each of these charges carries a maximum sentence of fifteen years to life in prison. Do you understand these charges?"

"Yes, you're Honor. I understand the charges," Vinny answered. He felt his heart skip a beat and sink.

"In addition, Mr. Denucci, you are under investigation for a possible connection with organized crime and for allegedly murdering Mr. Joe Loizzi. You are also under investigation for loan sharking and illegal sports betting, which are first degree felonies." She looked up from the papers in front of her and sighed.

"How do you plea to the charges of possession of cocaine and conspiracy to distribute cocaine?" She stared at him with no emotion showing on her face. Vinny was in shock and stood there silently. He could not think past the possibility of doing fifteen years. He noticed her gaze was on him and realized she was waiting for an answer.

"Not guilty!" he said abruptly but clearly.

The district attorney immediately stood up and cleared his throat. "Your Honor, we ask that bail be set at one million dollars. The prosecution believes there is a high risk of the defendant fleeing the country."

Judge Revitz nodded her head and verified the bail amount. Jack Calvin looked smug and quickly gathered up his paperwork and shoved it into his briefcase under the table. He turned and exited the courtroom followed closely by Agent Harris.

"One million dollars," Vinny thought. There was no way Vinny could raise that cash quickly. He felt his heart sink. He would have to rely on his father to bail him out and that was going to be a difficult thing. He still needed to call a lawyer, but now he could not think of one that could arrange bail money. Vinny could think of nothing but how disappointed his mother would be and how deeply embarrassed he was. Even though his mother was gone, he knew she could see him, and that hurt. The other problem he had was his father. He had disgraced and shamed himself and his family. He knew that according to the way his father would see this, Sonny would have no choice but to make an example of him. In other words, he was in deep shit. In addition, the worst part was yet to come. He still had to call his father and tell him he was in jail. He wondered if Sonny would help him or if he would leave him there to teach him a lesson because he had not listened to him. Vinny sat there listening to the bailiff read off the last of the closing information and prayed for this nightmare to be over.

An hour later, after seeing the judge, they had put him in a ten-by-six cell downtown in the Federal Building. He had not called his father when he had the chance to contact someone. He knew of no one that would come to his rescue and he still was not ready to confront his father. He knew if he called his people they would try to help him, but he did not want them involved anymore than they already were. They were his friends and he would not risk having them dragged into this mess.

He was lying on the bunk, trying to get his nerve up to call Sonny, when he heard footsteps stop outside his cell. A guard asked him if he was Vinny Denucci. Vinny sat up and swung his legs over the side of the bed.

"I'm Vinny Denucci."

"I have a message for you," the guard said. "Your father says, 'don't talk to anyone and be patient.' He's trying to put your bail together."

The guard turned and walked away before Vinny could say anything. He lay back down, stunned. How had Sonny found out? He should have figured he would. Sonny had contacts all through the police department, even up to the Commissioner's level. He did not know whether he should be glad or worried that he knew, but he wanted out of jail and he knew his father would arrange that. He sat most of the day waiting for someone to come for him, but no one showed. He had his dinner and he ate and paced the small cell, looking out the cell door and down the hall on each circuit, but there was nothing but the occasional drunk being brought in. Sleep sounded like a good idea to him, but he doubted he could even shut his eyes, his mind was in turmoil and he could barely keep himself from shaking with fear, anger and remorse at his situation. He threw himself on the cold, hard jail bed and rolled on his side. He punched at the poor excuse of a pillow they had given him, trying to gain some measure of comfort. He pulled the blanket over his back. He lay there staring at the wall, wishing for sleep, but terrified that it might bring him nightmares that were worse than his reality. Within minutes though, the emotional and physical exhaustion took their toll and he fell into a deep and dreamless sleep.

It seemed like only moments had passed when he awakened to the sound of a guard shouting to open up cell 131. In seconds, a guard appeared at his cell and said, "Okay, you made bail, let's go." Vinny glanced at the clock on the wall outside his cell and saw that he had been asleep for almost five hours. He was surprised that so much time had passed. The relief he felt flood through him at the thought of getting out of the hellhole he was in gave him an adrenalin burst and he shook off the last of his sleep and scrambled out of bed, almost sprinting to the cell door. The guard tossed in another pair of shackles and Vinny went through the same routine as he had when taken to the courtroom. As he shuffled down the hall with the guard at his side, he thought of nothing but sleeping in his own bed that night. Even the fear of facing Sonny was pushed aside at the thought of going home. Besides, he knew that once he got him out, his father would make sure he did not have to go back in.

Downstairs, they took off the shackles and cuffs and he signed out for his belongings. So far he had not seen anyone he knew that would have come to bail him out, but when he returned from changing into his own clothes he saw his father's lawyer, Max Delaney, waiting at the exit. Max was a sharp lawyer and had been handling his father's legal needs for years. He was tall and thin and took exceptional pride in his dress and the way he presented himself in court. When Max walked into a courtroom he had an uplifting charm about him that everyone liked. Vinny had watched him defend his father on several occasions. He had never lost, so he knew he could count on him.

Max smiled as Vinny walked up and shook his hand.

"Are you okay, Vinny?" Max asked.

"Yes. I'm fine. Tired and hungry and needing my own bed, but I'm oka," Vinny told him. "Did my father call you?"

Max nodded, "Your father's pretty upset right now, but he loves you. Hurry up and go home." Max escorted him outside and flagged a cab. He held open the door and as Vinny got in he said, "Get some rest and call me tomorrow so we can talk about the case."

Vinny nodded and said, "Thanks for everything, Max. I'll call first thing in the morning." The cabby looked at him in the mirror and asked him where he wanted to go.

"215 York Avenue. Take the long way." He was in no hurry to get home now that he was out; he had to think about what he was going to say to his father. He wondered what had happened to Frankie, Tommy and Henry. Were they in custody still or did they make bail somehow?

He leaned forward and told the cabby to pull over at a pay phone. He agreed, but said that he would have to keep the meter running.

"No problem. Just pull over when you see a phone," he said.

A few blocks up the cabby found a phone and pulled over to let Vinny out. He pulled some change from his pocket and he dialed Henry's house. The phone rang and rang. Then he tried Frankie's place. No answer there either. He figured they must still be in jail. He dialed Tommy's house to make sure they were not over there and Tommy's wife, Lorraine, answered.

"Hello, Lorraine. This is Vinny. Is Tommy there?"

"No!" she said. "He's still in jail. Did you just get out?"

"Yeah, is there anything I can do for you?"

Lorraine started crying. "Vinny, I know he's going to be in there for a long time. He doesn't have a father like yours to help him."

"Lorraine, please don't cry," he said. "I give you my word. I'll do everything I can to help him. I'll ask my father what's best to do."

"Thank you, Vinny," she said softly before he hung up.

Hearing Lorraine cry made him realize how stupid and careless he had been. It was his fault that all his boys were in jail. He got back in the cab feeling terrible.

They pulled up in front of the house and he paid the cabby. Opening up the front door, he heard voices inside. He barely had time to wonder who else was there before he caught a glimpse of his father's face. He was standing in the middle of the room with his arms crossed. He had a deadly look in his eyes. Vinny could feel his anger and he knew he was in for it.

Sonny spoke slowly but forcefully. "You have totally disgraced the Family and you have put me in an awful fuckin' position, Vincenzo."

The man with Sonny took a few steps toward the door and said "Okay, Sonny. I am leaving. We'll talk later." He ignored Vinny as he walked past him and opened the door. Vinny barely saw him; all he could see was the anger on his father's face. He automatically turned to lock the door as the man went out. He was turning back when he saw a fist fly at his face. He tried to duck but his father hit him squarely on the nose. He could feel the blood start to run down his face and the room sparkled as he saw stars for a few seconds. The force of the hit slammed him against the door. Vinny felt his knees buckle and he fell to the carpet. Sonny lost control and when Vinny tried to roll to the side and stand, he began to kick him repeatedly in the back and the head. The physical abuse of the last couple of days and the blows from his father were causing his back to spasm. The muscles contracted painfully and every time another kick reached him, he lost his breath. He cried out for Sonny to stop, but he just kept kicking. Vinny tried to crawl away from him, but Sonny followed. He was screaming at Vinny, each word punctuated by a sadistic kick to Vinny's back. "You're a loser, a fuckin' punk loser! You are a no good son-of-a-bitch! You have lowlifes for friends. Get rid of them, you little fucker, or I'll bury every one of them." Sonny finished his tirade with one final kick to the middle of Vinny's back, then turned and calmly walked away leaving Vinny in the middle of the hallway floor curled in a fetal position and gasping for air. Vinny could taste his own blood in his mouth and his eyes were squeezed shut against the tears that blurred his vision. He managed to pick his head up from the floor enough to see his father as he went to his room and slammed the door.

He rolled onto his back, but started to choke on the blood that flowed down his throat. He coughed and pain shot through him from one side to the other. He rolled gently back to his side then further over until he was on all fours. He pushed himself upward until he sat back on his heels, his hands reached for the floor, as he had to steady himself when the room began to spin. His mother had been right. There was no way but down in his father's world. Vinny felt dead inside. He finally got the energy up to go to his room and collapse on the bed fully clothed. He felt cold inside and out and pulled part of the blanket over him. He lay there shaking and trying to forget the past two days until finally exhaustion overtook him and he fell asleep.

Somewhere in that space between waking and dreaming, he heard his phone ringing. Rolling over, he painfully reached for the receiver to hear Debbie's anxious voice on the other end.

"Vinny! Oh, god, are you okay? You're all over the news!"

"What?" he was confused, still half asleep and not understanding what she was saying? Last night seemed unreal.

"Put the TV on! Channel 5," she said.

He turned on the TV and there he was, looking like a criminal. The anchor's voice continued, "The son of Sonny Denucci was arrested last night. Vinny Denucci, a high-ranking pre-law student, dropped out of law school to work for his father. The charges against him are possession and conspiracy to distribute cocaine. He is also under investigation for his connection with organized crime and the unsolved murder of a man found in the East River." Vinny sat on the end of the bed, shaking his head. This was all a bad dream.

He was clutching his right side of his ribs. His body ached all over. He just wanted to curl up and pretend none of this ever happened. He still held the phone to his ear. He could hear the TV on the other end and his own, and all he could think was that it sounded like stereo.

"Vinny?" Debbie said. "Are you still there?"

"Yeah, I'm here." Vinny sighed, "Just wondering what the hell is going on with my life, is all."

"Can I come over to see you? I would like to help." Debbie said.

He sighed. "I know you would, but I don't think this a good time, Debbie. Please call me later, okay?" Vinny said.

"Yes I will my love and remember that I love you." Debbie hung up the phone gently.

He was numb. He thought that nothing else could surprise him but here was a girl who does not even know him, hears terrible things about him on the TV and she says she loves him. He laid the phone back in the cradle. He was tired and disillusioned and hurt, but something inside him was still alive enough to like what she had said.

He heard a tap on the door and his father walked in.

"Are you okay?" he said.

"Fine," Vinny lied, not looking at him.

"About last night, Vinny, I'm sorry I did that to you. I was just so angry I was carried away. But you don't realize what you've done to me, to my reputation in the Family."

Vinny finally looked up at him. He tried to rise but the injuries of the past two days caused him to sink back onto the bed in pain. He was breathing heavily, trying to block out the aches and pains that threatened him. Between clenched teeth, he spit out at his father, "Dad, is this about you or about me? You fucked up my life! How can you stand there and tell me what I have done to you. Look what you have done to me! You know I never wanted this fuckin' shit. All I ever wanted was to become a lawyer and you stopped me. This isn't about your reputation."

"Vinny, let me explain something to you. I am still your father no matter what you think and I'm going to help you and my people will help you and you will repay the favor."

"You don't give a shit, do you Dad? You don't understand. I could care less about your organization or what you have to prove. What I do care about is if I have a father that loves me as his son and not as an extension of himself, someone to do your dirty work. Prove to me that you have a heart, if you can. I don't know. Maybe it's too late. I needed you, Dad, and you just wanted to make me like you, a hard and cold son-of-a-bitch." He felt guilty and sad about his uncle Joe, his mother's brother. He had killed him to earn his father's respect. He wanted to confront him, but the timing was not right. Would there ever be the right time, he thought. He turned away and laid down, rolling onto his side and pulling the covers over him again. He could feel his sore ribs pulling, his back was a mass of pain, and his jaw and nose hurt. He felt dead inside. "Get out of my room. I hate you. And I hate your precious organization."

Sonny sighed and when he spoke, again his voice was low, but hard, "Get dressed. We have to go see Max at eleven. Breakfast is on the stove."

Sonny left the room, closing the door gently behind him. Vinny lay on his bed, staring up at the ceiling. This is unbelievable! My father acts as if I owe HIM a favor for helping me out of the very mess he put me into in the first place. I never wanted this for myself, this terrible life thrust upon me. Vinny vowed immediately that if he got clear of this mess he was going to go straight. He did not want to end up dead on the street, or worse, trapped in his father's world forever.

On the way to Max's office, he did not speak to his father. Sonny was conducting business as usual on his car phone and ignored Vinny. Vinny was amazed. Sonny acted like nothing had happened, as if nothing bothered him. Vinny figured when you choose the life of a made guy you give up real life and real emotions.

They walked into Max's suite of offices and it was as if royalty had arrived. Everybody jumped to wait on Sonny. These people should know he was no fuckin' good, but there they were greeting him and smiling at him like fools. Power, even in its worst form, afforded privileges.

Max came out to greet them and said, "Hello, Sonny. Hi, Vinny, how are you feeling? Gentlemen, please come into my office." He ushered them into his office and closed the door behind them.

Sonny spoke first. "Well, Max, did you find out what happened?"

"Vinny was set up by an informant," Max said. He looked at Vinny. "That friend of yours, Henry, was pulled over about a week ago coming across the George Washington Bridge with ten pounds of marijuana and one million dollars of travelers' checks. The Feds put pressure on him, telling him he would be doing 35 years. So to lighten his sentence, Henry told them that he worked for you and they agreed to set him free on probation if he would set up the meeting where you were busted. He played their game. He set you up."

Vinny was totally still. He did not look at his father. His mind was confused, his heart pounded in his chest and he realized he was breathing hard. He did not want to accept that one of his friends would have set him up. Nevertheless, deep down he knew Max was telling the truth.

"Didn't I warn you?" said Sonny. "You don't trust anybody."

He ignored him, "Max, what about Frankie and Tommy?"

"Frankie's out. They cannot charge him because he was around the corner. He has a good defense so the DA dropped the charges. He saw Frankie as he left and told him you would contact him as soon as you could. Frankly, Tommy is fucked. They have him on a delivery charge. He's going to get fifteen years to life."

"Max isn't there anything you can do for him?" he asked.

"I can't promise you anything, but I'll see what can be worked out," Max said. He looked at his schedule. "Vinny, we have to appear in court at 10:30 Friday morning."

Max looked up. "Sonny, I know the judge real well and she's going to want a whole lot of money."

"How much, do you think?" Sonny asked.

"I don't know yet. I'll have to wait until I go to court and see if that murder charge is going to stick."

"What about the State's attorney?" Sonny asked

"He's easy," Max said, "$50,000 and he'll reduce the sentence."

Vinny sat there and looked back and forth between the two men as they calmly discussed paying off judges and lawyers and a high-ranking state attorney. Then, in his father's world, he figured it was normal. No one was above taking money, not even the people hired to protect the law. It was then that he realized what Max had just said and he felt panic rise in his gut.

"Wait a fuckin' minute!" he interrupted. "What do you mean reduce the sentence? I'm not going to fuckin' jail, no way!" Vinny pointed his finger at Sonny. "You're my father; I thought you're supposed to be the Number One Boss. I thought that meant you could pull some fuckin' strings!"

Sonny got a look on his face that resembled a statue. He stared at Vinny and finally said "You fucked up, Vincenzo, not me. You and those fucking' friends of yours. I will do the best I can and if you get a little jail time, it is because you fucked up and were caught. In this business, at some time or another, we all do time. It's a part of the risk we take and something that we wish we could do without." He shrugged. "But we do what we have to."

Vinny started to say something, but Max cut him off, "Vinny, don't worry. It will not be for long. You will have to do at least 3 years or more, depending on good behavior. You can handle it."

Vinny looked at Max in disbelief. He could not believe what they were telling him. They wanted him to accept going to prison, to lose years of his life behind bars. They must be insane! He could see that his life was one bad decision after another and he knew it could never be fixed. He had no choices. In addition, he realized he had never had a choice, because he was the only son of a mobster boss.

When they finally left Max's office, he and Sonny took the rest of the day off to spend it together. They had lunch and dinner at Vinny's favorite restaurants and sat around the house after talking about politics and nothing. Sonny was attempting to act as if he was the loving father, but Vinny could feel that he was just pretending. Vinny knew he was up to something. Sonny never did anything without a reason.

Vinny slept little on the night before he had to appear in court. On Friday, while they were standing outside the courthouse, waiting on Max, Vinny asked Sonny if he ever went to prison. Sonny stared off down the street as if he had not heard him. Vinny was about to ask again when

Sonny matter-of-factly said that he had to be detained once, but he would not describe it except to say that it was a 'short setback.' This only made Vinny more nervous. Max appeared around the corner and jogged up the sidewalk to them.

"Sorry I'm late. Traffic was a bitch this morning." The three men walked into the courthouse. "Well, Vinny, you ready?"

"Do I have a choice?" Vinny muttered. He was dreading this. He wondered if he would be in jail at this time tomorrow.

When they entered the courtroom, the atmosphere did little to lift his spirits. It was dark and gloomy, lit by weak florescent lights that made everyone appear to have a sickly white pallor to their skin. The first person Vinny saw was Tommy. He was standing off to the side of the room in handcuffs. His face was drawn and haggard and he looked as if he had not slept in days. Vinny could see the worry etched in the lines around his eyes and mouth so he smiled at him to let him know that things were under control. Tommy just stared at Vinny, almost as if he did not recognize him, and then looked away. Vinny saw tears in his eyes, and it hit him that he was responsible for this, that he was the one that had gotten them all involved. Now here was Tommy, paying for Vinny's greed and stupidity.

Judge Revitz entered the courtroom and the talking and shifting stopped. As soon as the ritual introduction was complete, they called Vinny's name. He could feel the blood rush to his head and hear his heart pounding. He thought he would faint, but Max touched his arm to steady him when he saw the look on Vinny's face.

Judge Marsha Revitz spoke, "Mr. Denucci, you are being charged with conspiracy and intent to distribute cocaine, which is a controlled substance. Do you understand these charges?"

"Yes, Your Honor," Vinny said.

Judge Revitz turned toward the prosecutor's bench. "How do the People want to proceed?"

Jack Calvin, the prosecuting attorney for the District Attorney's office, stepped forward and said, "Your Honor, we have a closely connected witness who will testify against Mr. Denucci. We are offering a plea bargain of seven-and-a half years to fifteen maximum."

Vinny tried to swallow, but his mouth was too dry. He was terrified—fifteen years maximum! He tried to say something to Max but could not speak.

Max shook his head at Vinny to wait and stood up. "Your Honor, Mr. Denucci is a good person. This is his first offense. Rather than waste the court's time, can we discuss this in your chambers? It's a matter of urgency for my client."

The judge nodded and took a ten-minute recess. She rose and went through the door behind the bench that led to her chambers. Max, Jack Calvin, and to Vinny's surprise, Sonny, followed her. Vinny sat there staring at the empty bench and wondering what was occurring behind that closed door. After a few minutes, the bailiff came and told him to follow him. The bailiff then escorted Vinny inside the judge's chambers as he halted just past the threshold in amazement. His father, Max, Jack Calving and Judge Revitz were sitting there laughing together as if this whole thing was one big joke. He wondered what could possibly be so fuckin' funny at a time like this. Max stood up and ushered him the rest of the way into the room. He introduced him to Judge Revitz and Jack Calvin. Vinny greeted them quietly as he took a seat beside his father.

Max said, "Vinny, because they have a strong witness, you're going to have to do some time."

"How much time?" he said.

"Two years."

Vinny felt as if his gut had just been ripped into a million pieces. Vinny dropped his head and tears ran down his face. His father looked at him and shook his head in disgust.

Vinny tried to compose himself and asked, "When would I have to go?"

"Well, since the holidays are coming up, we can arrange it to start in January, if that's okay with everyone here?" Max looked around the group.

The judge nodded and Jack Calvin said, "I think we should postpone the case until November. That'll give Mr. Denucci time to arrange things." Jack Calvin looked at Sonny and Sonny nodded to him. His face was grim and he looked as if he would explode any minute. Vinny did not understand this, but he was sure his father would tell him.

Judge Revitz called in the bailiff and arranged to have the case postponed until November 15. As they left the judge's chambers, Vinny overheard Max say to Sonny that there would be time to take care of the payoffs. Then in November, Vinny would plead guilty and begin his sentence. These people had his life all figured out, and although it was hard to believe, he knew he was going to prison.

On the courthouse steps, Vinny turned to thank Max and headed away from his father's car, which had pulled up out front.

"Where are you going?" Sonny demanded.

"None of your fuckin' business," he said.

"Hey, Vincenzo! Don't disrespect me in front of anybody!" he shouted.

"Why?" he asked and glared at him. "Are you going to have me killed? Well, fuck you!" Vinny flagged down a cab and jumped in. If Sonny said anything further, Vinny had not waited to hear it.

Vinny was angry. They were bargaining with his life and his freedom and he would be damned if he would spend what little time he had left under his father's rule. The thought hit him that two years was going to be a long time without a girl. He headed straight for Debbie's apartment, which was a small but cozy rent-controlled haven of bright colored fabrics and healthy plants. He loved her place.

She opened the door at his knock and jumped into his arms. She planted kisses all over his face and hugged him hard. It felt good and he was beginning to believe she might care for him. She led him into the living room and they sat on the couch. Debbie leaned into him and kissed him long and deep, running her hands over his chest and arms.

"Vinny, I thought I wouldn't see you again, not after what I was hearing on the news.."

"I know. I didn't think I would be coming back out either, but they moved my trial to the middle of November. I'm free till then." She snuggled into the nape of his neck and sighed. This feels good, he thought.

"Debbie, what are your parents like?" he asked.

"My parents died in my father's small plane when it crashed about eighteen years ago and I was raised by my mother's sister. I don't remember a whole lot about them. I was only three when it happened. My aunt and I never got along, so when I turned seventeen I moved in with this guy and tried to be a wife, but to him I was a punching bag." Her voice had gone flat, dead. "I don't want to talk about it anymore. It's in the past. I just want us to be together, Vinny." She moved closer, wrapped her arms around him, and held him tight. He hugged back and kissed the top of her head. She seemed so vulnerable curled against him and he felt like he should protect her.

They went upstairs and made love all night. He woke in the middle of the night with Debbie asleep in his arms. Lying next to her he wondered how she truly felt about him, and more important how he truly felt about her. After the last few days, he wasn't sure what he felt about anything. He settled back and closed his eyes but sleep would not come. So he got up and went into the bathroom to splash some warm water on his face and clear his head a bit. He stood there with the towel looking at his reflection in the mirror when he noticed the window behind him that overlooked the roof was partly open. Something did not look right so he looked at the windowsill and lock cautiously. Hmmm…looks like someone has come in this way. A thought flashed through his head that his father might have sent someone to snoop around Debbie's apartment. However, he shrugged it off—there was nothing here that would be of interest to his father, and if it had been a break-in he figured he could ask her about it in the morning. Bolting the window closed he went back to bed and curled up against Debbie's sleeping body. Within a few seconds he fell into a dreamless sleep.

The next morning he asked her, "Debbie, have you been robbed?"

"No, why do you ask?"

"Well, your bathroom window's a little loose. You should keep it shut so that it can't be cracked open all the time," he cautioned. It was better not to mention his suspicions. It would only make her nervous and upset her. He would have some guys come over and secure it before he left for prison.

He sat in her kitchen sipping the tea she had brewed for him and watching her as she made breakfast. She puttered around the kitchen in an oversized t-shirt and bare feet.

"Debbie, tell me something...what do you truly think about me?"

She pushed the pan of eggs off the burner and came to slide her arms around him. She kissed him on the cheek and said, "I love you. I love you because you make me feel good. Because I feel secure and protected when you're around—it's got nothing to do with your father's organization. Even if you were not a wiseguy, I would still love you. You're a wonderful man."

He held her around the waist and pressed his face against her. "Debbie, I have to go to prison for two years. I found out yesterday."

He felt her stiffen and then she started to cry. "Oh, Vinny, I just found you and now you need to go away. I'll miss you so much."

Vinny held her tighter as she continued to cry softly. God, why do the people in my life always get hurt? he thought.

"I'll visit you and I'll write you twice a week." Debbie said through the tears, "And I'll wait for you if you want me to, Vinny. I love you."

He kissed her gently, and then led her from the kitchen and back to bed. They made love throughout the day and into the night. He wanted to show Debbie his true feelings—how he wanted so much to stay with her. For three days, they barely separated. They went on long walks and talked long into the night. They talked about moving in with each other. When Debbie asked him to move in, he agreed without hesitation. His father would be upset but Vinny did not care.

When Vinny finally connected with his father and talked to him about it, he told him that he wanted to be happy and have fun before he had to go away. To his surprise, his father understood, but asked that he check in with him every day, which Vinny agreed to do.

Vinny and Debbie were happy with the time they had together. He asked her to quit her job and he set up a bank account for her that would take care of her even after he was gone. She balked a little, but when he assured her she could go back to work whenever she wanted, she agreed. Sometimes, being the son of a mob boss has its rewards—the company she worked for was one of his father's, but he never told her that.

He was not sure if what he felt for Debbie was love, but it was the closest thing to it. But he kept his feelings to himself. He had all these mixed emotions that he wanted to share, but did not know how to explain them to her. He had to deal with this problem alone. Going away to prison for 2 years is enough to make a man think twice about a commitment to a woman. He was frightened and confused, but this much he knew: his absence would be unfair to her.

Several weeks passed and Vinny and Debbie lived in their fantasy world where nothing else mattered. But things were getting hot. Day after day federal indictments were destroying Sonny's organization. It seemed that once the Feds had one Denucci, they wanted the rest. Max kept busy and Vinny had little time to talk with him about his case. Two days before he had to go to court, Max had him move back into his father's house. How strange to be back in his old room. As he looked around, he realized how much he had learned. He had grown up too fast, missed too much in his life. He held his mother's picture and felt a sadness deep inside because he realized he could not cry anymore. He was numb. He wondered if she would forgive him for killing her brother. He thought she would. However, how could God ever forgive him?

The day of the hearing came too quickly. Vinny found himself standing in front of Judge Revitz again. His name was called and he walked up to the bench with Max. Max asked to speak with her privately in her chambers. Judge Revitz agreed, just as Max had told him she would. Once again, Max, Sonny, Jack Calvin, and Vinny followed her into her chambers and closed the door.

"You're Honor; we have what we agreed on," Sonny said. He opened his briefcase and showed the judge the money. He removed several stacks totaling $100,000 and handed it to her —it disappeared quickly into the folds of her judicial robes. Turning to Jack Calvin, he tossed him $50,000. Calvin grinned and pocketed the cash. Vinny sat there in amazement. They each had such complete confidence in this transaction that he knew that this was nothing new to them. He began to feel like there was no such thing as justice and that the legal system was as corrupt as his father's organization.

They returned to the courtroom and Vinny took his place before the bench once again. Judge Revitz shuffled some papers in front of her and said, "Vincenzo Denucci, after a review of your case with the prosecution and your attorney, Mr. Delaney, I now sentence you to two-and-a-half to seven-and-a-half years in a maximum security prison. You must complete at least two years before you are eligible for parole. Sentence will begin December 1." She banged her gavel.

He looked at Max. "I thought we had agreed that I would start next year, after the holidays."

He shook his head. "Sorry, Vinny. Your father wants it this way."

Vinny turned to his father, "Why, Dad?"

Sonny did not answer. He stared straight ahead with a blank look on his face; his eyes never wavered toward Vinny. Vinny felt his heart stop and skip a beat. Every ounce of energy left his body. He wanted to die right there in the courtroom. His own blood had betrayed him.

CHAPTER 19
PRISON

* * *

IT WAS DECEMBER 1. Vinny stood outside the Federal Building once again, only this time he was entering through the area where they would begin his processing into prison. His Uncle Nunzi and Cousin Robert were there to see him off. Max was there too, to go in with Vinny and be with him during the formalities that would officially make him a prisoner. They stood there quietly. Debbie was leaning on his arm, crying softly.

Nunzi and Robert came up, embraced him, and shook his hand. When Sonny came to him and tried hugging him, Vinny stiffened and stood there like a statue. Sonny dropped his arms to his sides and said, "Vinny, I know this is going to be tough. Be strong and patient, and try not to worry. I've taken care of everything."

Vinny was afraid of what that meant. His father had not taken good care of him so far. He said final good-byes to everyone, but the only person who looked like they cared was Debbie. They clung together and he kissed her gently. She told him she loved him and kept promising she would write as Max pulled him away.

He did not look back as he and Max walked through the main gate. He did not want them to see the tears in his eyes. Two guards escorted him into a room where they fingerprinted him and took his picture. Max stood to the side while Vinny wiped the print ink from his fingers. As a guard came to lead him away, Max put up a hand to halt him and said, "Vinny, your father does care for you. Believe that. What he has done is what he thought was best. You may not believe that but maybe one day you two can come to terms with each other over this."

"I doubt it, Max. He promised I would be home until after the holidays and he screwed me. What am I suppose to think of him?" Vinny asked.

Max sighed. "I understand. However, he has made it as easy for you on the inside as he can. Give him some credit for that. And if you need anything you just call me, I'll arrange it."

Vinny stared at Max for a few seconds, then said "Good bye, Max. Take care of yourself."

The guards cuffed him and put shackles around his ankles. They led him into a holding cell where he would await transport to the Federal Penitentiary. He felt like an animal trapped in a cage. As they slid the door shut, one of the guards said "Nice to have such a celebrity in our little prison."

The other guard barked a laugh as they turned to walk away. "Yeah, crime sure doesn't pay, even when your daddy is the boss."

All Vinny heard was the laughter as the two men disappeared through the barred door at the end of the hallway. He felt like crying again as the final door clanged shut on his freedom.

He turned to look at the others in the holding cell with him. He counted fifteen other prisoners and to him they all looked like maniacs. He was so frightened he thought he was going to break down and cry, but he held back the tears and took a seat on the floor in the corner, the only place left to him. He knew this much about being in jail: if you show weakness you become a target, and tears would set him up with a big bull's eye on his forehead for whoever wanted to take advantage of him.

He sat and studied the other men, trying to figure out what they were thinking about him. If this was typical of the number of guys arrested in one day, it made Vinny suddenly realize just how many people were in the prison system! He knew they had passed four other cells identical with this one, and each was full of prisoners. He could not imagine living like this, but he knew until his parole, this was his life, jammed into an overcrowded room with a bunch of convicts.

Vinny sat there staring at his feet and feeling sorry for himself. Another pair of prison sneakers entered his view and he looked up to see a light-skinned black man staring down at him. "Hey, you got a cigarette?"

Vinny glanced at him and looked away. "No, I don't smoke."

He said, "Okay, that's cool. Uh, my name is Derek. What's yours?"

Vinny looked back up at Derek who was huge—built solid with well defined biceps and cords of muscle that strained at his shirt. About six foot two. Vinny figured around 240 pounds. Solid muscle. He grinned down at Vinny, exposing several gold teeth in his mouth. Vinny was not sure if he should be frightened of this guy. He just prayed the guy did not like him "too" much.

"Vinny."

"Is this your first bid?" Derek asked.

"What are you talking about?" Vinny asked, not understanding.

"I was right," Derek said. "Prison sentences are called bids. You don't look like you done time before."

"No," he said. "This is my first time."

"How long did you get?"

"Two years."

"I got fifteen years," Derek said. He just stared down at Vinny.

Vinny shifted uncomfortably on the floor and suddenly got frightened. Why was this man talking to me? Is he going to cause trouble for me? The last thing he wanted was to piss this guy off, so Vinny just sat there and listened to him talk. Derek rambled on about this being his second time in and was starting to say something else when he heard someone call his name.

"Talk with you later, Vinny." Derek said as he turned and walked away. Vinny slumped against the wall with relief. He realized he had been holding his breath.

A guard came over to the cell and called out Vinny's name. When he raised his arm to signal the guard, he was waved over to the bars. Vinny leveraged himself off the floor and saw a short, stocky-looking man with a crew cut at the bars. He wore a prison guard uniform and carried a clipboard in one hand.

"Vinny Denucci, I'm Danny," he said. "I'm a good friend of someone who knows your father. They have arranged it so that I can look after you while you're in prison." Danny explained. "So if you need anything, just ask and I'll take care of it." Danny kept his head down and his voice low. Every so often, he glanced at the clipboard as if he were checking something cautiously.

"Thanks, Danny." Vinny said. "Who is this good friend you know that is so concerned with my welfare?"

"No one you would know. They just want to make your stay a little easier, is all," Danny said. "Let's just leave it at that. It's better for us."

Vinny nodded and Danny walked away, peering in each holding cell as he passed until he exited the hallway. Vinny moved back to his corner and leaned up against the wall. It seems I have someone watching out for me, he thought. I wonder what else my father has arranged.

Derek walked back over. "You Vinny Denucci?" he said. "Are you connected to Sonny Denucci, the Mafia boss?"

"Yeah," he said. "He's my father."

"Well, I'll be damned! I read about you in the newspaper." Vinny looked at Derek with surprise. He could not believe this person could read, let alone keep up with what was in the newspaper. He reached out, grabbed Vinny's shoulder, and pulled him away from the wall. He turned around to the other prisoners and shouted, "Hey, listen up; this is Vinny Denucci, Sonny Denucci's kid. We got the Mafia boss's son doing time with us. So you all treat him nice." A few of the others made welcoming noises, but most just waved a hand or stared. Vinny felt slightly embarrassed by Derek, but he could tell Derek's word carried some weight with the others.

"If you need anything, you just let me know!" Derek said. For some reason, Vinny felt like he was back in high school when Henry approached him and he wanted to be his friend.

"Can I ask why? You don't even know me." Vinny was suprised.

"Your father helped out some people I know." Derek replied. "Most of us 'hoods have always been straight with the Italian boys."

Vinny nodded. He knew his father dealt with the black gangs on equal footing and respected their territory. Besides, the black gangs did not have the same type of businesses as the Italians, so there was never a real reason for war between them.

Vinny shook Derek's hand and said, "No problem. I could use a friend in here. How long do we have to sit here?"

"Could be one hour or it could be ten hours—it's all up to the guards." Derek shrugged. "In here they just take their time. It is not as if we have an appointment to keep. We have plenty of time."

Plenty of time...sure! Two years of time! He felt a tear start to well up and he quickly turned his head away and wiped it from his eye. What would these guys think of him if they saw the son of a powerful Mafia boss crying? He took a couple of deep breaths and felt a little better.

He turned back to Derek, who was staring down at his tennis shoes as if they held all the answers to the questions of the world. "If you don't mind me asking, what you are in here for?" Vinny asked.

Derek raised his head and grinned, "I killed my ex-girlfriend's boyfriend. When you live in a neighborhood like the one I grew up in, you only have one rule, survival. Sometimes you come across a nigger who wants everything you have, even your woman and your family. Therefore, you do what you have to do. I took him out of the game and now everybody knows I'm a bad motherfucker that takes care of his business."

Vinny stared at him as he explained. Derek stood there with no remorse. He seemed almost proud of what he had done.

"Derek, why would you give up your freedom over a girl?"

"When I was on the outside I was robbing people to stay alive, you know, taking down quick shops and tourists. It took care of me and it took care of my family. Living in hotels, condemned houses on the block, you know. My woman left me for a guy who had more money and she took everything I had with her, including my son. I had no family and no woman. So I killed the guy and took my money and my son. When they caught me, the Welfare people took him to a foster home. He is a cute kid and a family who can take care of him is adopting him. I take care of what is mine. She took off. Do not know where she is. Do not care. At least in here, I have a roof over my head and I get three square meals a day. do No pussy, but I can take care of myself if you know what I mean." He wiggled his fingers and laughed. "There are plenty of *Playboy* magazines around. In here, I have people to talk to. I get reports from the family that took my boy—he is doing much better. He won't grow up in the 'hood like I did, he's got a chance."

He looked at Derek and felt sorry for him. What a life to choose. However, in a way he admired him. He did what he had to do for his son, at least. It was more than Sonny did for him.

About that time, the guards started serving lunch. Each cell received a paper bag with a sandwich.

Thick-sliced bologna with cheese on white bread, an apple and cup of watered-down Kool-Aid. He couldn't stomach it so he gave it to Derek. Derek happily took the food and downed it with muffled thanks. Vinny asked the guard that delivered the food when they would move to better facilities.

The guard looked at him and grinned, "Better facilities? Right. Don't worry; you aren't going to your new home until some time late tonight."

The guard walked away laughing and Vinny could not figure out what was so funny about what he had said. He just shrugged and figured he would grab a few hours sleep, so he retreated to his corner and curled up on the floor.

The next thing he knew he felt someone kick his feet to wake him. "Get up, everyone! On your feet!" he heard. He jumped up and started shaking. In his sleepy confusion, he could not remember where he was. He stood there shaking and looking around nervously like a rabbit.

All a sudden a familiar face came into view. Danny, the guard he had met earlier, grabbed him by the arm and said, "Vinny! Vinny, its okay. C'mon, snap out of it. It's time to go." Danny reached around, grabbed his wrist, and handcuffed him to five other prisoners. "Sorry, Vinny. We must do this. It won't be for long," Danny murmured.

The guards escorted the prisoners outside and into a waiting bus. The bus windows had metal grates over them so the prisoners could see out but no one could see in. Vinny asked Danny what the time was.

"It's 8:30 p.m. and we got a bit of a ride ahead of us." Danny told him. Vinny felt totally disoriented. The bus driver yelled back that it would be two hours to Otisville Federal Prison, their new home. Vinny took a window seat and watched the world slowly disappear before his eyes. Nothing was familiar, the roads narrowed and wound through desolate countryside. The houses gave way to trees and grey sky. Vinny felt he was off to a distant planet where all communication with the world has stopped. This is surely the bus ride to hell!

They drove for almost two hours when he finally saw the sign that read 'Welcome to Otisville'. As they rounded a corner and approached the entrance, he could see it was surrounded with a twenty-foot high chain link and barbed wire fence. The first gate the bus stopped at was a regular sliding gate that groaned and rattled as it pulled back. The second gate was a solid partition, almost like a wall, and two stories high. A loud siren went off as the second gate slid slowly to the left on a hidden track. Once inside he could see the prison. It was a plain cement building painted beige and looked like a huge cement block with six floors of tiny little windows. Home for at least the next two years....

When they got off the bus, a guard shouted, "No fuckin' talking! Follow the yellow line. When you enter the building, look for the cell marked 'A'. Go inside and take off all your clothes. When you finish, wait for your name to be called and go into the next cell marked' "B'. Just to let you know, inmates, you will all have a physical and be taking a shower. Orange jump suits will be your attire in this facility. You also will be getting supplies for your cell. Then psychological testing and guidance to every one of you to help you adapt to the prison system. This process will take about three hours so don't plan on getting sleep."

Who could sleep? He could not see the main jail but what he did see scared the hell out of him. Derek walked over and asked how he was doing. Vinny told him he was hanging in there. Derek nodded and walked off. Vinny stared after Derek—why did Derek seem so interested in him? He couldn't figure it out.

The prisoner standing next to him leaned over and whispered, "Derek's okay. When guys are hit with heavy sentences they feel lonely so they try to get as many friends as they can to make their time go easier. If he comes on strong just let him know that he has a friend." Vinny nodded. It made sense. Besides, Derek did not seem as tough as he wanted everyone to believe he was.

All inmates in Cell A stripped off their clothes. Guards stood at either end of the room and hurried them through to Cell B where they all showered and dried off. With towels wrapped around their waists, they were ushered out of the shower into the next room. Each man was handed an orange one-piece jumpsuit with numbers on the back and the left front pocket. He wondered if this was what soldiers in boot camp felt like.

The inmates dressed and then were ordered to stand behind a red line painted on the floor where they would wait for their name to be called for their psychological evaluation. Three other inmates were ahead of Vinny. He felt like everybody was staring at him as he walked into Cell C to see the shrink. Her name was Mrs. Carmen. An overweight Latino woman in a blue jumpsuit and a white lab coat, she was mellow and seemed to like her job.

Mrs. Carmen shook Vinny's hand and said, "Vinny, I know this is your first time here so let me explain some things to make it easier for you. Go ahead and sit down." She pointed to a chair on the opposite side of her desk. Vinny sat and nervously folded his hands in his lap. "The first thing to understand is you have to put yourself in another frame of mind. Be patient. Things do not move as fast here as they do in the outside world. The second thing to remember is that you are incarcerated because you committed a crime. The third thing is that if you have a problem, you can come and see me."

Vinny stared at her. "Okay, I will. It sounds easy enough."

Mrs. Carmen smiled at him, "Not as easy as you think. This is a prison, and inside these walls, strange things happen to the mind. Some men are sent here for the rest of their life. Some, like you, are here for a few years. However, none of them want to be here and they are all a tough bunch. Do you understand?"

Vinny nodded. He understood. She was warning him to watch his back. Something he intended on doing.

She stood up and shook his hand again. Vinny then went to another cell where he had a physical and took a TB test. He could not believe how well the prison system worked. Although it reminded him of a conveyor belt for humans, they seemed to have the process down to a smooth efficiency.

It was 2:00am when the processing of the inmates finished. The guard escorted each inmate to a cell. Vinny walked slowly to his cell. It was unbelievably small, only six feet by eight feet. A toilet was in the corner and above it was a small sink with a button in the center. A bed that folded down from the wall was made of steel. He stood just inside the door in shock. The closet in his room at home seemed larger than this cell. There was no way he was going to stay sane in a place this size.

He heard a guard yell out "Lock up Cell 21!" and the door slid across and slammed shut with a sound like a gunshot. He jumped and turned to stare at the door. The lock connected and turned. The noise the door made sounded like a death rattle of a dying man. He never felt so cut off from the world. He wanted to grab the bars and scream as loud as he could even though he knew it would not have done any good. He climbed up into the top bunk. The mattress was about three inches thick and the pillow was as flat as a folded towel. The blanket was just big enough to cover his body but he was still cold. He began to cry silently and his body shook from the sobs he tried to hold inside. His stomach ached from tension and fear. Sleep finally came from exhaustion.

The next thing he knew it was morning, 5:00 am, and the guards rousted out the prisoners and ushered them to breakfast in the Mess Hall. They all stood groggily in line holding a tray like the ones they used at school. They were served watery oatmeal, hot tea, white bread and runny eggs. He stared at that slop numbly as he shuffled behind the next prisoner. At the end of the line, a guard handed each inmate a plastic spoon. They all sat at long tables that reminded Vinny of the college tables he used to sit behind in his lecture classes, except here, no one talked and no one moved, and there was no professor clearing his throat to give a lecture to a room full of students. No one ate until the guard gave the okay. The inmates had ten minutes to shove food down without choking on the sour taste of the eggs and the flat tea. They dumped the empty trays and filed over to a barrel where they dropped the spoons under the watchful eye of a guard.

Vinny saw Derek a few feet ahead of him and caught up to him.

"Hey, Derek, Can I ask a question?"

"Sure. What's up?" Derek said.

"Why do they watch the spoons?" Vinny asked.

Derek looked down at Vinny and grinned, "They got to. These cons in here will take the spoons back to their cells and make knives out of them. They use them to protect and kill. You be cool and keep your eyes open Vinny." Derek warned. "If anyone threatens you, you tell me, I'll see to it they don't mess with you." Vinny replied, "Okay, and thanks for looking out for me."

Vinny gave him a quizzical look before the guards separated them and sent them back to their cells. He still could not figure out Derek. Derek did not seem like the type to kill someone, and he without doubt was on the lookout for Vinny.

An hour or so after breakfast, Vinny was laying on his bunk when his cell opened to let in a scared Hispanic kid who looked like he was about sixteen. Vinny had himself a roommate.

Vinny jumped out of his bunk to greet the kid, but when his feet hit the ground, the kid jumped like a scared rabbit. Vinny tried to introduce himself, but the kid just stood and looked at him blankly.

"Hey, kid, don't worry, things aren't that bad," Vinny said.

The kid was scared. You could tell by looking in his eyes that he looked like he was ready to cry.

"This is my first time here. My name's Louie," he finally said.

"Well, the bottom bunk's yours—make yourself at home."

Vinny climbed back into his bunk and watched as Louie slowly walked over to the bottom bunk and laid his stuff on it. He looked like he had never seen anything like it before, and from the way he looked Vinny thought he was in shock. Finally, the kid lay down and Vinny heard his breathing become ragged. Louie was crying. Vinny tried to ignore it, but all he wanted to do was to go home and he had not even been there a full day yet. At last, the sound abated and Vinny knew Louie had fallen asleep.

As the day went on, the prison noise got louder and louder. Everybody was up and talking. Around 12:30, all the cells started to open up. Vinny jumped off his bunk and woke up Louie.

Louie stood up. "What's happening?" he asked. His eyes were wide and Vinny could see the kid was scared to death.

"It's okay. I think we're going to lunch." Vinny walked outside their cell and looked around. Inmates were everywhere.

Louie stayed back near the bunks and said, "Vinny is everything okay out there? I'm scared."

Vinny was, too, but he wanted to make Louie feel better so he turned to him and said, "Hey, Louie, I said its okay. I think there are many scared people in here. However, we are here so let us make the best of it. I think we both need a friend and since we're stuck together, I guess you're stuck with me." He still looked terrified. "Don't worry; I will look out after you."

"Thanks," he said. He seemed to relax a bit, and came over to the door and looked out. "I need a big brother."

Vinny grinned at him and asked Louie why he was there.

Louie leaned against the cell door and put his head down. "Me and some friends were hanging out on the corner when we saw an old man and we decided to rob him. Before we knew what was happening, Carlos, one of the guys, pulled a gun and shot him. They ran but I stayed there looking down at the old man and the cops came. I tried to explain, but they handcuffed me and charged me with first-degree murder. My public defender told him to plead guilty and he would get a good plea bargain for me but the judge gave me twelve years. So here I am."

"I'm sorry for you," Vinny said.

"Thanks. What got you here?" Louie asked. Vinny told him that he was set up. He told him that his father arranged a plea deal and that the judge only gave him two years. "That stinks," Louie said. At least you had a good lawyer. I think mine just wanted to get the case over with and didn't care what happened to me." There were tears in Louie's eyes again.

Vinny changed the subject—this kid was close to breaking, "So enough talking. Let's go and eat some lunch."

They lined up at the yellow line again and filed into the Mess Hall. Everybody looked angry as hell, as if they all wanted to kill somebody. For some reason they looked at Vinny like they hated him. He wondered what he had done, but then looked around and thought that maybe it was for the reason that he was white. He was not sure. The prison looked like it was about 80% black, 10% Latino and 10% white.

A guard shouted the lunch menu, Chicken, mashed potatoes, bread and Kool-Aid. Vinny ate a little because he was starving. It wasn't bad, but he just could not bring himself to eat more. Louie ate everything without question, shoveling it in as if it was the first good meal he had had in days. Vinny just shook his head and traded his half-full tray with Louie's empty one. The kid grinned at him and mumbled thanks in between mouthfuls.

After lunch, the inmates were taken outside, where they had basketball courts and weight benches. Some guys were playing handball against the wall. He had seen some giant body-builders at lunch and now he knew how they maintained their muscles. There was not much else to do around here anyway. He looked up and saw guards with rifles in the towers watching over the inmates.

It was good to be outside. The air was fresh and the sky seemed wide open. They stayed outside for about an hour, but it went by too fast. They were filed back inside to a large room they called the day room. It had a big TV, a couple of Ping-Pong tables, a pool table, games like chess and checkers, and many playing cards. He also saw some guys shooting dice. They were using cigarettes for money.

Derek saw him and shouted, "Yo, Vinny! Come over here!"

He walked over to him with Louie tagging along behind. "Hey, Derek what's up?"

"I want to introduce you to some people. This is String; this here's Deuce and the guy with the shades here is Romeo."

String was a tall thin black man with well-defined muscles and callused hands from lifting weights. Vinny figured he must have been doing time for a while when he said he was in for murder. He had his name tattooed on his right shoulder. Deuce was short and fat and you could tell he never worked out. He seemed a little feminine and was always raising his eyebrows for emphasis and he stood hitched to the side, like a woman. Romeo was big and solid. He wore dark glasses to hide his eyes. He was mean looking and said he was doing a life sentence for killing a cop.

"Yeah, they call him Romeo 'cause he's got himself a harem out on the streets," Deuce piped up.

Vinny looked them all over very cautiously, "This is Louie. He's my cell mate," Vinny said. "Are these your real names?"

"No, man," Derek laughed. "They're street names."

"So what do we call you?" String asked. "You got to have a name other than the one your momma gave you. In here, no one goes by their real name."

"No, I never had any other name." Vinny said.

Derek stared at him and screwed his face up in thought, "Well, now you have to have one. I know, how about Rico?"

The others immediately agreed but he asked, "Why Rico?"

"You're Italian, right?" Derek said. "Well, that's short for racketeer."

So that was how Vinny earned his prison name. It was his second day there and he tried to adjust. At least, that is what Derek thought. However, inside he was still scared, afraid he might break down. To many of the guys, prison was the only real home they had. For Derek, he was acting as if he had always been here. Vinny guessed he was right. He was better off here than on the outside—in here he had family and respect.

Vinny and Louie wandered around the day room, but did not participate in anything. Neither was sure what was going on. Later, Vinny met one of the guards who's name was Lt. Braverman and asked him to explain what goes on and what else there is to do.

Lt. Braverman looked at Vinny and then at Louie who was trying hard to hide behind Vinny. He had seen new guys come and go, and these two were about as new as they come. Braverman was a six-foot, 250 pound guard who had been working in the prison system for fifteen years and who had seen more cons come and go through the system than he could count, but he could always spot the new ones, the scared ones. He was bald and had a round face that was so innocent that only a mother could love it. He was laid back and easygoing, but far from stupid. He had seen every trick a con could pull and then some. Nevertheless, deep down he was a softy and when he saw guys like this, scared, alone, first-timers, he tried to help. Vinny was glad to have spoken to him first.

He said, "At 5 a.m. you eat breakfast. Then you go back to your cell until about 12:30, when you go eat lunch. After lunch, you get to go outside for about an hour and get some exercise. Then you come inside the day room until dinner. After dinner, you get to watch TV in here until about 10 p.m. Then you go back in lock-up. It is simple and very boring. Just follow orders and you will be fine. Pretend this is boot camp in the Marines."

"So that's it? Just follow orders?" Louie piped up.

We have school for those of you that want it and workshop and church and a library. You can use the phone to make calls but you have to walk a straight line to get these privileges. You have to earn points." Braverman told them.

"What're points?" Louie asked.

"If you don't get into fights and you keep your cell clean and you don't get smart assed with the guards, you earn points. You can turn in your points for privileges. By the way, we are called C.O.'s."

"What?"

"Correction Officer. C.O. is for short. So use that term from now on, okay?"

"No problem. And thanks," Vinny told him. "This might not be so bad if we watch what we do," he told Louie as they walked away.

"Yeah maybe Vinny, But I still don't want to be here." Louie muttered.

"Hey, call me Rico," he said. Louie looked at him. "The brothers named me Rico, so I guess I should use it. As soon as I think of a name for you, I will tell you. Oh, wait, I have one... how about Kid?

"I like it," said Louie with a grin. "I'm only eighteen, so I guess I'm still a kid to most of the guys in here."

It was getting late and they heard some inmates talking about dinner and making bets on what they were going to have. He could not even guess. A fight broke out over where some of the inmates were playing dice and it looked like the two guys were going to kill each other. The C.O.'s rushed over and broke it up. One C.O. said to take the fighters to the Hole.

"What's the Hole?" he asked a brother standing near him.

"Solitary confinement," he said. "Pray you never end up there. It isn't any Club Med."

"No shit," Vinny thought.

Dinner ended up to be hamburgers and French fries, tea and applesauce. Somewhere along the chow line he heard laughter and saw cigarettes flying through the air at one of the inmates, the winner of the 'Guess the dinner' contest he figured. By this time Vinny was so hungry he ate everything on his tray and wished he had more. When they finished they went back to the day room to watch TV. He sat and read a

Reader's Digest. It was almost time for lock-up and he started to get nervous. How would he handle being in the cell again?

Eventually, the guards turned the TV off and the inmates were lined up and taken back to their cells. He stood there staring around the tiny cell. He thought he was going to throw up. He felt so far away from home and he could not imagine 729 more days of this. He kept thinking that he was going to have a heart attack and the C.O.'s would just let him die. A thought raced through his head that they probably could not get him to a hospital in time. He started to panic.

Louie was watching him from his bunk and asked, "Vinny, are you okay?"

He said, "Like I told you, many people are scared in here. I am, too."

He heard a C.O. shout "Lock up 21!" He put his hands over his ears, but he could still hear that awful clang and grind as the cell door shut and locked. That noise seemed to echo through his entire body. He did not know how he was going to get used to that door slamming like that every night for two years.

He climbed up into his bunk and let the tears fall silently until he fell asleep.

The next morning when he woke up, he saw a box of stuff outside his cell. He jumped down and yelled for the C.O. to open 21.

A C.O. walked up and said, "Hey, Vinny, I'm Sgt. Roberts. Your father says hello and sent some things for you." Sgt. Roberts was a real redneck. He was tall, thin and had a southern accent. He could have used a tan—he was too white even for a white man.

Vinny thanked him, took the box in, and sat down on the edge of Louie's bed. Louie sat up and looked with interest at the box.

"What's in there?" he asked.

"I don't know. My father sent it in." He opened the box up and inside there were pens and writing paper, soap and toothpaste, brushes, shirts and underwear, chocolate chip cookies, fruit juice, a Bible, and a picture of his mother and father. Vinny almost started to cry again when he saw his mother's picture. He took the picture out of the box and put the rest of the things in his locker. He gave Louie some cookies then he got back into bed and stared at the picture until he fell back asleep.

The weeks passed slowly and turned into months. Vinny adjusted to prison life to some extent. It was the same thing day in, day out. The only things that changed were the faces of the inmates. Somebody new was always coming in and somebody was always going out. Every day he would write to Debbie but never got a letter back. He wrote his father, too, but never got anything but the boxes of supplies every few weeks. He even tried to call a couple of times, but he always got the answering machine. He was beginning to feel like he no longer existed.

Vinny kept his record clean and earned some points, so he asked to use the library. He figured if nothing else, he could educate himself; maybe learn all the things he missed when he was not able to go to college. He read a book about a soldier who was afraid to be away from home so he imagined he was at home while his body mechanically continued fighting in the war. Vinny thought that maybe he could do the same thing so every night he practiced. He pretended he was in a beautiful place, happy and free, while his body followed the routine of prison life. After a few days, it started to work, and he did not fight his prison term so much. He did not dwell on the fact that he was caged because he learned it was only his body that was in the cage, not his mind. He guessed he knew what the shrink was trying to tell him that first day.

He studied law books and cases and tried to learn the things he had always wanted about being a lawyer. Some of the guys started to call him Rico the Judge, because he gave them advice about their appeals and what to do as far as the law was concerned.

Being in prison teaches about survival, physical and mental. Prison can be a life or death situation if you get into a beef with someone. You are not just defending your honor; you are defending your life because there is nowhere to go. Inmates who are doing fifteen years to life mess with guys who were doing less than ten because they did not have anything to lose. If a person ratted on somebody, he got a name—Snitch—and everywhere he went the other inmates would find out and they would gang up on him.

Vinny never bothered anyone. Anytime someone wanted to mess with him, Derek or one of his boys would jump in and put a stop to it. It was like the old days when he had bodyguards. It was especially good when he got packages. It seemed Derek and the others had radar where his packages were concerned. They knew sometimes before he did that he had a box coming. He would give the guys cookies or candy, and help them write letters home. It surprised him how many of them did not know how to write and some could barely scribble their name. In exchange, they protected him and made his life a little easier on the inside. The black people hardly ever had family that would send them stuff like Vinny got. He felt sorry for them sometimes.

One day in the day room, a person asked him if he would like to play chess. Vinny told him he did not know how to play, but that he would like to learn. The guy grinned and said he would teach him. His name was Billy Bob and he was about as big a redneck as they come. Vinny started to introduce himself, but Billy Bob cut him off, "Yeah, I know who you are. You're with the Blackbirds."

"Who?" he said.

"You know. Derek. He has a group in here called the Blackbirds. They're a crazy bunch."

Billy Bob not only showed him how to play chess but he started to give Vinny a history of every gang in the prison. By the time they were escorted back to their cells, Vinny had a good idea of the pecking order in the prison. In addition, he knew Derek and his bunch were at the top of it.

The next day in the library, he picked out a book: Chess—Read To Understand The Game. He played every day until he got good. Then he got very good. Billy Bob was amazed at how fast he learned and Vinny told him about the book. He started to play for cigarettes and when he won, he would give them to Derek and the gang because he still did not smoke and they looked out for him. It got to a point when he had almost five cartons of cigarettes in his cell.

In prison, if you had cigarettes you were like a king. You could buy protection, favors, and almost anything else with cigarettes. His father did not send him anything but money. At the Commissary, you could buy paper, candy and cookies, other small stuff, and cigarettes. Inmates got paid $1.25 a day for working and that was put into their commissary account. When you went to the Commissary, you would ask first how much you had on account and then pick out the stuff you wanted. Still, many guys blew through their cigarettes and a fresh supply was as good as money.

He had become popular with the other inmates and they respected him because he was teaching guys to read. He started helping them with their appeal cases since he had planned on going to law school and had been studying the law books from the prison library. He gave advice and told them to push their lawyers, most of which were public defenders. He passed the rest of his time by writing to Debbie even though he never got a letter back and he left a message on his father's machine asking him to contact her for him. He never knew if he did or not.

One afternoon while seated in the library, a guard came over to him and told him he had a couple of visitors. He jumped up quickly, "Who is it?" he asked.

"Just go down to the visitation room," the guard told him. Vinny shot out of the library and hurried down the corridor. He kept hoping it was Debbie. Or even his father. He turned the corner and noticed two men in black suits standing in the visitation room. His heart dropped, the excitement he had been feeling dissipated. Were they here to give him bad news?

As he entered the room they turned. One of the men motioned him to have a seat. He sat down on one side of the table, while they sat on the other side. They looked to be in their forties with salt and pepper hair and looked too clean to be wiseguys.

"Vinny. I am Agent Jones and this is my partner Agent Harris. We are with the F.B.I., Special Investigations Unit.

He was surprised at first, and then answered sarcastically. "What's up?"

"Do you know a man named Henry?" Agent Jones asked.

"Who?" Vinny felt the hair on the back of his neck stand up. These guys wanted something from him.

"There was an informant in your case named Henry. Did you know him?"

"I don't remember," he said firmly.

Agent Harris made a disgusted sound and slid a manila envelope toward him. "Take a look at these pictures,"

Vinny opened it slowly, and slid out two photos. He saw Henry gagged and bound. There was blood all over his clothes. He stuck them back into the envelope. He sat back in the chair and took a deep breath. He felt an awful feeling inside. He looked up at the Agents. "What do you want from me?" he asked.

"We found his body in the trunk of a car with three shots to the head," Agent Jones said.

Vinny was not too surprised at the news, but he said, "So? Why ask me? I've been in prison for a year."

"Well, we think your father called the hit," Agent Harris replied.

"Fuck you," he said, getting up. "Why don't you go and ask him?"

"Hey, we are not here to give you a hard time. We're looking for some answers," Agent Jones responded in a conciliatory tone.

"Well I don't know shit, you guys are barking up the wrong tree. I have to go. This visit is over." Vinny told them. He turned and walked away leaving the two agents staring after him.

He didn't know what to do, so he headed for the chapel and asked to speak to Father Tom. Father Tom was a non-denominational minister and a quiet, scholarly man. Vinny had met him the first week and he was one of the reasons he had not flipped out in prison. He walked into his office, sat down, and started crying. He could not help it, it just happened and he was unable to control it.

"What's the matter, Vinny?" Father Tom asked.

"A friend who betrayed me a while ago was found shot to death in the trunk of a car. I am here because he informed on me. I think my father had him killed!" Vinny said in between the sobs that were wracking his body.

"Vinny, calm down and tell me why do you think that?"

"Because my father is a ruthless killer and he wouldn't hesitate to do that. I know him, Father; he would kill anyone that crossed him. He knew my friend ratted me out. He would have done this to prove a point. I can't tell you now... maybe later, maybe when I am free of this hell hole, but I know my father had someone kill him." Vinny had stopped crying but the tears were still in his eyes.

"I don't know what to tell you Vinny, except that God punishes those who do wrong. You know He will be the one your father has to answer to one day." The priest could see by Vinny's reaction that he was hurting, but nothing that he could do or say would make Vinny feel better.

"I know, Father. There are many things I have to get off my chest and I need to clear my head. But not now father! Not while I am stuck here. I have a frame of mind that I stay in and to change that would cause me to lose my mind in here."

"I understand, Vinny. When you need to talk, I am here for you. God is here for you. When you are ready, come to me and we will talk. Okay?"

Father Tom reached out a hand and squeezed Vinny's shoulder. "Just remember, anything you say to me is held in confidence, and in the word of the Lord. See you in church on Sunday."

Vinny got up and walked out after thanking him. He knew he had not told him anything important, but he still felt better for having expressed himself. From that day on, he swore that he would not miss one Sunday of church. He never did and he became close to Father Tom after that. Father Tom helped to guide him and made his stay in prison a little easier.

Sixteen months had passed and Vinny was happier because he knew that soon this nightmare would be over. One day he was holding out his tray for lunch and he asked Dillon, the head cook, why they never served pasta. Dillon laughed and said that no one knew how to make sauce.

"Well," Vinny said, "how about I give you one carton of smokes and you make me a head cook? I can make dynamite sauce. My mother was a real Italian cook and she taught me everything."

Dillon said, "You got a deal. You can start tomorrow. 4 a.m. sharp. I'll tell the C.O. on your floor and make the arrangements."

"Great!" Vinny said. This would give him something to think about for the next eight months. Moreover, this was a much better job than some guys had. In prison, you could clean bathrooms, do laundry, sweep and other boring work. Cooking—that was reasonably interesting.

The next day he showed up for work and Dillon introduced him to the crew. Like everybody else in this place, they were inmates, too. They said hey or waved their hand as he called out their names: French, Tit, Mickey, Jack and Burn. A scraggly looking bunch, but they seemed to like being there compared to some of the other jobs they could have had.

That morning he made tomato and potato omelets for breakfast and all the inmates went nuts. They were all shouting "Yeah for Rico!" and "It's about time we got a real fuckin' cook!" Dillon was happy, too, because some of the pressure to plan meals was off him. He could leave it up to

Vinny. Even the C.O.'s were impressed. For lunch, he made meatloaf, mashed potatoes and gravy. The gravy tasted like real gravy rather than tan colored water. He had bribed a C.O. to go buy some garlic and parsley and gravy mix. Everybody loved it! He finished the day with spaghetti and meatballs with garlic bread as a replacement for the plain old white bread they normally expected. He'd never seen them eat so slowly and with such enjoyment before. He was a success and it felt great.

Time was going by fast. He was up at 4 a.m. and back in lock-up by 11 p.m. Sleeping in the cell for five hours wasn't that bad and usually he was tired enough to fall asleep immediately. It got to the point where all his stuff was in the kitchen and he spent most of his time in there. Louie was upset that he had practically moved out, but he told him to come by and see him as much as he wanted.

One afternoon while he was playing chess with Derek in the day room, Billy Bob came running in.

"Rico come quick! They've got Louie!"

"What?"

"Ken and Tuna got him in the cell."

Vinny and Derek jumped up and raced down the corridor to the cell. Derek was shouting for his boys to get together and follow him. They raced up the staircase to the second floor cells. They could see a crowd around his cell and he made a quick prayer that everything was okay. All of a sudden, the prison siren went off. Vinny tried to get through the crowd in front of his cell but String and Deuce, who had gotten there first, grabbed him and pushed him back against the wall.

"Rico, it's over," String said. "The Kid's dead."

Vinny looked at him like he did not understand the words. He jerked free and pushed through to the railing in front of his cell. He looked over and saw Louie lying face down on the concrete below.

"What happened?" he asked String.

"Ken and Tuna raped him and Louie ran out and jumped over the railing," String explained.

He looked around and saw Ken and Tuna watching him. They knew Louie was Vinny's friend and had never bothered him before. Vinny felt sick to his stomach. He knew he had left him alone too much, working in the kitchen, but he never thought anything like this would happen to him. He blamed himself for not protecting him better. He started to move toward Ken and Tuna but a firm hand on his arm held him back. He looked around and saw Derek standing beside him.

"Rico, I'll take care of this. Hey, man, you are out of here soon. Don't fuck up now. I am here for a long time. I promise I'll find a way to kill those bastards for you."

"I want them dead, Derek this is my fault this happened...he was just a kid, he couldn't take care of himself. I should have been here," Vinny said.

"It's not your fault. It would have happened eventually. The Kid was a target from the day he walked in here. You couldn't have stopped this," Derek told him. "Just let me and the boys take care of it. Don't blow your chance to get out of here."

Everybody was sent to lock-up to calm down until the C.O.'s could come get Louie. When the cells opened back up, Vinny went to the chapel to say a prayer for Louie and to ask God to forgive Derek for what he was going to do. Vinny never liked to kill but this time it was all he wanted to do. He had spent a lot of effort in here to teach himself to be a better person, but he wanted those guys dead. He knew nothing was going to be the same. He had lost the low-key outlook that enabled him to be content in jail and went back to being anxious and upset again.

The days passed. One month before his release, he got a visitor. He was standing in the kitchen cooking and a C.O. came to tell him to report to the visiting room. He hoped it was not those detectives asking about Henry again. He walked into the room and there was Debbie, looking like the most beautiful woman in the world.

"Debbie!" he shouted! He hugged her so hard that she started crying.

"Vinny, you look great and you put on some weight," she observed. There were tears in her eyes as she looked at him, but the smile never left her face.

"I'm in charge of the kitchen and all I do is eat and then workout every day to burn off all those calories." He grinned down at her. "How are you?"

"I'm okay, I miss you a lot."

"Why didn't you write me?" he asked her.

"I did!" she said. "You didn't write back so I had to come see you."

"I never got your letters. Why didn't you come to see me sooner?"

"Vinny, this might shock you but your father told me if I came to see you he would have me killed. Then they found Henry and I was scared. Finally I couldn't wait any longer, so I came anyway."

Vinny felt his anger rise at his father, but he smiled at Debbie and said, "Don't worry. Friday I am being transferred to Manhattan Correctional Center to finish my sentence. You can come and visit me every day."

"Oh, Vinny, that's wonderful! I promise I'll try to be there every afternoon," she said. She hugged him again and Vinny stroked her hair.

"I am so glad you came. I missed you. When I didn't hear from you I thought you didn't care about me."

"Oh, Vinny," she said. "I missed you, too. I love you so much. I never stopped loving you."

He had just enough time to kiss her before the bell rang to announce that visiting time was up. She pulled away whispering she loved him and was escorted through the visitors door and out of sight. Vinny stood there and stared after her. He could feel the softness of her in his arms still, and the scent of her perfume clung to his clothing. It was the happiest he had been since he first came to this place.

That night they threw Vinny a going-away party. He gave all his cookies and cigarettes to Derek and String. They had gotten close in those two years. He told them that he would write and send money if they needed it. They told him to stay out of trouble and to become the lawyer he wanted to be so he could defend them. They all laughed at that.

That last night in his cell he could not sleep so he lay there thinking about how much his life had changed. He was a better, stronger person because the things he had to learn to survive. The prison system works if you do not fight it and you let it help you. Even though it is not the same world, as on the outside, he knew that a person could come out straightened up if he tried.

The next morning he said good-bye to everybody and started walking toward the door to the outside gate. He was almost there when he heard the prison siren go off. He turned to see Deuce running toward him.

"Rico!" Deuce yelled at him, "Revenge has taken place."

Vinny knew what he meant and when Deuce reached him he thanked him for telling him. Ken and Tuna were in hell and he was glad.

The bus ride was so nice that it was as if he was going home even though he still had thirty days left at the Manhattan Correctional Center. The trees and hills were beautiful. He stared at all the cars and houses the bus passed. He felt like he was going back to Earth after being on a desolate and colorless planet for years. They drove into Manhattan and he thought the skyline was beautiful. The variety of people and things to look at was overwhelming.

At the downtown jail, Vinny had no one to share his cell. It felt lonely but he dealt with it. The food was back to being the tasteless muck of the prison system, but he did not complain. He knew the nightmare was almost over so he just wanted to wait it out.

Danny the guard came over to his cell and said, "Hey, Vinny you remember me?"

"Yeah, I never forget faces." Danny was the guard on duty the night he was arrested.

"How are you?" he asked.

"I made it through if that's what you mean."

"Well, welcome back. I'll see you later," he said. "Ask for me if you need anything."

For the next few weeks, Debbie came to see him twice a week, on Tuesdays and Thursdays. It was wonderful. He kept leaving messages on his father's machine but he would never pick up the phone. He wondered why he never visited him or called him. The days went fast. All Vinny could think about was getting out of this nightmare he had been in for two years. Finally, it was the night before he was to be set free. Vinny could not sleep—his adrenaline was pumping. He thought about the future and about his father. What was he going to do? He prayed to God for the strength not to get involved in the same things that put him behind bars in the first place.

December 1, two years after he went in, the air was cool and it felt refreshing. He was twenty-four years old. This was going to be the best Christmas. He had missed the last two and was looking forward to having some fun. He heard the C.O. shouting to open his cell and he walked out with a huge smile on his face. He walked over to the counter where a guard handed him a brown paper bag. Vinny opened it up. The night he was arrested his personal property had been taken away. It had been stored somewhere in the prison system. Vinny looked at his pinky ring. He looked through his wallet. He pulled out a picture of his mother. He took a deep breath and grinned at the guard holding back the tears. The guard then handed Vinny a check for $365.00 dollars. Danny the guard then escorted him down the hall to the main gate where he was set free.

As Danny shook his hand he said, "Vinny, whether you know it or not, your father kept track of you. I had friends inside, I got reports that I passed on to my contacts. He knew what you went through in there."

Vinny looked at him with surprise. "He never once contacted me, Danny. He never answered any of my phone calls or my letters. How would he know anything?"

"Trust me; he knew everything that went on." Danny said. "Well, good luck Vinny. I hope we meet under different circumstances."

Danny waved a hand as Vinny walked through the gate. When the gate slid shut behind him, this time it sounded like freedom when the lock clicked behind him.

He could see Debbie and his father waiting for him. He was crying as he bent down to kiss the ground. Debbie ran over and hugged him. Then she stood back and his father grabbed him and kissed him.

"I'm sorry, Vinny," he said in spite of everything, Vinny was so happy to see him that he forgot all the things he had done. "You look good, Vincenzo. You've put on some weight."

"Yeah," he said. "I was a cook."

"So I heard," he said, smiling. "Your Uncle Nunzi reserved a hotel for you and Debbie in Atlantic City. Call me in a couple of days." He kissed him again and got into his limo.

He watched his father's limo drive off and shook his head. He did not make sense, but then nothing in the last few years had made sense where Sonny Denucci was concerned. He turned to Debbie, gathered her up in his arms, swung her around, and said, "Baby, I've got to make up for two years. Let's go have some fun. Atlantic City, here we come!"

CHAPTER 20
THE TRUTH ABOUT FAMILY

* * * *

THEY MADE LOVE ALL NIGHT and spent the week between the bedroom and the gambling halls. Vinny had two years to catch up on and he wanted to see it all and do it all. He ran room service ragged with delivering gourmet meals around the clock. He could not get enough food, drink or sex. The week went by too fast and soon it was time to go home. Time to go back to a life he dreaded almost as much as prison. He had made many decisions while he laid in bed watching Debbie sleep. He needed to get his life back on track. When they finally returned to the real world, he knew it would be a different world, one where he was in charge of his future, not his father.

The limo took them home and he dropped Debbie off at her apartment, kissing her good bye and telling her he would call later. When he arrived at home he walked in and shouted for his father, but there was no answer. He checked the house, but quickly realized his father was not home. He walked in to his bedroom and stood in the doorway staring, he had never seen anything look so good. Like some little kid on holiday, he ran and belly-flopped on his bed, bouncing around until he landed on his back staring at the ceiling. God, it was good to be back home. He laid there thinking about all the unanswered questions that he wanted to ask Sonny. He wondered if he would tell him the truth. He thought about what Danny had said when he walked out of the gate, maybe he was wrong, maybe his father cared. He wanted to understand him better, to know why he would send him stuff in prison, yet not answer his calls, why he threatened Debbie then brought her with him and then allowed them go away together for a week. However, most of all, why was he so unfeeling that he would have his only son murder his own uncle?

Vinny thought about Henry, about the pictures the F.B.I. agents had shown him. Even though Henry was the reason Vinny had to go to prison, how could Sonny kill without concern for his victim's family or even for his own soul? He realized that Sonny had always gone to church even if he had casually murdered someone the night before. Did he think about God? On the other hand, was he just a hypocrite, paying mock tribute? He was not too worried that he would die without Last Rites or the Act of Confession and go straight to hell. Maybe he just paid his debt and thought that was enough.

Vinny had had time to think in prison, and he realized that his father was the boss of a self-destructive empire. Why would he want that? It gave him nothing—even the power was an illusion. In the end, Sonny would end up in jail or found dead and no power in the world would help him. Vinny had talked a lot to Derek about his son. Derek had killed to take back what was his, and had made sure his son would not suffer the same fate as he had. "Why couldn't Sonny be the same," Vinny thought. Derek had made sure his son was safe, where Sonny put his family in danger. This brought him to the biggest question on his mind: Why would he put his only child's life in jeopardy?

Vinny had been a normal kid until he was dragged into an unfulfilling life that he never wanted. He had been taught just enough to be dangerously impulsive, but not enough to be just. He went to prison, which restored him to normal but left him with a phobia about being enclosed. He mostly wanted to know why his father had not once visited or written.

He lay in bed feeling depressed, unsure of how he was going to handle the situation. He had made up his mind in prison that he would never go back there again. He could still become the lawyer that he wanted to be. Once you have served your time, you are free to start over and he knew plenty of people who could use his services and would not mind his background. Vinny needed to prove he could be a better person and conduct himself as a man who knew life was precious. Father Tom told him in jail that God forgives everybody no matter what they did. He had renounced his sins and in his heart, he felt that God had forgiven him. It was up to him to show God that he had a good heart and he could be strong. Vinny's faith in God would never let him down. He picked up the prayer book that Father Tom had given him and recited prayers until he fell asleep. That night he dreamed about his mother.

The next morning he woke up refreshed and feeling as if he could face whatever the world was going to give him. He walked into the kitchen and found his father just finishing breakfast.

"Good morning, Dad."

"Good morning, Vinny. It's good to have you home finally." he said, putting down his coffee cup.

Vinny poured a cup of coffee and kept his back to his father, he did not want to face him just yet. "Dad, when you get some time, I would like to sit down with you and talk about some things that I want to get off my chest."

"Fine," he said, "I'll be busy until noon but when I come home, we'll talk."

"Great," Vinny replied.

Sonny rose to leave, then turned and said, "And, Vinny? Call your Grandma. She wants to talk to you."

"Okay, I will," he said, "Have a good day."

He sat down at the table with his coffee and a glass of juice and picked up the paper. The headlines read, Denucci under Investigation. "Mafia Boss Sonny Denucci is under investigation again for racketeering and possible murder charges. Several other crime boss figures in other states are also being sought for questioning."

Vinny shook his head and wondered if Sonny would be able to buy his freedom or if he would have to go to prison. In a way, it was poetic justice. Like father, like son.

He heard his father come out of his bedroom dressed for the day and Vinny shouted out to him, "Are we going out for dinner tonight?"

"No," Sonny shouted back. "We'll order out. And don't forget to call your Grandma Gina."

He heard the door slam and then reached over and picked up the phone. His grandmother's phone rang and rang and he was almost ready to hang up when he heard a weak voice say, "Hello."

"Grandma Gina, it's me, Vincenzo! Can you hear me?" he said. She sounded so frail and old.

"Vincenzo, My grandson, what is the matter with you? You never call me no more. You are a big shot like your father. You forget about your grandma in Queens." Her voice was getting stronger as she went on.

"No, Grandma. It's just that I don't get out much," he replied.

"Well, I should think you wouldn't. Do not think I do not know where you have been the last two years. However, that still is no excuse for you not to call. They have phones in those places," she berated.

Vinny gave a little laugh, "Yes, Grandma, they had phones, and I'm sorry I didn't call. Don't worry, I'm home to stay and I'll call you every day."

"Why don't you come over, visit me before I die?" she said.

"Yes, Grandma, I'll come over tomorrow around noon. We can have lunch." Vinny said.

"Okay, Vincenzo. I will wait for you. I will make you your favorite dish, pasta and peas."

"Great, Grandma. That sounds good. I love you."

He hung up the phone. Tears were in his eyes. His grandmother was the sweetest old woman and he knew he never spent enough time with her. Grandpa passed away ten years ago from a heart attack and she liked to have someone over to cook for, and Vinny was her favorite.

He went to his room and picked up his prayer book. He prayed to God to help his Grandma. He prayed that He would guide him in the right direction, and strengthen him. He also prayed that He would touch a place in his father's heart so that when they talked later he would tell him the truth.

He called Father Tom over at St. Joan of Arc Catholic Church in Jackson Heights, where he worked when he was not at the prison. He was so happy that his heart was soaring. He hummed while the phone rang. The receptionist answered, asked his name and transferred him immediately. Vinny felt honored to be speaking with father Tom.

"Hello, Vinny. How are you, my son?" Father Tom said. He sounded as happy as he felt. It was great to hear from Vinny again. "I was wondering when you were going to call."

"I'm fine, Father. I went on vacation when I got out. I missed talking to you, though. You helped me a lot in prison."

"No, Vinny, you helped yourself. I just showed you the right path and encouraged you to talk to God."

"I pray twice a day Father," he said.

"That's good. Well, Vinny, when are you going to come see me?" Father Tom asked.

"How about tomorrow around 2:00 p.m.?"

"That would be fine," Father Tom said.

"Okay, I'll see you then…Father Tom?"

"Yes Vinny…"

"Thanks for everything. I just wanted to let you know that I'm grateful for your help and support."

"You're most welcome, Vinny. I'll see you tomorrow."

He hung up and went to take a shower. He was already wet and soapy when the phone rang so he couldn't get out of the shower to answer it. A couple minutes later, there was a loud knocking at the door. He had shampoo running into his eyes so he quickly rinsed his hair, wiped his face with a towel, and then wrapped it around him as he walked to the front. He looked through the peephole and saw Debbie raising her hand to knock again.

He opened the door and said, "Hi, babe. I was in the shower."

"I can see that," she said, hugging him tightly. "I'll help you rinse off. But first I wanted to tell you how much I love you and miss you."

"You just saw me yesterday," Vinny said.

"I know. But can't I miss you even after a day?" Debbie's voice started normal, and then dipped into a seductive purr. She ran her hands up and down his arms and shoulders. He could feel the heat from her body as she leaned into him and the chill from the cooling water was quickly becoming an answering heat. He looked down at her and could see the lace outline of her bra through her blouse where she had hugged him to her. He reached out and pulled her toward him, shoving the door closed behind her. He kissed her passionately, unzipping her black leather mini skirt with one hand. She stepped out of it and stood in front of him with her high heels on, a satiny pair of underwear, and her blouse clinging to her. He grabbed her by the hips and pulled her to him, rubbing against her. She moaned and leaned back a little, stroking his neck and shoulders as he reached to unbutton her blouse. The buttons came free and he pushed it off her shoulders and let it drop to the floor. He bent his head toward her and kissed the soft creamy tops of her breasts, burying his face between them and licking the dampness that his wet body had caused. The water had caused her black lace bra and panties to cling to her and outline her hidden shape. Debbie curled one leg around his thighs and wiggled to get closer. The movement sent desire racing up his spine and he struggled to control himself.

He unsnapped her bra and tossed it aside. She leaned back against his arm, inviting him as she thrust her full breasts toward his lips. He kissed one breast hard and then flicked his tongue across it repeatedly, suckling her and drawing her nipple to a point with his teeth. His hand cupped her breast and massaged it until he could feel the heat like a fire in his hands. He kept one arm wrapped around her waist, giving her support as she leaned further back, offering more of herself. He licked his way across one breast to the other one and tugged at it, too. She had become so relaxed and limp that she could not keep her leg around him anymore. As it slid down, he moved his hand from her breast and ran it from the inside of her knee to the edge of her panties. Kissing her deeply, he rubbed his hand between her legs.

He set her on her feet and stood back just a little to look at her. She looked so sensational in high heels and black panties, all the rest of her white, smooth and lush.

Debbie smiled with drowsy eyes when he pulled her to him and pushed down her panties. She leaned her head against his shoulder and panted softly as he touched her gently at first, and then with silky wet insistence. She pushed up at him and began kissing and biting his neck and chest. She grasped his nipple in her mouth and ran her tongue over it, gently sucking and drawing a gasp of pleasure from him. Her hands roamed further down and she tugged at his towel, letting it drop to the floor. She stroked him from shoulder to leg, running her nails in a gentle pattern on his back.

Her hands moved to the front and scratched lightly down his belly to grasp his hardness. His legs almost buckled and she knew it and smiled. She knelt before him and touched the tip of him with her tongue. He felt her warm breath and lips as she kissed it lightly and then closed like liquid fire around him. She ran her tongue around the head and over the bulging vein, flicking and sucking until he thought he would explode. Her hands gently lifted his balls and she ran her tongue around them and under them, sucking one into her mouth before she returned to his member. When she bit him gently on the abdomen, he grabbed her by the shoulders and pulled her up to kiss her, pressing her hips into him.

He picked her up and carried her into the shower. He turned the water on full and pressed her against the back wall. He ran his hands down her back until he lifted her up by the ass and she wrapped her legs around him. She reached up to hold the towel bar and arched as he thrust deep and fast inside her. They cried out with the shock of sensations they felt. In half-formed words, she told him to come with her and he pushed even deeper. She opened her legs wider and slid downward just a little bit to take him all inside, it was more than either could handle and they went over the edge together. He rested against her and the wall for a minute before he unpeeled her legs and set her down.

They stood in the water and held each other and she whispered in his ear that she loved him and for the first time since he had met her told her he loved her too. She smiled and grabbed the soap to wash him. She scrubbed and massaged his body and then washed hers. He thought about what he had said. He knew he loved her in some ways because she cared about him, the real him, but he was not sure he was in love with her.

When they had dried off and were lying together in bed, Debbie looked at him and said, "Can I ask you a personal question?"

"Sure, go ahead."

"Did you ever kill anyone?"

He lay there quietly for a moment. Why would she ask a question like that? "Would you like me less if I did?" he asked her.

"No."

"I never killed anybody," he lied. He felt guilty but he thought it was best and the time was not right for confession. She kept her head on his chest, rubbing her fingers lightly on his leg and did not say anything. He had a feeling she knew he was lying, but it did not matter to her.

He heard his father come home and told Debbie she would have to leave because he had to discuss business with him. As they got dressed, he watched her and for some reason he had a feeling things were going to change with her. He did not know why, but he wanted to be able to remember her, as she looked, fresh and clean and happy with love.

"Vincenzo!"

"Yeah, Dad, I'll be right out! Debbie is over, but she's leaving." Vinny replied.

"Okay, Vincenzo. I'll be on the terrace."

He turned to Debbie, "You got to go, baby. I'm sorry."

She stood on tiptoes and kissed his cheek. "I know, Vinny. I will call later. You better go to your father."

He hugged her and escorted her to the front door. She kissed him good-bye and he watched her until the elevator doors closed on her. Walking toward the terrace, he prayed that God would give him the courage to talk to his father. Sonny looked up when he stepped outside.

"Well, Vinny," he said. "What's on your mind?"

He sat down facing him. "Dad, this is hard for me, but I'll do my best to stay calm." He paused to look at him. Sonny seemed to be listening. "Why didn't you ever visit me while I was in prison? Or call?"

"Vinny, our culture...," he broke off and then started over. "In our Family, we have a rule: If you have to do some time, you take it like a man and do it —alone. I don't like prison so I didn't come to visit you. It's against my standards as a boss. Who the hell has time to write? I spent a lot of time out of town and that's why I wasn't here to accept your phone calls."

"Dad, how can you call those reasons?" Vinny yelled. He started to cry. He knew Sonny was trying to bullshit him and it made him feel like he was just another soldier in his squad. "All I wanted to hear from you was that you cared about me. Don't you care about anyone?"

Sonny sighed and shook his head, "I'm sorry, Vinny. What do you want me to do? It's over and you're home. Put this behind you and we can move on. So many things have changed and I need to prepare you for your position in the Family." The two men stared at each other. Vinny could see his father was getting upset.

Sonny started to talk but Vinny interrupted him. "Dad, I'm not finished talking. Why did you try to keep Debbie from visiting or writing me? Why did you threaten her?"

"Vinny, she's a whore. She's only with you to see what she can get."

"Fuck you. You don't even know her! She cares about me." Vinny yelled.

"Vinny, my boy," he said, with a small smile.

"What?" Vinny snapped.

"Does she fuck well? All whores do it good. I've had a few dozen whores myself," Sonny said.

"Dad, if you call her a whore one more time, I'm going to marry her just to piss you off," he hissed.

Sonny did not say anything but stared at him with those cold dark eyes Vinny had always hated. Sonny did not take well to back talk, even from his only son. Vinny shifted in his seat and changed the subject.

"What happened to Henry? I got a visit from two detectives in prison. They asked me if I knew anything."

"That rat bastard sent you to prison. He got what he deserved." Sonny shrugged.

"Is that the answer to all your fuckin' problems, Dad? If someone gets in your way just kill him or her. Is that what happened to Uncle Joe? Did he rat? Did he deserve to die by my hand? Is that why you made me kill him?" Vinny was on his feet shouting by this time. His heart was racing. He wanted to reach over, punch Sonny, and wipe that superior expression off his face.

Sonny jumped up, grabbed him by the neck, and slammed him against the wall. His hand tightened around Vinny's throat, choking off his airflow. "Don't you dare question my authority you little bastard! I run this fucking organization and it is none of your fucking' business who the hell I kill or what I do! You shut up and do what I tell you or I'll stick you in the fuckin' ground!" Sonny let go of his throat and left him gasping for air. He fell to the floor and sat up against the wall.

Sonny turned his back on Vinny and began to pace, "You hear me? Let me tell you about your low life uncle. I gave him a job to earn some money because he was your mother's brother. He stole from me. I told him not to do drugs, he lied to me about that, and I caught him. He had a big mouth and sooner or later he would have fucked up."

"So you had me kill him because you felt threatened," he said with a sneer even though his heart was racing. He knew he was pushing Sonny to the edge.

"Vinny, that's enough. This conversation is over. The next time you talk to me it better be something important and not the third fuckin' degree. When you're boss, you can give the fuckin' orders."

"But I don't want to be boss and I don't want to be like you!"

"It's too late," Sonny, said. "You're fucked and there's no turning back. You already are me."

Fuck him, he thought to himself as he walked away from him angrily. From this day forward, he was not going to try to pretend that his father loved him or that he would ever let him do what he wanted. He walked into his room and slammed the door.

It was quiet and he could feel his heart pounding. His face burned with humiliation and rage. He knew what it was like to have his father's killing rage directed at him. Son or not, Sonny would kill him if he were trouble enough. He lay face down on the bed; his mind flip-flopped between frustrated thoughts of vengeance and anxious prayers to control his wish to hurt his father.

There was a knock on his bedroom door. "Vincenzo, are you hungry?" Sonny asked.

"No."

"I want to come in and talk to you."

"No! I don't want to talk to you. Just leave me alone."

He lay there silently, holding his breath, waiting to see if he would leave. He did and, in a way, he was disappointed and relieved. He agonized for hours about what he should or even could do until, lastly, he was too exhausted to think, and fell asleep.

The next morning he felt better and decided he was not going to get upset over this because he was going to do what he wanted no matter what his father said and that was that. He walked into the kitchen and saw his father sitting there, reading the paper. He said good morning to him.

He looked over the top of his paper at him, hesitated and said, "Yeah. Good morning, Vinny," and asked him to come to the city with him but Vinny told him he had other commitments.

"Okay, Vinny, but you have an obligation to the Family."

"Dad, I don't want to fight with you but I'm only going to say this once more. I do not want any part of the Family. I don't want to go to prison again or end up dead."

"Vincenzo let me explain something to you in case I wasn't clear enough last night. You have no fuckin' choice. If you decide to get out, the only way is death. Don't put me in the position where I have to do something I don't want to do."

Vinny looked at him and realized that the time had come to put his cards on the table. "Do what you have to do," he said quietly and then walked out.

In the cab, he thought about what he said to his father and he knew he meant it. After he told him that he was not going to give in, Sonny had just sat there, resigned to the inevitable, resigned to killing his only son. He had made a decision and no need to think about it, or Vinny, further. He went back to reading the paper.

Vinny looked out the window and thought how wonderful life and freedom were. He was never going to let anybody take that away from him again—especially the man he called father.

When he arrived at his grandmother's, she was overjoyed to see him. She hugged him and kissed him on the cheeks, "Vincenzo, you look like you put on some weight."

"Yes, Grandma I did. Sometimes prison does that to you."

"So, Vincenzo how's your head? You okay inside there?"

"I'm fine. I found God and I'm going to put my past behind me," he said.

"Good! Good! I'm so happy," she smiled and patted his hand.

"Well, Grandma, what about you? How are your doing"?

"Okay," she said. "I'm an old woman. How am I supposed to be doing? I am not dead yet, so I guess that is something in my favor. C'mon, Vincenzo Come sit down. Eat some pasta I made just for you. I have to tell you something but I don't know if this is the right time."

Vinny followed her into the immaculate kitchen and sat down at the table. Hand-made Italian glass bowls held his favorite food, pasta and peas. Tea was in the clear pitcher in the middle of the table and two plates of the same Italian glass were on the table. He dug in immediately and savored the taste he knew he would always associate with his mother's cooking.

"What did you want to tell me, Grandma?" he asked while he ate.

She looked away and spoke as if she was talking to herself, "I want to tell you before I die so you know the truth. But I don't know if it's time yet."

He looked at her quizzically and wondered what it was, but she was not ready to tell him and kept urging him to eat. They talked about non-committal things while they ate. She asked him when he was going back to school. He told her he planned to meet with his old advisor next week to discuss it. "Good," she said and he finished eating and cleaned up the dishes. He noticed then that she had barely touched her food. It must be something bad, he thought, she normally loves to eat.

She led him into the living room and patted the couch cushion beside her, motioning for him to sit. She pulled out an old picture album from the end table drawer and showed him a picture of his mother and his uncle as children. They were windblown and sandy from being at the shore and they looked happy. She had tears in her eyes when she spoke.

"Your father took the two most special children away from me," she said.

"What do you mean, Grandma?" he asked, puzzled.

"He had my son killed. My baby boy and for nothing! I can't prove it. But I know he did it," she spit out in anger.

He knew why, he also knew how, and he did not want Grandma Gina to know what he did. She was already upset enough and he did not think she could forgive him even though she would probably try. Tears began to roll down his cheeks. He was silent, not knowing what to say that would ease her pain.

She drew a ragged breath and fought back her own tears, "Vincenzo, the day your mother was rushed to the hospital, do you remember?"

"Sort of."

"Vinny, your mother and my only daughter, she didn't die of cancer!"

"What? Yes, she did, Grandma. I read the reports from the doctor," he said gently. He wondered whether Grandma Gina was confused because she was so old.

"No, Vinny," she said. She squeezed his hand and looked him in the eyes to make sure he knew she was telling the truth. "You read a phony report that your father paid a bundle of money for so he'd have something to show everyone."

"Wait a minute, Grandma! What are you trying to say?"

"Your mother found out your father was cheating on her. When she confronted him, he denied it. She told him she had proof and he told her to go to hell. Then she told him that if he did not admit it she would call the police and tell them he was a murderer and a dope dealer. She had something on him, he felt threatened by this, and that night he shot her twice in the chest. Then he set up the cancer story."

He could not believe what he was hearing. Was Grandma Gina going senile or was she right? He was unsure what to believe because he had seen the doctor's report.

Gina saw the doubt in his eyes. "Vinny, it's true. I am not so old that I am losing my mind yet. Your father killed her! Look at this!" She pulled a manila envelope from the drawer and handed him the coroner's autopsy report. On the line for cause of death, it said, "gunshot wound." He stared at it until he started to feel dizzy. He realized he was holding his breath and when he took a gasping breath, he began to cry. He was hysterical. He jumped to his feet and paced around the room, wailing. He threw the report against the wall. Papers fluttered to the floor. He cursed his father and swore to kill him in the most brutal and painful way he could think of. Gina was crying, too, watching him stomp around and feeling his pain.

"Vinny, Vinny! Please. None of this is going to help. Killing him will not help your mother's memory... it will only dishonor her. Stop. Think about this." Her last words got through his pain and she calmed him down enough to sit down beside her again.

"I'm so sorry, Vincenzo. He has hurt us. What he has done can never be fixed." She held him tightly and forced him to look at her. "I know you want revenge but please don't try it. Nothing will bring her back. He is no good. He is a real bad man. Vincenzo, are you listening to me? He will hurt you, too. If he finds out that I know this and that I told you, he'll kill me, too."

Vinny started to cry again but she put her hands on his shoulders and shook him. "Listen to me, Vincenzo. You have to listen to me. I have been thinking about what to do. I have a friend in the FBI who is close to me.

His name is Richard Carr. He has been trying to build a case against your father for years, but Sonny always manages to buy his way out. He is still looking for Joe's killer. He thinks your father did it but he has no proof."

Vinny stared at his grandmother in shock. She wanted him to talk to an agent who was trying to figure out who killed his uncle. He was confused. Nothing was making sense to Vinny.

"FBI agent? Grandma, how can you be friends with an FBI agent? What if Sonny found out, he would kill you!"

Gina smiled at him and nodded, "Yes, I know he would kill me. Vinny... I am an old woman... I will die one day anyhow. Except for you, Sonny has taken everything away from me. What do I have to lose?"

Vinny stared at his grandmother with amazement, "But how? I mean, how do you know someone from the FBI?"

Gina leaned back on the couch and laughed, "What, you think an old woman never leaves her home? After your mamma died, I got that report from a friend at the hospital—some nurse that I knew who cared for me when I had pneumonia. Remember?"

Vinny nodded. He remembered when she had been so sick that they had thought she would not live. She gave credit to her recovery to a nurse at the hospital that cared for her around the clock.

"Well, I was heartbroken to know what he had done. I always knew he was an evil man, but your mother loved him no matter what he did. She found out about his mistress. That hurt her more than anything he had ever done. After she died, Richard Carr from the FBI contacted me. He suspected your mother was murdered. They had always watched your father's dealings, and this time he thought he could catch him. However, your father had too much money and too many connections and your mother's murder was swept under the rug. Richard came to me to see if I knew anything and I showed him the report I had received. It was not enough to put your father away, but it was enough to keep the case open. He asked me to help him, but there was little I could tell him. I will admit, Vincenzo, I was afraid. Afraid your father would kill me too if I told anything. I still had your uncle and you to think about. Can you understand?" she looked at Vinny with tears in her eyes and he realized how hard it must have been for her to know Sonny had killed her daughter and not to be able to do anything about it.

"I understand, Grandma. It's okay. I know Mom would have understood too." He patted her hand and she smiled sadly at him.

"I kept quiet with what little I knew, but kept contact with Richard, just in case. Then your uncle was found dead and you went to prison. I had nothing left to lose. I told him everything I knew, which was not much, but it was enough to keep him trying to find out things against your father. He has been a good friend over the years. He would let me know how you were doing in prison; it was the only way I was able to find out things about you."

"Grandma, I am sorry. I will see what I can find out. Sending my father to prison is probably the only way I will ever be free of him anyway. Grandma, just remember no matter what happens I love you."

"I love you, too, Vincenzo. Don't do anything stupid, okay? He's a smart man." Grandma cautioned Vinny.

"Don't worry about me," he assured her. "But I have to go. I have an appointment at the church with the priest."

She nodded her head, "That is good, Vincenzo. Pray to God. He will help both of us through this." She reached in the drawer one more time and handed him a business card. "This is Richard Carr's number. Call him, Vinny, he can help you." Vinny took the card and stared at it. The seal of the FBI was on one side and the agent's name and a phone number were beside it. He tucked it in his pocket and kissed her good-bye. He ran down the steps to flag a cab. He was glad he had an appointment to see Father Tom, because what he wanted to do was go home and kill his father. But he knew that would have achieved nothing except to put him back in prison. One part of him thought it would be worth it, but his calmer self knew that the way to defeat his father was to put him in the place he hated—prison, for life! He hated the bastard. He hoped Father Tom could help him resist and guide him to choose the right decision. When he got to the church, Father Tom was waiting for him outside. His welcoming smile went to a look of concern when saw that Vinny had been crying.

"Vinny, what's the matter?" he asked. He put his arm around him and led him inside his office.

"Okay," he said, "What happened?" He motioned Vinny to the couch in his office and took a seat at the opposite end.

"I just found out that my father killed my mother! He shot her twice in the chest. I want to kill him!" Vinny blurted out.

Father Tom got a stunned look on his face, but recovered quickly. "No," he said, "That's not the answer."

"Well, what should I do? He told me this morning that if I don't do what he says he'll do the same to me!"

"Are you sure he wasn't just angry? Saying something he regrets?"

"No, Father. He meant it. I could see it in his eyes. He's made his decision that if I don't go along with his plans for me, I'm a liability, and I need to be removed."

"Vinny, God would not want that to happen. I think you should distance yourself from him and make the best of your life, alone."

"That's hard to do, Father. You, of all people, know you just don't walk away from the Mafia."

Father Tom nodded. "I know that Vinny. However, there has to be a way for you to get out from under this. Pray to God, He will help you to find the answers you need."

Vinny wanted to tell Father Tom about Grandma Gina and the FBI agent but he kept quiet. This was not the time, and he needed to think this through.

"Vinny, pray to God to give you direction. I also think you should consider moving away from your father."

"Maybe you're right. Maybe moving away will help me to stay out of the plans he has for me. I just don't know what to do."

"I understand. Think on this. Pray. You are a good man; you will do what is right," Father Tom told him.

Vinny stared down at his hands that he had just noticed were clenched into fists on his knees. He uncurled his hands and flexed the fingers to bring life back to them. He thanked him for his support and promised to keep him informed. He went into the church and lit candles for his mother, his uncle and his grandmother. He knelt and prayed for a sign from God. Vinny thought about the law and how his father's law was going to get him killed. God tells us to leave justice to him and obey His laws, which are universal and constant. He remembered being at his trial and seeing the words "In God We Trust" on the wall above the judge. Even in the courtroom, he felt that the laws were clear and fair and that evil people only corrupted them. He believed this because society's rules are roughly the same as God's rules, but the difference is that God's rules cannot be bought. In the past, he had chosen Family law and tradition as the most important guidelines but he would not allow himself to be forced to choose that way. God had given him a second chance by opening his eyes to His way in prison. Maybe going to prison saved him from an early death. He did not know for sure but he knew that he wanted to live a good life, by the laws of God and good people. He trusted God to protect him, to love him, and to be just. He could never trust Sonny Denucci about anything ever again. He made the Sign of the Cross and left the church.

Outside he kept walking until he found a phone booth. He pulled out the card his Grandma had given him and called Agent Carr.

The phone rang twice and then a voice said, "Richard Carr speaking. Can I help you?" Vinny could not speak and he heard Agent Carr ask, "Hello? Can I help you?"

"Uh, hello, I'm Vinny Denucci. Sir, my grandmother gave me your card."

"Vinny, are you okay?" Agent Carr asked.

"I guess so, Mr. Carr."

"Call me Rick, okay? Can we meet somewhere, Vinny?" he asked.

"I don't know. I know about my mother's death. My grandmother told me today. I want to bring my father down and," he paused, ."..and I want out altogether."

"Maybe we should meet to discuss this," Rick said.

"If Sonny finds out, he will kill me. He knows I do not want to be part of his business. You know that, Rick?"

"Yeah, I know, Vinny. Where should we meet?"

He thought for a minute. "How about the diner on 53rd and 5th Avenue? One hour from now," Vinny said. I'm wearing a black sweat suit with a tiger on the back."

"Okay, Vinny. I will be there, waiting. I am wearing a yellow shirt with blue jeans, okay?" Rick said.

"Yeah, okay. See you." He hung up and he went over to a cafe in that area to have some hot tea. He could just see the entrance to the diner from his table. About fifty minutes later, he saw a man in jeans and a yellow sport shirt waiting out front. He was middle-aged and he looked like a regular guy. He walked up to him and asked if he was Rick.

"Yes, I am. Vinny?" he asked.

"Yeah." They shook hands.

"I'm glad you called, Vinny. Shall we go inside?"

"Uh, no, do you have a car?" Vinny asked him.

"Yes, that red Thunderbird over there."

"Well, I think it would be better if we drove around for a while." Vinny kept looking around. He didn't think his father was having him watched, but he wanted to be cautious.

"Sure, we can do that," he said. They got in his car and he asked him where he wanted to go.

"Let's drive over to Calgary Cemetery where my mother's buried, okay?" he said.

"No problem," Rick said.

It was quiet for a few minutes, and then Vinny said, "What do I have to do?"

"First things first," agent Rick said. "Are you extremely positive you want to do this?"

"Yes, I had two years to think about it and the fact that he killed my mother just strengthens my resolve."

"Okay, Vinny. I know this is not easy for you but here is what you have to do. You have to get close to him and make him think he was right about everything and that you have changed your mind. Make him forgive you and want to include you in running the organization. Every time he makes a move, you call a number that I will give you. Your calls will have to be taped and documented. When we are ready and have enough evidence on him, I will have my men take him and everybody down. He'll never know who's doing what unless you slip up."

"Will I have to testify?" he asked.

"No, if we can link him to a murder case, catch him in the act of doing something himself, or have one of the guys we arrest testify against him, you won't have to. However, if we do not have enough evidence, there is a possibility you might. Are you willing to do that?" He glanced quickly at him.

"I don't know, Rick. Right now I just want him to suffer."

"Okay, we'll worry about that later. The only agent you will ever talk to is me. Be careful and I will try to help you. Vinny, I want to tell you that I know about your uncle and I know you did it. Nevertheless, I also know that Sonny forced you into that hit. I am overlooking that because I want your help. I will not tell your grandmother because you are all each other has left. It is our secret. Gina does not know and I will not tell her. You have my word on that, okay. Do you understand everything? Do you want to ask me anything?"

He turned in his seat and looked him in the eye. "Yeah, I understand. And, Rick, you have my word that I will help you take down his fuckin' empire."

We had arrived at the cemetery by that time. He wrote down the undercover number and they shook hands again.

"Good luck," he said. "Be alert."

Rick let him out and he walked over to his mother's gravestone. He kneeled down and stared at the inscription, which read, "Loving wife and mother."

"Don't worry, Mom," he said to her. "Sonny is going to hell, I promise you."

CHAPTER 21
NO TURNING BACK

* * * *

THE NEXT MORNING, Vinny lay in bed staring at the ceiling and thinking about his life. He wanted to erase the past and put his new life in a better perspective. He wanted all the hate and anger to dissipate. He wanted to be free. He knew God had helped him throughout his life, and here he was going to ask him to help him to destroy his father and his empire. He wondered if God would want him to do it this way. Would God forgive him one more time?

He knew something had to be done. He had the intelligence and the training to play his father's game and if anybody could hurt Sonny Denucci, it was Vinny. He did not have the heart anymore to kill him, so he decided to beat him at his own game. He had to be smarter than him! One more time, one last time, he had to put himself in a position he did not want to be in. He had to think and act like a killer and a person with no morals or gratitude. He had to get inside his father's mind and think like him. This would be hard, because he was always unpredictable, and you could never trust him. He would have to rely on instinct.

He got out of bed and knelt on the floor. He made the sign of the cross and clenched his hands tightly together. He prayed, "Dear God, forgive me for what I'm about to do. I know the feeling I have is not what you would want, but I care for other human life and I do not want my father, this maniac, destroying anybody's family or taking someone's life. A life should not be taken to gain respect or because someone misses a vig payment. I pray you will protect me and guide me through this journey of destruction against my father. In the end, I hope it is best for everyone. Amen."

He put his body and mind in a state of vengeance. He became a machine that had to tear down a building. He had to start at the top and take it piece by piece until he tore it down to the ground. He dressed and went over to Central Park, to a place where he used to visit with his mom. There was a park bench with huge rocks behind it and there was a lake off to the side, which was filled with goldfish. It was a place where he knew he could think and plan his father's destruction.

The first thing he had to do was gain back his father's respect, and put him in a position where he could only trust him and no one else, even though he knew he would never trust him fully. He was smart enough to know that the Mafia Bosses trust no one, not even their Family members. For them, if they needed you, they'd keep you alive, and if they did not, they would have you killed. You were just a pawn in a game they controlled. However, Vinny was going to make him think the only person he could depend on was his only son. He was going to think like him. He was going to feel his emotions. He was going to know all the answers. His father was going to be impressed. He knew his father was smart, but he would pretend not to be too smart so his father would not be able to see through it. The last thing he wanted was for Sonny to catch on. He would be dead if he did. This would be a hard task, but he knew what he had to do. He knew it was going to be stressful and emotionally hard for him, but he was going to prepare himself.

As he was growing up in his father's house, his father taught him that if you want to hurt someone, you hurt their cash flow and take away their power. You take away what they value: money and power. One thing he learned about the Mafia is they are all greedy sons-of-bitches. Money is the only thing they care about, with that they could buy the power they coveted. Once you take away the money, they lose their power. When that happens, you find out if they are making illegal earnings, and you report them to the IRS. This would be an easy task for him since he knew his father's operations. The hardest part for him was choosing which way was the most valuable. He wondered if he should have his illegal casinos raided and shut down, or have his drug selling on the corners stopped. He had so many choices, and so little time, but the best way, the quickest way, was his father's gambling and his loan sharking. He felt this would hurt him terribly.

As he sat there on the bench, he thought cautiously about the plot to destroy this king's empire. He wanted a complete plan that would see the end of Sonny Denucci. If he planned to take him down, he might as well take the whole organization too. Otherwise, someone would step up into his position and everything would continue. Therefore, he plotted in his mind how best to hurt the other Bosses and their empires, from which they and Sonny profited. If they knew what he was thinking he would be a dead man, but it was worth the risk.

He sat there for a while and kept asking himself if he had covered everything needed to make sure that every time the Feds made an arrest or raided one of his father's joints it would look like another Family member was trying to take over. He was going to set it up where his father was going to think it was one of his other Family members wanting to dethrone the big king. In this lifestyle, you always made enemies because somebody always wanted to take your place and he knew this was his father's biggest fear. He also thought about how his father hated rats and prison. The worst thing you could do to a Mafia boss is to rat on them, testify against them. He could not imagine what his reaction would be when he finds out it was his own son. Set up by his own flesh and blood. His father would kill him right away or, if he couldn't do it, he would have a contract put out on him and hire a hit man to come and find him and kill him. Vinny's death would merely be satisfaction, a way of justifying his belief that he was right in killing his own son. He knew his father and he knew that is what he would do.

He thought, "What am I going to do if he ever finds out before I get started? Would he ever be able to find me? Is he too powerful for me to take such a risk?" At that moment, he did not care, nor did he have second thoughts. All he wanted was for him to suffer. A prison cell for Sonny for life would satisfy Vinny's yearning for revenge.

He remembered what Rick said, "We need Sonny on tape. The more information you can get the better for our case." That requirement was going to be tricky. How was he going to pull this task off? He would be nuts to wear a wire device; he would be too nervous. Therefore, he just sat there, thought, and decided that when the time was right he would buy a pocket tape recorder and plant it somewhere, maybe in his bedroom in the condominium. He had many ideas, but nothing made him feel comfortable. He knew getting evidence was something he had to work on, but he was determined to make it happen, now that he seemed to have a good picture of what he was going to do.

The only question was when to start. He wanted to destroy him, but it would pay to be patient. The more damning evidence he could gather on Sonny, the better the case against him would be. It was getting late, so he decided to review his plan one more time to see if he had left out anything. He knew he would have no time to be alone and think once he started the destruction. There was no turning back, so he went over it again in his head. The plan was to raid the casinos first, and then stop his illegal dope houses, tape some conversations about murders or his plan to kill someone. In a way, this all seemed like a movie to him, but he knew it was not. The only thing left for him to do was to make sure he had the information on when the drugs were coming in from Florida and the schedules for the casinos and tell Agent Rick. He would need to use out-of state Feds that no one knew so he could get him or her inside the casinos for the raids. He would have Agent Rick make some big bets with the bookmakers and not pay them. That would entice his father to send his boys to collect. Finally, yet most importantly, he would have to get some good conversations on tape.

Tomorrow would be the day his father was going to be the target of the first successful FBI investigation against a Mafia boss...if all goes well...

The entire organization will be destroyed by one of their own members. He knew some people would go down that maybe did not deserve it, and he was sorry for that, but he also knew that it was something that had to be done. The only thing that mattered to him was having his father destroyed and imprisoned for life. He did not want him hurt physically. He wanted him to hurt mentally and to see what it feels like when someone else makes decisions regarding your life. When to eat, when to sleep, the slamming of a prison door every night for the rest of your life. He wanted him to suffer emotionally the way he had. He knew he finally had the chance to get even. Ever since he came out of prison, he had an emotional scenario playing within him that would never leave. However, he was never totally like his father. He remembered who he was in prison and with help, he could put himself back on the right road to success. To build the perfect setup he would only have to live in the past for a little while, before he could move on. He fully understood the plan in his mind and his thoughts and emotions were calm.

"God forgive me, please, and guide me. I know this is not the answer, but maybe it will be a lesson for my father. Maybe the entire organization will break off at the base, and some people will be free to untangle themselves from the knot. Amen."

He went to the nearest phone booth and dialed Agent Rick's number. After three rings a machine answered, "I'm not available, leave your name and number and I'll return your call." Beep.

He hung up.

CHAPTER 22
THE SETUP

* * * *

THE FOLLOWING DAY he woke up a little earlier than usual to prepare breakfast for his father, hoping the surprise would help convince him that he was truly repentant and longing for his approval. He had rye toast in the toaster, sunny side up eggs with a little fresh pepper, extra crispy bacon, and light sweet coffee. The newspaper was on his chair and he had Frank Sinatra playing on the radio. It was a good setup.

Sonny walked into the kitchen and looked at the table loaded with his favorites. "What's this, Vinny?" he warily asked.

"Dad, I'm sorry for the way I've been acting lately. I was just afraid I might end up in prison again." Vinny put on his most serious face. He had to convince Sonny that everything he said and did was true.

"Vinny, if I didn't know better I think I was being setup."

He stood in shock! He stuttered for a moment, "What do you mean?"

"When somebody wants something they suck up to you." Sonny said.

"Do you think I want something?"

"Vinny, come here." He put his arm around Vinny and kissed him. "I'm glad you changed your mind. You're my son and I want you to be with me."

Vinny untangled himself, feeling a shiver of disgust. It was amazing how he had lost his love for his father so totally. He had been working free of him emotionally for a long time, but just needed the edge of anger to finally break away. He held his chair for him and said, "Come on, sit down, Dad. Let's eat."

As he fixed his toast, he said, "Vinny, we have a bunch of work to do today, so after you clean up, we need to leave."

He sat on the opposite side of the table and fooled around with his food to avoid looking at him. His muscles were tense with the effort needed to continue sitting still looking cool and enjoying breakfast, when all he wanted to do was to rip Sonny's head off. Maybe he should have poisoned him. It would have been a lot faster, but probably not as satisfying as seeing him realize his kingdom was destroyed and he was jailed forever. Sonny destroyed by his only son.

He was glad of the anger because if it were not for that, he would be shaking and visibly terrified of him. Sonny would really start to wonder what was going on. He remembered what Grandma Gina said, that he was smart. He knew it was true and he knew that if Sonny caught on to what he was doing, he would kill him himself without regret.

Vinny was thinking so hard that when Sonny spoke to him he almost jumped out of his skin.

"Vinny, I'm curious why the change? Yesterday you were hysterical and today you want to be a part of me. Are you doing this because you're scared, or because of the power?"

This was a trick question. If he answered that he was making up with him because he was scared, it would give Sonny the advantage, knowing that he had manipulated his son. On the other hand, if he answered that he wanted the power, then Sonny would have to regard him as ambitious and wonder what his next move would be.

"Power and respect, I want to be like you," he said, looking at him in what he hoped appeared to be sincere admiration. "I know you could teach me a lot if you want to."

He smiled. "Good answer," he said, wiping his mouth with a napkin. He stood up. "Clean this up and get ready. We need to be in Brooklyn in an hour."

He took care of the dishes then went into the bathroom. He locked the door and pulled out the card Rick gave him. He memorized the number, tore it up and flushed it. He watched the water to make sure no pieces of paper were left swirling around. It was a relief to get rid of the card. He felt as if it had been burning a hole in his shirt pocket during breakfast.

In the car on the way over to Brooklyn, Sonny told him Vinny would be his new bodyguard and under boss. An under boss is someone who takes over if the boss is killed or cannot be reached in jail. Bosses can still run things from jail, but sometimes it takes a couple of days to set up the communication system. He was going to try to remember what he taught him even though there would soon be no organization to run. You never know when the inside information that he would be learning might come in handy. He wanted to know everything so that he could set-up Sonny good. He did not want him buying his way out this time as he had with his mother's murder.

"I have to go pickup some money that a guy owes me," Sonny said.

"Yeah, okay, Dad."

"Vinny, from now on, I want you to call me Sonny. I cannot have my under boss calling me Dad. Okay, Vinny?"

"Yeah, no problem," he said. Vinny was glad he asked him to call him Sonny because he didn't want to believe this man sitting beside him was his father anyway. Besides, it would make the set-up a lot easier if he was not always reminded of the relationship.

"And, Vinny? I am going to give you a gun to carry. From now on, you take it with you wherever you go. You got that?"

"I'm on parole. You know that. I go back to prison if I get caught with a gun," Vinny said.

"Well, just don't get caught. There is some bad blood between some families and I want you to be prepared for anything. I would rather it be them than us. Besides, would you rather have twelve men convict you or six men carrying you?"

They drove a little further when Sonny said:

"There's a guy named Joey Forte that's working with the Feds to get a reduced sentence and he's ratting people out. It is causing many bad feelings between some of the families. But don't worry, Vinny," Sonny said. "We're close on the inside and his fuckin' days are numbered."

Vinny got scared when he saw the look on Sonny's face when he said that last bit about being close. He wondered if Rick knew about Joey Forte. Maybe he should warn Rick.

As he was thinking this over, they arrived in Brooklyn. Sonny said, "Look for 7901 Seneca Ave."

Vinny spied it first, "There it is... the white one with the blue trim. It's the two story house with the big wooded fence around it."

They pulled up in front. He got out first and looked up and down the street. He tapped on the hood to let Sonny know it was okay to come out. Sonny got out and stood by the car, protected by the open door. He told him to go and check things out. Vinny walked up to the fence and peeked through a crack between the wooden slats. He motioned to Sonny, all clear—no dogs. He reached around, pulled out his gun, and cocked it. He was not taking chances. Who knows what Sonny had up his sleeve? They walked up to the entrance and rang the bell.

"Get ready. Be alert. This guy is a two-bit hustler," Sonny said, just before the door opened. The door swung open and to Vinny's surprise, it was Dino the owner of the pizzeria. "Sonny, why didn't you call? I got your money." Dino was a six-foot-four, 185-pound scruffy looking guy. He had not shaved in a few days; he had dark circles under his eyes and his breath smelled of liquor. His hair was greasy looking and he looked like a real scumbag. He was wearing black silk boxer shorts and had a cigarette dangling from his mouth.

"Good," Sonny said, as they stepped inside, stopping near the door.

"Let me go get it," Dino said.

"No," said Sonny. "Call your wife and tell her to go get it."

Dino laughed and said, "Hey, Sonny, don't you trust me?"

"No, you cocksucker! Stop stalling. Where is my fuckin' money? $50,000 you owe me."

Vinny knew what a bodyguard would do at this point so he grabbed Dino and twisted his arm behind his back. He held it ready to break. "Call your wife," he said.

"Okay, okay. Don't break my arm," he said. "Nancy, honey, bring down my black duffel bag, please."

Nancy came downstairs. She was a skinny woman with enormous breasts, scraggly blond hair and black eyeliner on her eyelids. She kept sniffling her nose every couple of seconds, probably cocaine, and her breasts barely fit in her dingy white terry-cloth robe. She looked terrified and disheveled. With one hand, she nervously held her bathrobe closed and with the other she carried the black duffel bag. She set it down in front of Sonny and scurried back to the stairs. She was shaking in fear, but she glanced at Sonny and then looked at him and said, "Please don't hurt him."

"Don't worry, doll," Sonny said. "He's not worth killing."

She started crying and Dino said, "Go on back upstairs, Nancy." She just sat down on the stairs and cried harder.

Sonny looked disgusted, but he ignored her and bent down to unzip the duffel bag. He pulled out the money and quickly counted it.

"Okay, Vinny let him go. It's all here."

Vinny shoved Dino onto the couch and stepped back. Nancy ran over to Dino and he put his arms around her.

"The next time you're late with my money, I'm going to kill her first, then you. C'mon, Vinny. Let's go." Sonny turned to go.

Vinny breathed a silent sigh of relief. Those two were lucky Sonny just accepted the money and left. Lately there had been a string of accidental killings of innocent bystanders like wives and kids. The old Mafia bosses would never have killed a woman or a child for any reason, but now, with the younger, hard-ass bosses, the popular way of whacking a boss and his bodyguard was in a restaurant, and sometimes his family was killed, too. Some hard bosses liked to kill or threaten the women, partly for the thrill of making them grovel, but mostly because it was effective in keeping low-level guys in line.

They got back into car and Sonny handed him a couple packs of bills.

"Here, this is for you," he said, "To thank you."

"For what?" Vinny asked.

"Vinny, you showed me something inside that house that I didn't think you had in you. I am very proud of you. You're going to be a great boss."

He thought he was going to get sick. He wondered what he would have done if Dino did not have the money. Sonny probably would not have killed him because he still wanted to get his money, but he would have done something cruel to show his power, like break the woman's arm.

Next, they drove down to some restaurant in East Manhattan. Apparently, the owner needed a loan bad. He always wondered why people did business with Sonny when they knew how he operated. They always think they can play the game safely just this once and if they screw up, well, everyone makes mistakes and surely, they have time to fix it. However, Vinny knew that Sonny does not give many second chances. As he drove he thought about how he used to feel about his place in the Family and as Sonny Denucci's son, but that was before he knew what had happened to his mother. . He bet his mother and uncle thought they were safe from Sonny's anger. You never believe that someone might kill you until it's too late.

No one was safe from Sonny.

"Vinny!"

"What?" he asked startled.

"Are you okay? I've been talking to you and you just keep staring at me."

"Sorry, Sonny. I'm just thinking about the Family."

"What are you thinking about?" he asked.

He thought for a second. He wanted to tell him that he knew everything and he was going to fuck his life up and stand there and laugh when they led him away, but instead he told him some bullshit excuse that sounded good. "Do you think I'll have a problem with my cousin Robert if something should happen to you? Do you think he would have me bumped off?"

Sonny looked him over a bit while he thought. "No," he said at last, "I don't think so. He would have to kill his father first and I don't think he would do that."

"That's good to know."

"Is that all you're worried about?"

"Well, no. I think you might be right about Debbie, she's just out for herself and I'm too young to be exclusive."

"Well, Vinny, I'm glad you thought about that. Everybody is your enemy. Do not trust anyone. And especially don't trust some whore." Sonny nodded his head in approval and Vinny thought to himself, you are right you stupid fuck. The one you had better not trust is your own son.

They finally arrived at a place called Anna's Cafe and Restaurant and Sonny told him to park out front on the street. One of the few good things about being in Sonny's organization is that you never got a ticket. A cop knew the deal about Lincolns and if they had any doubts they would stick their heads in a restaurant or wherever and ask the bartender whose car was out front. The bartender would shake his head or say "VIP" or something and the cop would go away. They knew better than to leave a ticket on Sonny's car.

Vinny repeated the same bodyguard routine he had before and then escorted Sonny into the restaurant. Inside they met Dominic Carletta, the owner. "Hey, Sonny," he said, shaking hands. "Thank you for coming on such short notice."

"Hey, Dom. Meet my son, Vinny."

"Hello Vinny, how are you doing?" he asked.

"Good, thanks," Vinny replied.

"Do you have a place where we can talk?" Sonny asked.

"Yeah, follow me." They filed into the back room and sat down at a table.

Dominic pulled out a picture and passed it to Sonny, then pulled out a wad of cash. "That's Ralph Morales. How much is it going to cost to have that guy out of my life?"

Sonny looked the picture over. "Dom, you know I don't do these kinds of hits. Why do you want this guy whacked?"

"He's going to testify against me on Thursday. I loaned him some money but he could not pay me back. So I scared him a little and he ran to the fuckin' cops!"

"You have a problem, Dominic, you do. Here, talk to Vinny. He likes these kinds of jobs."

Vinny was surprised, but all along, he should have remembered. Do not trust this piece of shit excuse for a father. He fell right into the trap. There was no way out without risking his cover.

He looked at Dominic and said, "$50,000 and your problem is over." Sonny's eyebrows went up as if to say, hey, you are going to do this.

"I'll give you $25,000 and when I read about it in the paper I'll give you the rest." Dominic said.

"Fine," he said. He picked up the picture and the money and stashed them inside his coat.

Dominic gave Vinny some other information to help him find the person and said, "I appreciate this, Vinny."

He nodded and Sonny and Dominic embraced. Back in the car, Sonny said, "I'm impressed. Let's go home. I'm tired and you have work to do."

He was breathing a sigh of relief that Sonny was not going to try to go with him. This would give him the chance to call Rick and let him know what he got and ask him how to proceed. He dropped Sonny off, told him he was going to look into the Morales situation, and went to a pay phone out of the neighborhood. He dialed the number Rick gave him. He was surprised when he answered.

"Hello, who is this?" he said.

"Rick?"

"Yeah."

"It's me, Vinny."

"Hey! How are you, Vinny?"

"Okay."

"I was just leaving; making sure the tape was set up for you."

"Well, I have something for you," he said.

"Good. What?"

"I've been ordered to make a hit."

"You?"

"Yes, me. I have been paid $25,000 up front. Another $25,000 when it's done."

"Who's it for?" he asked.

"A guy named Dominic Carletta."

"Say no more, Vinny. I know who he is. We have a case against him. He is looking at a long vacation. We also have a witness."

"Rick, the witness, Ralph Morales, is the man I have to hit."

"Holy shit! You are right, that is who it is. And he's our key witness." He paused to think it over. "Okay, here's what we're going to do. You go as planned and act like you whacked this person. It will be in the newspapers as soon as you give me the details. I will put him somewhere safe in another state. When we have enough evidence against Sonny, we'll bring him back and get Dominic too."

"Okay, Rick. Two more things: I don't know if you know Joey Forte or not, but Sonny mentioned that he was closing in on him."

"Fuck! Oh yeah, I know that guy. Okay. Thanks, that is very good. I would hate to fuckin' lose that guy. Anything else?"

"Yeah. Sonny has many cops on the payroll. I hope you realize that," Vinny warned.

"Yeah. Don't worry, Vinny. I'm extremely careful. Does Sonny know about the hit?"

"Yes, he was there. Dominic is one of his capos."

"Is there anyway you can get Sonny to talk on this tape?"

"Rick, you're asking a lot. But I have an idea so let me look into it."

"Okay, Vinny. All we need is a little conversation on tape, a couple of good busts, maybe a witness, and he is history. Be careful, okay?"

"Yeah, okay."

"Thanks again, Vinny. Keep up the good work."

He hung up the phone and stood there for a few minutes, thinking about how he was going to have Ralph Morales die. He spotted an electronics store across the street and he walked over to check it out. Inside, he asked the sales clerk if they had a small tape recorder that he could hide and record for about two hours. He showed him a flat mini-recorder that came with a tiny microphone on a wire you could clip inside your shirt. He set the tape speed for him and inserted the batteries and tape. He paid in cash and told him to keep the boxes and the change. The clerk threw away the boxes with no change of expression. Apparently, this happened a lot in New York.

Vinny got in the car, drove a couple blocks away, and pulled over. He pulled the leather headrest off on the passenger side. He ripped out some of the foam, put the recorder inside, and forced it back on the seat. He could just reach the on/off switch from underneath. Sonny liked to talk in the car and he usually sat in the passenger seat. He hoped this would work but he was too tired to think about it anymore and he drove home.

When he got home, Sonny was sitting inside, watching the news. He walked in and he said, "Did you get everything worked out?"

"What? Do you want a written report?" he said.

"Don't get smart assed with me, Vinny. I'm still your father."

"Well, Sonny, the way I look at is, the less people who know, the better off I'll be. Is this what you have always taught me? If you are going to do something, do it by yourself and don't talk about it. So goodnight. I'm going to bed."

He took a shower and lay down. Leaning over, he opened his bedside dresser drawer and pulled out one of his favorite photos of his mother and him. He had just turned fifteen and she had taken him for an early morning horse and buggy ride in Central Park. He used to love to ride through Central Park in the wintertime. The air was clean and cool, the leaves were still colorful and usually there would be a thin layer of frost. The park always made him forget his problems and he could just be happy like a child without responsibilities or regrets. The picture was of them sitting on a bench with these huge rocks behind them. They almost looked like mountains in the background. Looking at her face, he started to cry, because he knew that he wanted to get revenge for her but that she would have told him to leave and start over somewhere else like Father Tom said. However, he knew that was impossible. Despite wanting to do what he thought his mother would want, he knew he was still going to continue with the plan.

The phone rang. It was Grandma Gina. He was surprised that she was calling so late.

"Hello, Grandma," he said. "What's wrong? Are you okay?"

"Hello, Vincenzo. I'm waiting for the ambulance to get here."

"What do you need an ambulance for?"

"I'm not feeling good and I don't want to die here alone."

"Don't talk like that, Grandma. I'll meet you at the hospital."

"No, Vinny. You come see me tomorrow. I will be at Flushing Hospital. Did you write that down, Vinny?"

"Yes, Grandma."

"Where's your father?"

"He's sleeping, I think. Grandma, you can talk to me. I have my own private line. Sonny can't listen in."

"Good. Vinny, I want to tell you that you are special to me. I know what you have to do is hard and you might think that it is not the right thing to do but just remember your father took your mother away from both of us. He is rotten and he will hurt you, me, and anybody else who gets in the way. Do it for me, Vincenzo. Please do it for me."

He felt relieved that she had told him this; he felt he had gotten the answer he needed. "Okay, Grandma. I promise I will do it. I hope you will feel better. I'll see you tomorrow."

"Okay, Vinny. We'll talk tomorrow."

He hung up, his determination to destroy Sonny stronger than ever. He prayed that God would forgive him. He was totally committed and he knew what he had to do next. He called Debbie and she answered on the second ring.

"Hi, Debbie. It's me, Vinny."

"Vinny! I was hoping you would call! I miss you. When can I see you?" She was excited to hear from him and he dreaded telling her his news.

"Debbie, I have to tell you something. I know it'll hurt you and it hurts me, too." He paused to think of the right words. "Debbie, we can't see each other anymore."

"Why? Vinny, why are you saying this?" She started crying.

"I have to take care of something and I have to do it alone. It is better like this. Please understand."

"I don't want this but I think I understand," she said. "Vinny, I'll always love you. I'll wait for you."

"I know, Debbie... good-bye for now. I promise I will call you when I can." He gently put down the phone. He felt terrible about making her cry but it was for her own good. He was going to miss her, too. He felt so alone at that moment.

The next morning yelling awakened him. He struggled out of bed and ran into the kitchen. Sonny was holding the phone away from his ear and screaming words that even he could barely understand. He was so mad that his face turned the color of a raspberry and he was spitting as he tried to scream at the person on the other end of the line. He slammed the phone down and started pacing and muttering. He looked up at him and glared.

"What? What's the matter?" he said.

"That no-good, son of a bitch brother of mine won't do me a favor," Sonny roared.

"What favor do you need?" he asked, wondering how Uncle Nunzi could possibly refuse Sonny anything.

"Nothing! Not a goddamn fucking thing! Go and get dressed. I have to go to Staten Island today. We'll get breakfast on the way."

Vinny made a hasty exit and went to take a shower. He wondered if he should call Uncle Nunzi to see what the problem was. He decided he better stay out of it. He had wanted to go to the hospital to see his Grandma Gina, but in the mood Sonny was in he figured he better not say anything to him about it.

As soon as he was ready, they left. As they rode down the elevator, he could see that Sonny was still agitated. He wondered what action he was going to take against his brother. Was Sonny angry enough to have his brother killed?

When they got down to the garage, Sonny said, "That problem you have to take care of, I want it done today."

"Okay, Sonny."

"And drive over to Frank's Deli so we can get a coffee and a bagel."

Frank's was only a few blocks away. When they stopped, Vinny jumped out of the car and ran in to get the food and a newspaper. George, the owner, saw him come in. He waved away the waitress telling her, "Don't worry, honey, I'll take care of Vinny."

George was a good deli owner, he would make them special pasta or sandwiches when they came in. Today he took one look at Vinny and fixed the order without asking questions. As he waited, he tried to figure out how he could get the recorder on, now that Sonny was in the car.

On his way out, George's son Pete came in and said, "Hey, how you doing, Vinny?"

"Okay, Pete Have to go... Sonny's waiting." Vinny said.

"Give Sonny my regards, will you?"

"Yeah." It was amazing how much respect Sonny got. The difference between Pete and George was that Pete admired Sonny where George was respectful but cautious. Both of them had a pretty good idea what Sonny did for a living.

Back in the car, Sonny grabbed the bag and said, "Didn't you get anything for yourself?"

"No, I'm fine."

"Okay, then. Head over to the Island." Sonny was eating and as Vinny reversed the car, he put his right hand across the back of the passenger seat and flipped on the recorder. He glanced at Sonny to see if he noticed but he did not even look up. He smiled to himself at how smoothly he handled that. Now he had to get Sonny to talk about his empire.

At that moment, Sonny turned to him and said, "Do you have your gun with you?"

"Yes," he said. His heart was pounding.

"Good. I have to teach someone a lesson today," Sonny stated.

Oh my God. It must be fate that I just turned on the recorder and Sonny immediately starts convicting himself. Vinny thought.

He was still talking. "I'm going to have to put a couple rival bosses out of commission because they're getting sloppy with the private casinos and making trouble for the rest of us. Johnny Delacrue wants a bigger cut, but I told him to go fuck himself. However, I think he needs a reminder of who is in charge. I also need you to make a stop on your way to complete your business."

"What's that?" he asked.

"I need you to take something to Detective Calloway." Sonny laughed. He pulled a wad of money out of his coat and handed it to Vinny. "He'll meet you at Dino's, around eight o'clock tonight. Just hand him the cash and leave, he's expecting you."

"No problem. I will take care of it. Anything else?"

"No. Just take care of your business. I want that fucker dead."

So, that's why we were going to Staten Island, Vinny thought, One of Sonny's capos was getting too strong and Sonny wants to explain a few facts to him, probably violently. At the present, he has me running payoffs to the cops. He wanted to take advantage of Sonny's bad mood by questioning him about the organization. He thought he was too angry to control himself and he might spill his guts, but he just sat back and kept quiet. He casually reached over and turned off the recorder while pretending to stretch his arm muscles.

They arrived at Johnny Delacrue's house. At the door, a bodyguard greeted us.

"Sonny, Johnny said he'll take a ride with you, if that's okay?"

Vinny was thrilled. He would get Sonny talking to one of his own capos on tape. Johnny came out of the house and got in the back seat. He told his bodyguard he would be right back and the guard shut the car door. Vinny took the chance to reach around and click the recorder on again as he pretended interest in the man getting in the back seat. Sonny told him to drive around the block.

"Hey, Johnny. This is my son, Vinny."

"Hi, how you doing, Vinny? You look just like your father. I hope you don't have his fuckin' hard head, though." Even though it was not a diplomatic thing to say, Vinny had to smile at that.

"Okay," said Sonny. "Cut the bullshit. What is the fuckin' problem, Johnny? You want my fuckin' money. Why? I gave you Staten Island and a piece of the action. You are getting fuckin' greedy. Don't you forget where you came from?"

"Hey, Sonny, I run forty-five casinos for you in Brooklyn, Bronx, and Queens. All over the fuckin' place. I sell your drugs and make sure the numbers all come out right. All I get is a lousy seven thousand a week and I have to take care of my men. Every time there is a problem, I don't call you up, whining about it. I take care of it. I never ask you for a fuckin' dime."

"So, how much do you want? What do you think you fuckin' deserve?" Sonny said as sarcastically as possible.

"I want fifteen grand a week."

Sonny whipped around and looked right into Johnny's eyes. "Are you fuckin' crazy? I should kill you right now, cocksucker!"

He could see Johnny's face in the rearview mirror. He looked scared but determined.

Sonny sighed. "Ten thousand. Take it or you're through." He brought his gun out almost as an afterthought and pointed it right at Johnny's forehead.

Johnny closed his eyes and said, "Okay, okay. I'll take ten." He was holding up pretty good considering how much danger he was getting himself into.

"The next time I have to come down here over this bullshit, I'm going to kill you," Sonny warned.

Johnny did not say anything and they made the ride back toward his house in silence. Sonny told him to pull over at the end of the block and they dropped Johnny off at the corner. Sonny told him to walk home. It was not far, but Sonny liked his petty humiliations.

"Let that be a lesson for you when you become boss, Vinny. I arrange for him to sell my drugs, run my numbers houses and my casinos, and he makes a good fuckin' living out of it. However, let me warn you, they always want more of the cut. Also, learn that sometimes you got to compromise with your people. I'd have given him twelve thousand if he'd pushed it, but the fucker didn't have the balls to stand up for it."

"Would you have killed him?" Vinny asked.

"Yes, and he knew it. But he could have asked for more and gotten it, he was just a fuckin' coward," Sonny said. "There are times that even bosses have to bend a little to keep the cash flowing. I gave him more than what he expected and did not blow his head off. He's happy with that."

Vinny just shook his head. His father would have killed a man for a couple thousand dollars of dirty money, but could still sit there and tell him how nice he had been by not blowing some guy's head off.

"Vinny, drive over to Queens. I have to collect some money."

"Sonny, I can't stay with you all day because I have that problem to take care of," Vinny told him.

"Okay, just one more stop then you go do what you've got to do."

What he had to do was pass on the information that he learned and switch tapes. There was no traffic and they got to Queens quickly. Sonny directed him to some bar named Conchetta's.

"Pull up in the front," Sonny said, "this isn't going to take long." Sonny went in and came out quickly.

"Everything okay?" Vinny asked as he got in.

"Yeah. Everything is fine. Take me home."

It was about 3:00 p.m. when he dropped off Sonny. Sonny hesitated when he was getting out and said, "Keep your word and bury that bum.

When you whack that guy, Morales, stick an extra bullet in his head for me. I can't stand fuckin' rats."

"Okay," he said with hardly a tremor in his voice. He drove about ten miles away to a pay phone. He got the answering machine, so he left a message for Agent Rick to call him right back. The phone rang within two minutes.

""Vinny, that you?"

"Yeah. Rick, I got some great conversation with Sonny on tape. Can you arrange tomorrow's headline to read that Morales was found in his car, shot twice in the head?"

"Yes, I can do that."

He told him about the conversation with Johnny.

"Perfect. Where are these casinos that Johnny runs, Vinny?"

He gave him about thirty locations. "That's all I can think of right now."

"Okay, that's good enough. It is enough to hurt Sonny where it counts. Are they all running tonight?" Rick asked.

"Yeah. It's Friday. Payday, you know? All the casinos are open on payday."

He told him that Sonny also admitted to selling and distributing drugs on the tape. He gave him all the information he could remember about the connections and the places that were constant spots for selling. Rick asked him about the numbers houses. Vinny gave him the locations of each and every one. "Okay, Vinny. That's enough for now. We will start raiding these places and busting everyone we can. Maybe we can get some witnesses against Sonny. We will be ready to indict him by Monday at the latest.

"Good. What do I do with the tape?" he said.

"Leave it behind the phone book and I'll send someone to come get it."

"Do you know where I am?"

"Yeah, well, you've been on the phone long enough for me to trace it." Rick sounded somewhat embarrassed but Vinny did not mind. He was already on the team.

Rick started to say good-bye, but Vinny interrupted him. "I have one more thing for you."

"What's that?"

"Sonny wants me to pay off a cop tonight, it's on the tape. What should I do?"

He heard a low chuckle from the other end of the line, "Keep the appointment, right now I want Sonny for the main course. A dirty cop will be the desert."

Rick wished him luck and he said, "Yeah, you, too." He hung up and headed for the hospital to see his Grandma. He had a couple hours to kill before he had to meet up with Detective Calloway and make the payoff, then he could go home.

At the hospital, he was not able to talk with his Grandma Gina, she was sleeping and he did not want to disturb her. Vinny found the doctor and he told Vinny that she had a mild stroke, but that she would be fine in a few days. Vinny breathed a sigh of relief. He went to the hospital gift shop and bought her some flowers to put in her room. By this time it was almost 8 pm, so he headed out for his meeting with Detective Calloway after making sure the hospital knew to call him if anything happened. When he met up with Calloway a few minutes after eight, the payoff went smooth and he headed for home. He walked into the condominium and found Sonny was waiting.

"Well, Vinny, how did everything go?" he asked.

"You'll read about it in tomorrow's paper." Vinny said. He gave Sonny a grin that he hoped was convincing. Sonny smiled back at him and proudly hugged him. Vinny could barely look at Sonny without wanting to get sick.

"Listen, I'm tired and need a shower. I'm going to call it a night," he told Sonny. He had to get away from him.

"Sure, Vincenzo. You did very well today. I'll see you in the morning."

Vinny walked away and went into his bedroom. He quietly shut the door, stripped out of his clothes, and climbed in a hot shower. He had never felt so dirty in his life. He leaned his head against the shower wall and let the hot water flow over his back and shoulders. God, he prayed, please help me through this. Give me the strength to continue.

He showered and crawled into bed, falling asleep before his head hit the pillow.

About midnight the phone rang. He heard Sonny pick it up and then heard him swearing. Curiosity got the best of him and he threw on a bathrobe and headed for the kitchen. He figured he was thirsty anyway so it would give him a good reason to be there.

Halfway to the kitchen, he heard Sonny shout, "How could they raid us? I paid off all those fuckin' pigs! Son of a bitch!"

He heard Sonny slam down the phone as he came in the kitchen.

"What's the matter?" he asked him.

"They just raided fourteen of the casinos."

"Fourteen?"

Sonny shouted at Vinny, "Did you pay off Detective Calloway like I told you to?"

"Of course I did!"

"You better be fuckin' sure, Vincenzo."

"I'm sure. Who raided the casinos?" he asked.

"It was the Feds. Who else would have balls enough? We must have a leak or somebody turned out to be a rat. Son of a bitch, what else is going to happen?" It was almost pitiful how weak his father seemed at that moment.

"Who do think it could be?" he asked him.

Sonny started to answer but the phone rang again. He grabbed it. "What? You are fuckin' kidding! Shit!" He hung up.

"What?"

Vinny had made him a cup of espresso. He took it, gratefully. "Thanks." He sat down heavily at the table and stared at his cup.

"Well, who was that?" Vinny asked.

"The gang from the Lower East Side. Four drug houses just got raided and they confiscated 27 million dollars in cash and drugs." Hearing the depressed tone of Sonny's voice made him realize how bad it was and that Sonny was getting pissed off. "Vinny, it might get rough so be prepared."

Saturday morning came and Sonny was back on the phone, yelling. As he came into the living room, Sonny threw the phone against the wall and pieces flew around the room.

"Shit, they're fucking busting everybody. Somebody leaked out a lot of information. They know too much about everything. Vinny call a meeting with all the Families. Tell them it is at the Waldorf on Sunday at 10:00 a.m. I will book a room. I have some connections over there. We had better stay home today, Vinny. You call Max and tell him to get over here."

All day Sonny got calls from even the most distant houses. Detroit called and said the Feds were raiding everybody. The guys from Florida said that all their places were being hit. Everyone who went by or called a drug house was arrested. Sonny knew for sure there was a rat, but he could not figure out who it was. He thought none of the top guys would do this because they had too much to lose. He turned on the TV. The news on every channel was about the sting the Feds had going and how they were going to break the back of organized crime.

They went on to say that according to inside sources at the Federal Building, Sonny Denucci, the so-called head of the Syndicate would be indicted. Task forces across the nation have been raiding all the drug houses, casinos and other illegal operations run by the Denucci Crime Family and 115 arrests had been made, over 300 million in cash and property had been seized, and 24 million dollars in heroin and cocaine had been retained by law enforcement agencies as evidence.

All of the news agencies reported the background on him. They told how Sonny became boss over fifteen years ago, when he allegedly shot and killed former Mafia boss Vito Scarabelli. Sonny was never convicted of the murder due to lack of evidence but sources inside the Mafia say he pulled the trigger. They gave details of how Sonny went on to organize the New York Families under his leadership. Vinny sat there listening to Sonny flip from one channel to the next, always encountering the same thing.

A reporter said, "He quickly strengthened his position because although he was well liked, he would kill anyone he perceived as a threat to his power..." Sonny snapped off the TV. He was furious with the stories. He hated publicity.

Vinny knew better than to antagonize him in any way so he started making calls to all the under bosses and capos to tell them about the meeting. He tried calling Max but he could not get hold of him so he left a message. Even if he were out for the weekend, eventually he would call in or see the news. Sonny went into his room and locked the door. He did not come out again that evening although Vinny knocked to see if he wanted dinner. A muffled "no" was all the answer he got.

About 2:00 a.m., Vinny took a chance and called Agent Rick from his private line. He did not get anything except for the answering machine, so he left his number and hoped he returned the call soon.

The phone rang a few minutes later and Vinny snatched it up before the first ring died.

"Hey Rick is this you?" he said.

"Yeah, Vinny, Its agent Rick. Are you okay?"

"Yeah. What is happening? The shits hitting the fan all over the place."

"We're still making arrests. Mob guys are hearing about the raids and they are rolling over. The grand jury is listening to the tape and their statements right now. Don't worry, we've got him"

"Rick, I wanted to tell you, there's a meeting tomorrow at 10:00 a.m. at the Waldorf Astoria. Everybody will be there to come up with a plan. Sonny, Vinny and the bosses from the five families. He wants to confront everybody and find the rat."

"Good. We will raid the hotel and get everybody all at once. We are going to take you into custody as well. We do not want Sonny thinking it was you. Then I will come and get you. Vinny, you did a great job. Be careful tomorrow. Hit the floor and stay down when we come in. There may be trouble," Agent Rick warned.

"Okay. I won't call you anymore because it's too risky. I'll see you later." Vinny told him.

"Bye, Vinny. And good luck."

He gently replaced the receiver and lay in bed thinking that there was no turning back. Sonny Denucci was history. He smiled in the darkness.

Sunday morning, Sonny came in and woke him. "Vinny, its 8:00am Get up and get dressed or we're going to be late." Shit! He had forgotten to set his alarm. He threw on some clothes and met his father downstairs. They hurried to the hotel and arrived only a few minutes before the set time.

The place was mobbed with Family members. Everyone looked serious and greeted Sonny formally with an embrace. They went into a conference room that held a big oval table. Vinny was getting anxious and tried to nonchalantly look for a hiding place before for the raid. Sonny took his place at the head of the table with about 50 other bosses seated around the table. Everyone else stood respectfully against the wall. Vinny stood to his right-hand side as a sign of support and protection. Sonny did not have to shout because everyone was tensely waiting for him to speak. He stood up and paced around the table.

"Gentlemen, we have a rat among us. The Feds could have never figured out this much about me, or the Family's business." He stopped and stared directly at Vinny.

Vinny felt his heart drop and thought he would have a heart attack. He thought he had slipped up somehow and Sonny had found out he was the rat. Whether he had or not, it did not matter anymore. Sonny was doomed and he knew it. Vinny had to lock his knees to stay erect while he met his father's gaze.

Sonny continued, "I'm going to give everybody a chance in this room. Stand up and admit who you are, you fuckin' rat. Did I not make money for all of you? Didn't..." He was interrupted by a knock at the door. Sonny nodded at the person nearest the door to open it. Even after all the shit that had happened last night, he was still unafraid that anyone could touch him personally. A waiter came in with coffee. Vinny did a double take. It was Agent Rick Carr wearing a waiter's outfit and serving the coffee. Rick asked him if he wanted coffee and he about choked.

Sonny went back to his quest for the rat without a break. He looked around the room and said impatiently, "Well, who was it?"

Everybody stood or sat quietly, but their eyes were darting from person to person wondering if the man next to them was the rat. Vinny was crumbling from the pressure and he felt himself rise to his feet. Sonny looked at him like, what the fuck are you doing and Vinny could see agent Carr slightly shaking his head. However, he could not sit back down, his anger and hate was too intense. His heart was pounding too fast and he wanted to get this over. He wanted his father to know who had destroyed him. He wanted to show him how much he hated him.

He stood up and shouted, "It was me, you no-good fuckin' killer!"

There was complete silence for a minute. Sonny was shocked and could not speak for a moment. Then he calmly said, "Vincenzo, you betrayed me and the Family. Why?"

Insanely furious that Sonny would ask that so sincerely, he pulled out his gun and pulled the trigger back. He had everyone's attention, but the only one that mattered was Sonny. He felt a calm steal over him. His voice was low, but carried throughout the room, "You killed my mother over a fuckin' whore. You made me kill my uncle for the sake of the goddamn Family. I went to prison for you and you didn't even visit me once! You fucked up my life for the sake of your personal power and money. You always used the Family as an excuse for everything, but you are very selfish. You would do anything to maintain your empire. Yours! Not the Family's! The Family never meant fuck to you as long as you could control it!"

"I know I'm as good as dead, but then you killed me the day you put my mother in the ground and took away my life. So I had to take you down so you know what it feels like, you low-life murderer."

Vinny raised the gun and pointed it at his father, then put the gun to his own head. He could see that his father was indifferent to his pain. This was no fairy tale where his father would apologize to him. No tearful moments of forgiveness or love. Vinny was less than nothing to Sonny—nothing had changed! He knew it a long time ago. He looked at agent Carr and saw the saddest expression in his eyes. He shook his head, no, but he knew it was too late to stop what Vinny had put in motion.

The room suddenly exploded as everybody started to get up and tried to see what was happening. They were all cussing, yelling, and pointing angry fingers at him.

"Sonny, did you raise a fuckin' rat?" said one capo.

"Hurry up and kill yourself or I'll do it for you, you fuckin' rat bastard!" someone shouted near the wall.

"Go to hell, you dumb fuck!" Vinny yelled back.

He saw Agent Carr signal for his men to enter the room. The door flung open, and about a hundred agents with readied guns came pouring in.

"FBI! Everybody freeze!" they shouted as they entered. He saw Agent Carr go over to Sonny and restrain him from behind. Sonny would not look at Vinny and seemed numb as he passively let Agent Carr push him toward the door.

Everyone froze in surprise as the FBI agents surrounded them. All of a sudden, his cousin Robert came unhinged and rushed at Vinny, intending to strangle him, break his arms, anything. He screamed, "Vinny, you fuckin' rat. I knew you were a no-good son-of-a-bitch from when we were kids. You had everything and what did you do, you fuckin' threw it away! You had better kill yourself right now, Vinny, 'cause if I can I'm going to fuckin' pull you apart, one bone at a time."

Uncle Nunzi ran over to Robert before he could reach Vinny and put his arms around him to hold him still. Hoarsely, he said, "Robert, stop it! I understand. However, save your strength. With Sonny in jail and Vinny dead, I will pull us all together. There will always be enough of us to carry on. To the patient go the spoils, remember that, Robert."

Robert stared unwaveringly at him, intense hate in his eyes, but Vinny could see him considering his father's argument and relaxing. He stared at Vinny with a hatred Vinny had never seen before.

"Yeah, Vinny, hear that? Long after you are fish food, we will still be here, stronger than ever. Think about that."

"Vinny!" Vinny turned to look at agent Carr ."It's over. Put the gun down!"

Vinny stared back at him and shook his head, no. He looked right at his father who had recovered his usual cold-hearted expression on his face. Sonny was standing by the doorway between two FBI agents. He looked like he did not even care—it was as if he was ready for this.

"Sonny!" Vinny shouted.

Sonny slowly looked over at his only son. The room was silent for a moment before Vinny spoke.

"Sonny, I'll leave you with this. I am going to end my life right here in front of you because I don't want to give you the satisfaction of having me killed like the rest of my Family. But just knowing you're going to rot in prison is good enough." The room filled with silence. Sonny put his head down and closed his eyes.

Vinny pulled the trigger.
CLICK! CLICK! CLICK!

* * *

Made in the USA